DISCARD *The Iron Duke*

"I loved it! As far as I'm concerned, with *The Iron Duke*, Meljean Brook has brilliantly defined the new genre of steampunk romance. From now on, everyone will compare other writers in the genre to her."
—Jayne Ann Krentz, *New York Times* bestselling author

"A stunning blend of steampunk setting and poignant romance— smart, sexy, breathtaking, and downright addicting. I'm ready for the next book or anything else Meljean Brook writes."
—Ilona Andrews, *New York Times* bestselling author

"Engrossing steampunk adventure . . . [A] complex, gripping read."
—*Publishers Weekly* (starred review)

"With adept writing and a flair for creating believable worlds, Brook's first in the Iron Seas series showcases her masterful storytelling."
—*Booklist*

"A high seas/airborne adventure that's filled with zombies, pirates, and deadly betrayal. Along with the pulse-pounding adventure, there's plenty of serious sizzle for readers to enjoy."
—*RT Book Reviews* (4½ stars)

"I absolutely loved this book . . . Everything from characters to world was done with care and precision . . . Any current fan of Ms. Brook has to read this one, and those who aren't fans should. Steampunk has never been written so well."
—*Night Owl Reviews*

continued . . .

Demon Forged

"Dark, rich, and sexy, every page makes me beg for more!"
　　　　　—Gena Showalter, *New York Times* bestselling author

"Another fantastic book in a beautifully written series. [It] has all the elements I love in Meljean's books—strong, gorgeously drawn characters, a world so real I totally believe it, and the punch of powerful emotion." 　　　　　—Nalini Singh, *New York Times* bestselling author

"A dark, gripping read . . . The characters are brilliant, and the breathtaking romance, vivid setting, and darkly delicious adventure will immerse readers in this spellbinding world until the satisfying conclusion." 　　　　　—*RT Book Reviews*

Demon Bound

"An excellent entry in a great series . . . Another winner as the multi-faceted Guardian saga continues to expand in complexity while remaining entertaining . . . As complex and beautifully done as always."
　　　　　—*Book Binge*

"Be prepared for more surprises and more revelations . . . Brook continues to deliver surprising characters, relationships, paranormal elements, and plot twists—the only thing that won't surprise you is your *total* inability to put this book down." 　　　　　—*Alpha Heroes*

"Raises the bar on paranormal romance for sheer thrills, drama, and world-building, and hands-down cements Brook's place at the top of her field." 　　　　　—*Romance Junkies*

Demon Night

"Meljean is now officially one of my favorite authors. And this book's hero? . . . I just went weak at the knees. And the love scenes—wow, just wow." 　　　　　—Nalini Singh, *New York Times* bestselling author

"This is the book for paranormal lovers. It is a phenomenal book by an author who knows how to give her readers exactly what they want. What Brook's readers want is a story that is dangerous, sexy, scary, and smart. *Demon Night* delivers all that and more! . . . [It] is the epitome of what a paranormal romance should be! I didn't want to put it down."
                                                    —*Romance Reader at Heart*

"Poignant and compelling with lots of action, and it's very sensual. You'll fall in love with Charlie, and Ethan will cause your thermometer to blow its top. An excellent plot, wonderful dialogue . . . Don't miss reading it or any of Meljean Brook's other novels in this series."
                                                    —*Fresh Fiction*

"An intense romance that will leave you breathless . . . I was drawn in from the first page."
                                                    —*Romance Junkies*

Demon Moon

"The fourth book in Meljean Brook's Guardian series turns up the heat without losing any of the danger."   —*Entertainment Weekly*

"A read that goes down hot and sweet—utterly unique—and one hell of a ride."   —Marjorie M. Liu, *New York Times* bestselling author

"Sensual and intriguing, *Demon Moon* is a simply wonderful book. I was enthralled from the first page!"
                                                    —Nalini Singh, *New York Times* bestselling author

"Brings a unique freshness to the romantic fantasy realm . . . Action-packed from the onset."   —*Midwest Book Review*

"I loved every moment of it."   —*All About Romance*

continued . . .

"Fantastically drawn characters . . . and their passion for each other is palpable in each scene they share. It stews beneath the surface and when it finally reaches boiling point . . . OH WOW!"

—Vampire Romance Books

Demon Angel

"I've never read anything like this book. *Demon Angel* is brilliant, heartbreaking, genre-bending—even, I dare say, epic. Simply put, I love it." —Marjorie M. Liu, *New York Times* bestselling author

"Brook has crafted a complex, interesting world that goes far beyond your usual . . . paranormal romance. *Demon Angel* truly soars."

—Jennifer Estep, author of Kiss of Frost

"I can honestly say I haven't read many books lately that have kept me guessing and wondering 'what's next,' but this is one of them. [Brook has] created a unique and different world . . . Gritty and realistic . . . Incredibly inventive . . . This is a book which makes me think and think about it even days after finishing it." —*Dear Author*

"Enthralling . . . [A] delightful saga." —*The Best Reviews*

"Extremely engaging . . . A fiendishly good book. *Demon Angel* is outstanding." —*The Romance Reader*

"A surefire winner. This book will captivate you and leave you yearning for more. Don't miss *Demon Angel*."

—Romance Reviews Today

"A fascinating romantic fantasy with . . . a delightful pairing of star-crossed lovers." —*Midwest Book Review*

"Complex and compelling . . . A fabulous story."

—Joyfully Reviewed

Heart of Steel

MELJEAN BROOK

BERKLEY SENSATION, NEW YORK

THE BERKLEY PUBLISHING GROUP
Published by the Penguin Group
Penguin Group (USA) Inc.
375 Hudson Street, New York, New York 10014, USA
Penguin Group (Canada), 90 Eglinton Avenue East, Suite 700, Toronto, Ontario M4P 2Y3, Canada
(a division of Pearson Penguin Canada Inc.)
Penguin Books Ltd., 80 Strand, London WC2R 0RL, England
Penguin Group Ireland, 25 St. Stephen's Green, Dublin 2, Ireland (a division of Penguin Books Ltd.)
Penguin Group (Australia), 250 Camberwell Road, Camberwell, Victoria 3124, Australia
(a division of Pearson Australia Group Pty. Ltd.)
Penguin Books India Pvt. Ltd., 11 Community Centre, Panchsheel Park, New Delhi—110 017, India
Penguin Group (NZ), 67 Apollo Drive, Rosedale, Auckland, New Zealand
(a division of Pearson New Zealand Ltd.)
Penguin Books (South Africa) (Pty.) Ltd., 24 Sturdee Avenue, Rosebank, Johannesburg 2196,
South Africa

Penguin Books Ltd., Registered Offices: 80 Strand, London WC2R 0RL, England

This book is an original publication of The Berkley Publishing Group.

This is a work of fiction. Names, characters, places, and incidents either are the product of the author's imagination or are used fictitiously, and any resemblance to actual persons, living or dead, business establishments, events, or locales is entirely coincidental. The publisher does not have any control over and does not assume any responsibility for author or third-party websites or their content.

PRINTING HISTORY
Berkley Sensation trade paperback edition / November 2011

Berkley Sensation trade paperback ISBN: 978-0-425-24330-5

An application to register this book for cataloging has been submitted to the Library of Congress.

PRINTED IN THE UNITED STATES OF AMERICA

10   9   8   7   6   5   4   3   2   1

Archimedes Fox and the Last Adventure

London, England
May 23

O! brilliant Zenobia,

It is time to brush up on your knowledge of Venice, for I have determined that it will be the site of my next adventure. As a practical man of good sense and judgment, I am well aware that it might be my last adventure (as all of them might have been) so please forgo the warnings, lamentations over daft brothers, insults to my intellect, and etc. in your reply. The moment after I post this letter I will be en route to Bath, where I am boarding the first available passenger flight to the New World and the University in Wien, where I will waltz through their lovely map archives. Please pray that the airship does not combust over the Atlantic, that I do not have to share a cabin with a minister or one of those absurdists who believes he can discern a man's character by studying the shape of his skull, and that we are not beset upon by pirates or mercenaries—unless that mercenary is she who freed us from patriarchal tyranny, because I would like to finally express our gratitude. I should do it while wearing my yellow waistcoat. Do you think she would fall immediately in love with me, or would I need to charm her for a full hour?

I have delivered your manuscript to The Lamplighter Gazette *and enclosed their bank check. You ought to begin asking them to pay in livre; English money is worth nothing, and will not be until they are better recovered from the Horde occupation.*

I am off! Yours,
Archimedes

P.S. *You should title it* Archimedes Fox and the Ravenous Cadavers of Venice.

Fladstrand, Upper Peninsula, Denmark
June 7

My dearest brother,

When you meet our favorite mercenary, I recommend wearing only your yellow waistcoat—her hysterical laughter will afford you another thirty seconds of life before she recovers her wits and runs you through.

I will not stab you, but my *hysterical laughter began at the word* rational *and continued on for a good hour after finishing your letter. Do you not remember that you considered Venice before? Not long after poor Bilson ran off, and you still feverish and vomiting from an assassin's poison.* Venice! *you cried. Marco Polo was imprisoned there after he returned from the Mongol territories along the Silk Road, and in prison he penned his mad writings about the machines of war the Horde were creating!* And then, *Leonardo! While the Horde's war machines were held back at the Hapsburg Wall, the great men of Europe convened in Venice, and da Vinci was among them, inventing weapons* to hold back the Horde! Surely there must be something left in the city!

How is it that you are as stupid now, in your full senses, as you were half out of your mind with sickness? Must I remind you that when the zombie infection came across the Hapsburg Wall and it was discovered that the creatures would not cross water, almost everyone in that region fled to Venice? Must I also remind you that blowing the bridges did not save them—and that once the infection reached the city, only the few who made it to a boat escaped? There is not a building or a foot of dry land in Venice that a zombie does not stand upon, and they are more numerous there than anywhere else in Europe. Only a few years ago, even you *in all of your dim-witted, thick-skulled rationality deemed it too dangerous.*

No, I cannot believe that you've forgotten. So although you do not mention it, your Awful Dilemma must have raised its ugly head again. You must be desperate indeed. You also had planned to go to the Ivory Market, not to the New World after London. Did an assassin find you? It is the only explanation I can find for such a foolish move, even from you. Does he know the name you travel under now? Should I be looking out my window for a sign of the Horde's elite guard?

Lovingly,
Zenobia

P.S. *I intend to call it* Archimedes Fox and the Idiotic Impossible Quest. *Anyway, there is no point. A survey by Bishop Mendi reported that most of the buildings along the canals were all underwater, as were the streets, and that zombies filled every inch of dry land. Overgrown with moss and vines, nothing on paper could possibly have survived. It is a fool's errand, brother.*

Wien, Ludwig Principality, Johannesland
June 27

Z—

Regarding the Awful Dilemma: So far, he has sent only bumbling fools to kill me. You know that he has much better at his disposal, who will not give any sign of their coming. I cannot return his goods, but returning their value may appease him—and I'm far more likely to find such a treasure in a city that I haven't already picked over, and that wasn't emptied while its population fled to the New World.

Tomorrow I am bound for Copenhagen. A man claims that he's developed a breathing device for underwater that doesn't take two to operate. If I keep to the canals, I will avoid the zombies.

What airship captain dared to take Bishop Mendi to Venice? My only worry was finding someone to take me directly to the city, because they must fly too close to Horde outposts and the occupied territories across the sea. Now you say someone did?

Archimedes

P.S. *It will be* Archimedes Fox and the Astonishing Discovery.

Fladstrand
July 3

Idiot,

By now you will have looked up the scientific article and know that Mendi was aboard Lady Corsair. *Do not do the same, brother. You will never reach Venice. If you are lucky, she will only hang you naked and upside down from her bow like she did that Castilian comte—but more likely, she will open you from gut to gullet like she did Bloody Bartholomew, then feed your dismembered limbs to megalodons.*

Zenobia

P.S. Archimedes Fox and the Merciless Mercenary.

Copenhagen
July 19

O! doubting Zenobia,

How will she know who I am? Like you, I resemble our departed Mother, and no one suspects anything of Archimedes Fox, Adventurer. Even if I do see someone I knew, I no longer wear a beard and have dropped two stone since my last run to Horde territory.

I have purchased the underwater breathing device, along with a glider contraption that converts into a waterproof satchel to carry any letters or writings, so that it is useful after I leave the airship rather than dead weight. I have already jumped from a balloon and the glider maneuvers perfectly. You can see for yourself when I visit next week. You will not be able to resist taking a jump.

He has also repaired my grapnel and spring-loaded machetes at my wrists. I am ready to flee from zombies—though I much prefer it when you write me fighting them.

Yours,
Archimedes

P.S. Archimedes Fox and His Brilliant Acquisitions.

Chatham, England
September 6

Zenobia—

Quickly, for Lady Corsair *is about to depart, and I must hand this letter over to the porter before the captain fires the engines.*

The Iron Duke is aboard. I have been recognized and exposed by that damned pirate, but I still live. I wore my yellow waistcoat. I'm certain that our favorite mercenary rather fancied me before she threatened to slit my throat. She relented when I reminded her that she would lose out on the price of my passage—and I am certain that she also recalled that she will receive a quarter of my salvage, if any.

I have learned her name: Yasmeen. She's as magnificent as I'd hoped, and I'm tempted to write poetry celebrating her green eyes, tight breeches, and sharp blades. If she gives me the least bit of encouragement, I will fall in love.

If I do not return, you should make an arrangement with her to provide stories for new adventures. I am certain that she would agree, as long as she receives a percentage of your royalties—and as long as those royalties don't come in English pounds. She is a mercenary, not a fool.

Completely wrecked and ridiculous,
Archimedes

P.S. Do not begin scheming yet! I shall return, of course. I will be three weeks in Venice, add on a few days for the flight; you should expect a letter this time next month, and my visit a few days after—unless I have found something worth taking to auction. If

I have, I will head directly to the Ivory Market, but I will send a letter regardless, including every detail of the encounter between Archimedes Fox and the Captivating Captain Cutthroat.

Venice
October 8

Zenobia,

You are expecting a letter this week, but I am only now writing it. I've little hope that you will be able to read the words when you eventually receive it; the ink bleeds on the damp paper even as I stroke my pen. Everything in Venice is damp, grown over with mold and ivy.

It has taken me almost seven days to travel half a mile, though when I first arrived, I was traveling the same distance through the canals in an hour. The breathing apparatus works perfectly. The food pack that the inventor in Copenhagen promised was watertight began leaking swamp water within a day, however, and my supplies rotted within a week—even my gunpowder is soaked and my pistols are useless. I dare not risk the same leaks in my satchel. I have made an Astonishing Discovery, one that will solve my Awful Dilemma. Yet it will be all for naught if my discovery becomes wet.

If I were a practical man of good sense and judgment, I would abandon the treasure and make an attempt to recover it later, or take the risk that the satchel would remain watertight. But we both know that if I do not pay off this debt soon, I will not have another chance. I have killed too many of his assassins. Soon, he will send one that I cannot possibly defeat.

So I am on foot, traveling from deteriorating roof to deteriorating roof. Fifteen minutes ago, it began raining, and I've taken shelter in one of the upper chambers of a palazzo. Water has flooded the ground levels, and so the zombies are trapped in the building—God knows how long they have been trapped here, three hundred years perhaps—and I have provided them their first entertainment in as long. I can hear them mobbing the door. But I am in luck. Unlike most of the houses, the wood has not rotted, and the interior walls still stand. I will try to take a rest while it rains, but I fear sleeping too long.

I am late returning to the airship. By some miracle, Lady Corsair still waits for me. I can see her white balloon from my window, hovering over the rusted ruins of the great basilica, exactly where I asked her captain to meet me a week ago. Was it only my waistcoat, is it the remainder of my payment, or does she have tender feelings for me? If it is not that, I must make certain that she eventually comes to care for me. I have had much time to think, and I have heard that extreme hunger clears the mind. I have seen that she respects the Iron Duke—a man who Gives Orders—and so to win her heart, perhaps I will affect the same attitude when I next see her.

That must be soon. I cannot hold out hope that she will wait much longer.

The airship is only a mile away. I have searched for a boat or a gondola, but every one of them must have been taken centuries ago when people fled the zombie infection, or has sunk. I think that the chamber door might serve as a raft, however—keeping me dry while I paddle through the canal, where the aviators will certainly see me. I will only have to remove the hinges and throw it over the balcony into the canal. If it floats, I will lower myself on top of it. When I remove the hinges, however, I will have no protection— and I do not know how many zombies are in the palazzo.

Night approaches, and the light grows dim. I would continue, but my spark lighter is also damp. Rusted iron hinges and a val-

iant fight await. What an adventure that will be, Geraldine—and I trust that you will write a fine ending for me.

With love and affection, always,
Wolfram

P.S. You will never read this, of course, because I will prevail, and paddle my door to the airship, where I will take charge and give orders. Once there, I will discard this letter and write another. Do not despair, sister! Soon, you will hold in your hands the adventures of Archimedes Fox and the Mysterious Lady Corsair.

Chapter One

Yasmeen hadn't had any reason to fly her airship into the small Danish township of Fladstrand before, but her reputation had obviously preceded her. All along the Scandinavian coast, rum dives served as a town's only line of defense against mercenaries and pirates—and as soon as the sky paled and *Lady Corsair* became visible on the eastern horizon, lights began appearing in the windows of the public houses alongside the docks. The taverns were opening early, hoping to make a few extra deniers before midday . . . and the good citizens of Fladstrand were probably praying that her crew wouldn't venture beyond the docks and into the town itself.

Unfortunately for them, *Lady Corsair*'s crew wasn't in Fladstrand to drink. Nor were they here to cause trouble, but Yasmeen wasn't inclined to let the town know that. Let them tremble for a while. It did her reputation good.

Dawn had completely faded from the sky by the time *Lady Corsair* breached the mouth of the harbor. Standing behind the windbreak on the quarterdeck, Yasmeen aimed her spyglass at the skyrunners tethered over the docks. She recognized each airship—all of them served as passenger ferries between the Danish islands to the east and Sweden to the north. Several heavy-bottomed cargo ships floated in the middle of the icy harbor, their canvas sails furled and their wooden hulls rocking with each swell. Though she knew the skyrunners, Yasmeen couldn't identify every ship in the water. Most of Fladstrand fished or farmed—two activities unrelated to the sort of business Yasmeen conducted. Whatever cargo the ships carried probably fermented or flopped, and she had no interest in either until they reached her mug or her plate.

When *Lady Corsair*'s long shadow passed over the flat, sandy shoreline and the first rows of houses overlooking the sea, Yasmeen ordered the engines cut. Their huffing and vibrations gave way to the flap of the airship's unfurling sails and the cawing protests of seabirds. Below, the narrow cobblestone streets lay almost empty. A steamcart puttered along beside an ass-drawn wagon loaded with wooden barrels, but most of the good people of Fladstrand scrambled back to their homes as soon as they spotted *Lady Corsair* in the skies above them—hiding behind locked doors and shuttered windows, hoping that whatever business Yasmeen had wouldn't involve them.

They were in luck. Today, Yasmeen only sought one woman: Zenobia Fox, author of several popular stories that Yasmeen had read to pieces, and sister to a charming antiquities salvager whose adventures Zenobia based her stories on . . . a man whom Yasmeen had recently killed.

Yasmeen had also killed their father and taken over his airship, renaming her *Lady Corsair*. That had happened some time ago, however, and no one would consider Emmerich Gunther-Baptiste *charming*, including his daughter. Yasmeen had seen Zenobia Fox once before, though the girl had been called Geraldine Gunther-Baptiste then. As one of the mercenary crew aboard Gunther-

Baptiste's skyrunner, Yasmeen had watched an awkward girl with mousy-brown braids wave farewell to her father from the docks. Zenobia had been standing next to her pale and worn-looking mother.

Neither she nor her mother had appeared sorry to see him go.

Would Zenobia be sorry that her brother was dead? Yasmeen didn't know, but it promised to be an entertaining encounter. She hadn't looked forward to meeting someone this much since Archimedes Fox had first boarded *Lady Corsair*—and before she'd learned that he was really Wolfram Gunther-Baptiste. Hopefully, her acquaintance with his sister wouldn't end the same way.

A familiar grunt came from Yasmeen's left. *Lady Corsair*'s quartermaster stood at the port rail, consulting a hand-drawn map before casting a derisive look over the town.

Yasmeen tucked her scarf beneath her chin so the heavy wool wouldn't muffle her voice. "Is there a problem, Monsieur Rousseau?"

Rousseau pushed his striped scarf away from his mouth, exposing a short black beard. With gloved hands, he gestured to the rows of houses, each one identical to the next in all but color. "Only that they are exactly the same, Captain. But it is not a problem. It is simply an irritant."

Yasmeen nodded. She didn't doubt Rousseau could find the house. Though hopeless with a sword or gun, her quartermaster could interpret the most rudimentary of maps as if they'd been drawn by skilled cartographers. That ability, combined with his expressive grunts and eyebrows that could wordlessly discipline or praise the aviators—and a booming voice for when nothing but words would do—made him the most valuable member of Yasmeen's crew. A significant number of jobs that Yasmeen took in Europe required *Lady Corsair* to navigate through half-remembered terrain and landmarks. Historical maps of the continent were easy to come by, but matching their details to the overgrown ruins that existed now demanded another skill entirely—that of reading the story of the Horde's centuries-long occupation.

Though not ruins, Fladstrand's identical rows of houses told another tale, one that Yasmeen had seen repeated along the Scandinavian coastlines.

In one of her adventures, Zenobia Fox had written that the worth of any society could be judged by measuring the length of time it took for dissenters to go from the street to the noose. Zenobia might have based that statement on the history of her adopted Danish home; a few centuries ago, that time hadn't been long at all. Soon after the Horde's war machines had broken through the Hapsburg Wall, they'd deliberately created a zombie infection that had outpaced their armies, and the steady trickle of refugees from eastern Europe had opened into a flood. Those who had the means bought passage aboard a ship to the New World, but those without money or connections migrated north, pushing farther and farther up the Jutland Peninsula until they crowded the northern tip. Some fled across the sea to Norway and Sweden, while others bargained for passage to the Danish islands. Those refugees who were left built rows of shacks, and waited for the Horde and the zombies to come.

Neither had. The Horde hadn't pressed farther north than the Limfjord, a shallow sound that cut across the tip of Jutland, separating it from the rest of the peninsula and creating an island of the area. The same stretch of water stopped most of the zombies; walls built near the sound stopped the rest. Poverty and unrest had plagued the crowded refugees, and the noose had seen frequent use, but the region slowly recovered. Rows of shacks became rows of houses. Now quiet and stable, many of the settlements attracted families from England, recently freed from Horde occupation, and from the New World. Zenobia Fox and her brother had made up one of those families.

"We are coming over her home now, Captain." Rousseau's announcement emerged in frozen puffs. "How long do you intend to visit with her?"

How long would it take to say that Archimedes had discovered a valuable artifact before Yasmeen had killed him, and then pay the woman off? With luck, Zenobia Fox would send Yasmeen on her way in a fit of self-righteous fury—though it might be more entertaining if she tried to send Yasmeen off with a gun. In both scenarios, Yasmeen would hold on to all of the money, which suited her perfectly.

"Not long," she predicted. "Lower the ladder."

Rousseau relayed the order and within moments, the crew unrolled the rope ladder over *Lady Corsair*'s side. Yasmeen glanced down. Zenobia's orange, three-level home sat between two identical houses painted a pale yellow. Unlike many of the houses in Fladstrand, the levels hadn't been split into three separate flats. The slate roof was in good repair, the trim around the windows fresh. Lace curtains prevented Yasmeen from looking into the rooms. Wrought-iron flower boxes filled with frosted-over soil projected from beneath each windowsill.

Large and well-tended, the house provided ample room for one woman. Yasmeen supposed that much space was the best someone could hope for when living in a town—but she couldn't have tolerated being anchored to one place. Why would Zenobia Fox? She had based her adventures on her brother's travels, but why not travel herself? Yasmeen couldn't understand it. Perhaps money had been a factor—although by the look of her home, Zenobia didn't lack funds.

No matter. After Yasmeen paid her off, Zenobia wouldn't need to base her stories on Archimedes' adventures. She could go as she pleased—or not—and it wouldn't be any concern of Yasmeen's.

As this was a social visit, she removed the guns usually tucked into her wide crimson belt. At the beginning of the month, she'd traded her short aviator's jacket for a long winter overcoat. The two pistols concealed in her deep pockets provided enough protection, and were backed up by the daggers tucked into the tops of her boots, easily reachable at mid-thigh. She checked her hair, making certain that her blue kerchief covered the tips of her tufted ears. If necessary, she could use her braids to do the same, but the kerchief was more distinctive. There would be no doubt exactly who had dropped in on Zenobia Fox today.

The ladder swayed when Yasmeen hopped over the rail and let the first rung catch her weight. Normally she'd have slid down quickly and landed with an acrobatic flourish, but her woolen gloves didn't slide over the rope well—and Yasmeen didn't know how long she would be waiting on the doorstep. Cold, stiff fingers made drawing a knife or pulling a trigger difficult, and she wouldn't risk them for the sake of a flip or two.

The neighbors might have appreciated it, though. All along the street, curtains twitched. When Yasmeen pounded the brass knocker on Zenobia's front door, many became bold enough to show their faces at the windows—probably thanking the heavens that she hadn't knocked at their doors.

No one peeked through the curtains at Zenobia's house. The door opened, revealing a pretty blond woman in a pale blue dress. Though a rope ladder swung behind Yasmeen and a skyrunner hovered over the street, the woman didn't glance up.

A dull-witted maid, Yasmeen guessed. Or a poor, dull-witted relation. Yasmeen knew very little about current fashion, but even she could see that although the dress was constructed of good materials and sewn well, the garment sagged in the bodice and the hem piled on the floor.

The woman must have recognized Yasmeen as a foreigner, however. A thick Germanic accent gutted her French, the common trader's language. "May I help you?"

"I need to speak with Miss Zenobia Fox." Yasmeen smoothed

the Arabic from her own accent, hoping to avoid an absurd comedy of misunderstandings on the doorstep. "Is she at home?"

The woman's eyebrows lifted in a regal arch. "I am she."

This wasn't a maid? How unexpected. Despite the large house and obvious money, Zenobia Fox opened her own door?

Yasmeen liked surprises; they made everything so much more interesting. She'd never have guessed that the tall, awkward girl with mousy-brown braids would have bloomed into this delicate blond thing.

She'd never have guessed that her first impression of the woman who penned clever and exciting tales would be "dull-witted."

Archimedes certainly hadn't been. Quick with a laugh or clever response, he'd perfectly fit Yasmeen's image of *Archimedes Fox, Adventurer.* She could see nothing of Archimedes in this woman— not in the soft shape of her face or the blue of her eyes, and certainly not in her manner.

Blond eyebrows arched ever higher. "And you are . . . ?"

"I am *Lady Corsair*'s captain." Kerchief over the hair, indecently snug trousers, a skyrunner that had once belonged to Zenobia's father floating over her house—was this woman completely blind? "Your brother recently traveled on my airship."

"Oh. How can I help you?"

How can I help you? Disbelieving, Yasmeen stared at the woman. Could an aviator's daughter be this sheltered? What else could it mean when the captain of a vessel appeared on her doorstep? Every time that Yasmeen had knocked on a door belonging to one of her crew members' families, the understanding had been immediate. Sometimes it had been accompanied by denial, grief, or anger—but they all knew what it meant when Yasmeen arrived.

Perhaps because Archimedes had been a passenger rather than her crew, Zenobia didn't expect it. But the woman should have made the connection by now.

"I have unfortunate news regarding your brother, Miss Fox."

The "unfortunate news" must have clued her in. Zenobia blinked, her hand flying to her chest. "Archimedes?"

At a time like this, she called him "Archimedes"—not Wolfram, the name she'd have known him by for most of her life? Either they'd completely adopted their new identities, or this was an act.

If it was an act, this encounter was already turning out better than Yasmeen had anticipated. "Perhaps we can speak inside, Miss Fox."

With an uncertain smile, the other woman stepped back. "Yes, of course."

Zenobia led the way into a parlor, her too-long skirts dragging on the wooden floor. A writing desk sat by the window, stacked with blank papers. No clickity transcriber's ball was in sight, and no ink stained Zenobia's fingers. Obviously she hadn't been busy penning the next Archimedes Fox adventure.

A shelf over the fireplace held several baubles, some worn by age, others encrusted with dirt—a silver snuff box, a lady's miniature portrait, a gold tooth. All items that Archimedes had collected during his salvaging runs in Europe, Yasmeen realized. All items that he'd picked from the ruins but hadn't sold. Why keep these?

Her gaze returned to the lady in the miniature. Soft brown hair, warm eyes, a plain dress. The description seemed familiar, though Yasmeen knew she hadn't seen this portrait before. No, it was a description from *Archimedes Fox and the Specter of Notre Dame*. In the story, he'd found a similar miniature clutched in a skeleton's fingers, and the mystery surrounding the woman's identity had led the adventurer to a treasure hidden beneath the ruined cathedral.

How odd that she'd never realized that fictional miniature had a real-life counterpart. That she'd never imagined him digging it out of the muck somewhere and bringing it to his sister. That he'd once held it, as she did now.

The stupid man. Yasmeen lied often, and so she didn't care that he'd lied about his identity when he'd arranged for passage on her airship. It *did* matter that she'd allowed Emmerich Gunther-Baptiste's son aboard her airship without knowing who he really was. A threat had sneaked onto *Lady Corsair* right beneath her nose.

She couldn't forgive him for that. Too often, she led her crew into dangerous territory, and they would only be loyal to a strong captain. A captain they could trust. She'd invested years making certain that her crew could trust her, and rewarded their loyalty with piles of money. There wasn't enough gold in the world to convince a crew to follow a fool, and Archimedes Fox had come close to turning her into one when he'd boarded her ship. She'd only been saved because he'd openly thanked her for killing his father, negating his potential threat. He'd become a joke, instead.

And later, when he *had* threatened her in front of the crew, she'd gotten rid of him . . . maybe.

Yasmeen turned to Zenobia, who stood quietly in the center of the parlor, tears trailing over her pink cheeks.

"So Archimedes . . . is dead?" she whispered.

Funny how that terrible accent came and went. "As dead as Genghis Khan," Yasmeen confirmed. "Unfortunate, as I said. He was a handsome bastard."

"Oh, my brother!" Zenobia buried her face in her hands.

Yasmeen let her sob for a minute. "Do you want to know how he died?"

Zenobia lifted her head, sniffling into a lace handkerchief, her blue eyes bright with more tears. "Well, yes, I suppose—"

"I killed him. I dropped him from my airship into a pack of flesh-eating zombies."

The other woman had nothing to say to that. She stared at Yasmeen, her fingers twisting in the handkerchief.

"He tried to take control of my ship. You understand." Yasmeen flopped onto a sofa and hooked her leg over the arm. Zenobia's face reddened and she averted her gaze. Not accustomed to seeing a woman in trousers, apparently. "He hasn't come around for a visit, has he?"

"A visit?" Her head came back around, eyes wide. "But—"

"I tossed him into a canal. Venice is still full of them, did you know?"

Zenobia shook her head.

"Well, some are more swamp than canal, but they are still there—and zombies don't go into the water. We both know that Archimedes has escaped more dire situations than that, at least according to his adventures. You've read your brother's stories, Miss Fox, haven't you?"

"Of . . . course."

"He mentions the canals in *Archimedes Fox and the Mermaid of Venice*."

"Oh, yes. I'd forgotten."

There was no Mermaid of Venice adventure, yet the woman who'd supposedly written it didn't even realize she'd been caught in her lie. Pitiful.

But the question remained: Did that mean Zenobia wasn't the author after all, or was this not Zenobia? Yasmeen suspected the latter.

"So he might be alive?" Zenobia ventured.

"He still had most of his equipment and weapons. But if he hasn't contacted you after two months now . . . he must be dead, I'm sorry to say." Yasmeen meant it, but she wasn't sorry for the next. "And so he is the second man in your family I've killed."

Surprise and dismay flashed across her expression. "Yes, of course. My . . ."

She trailed off into a sob. Oh, that was good cover.

"Father." Yasmeen helped her along.

"Yes, my father. After he . . . did something terrible, too."

That was good, too. Smart not to suggest that the armed woman sitting in the room had been at fault.

Obviously this woman had no idea who she'd targeted by taking Zenobia Fox's place. If asked, she'd probably say that her father's surname had been Fox, as well. She wouldn't know that Emmerich Gunther-Baptiste had once tried to roast a mutineer alive. Yasmeen hadn't had any love for the mutineer—but she'd shot him in the head anyway, to put him out of his misery. She'd shot Gunther-Baptiste when he'd ordered the other mercenaries to put her on the roasting spit in the mutineer's place. When Yasmeen realized that she'd attained a beauty of an airship in the process, she'd shot every other crew member who tried to take it from her.

After a while, they'd stopped trying and began taking orders, instead.

"Did he do something terrible? I've killed so many people, I forget what my reasons were." A lie, but Yasmeen wasn't the only one telling them. Now it was time to find out this woman's reasons. With a belabored sigh, she climbed to her feet. "That's all I've come to say. A few of Archimedes' belongings are still in my ship. Would you like to have them, or should I distribute them among my crew?"

"Oh, yes. That's fine." For a moment, the blond seemed distracted and uncertain. Then her shoulders squared, and she said, "My brother hired you to take him to Venice, and was searching for a specific item. Did he find it . . . before he died?"

Ah, so that's what it was. Yasmeen had spoken to three art dealers about locating a buyer for the sketch Archimedes Fox had found in Venice. A flying machine drawn by the great inventor Leonardo da Vinci, the sketch was valuable beyond measure.

She'd demanded that the dealers be discreet in their inquiries. Not even Yasmeen's crew knew what she'd locked away in her cabin. But obviously, someone had talked.

"It was a fake," Yasmeen lied.

No uncertainty weakened Zenobia's expression now. "I'd still like to have it. As a memento."

Yasmeen nodded. "If you'll show me out, I'll retrieve it for you now." She followed the woman from the parlor and into the hallway. "Will you hold the rope ladder for me? It's so unsteady."

"Of course." All smiles, Zenobia reached the front door.

Yasmeen didn't give her a chance to open it. Slapping her gloved hand over the blond's mouth, she kicked the woman's knees out from beneath her. Yasmeen slammed her against the floor and shoved her knife against the woman's throat.

Quietly, she hissed, "Where is Zenobia Fox?"

The woman struggled for breath. "I am Zen—"

A press of the blade cut off the woman's lie. Yasmeen smiled, and the woman's skin paled.

Her smile frequently had that effect.

"The dress doesn't fit you. You've tried to take Zenobia's place but you've no idea who you're pretending to be. Where is she?" When the woman's lips pressed together in an unmistakable response, Yasmeen let her blade taste blood. The woman whimpered. "I imagine that you're working with someone. You didn't think of this yourself. Is he waiting upstairs?"

The woman's eyelids flickered. Answer enough.

"I can kill you now and ask him instead," Yasmeen said.

That made her willing to talk. Her lips parted. Yasmeen didn't allow her enough air to make a sound.

"Is Zenobia in the house? Nod once if yes."

Nod.

"Is she alive?"

Nod.

Good. Yasmeen might not kill this woman now. She eased back just enough to let the woman respond. "Where did you hear about the sketch?"

"Port Fallow," she whispered. "Everyone knew that Fox boarded your airship in Chatham. We realized he must have found the sketch on his last salvaging run."

Yasmeen had only spoken to one art dealer in Port Fallow: Franz Kessler. Damn his loose tongue. She'd make certain he wouldn't talk out of turn again—especially if this had been his idea. This woman certainly hadn't the wits to connect the sketch to Zenobia.

"You and the one upstairs. Was this his plan?"

Yasmeen interpreted her hesitation as a yes—and that this woman was afraid of him. She'd chosen the wrong person to fear.

"What airship did you fly in on?"

"*Windrunner.* Last night."

A passenger ship. "Who's upstairs?"

"Peter Mattson."

Miracle Mattson, the weapons smuggler. A worthy occupation, in Yasmeen's opinion, but Miracle Mattson sullied the profession. He always recruited partners to assist him with the job, but as soon as the cargo was secure, the partners conveniently disappeared. Mattson usually claimed an attack by Horde forces or zombies had killed them, yet every time, he miraculously survived.

No doubt that if this woman had secured the sketch for him, she'd have disappeared soon, too.

"Did he hire you just for this job?"

"Yes. I'm grateful. I've been out of work for almost a full season."

A full season of what? This woman's soft hands had never seen any kind of labor. Only one possibility occurred to her.

"Are you an *actor*?"

The blond nodded. "And dancer. But the company replaced us all with automatons."

If this woman's performance was an example, Yasmeen suspected that the automatons displayed more talent. "All right. Call Mattson down."

"Why?"

"Because I'll make you a better deal than he will." Yasmeen wouldn't kill her, anyway. Probably. "And because if I go upstairs holding a knife to your throat, he might do something stupid to Miss Fox."

"Oh." Her eyes widened. "How do I call him?"

God save her from idiots. "I'll let you up. You'll open and close the door as if you've just come in from outside, and yell, 'I've got it! Come see!' You'll be very excited."

"And then?"

"I'll do the rest." She waited for the woman to nod, then hauled her up. "Now."

Yasmeen had to give the actress credit; even with a knife at her throat, she played her part perfectly. Mattson must have realized that something was amiss, however. No answer came from upstairs. Perhaps he'd taken a look out the window and saw that Yasmeen had never climbed back up to the airship. She didn't think he'd heard their whispers. When noise finally came from above, the walls and ceiling muffled Mattson's low voice.

"Get up." A thud followed the rough order, the sound of a body falling onto the floor, then the slow shuffle of feet and the heavy, regular tread of boots. *"Stay quiet. Don't try anything stupid."*

Ah, Mattson. Always predictable. Of course he wouldn't come down alone and risk his neck. He was bringing Zenobia with him, probably with a gun at her head—and he likely intended to offer the woman's life in exchange for the sketch. Yasmeen couldn't imagine why he thought it would work. Did she look that foolish? After she handed over the sketch, nothing would stop him from shooting them all.

No, Mattson was the only fool here. Knife still at the actress's throat, Yasmeen dragged her into the parlor. She stopped with her back to the window, the actress in front of her and facing the parlor entry—an escape in one direction, a shield in the other. If Mattson began firing, Yasmeen preferred that the bullets didn't hit her first, and the actress's body hid the gun Yasmeen tucked into the sash at her waist. No need to draw it yet. Her blade would do until she tired of talking.

As if suddenly realizing what her position meant, the actress emitted a desperate squeak. Yasmeen hissed a warning in her ear, and the woman fell silent, trembling.

The tread of boots reached the stairs. Slowly, they came into view, Zenobia's pale bare feet and Mattson's shining black boots. Her hands had been bound at the wrists. He must have surprised Zenobia while she slept. Rags knotted her brown hair, and she wore a sturdy white sleeping gown. A wide strip of torn linen served as a gag, stretched tight between dry lips and tied behind her head. Her eyes were the same shade as Archimedes'—emerald, rather than the yellowish-green of Yasmeen's—and bright with anger and fear.

Zenobia's gaze locked on Yasmeen's, but aside from a quick glance at the woman's face and at the revolver that Mattson held to the side of her throat, Yasmeen didn't bother to pay her any attention. Mattson served as the greater threat here, and Yasmeen wasn't a fool to be taken unawares while making cow-eyes at a writer whose work she adored.

Though Zenobia was a tall woman, Mattson's height left him completely exposed from chin to crown. Idiot. He ought to have been crouching, but perhaps he considered any sort of cower an affront to his dignity. Sporting a neatly trimmed blond mustache and wearing a pressed jacket and trousers, he stood straight as any soldier, but Yasmeen had never known any soldier who took offense as easily as Peter Mattson. The sun reddened his skin rather than tanned it, so that he always appeared flushed with anger—as he often was, anyway. Belligerent the moment anyone questioned his character and big enough to pose a challenge, he'd become a favorite amongst the regulars at the Port Fallow taverns who found their entertainment by picking fights.

He stopped just at the entrance to the parlor, standing in the foyer and with Zenobia filling the door frame. He'd have a direct line to the front door—so he also kept a shield and an escape. The fool. If Mattson didn't want to be shot, he shouldn't have come down the stairs with his gun already drawn.

Pale blue eyes met hers. "Lady Corsair."

Captain Corsair. Her airship was a lady, but Yasmeen certainly wasn't. She didn't bother to correct him, however. Everyone called her by the wrong name. No surprise he did, too.

"Mr. Mattson," she said. "I believe you are here to make an exchange. Your woman for mine, perhaps?"

"I want the sketch."

Of course he did—and of course he'd never get it. But as a woman of business, she was curious as to what he'd offer. "In exchange for what?"

"Nothing."

"So generous, yet I'm not tempted to accept."

"You should be. Give the sketch to me now, and my associates might let you live. I'll tell them you cooperated."

Yasmeen couldn't have that. "And ruin my reputation? I don't think so, Mr. Mattson—especially since *you* usually kill your associates. I doubt I'll have much to fear from them."

"You have no idea who you're up against." His gaze left Yasmeen and fell to the knife at the actress's throat. His lips curled. "Do you think I care whether she dies? Go on, slit her—"

The crack of Yasmeen's pistol cut off the rest. Mattson's brains splattered against the foyer wall. His body dropped, gun clattering against the wood floor—and luckily, not discharging on impact.

Eyes wide, Zenobia lifted her bound hands and touched the blood sprayed across her cheek and temple. She startled from her stupor and almost tripped over Mattson's boots when the actress suddenly shrieked, ducking and covering her ears. A bit late for that—though if she kept screaming, Yasmeen might shoot her just to shut her up.

She tucked the weapon back into her sash and crossed the room to nudge Mattson's thigh with her toe. Dead. Yasmeen knew many people who seemed to function well without brains, but her bullet had definitely done this one in. Blood pooled beneath his head.

"A hell of a mess," Yasmeen said, and slipped her blade between Zenobia's wrists, slicing through the ties. She did the same to the woman's gag. "If you need to vomit, I suggest you do it on him. There's less to clean up."

"Thank you," Zenobia rasped. The corners of her mouth were raw. "But I don't need to."

Then she glanced down at Mattson's face, bent over, and did.

Chapter Two

Yasmeen found the maids tied hand to foot on the floor in a bedroom upstairs. She cut through the ropes, accepted their thank-yous, and when Zenobia rushed into the room a moment later, left them to do their weeping and dressing.

She retreated downstairs, where the actress had finally stopped screaming. Yasmeen led her outside and signaled to Rousseau. He sent down two aviators to escort the woman up to the airship while Yasmeen returned to the parlor. Her cabin girl, Ginger, brought Yasmeen's favorite mint tea down from *Lady Corsair*, and relayed that Rousseau had locked the actress in the stateroom. Good enough for now. Yasmeen would let Zenobia decide what to do with her.

When Zenobia came downstairs, she stopped and studied Mattson's body for a long moment. Jaw set, she stepped over him and poured herself a cup before sitting on the chair opposite Yasmeen.

"You've come to tell me that Wolfram is dead," she said.

"Yes." Yasmeen studied the other woman's expression. She saw resignation. Sadness. But no sudden grief. "You aren't surprised."

"I was supposed to receive word from him two months ago.

By the third week, I had to accept that a letter wasn't coming. So I have had some time to accustom myself to the idea that he wasn't returning." She sipped her tea before leveling a direct stare at Yasmeen. "Wolfram isn't part of your crew. So why have you really come?"

"He was on my ship. He wasn't my crew, but he was my responsibility," she said, marveling at the other woman's composure. How was it that Yasmeen didn't feel as steady as his sister looked? She slipped her fingers into her pocket, producing her cigarillo case and lighter. "Do you mind if I . . . ?"

"Yes," Zenobia said bluntly. "It reeks."

"If you smoke one, too, you won't notice it as much." Yasmeen smiled when the other woman only fixed a baleful look on the proffered cigarillo. She slid it back into the silver case. "I have his belongings and his purse—minus the five livre he owed to me for his passage."

Five livre was a large sum of money, but Zenobia didn't blink. "I'll take them. And the da Vinci sketch?"

"You'd be a fool to keep it in your possession."

"As aptly demonstrated today."

Though dryly stated, Yasmeen could see that the other woman knew it was the truth. "Mattson will only be the first."

"Yes." Zenobia took another sip before coming to a decision. "Sell it, then."

Exultation burst through Yasmeen's veins. She contained it, and merely nodded. "I will."

A tiny smile curved the woman's mouth. "I understand that on dangerous flights, the airship captain receives twenty-five percent of the salvage."

Yasmeen met Zenobia's steady gaze. "For this job, I'll take fifty percent."

Zenobia studied her, as if weighing the chances of coming to a different agreement. Finally, she took another sip and said, "I suppose fifty percent of an absurd fortune is still a ridiculous amount of money."

Clever woman. *This* was the Zenobia that Yasmeen had expected to find. She wasn't disappointed. "I'll see that you receive your half when the sale is finalized."

"Thank you." She hesitated, and some of the hardness of negotiation dropped from her expression, revealing a hint of vulnerability. "I heard a little bit of what you said about the zombies, Captain. Is it true that you deliberately threw him into a canal?"

Yasmeen shook her head. "It was the middle of the night. I couldn't know where he landed."

Lies. Her eyes saw well enough in the dark. She'd watched him splash into the canal. She'd known that with luck and brains, he'd survive—and her crew wouldn't think she'd gone soft.

But even for Archimedes Fox, his chances of survival were slim. She wouldn't give this woman any more false hope than she offered herself.

"I see." Zenobia's fingers tightened on her cup. "If, on your travels, you see him with the other zombies . . ."

"I'll shoot him," Yasmeen promised.

"Thank you." The vulnerability left her face, replaced by sudden amusement. "Speaking of your travels, Captain . . . you've tossed the source of my stories overboard."

Yasmeen looked pointedly at Zenobia's fingers. Unlike the actress's, ink stained their tips. "You're writing."

"Only letters."

"You won't need the income when I've sold the sketch."

"You misunderstand me." Zenobia set her cup on the table and leaned forward. "I don't need the income now. I write because I enjoy it. Will you leave your airship when you've received your portion of the money?"

"No." When she left her lady for the last time, it would only be because her dead body had been dragged away.

"It is the same with me for writing. I won't stop, not voluntarily. But I do need inspiration for the stories. With the basis for Archimedes gone, I'll have to create another character. Perhaps a woman this time." She sat back, her gaze narrowed on Yasmeen's face. "What about . . . *The Adventures of Lady Lynx*?"

Yasmeen laughed. Zenobia didn't.

"You're not joking?"

The other woman shook her head. "You live a life of adventure and meet with many different people, particularly the villainous sort."

Yasmeen *was* the villainous sort. "Yes, but—"

"I'll write them. You receive twenty-five percent of royalties."

The sudden need for a cigarillo almost overwhelmed her. A drink, a hit of opium. Anything to calm her jumping nerves. Was she going to agree to this?

Yes. Of course she was. Even without royalties, she would have.

But still, no need to be stupid about it.

"Fifty percent of royalties," Yasmeen countered. "Paid quarterly in French currency or gold."

"Twenty-five percent. You send me reports of where you go, who you see, what you eat. I need to know how long it takes you to fly to each location. I want your impressions of your crew, your passengers, and everyone you meet."

Impossible. "I won't share everything."

"I won't name them. I only seek authenticity, not a reproduction of the truth."

"I *won't* share everything," Yasmeen repeated.

For a moment, Zenobia looked as if she'd try to negotiate that, too. Then she shrugged. "Of course you can't. But let us begin with your background. Thirteen years ago, you joined my father's crew. After you killed him—well done, by the way—you sold *Lady Corsair*'s services as a mercenary in the French and Liberé war, where you worked both sides, depending upon who paid the most. You earned the reputation of being willing to do anything for money. But what happened before that? Where were you before my father's ship?"

In a very pretty cage. But did she want to share that? Yasmeen shook her head. "As far as I'm concerned, my life started when I boarded *Lady Corsair*. Make up what you like about what came before."

"All right. A mysterious past will only make Lady Lynx more fascinating," she mused. "I could deliver the background in bits, like crumbs."

"Whatever you like." Yasmeen stood. "I'll send the other reports to you regularly."

Zenobia's expression sharpened as she rose. "Where are you heading after you leave Fladstrand? Do you have a job now?"

"No. We'll spend the day traveling to Port Fallow. Mattson was only here because an art dealer talked about the sketch. I need to have a conversation with him."

Then she'd fly to England, and ask the Iron Duke to hold the sketch safe at his London fortress until she found a buyer. If word of the sketch had begun to spread, she couldn't risk carrying it with her any longer.

Zenobia glanced at Mattson's body. "A man has been killed in my house, and I suppose I must explain it. Will you come with me to speak with the magistrate? This time of morning, he's always at the Rose & Thorn taking his breakfast. You can give him your account and I'll buy drinks for your crew afterward."

And let word spread that Yasmeen had run to the authorities after Miracle Mattson had threatened her? That she'd answered to a magistrate? Not a chance.

"He'll believe that I shot Mattson without my word on it," she told Zenobia. "But if you like, I'll have the actress taken to him. She's on my lady now, and we can fly her wherever you wish— whether to the Rose & Thorn or to a mob of zombies in Paris."

Zenobia smiled. "The magistrate will do, thank you. May I come with you? For research."

Yasmeen didn't care. She nodded, then waited outside while the other woman retrieved her coat. The frigid air shivered through her. Lighting a cigarillo, she let the smoke warm her lungs and ease the tiny shakes.

A few neighbors had ventured outside, gaping up at *Lady Corsair*. When Zenobia finally emerged, she waved to them and called a good morning, and Yasmeen couldn't decide whether surprise or relief added such volume to the "Good morning!"s they called to her in return. Feeling the cold down to her toes, she started for the rope ladder.

"Captain Corsair?" When Yasmeen turned, Zenobia avoided her gaze. She seemed to find the act of pulling on her gloves either fascinating, or extraordinarily difficult. "I thought we might walk rather than fly."

"I thought you might want to have a look at my lady. For authenticity." And because the boilers kept the cabins heated and the deck beneath her feet warm.

"I've seen her." She shot a glance upward. "When she was my father's."

Damn it. Yasmeen wouldn't ask what had happened. She'd seen enough of Emmerich Gunther-Baptiste's cruelties to guess.

"We walk, then."

She signaled for Rousseau to follow overhead, then started for the taverns along the bay. Zenobia's boot soles clipped across the cobblestones as she matched Yasmeen's long stride. So loud. Yasmeen's soft leather boots weren't as warm, but at least they were quiet—and didn't announce her approach from hundreds of yards away.

"I can't remember if I've thanked you for saving us." Zenobia's cheeks had already flushed with cold. "That was quite the crack shot. I never saw you draw your weapon or aim."

That was the point. "If Mattson had seen it, you'd be dead."

"Are you infected, then? I have heard the bugs make a person stronger and quicker."

Infected with Horde nanoagents, the millions of tiny machines that lived in her body like industrious little ants. Though Yasmeen's nanoagents weren't exactly like the two strains Zenobia was probably familiar with—the "bugs" used by the Horde to control large populations, or the ones that infected the zombies—Yasmeen didn't bother to explain the difference. The woman had only asked if they'd made her fast and strong—and they had.

"Yes," she said.

"Mattson must not have been, then."

Oh, he had been. His bruises had always healed too quickly after each tavern brawl for him to have been anything but infected. But Yasmeen only nodded. "He was slower," she said.

"Are you originally from one of the occupied territories, then?" Zenobia asked. "Or did you take a blood transfusion and infect yourself later?"

"Is this a search for a crumb?"

"For your background? Yes."

"Surely you've already picked up a few."

"Yes, but they tell me little. Your accent, for instance. Perhaps you were born in the occupied territories of northern Africa or farther east. Perhaps you came from one of the tribes who fled to the southern American continent when the Horde moved across the Arabian Peninsula."

Only her accent was of note? Was Zenobia trying to be delicate?

Or, considering the woman's hatred toward her father, perhaps she simply didn't want to echo him. "And my complexion?"

"Tells me nothing. In the New World alone, I cannot name a city that you couldn't have hailed from. Who does not have family that is native or African, or some mix of both in their blood?"

Spoken like a true Liberé supporter. "As your father often pointed out, your family doesn't."

"Yes, well. Even that means little as far as discerning your origin by complexion. Without the sun, Wolfram is as pale as I, yet after a summer spent diving along the Gold Coast, he returned as dark as you. How many of your own crew are, too?—and how many are from the New World?"

Most of them. "So I could be from anywhere. Your options are open. You cannot make a story out of that to please your readers?"

"Of course, but it does not satisfy *my* curiosity." She huffed out a breath. "At least tell me how you became such a crack shot. Did you learn before you joined my father's crew? Of course you did, since you shot him in the head, too. You must be from the New World, then—perhaps along the frontier borders, or in the disputed territories. I cannot imagine anywhere in the Horde empire that they would teach a young girl to fire a gun."

"Can't you? I imagine they'd have reason to in the walled cities. If a zombie came over the barrier, a girl's ability to shoot it in the head might be her—and the city's—only chance of surviving."

"That is true enough. But I didn't realize the Horde armed the citizens in the occupied cities. They didn't in England."

"They don't. But they should." Amused by Zenobia's second exasperated huff, Yasmeen smiled and blew a stream of smoke through her teeth. "I think every woman should be armed, including writers in quiet little townships like Fladstrand."

The woman's color deepened. "I have a weapon. But I don't sleep with it."

"I do." Yasmeen kept so many weapons in her bed that her friend Scarsdale had once called it an orgy.

"And I am grateful that you were so well prepared. I'll admit that I despaired when I thought you only had a blade."

"I never *only* have a blade—but the only weapon I bring to a conversation is a knife. A gun means the talking is over."

"Oh. Oh! I must make Lady Lynx say that." Without a break in her stride, Zenobia tore off her right glove with her teeth before digging out a paper and pencil from her pocket. She scribbled the line as she walked.

Inspiration was to be taken so directly? Yasmeen slowed to accommodate the other woman's preoccupation, wondering if she'd often done the same when walking with Archimedes . . . who was charming and fun, much like the character Zenobia had created. Yasmeen had assumed it also reflected the sister, but Zenobia seemed far more sober and practical than her brother had been.

"How much of Archimedes came from Wolfram, and how much was you?"

Zenobia tucked her notes away. "All Wolfram. It was easy, though, because I know him well. Lady Lynx will likely have more of me in her."

Because she didn't know Yasmeen as well. Fair enough. "And so she'll be French? Prussian?"

"Oh, no. English again, probably, just as I made Archimedes."

She'd already decided? "Then why the interrogation about my background?"

"My own curiosity, as I said—and to build a better character. But the English bit, it's the audience, you understand. The New World is fascinated with the Horde occupation and those who've lived under their heel, and the English like to see themselves as heroes—and I sell more copies all around."

Which meant more money for Yasmeen, too. The mention of

heroes worried her, however. She'd carefully cultivated her reputation to protect her lady and her crew; she wouldn't see it destroyed with a stroke of a pen. "They won't know she is me, will they?"

"No. They'll assume it is based on that lady detective, the one every newssheet from London has been writing about. She was your passenger once, I believe?"

Ah, Mina Wentworth. Yes, the detective had spent some time on *Lady Corsair*. Yasmeen liked her, even though the woman had been idiot enough to go soft for a man—especially a man like the Iron Duke. He captained a ship well, and was one of the few people Yasmeen would trust at the helm of her lady, but in pursuit of the detective he was as dense and as possessive as any man who ever lived.

Yasmeen nodded. "She'll do."

"Perhaps I will give Lady Lynx a background connected to the Horde rebellion—I could use some of Wolfram's old letters to establish that, and the stories would be of her current adventures." She paused, as if considering that, before continuing. "Yes, that will work very well. Were you ever part of the rebellion, Captain?"

More crumbs? This trail would lead Zenobia all the way to Constantinople—what little remained of it after the Horde had crushed the rebellion there.

"I've never been a part of it," she said truthfully. "But I've had business dealings with the rebels. I'll share the details with you in my letters."

"Thank you. If there is anything that you think she *shouldn't* be, Captain Corsair, I would appreciate you telling me now. I can't promise that you'll like what I write, but I prefer not to be . . . inaccurate."

Or to offend her, Yasmeen guessed. She appreciated that. "Don't let her be an idiot, always threatening someone with a gun. Only let her draw it if she intends to use it."

Zenobia blushed again. "Unlike Archimedes Fox?"

In her stories. "Yes. You *have* to assume that someone will try to kill you while you're deciding whether or not to shoot them. So by the time the gun comes out, that decision should have been made."

"I see." Her notes were in her hand again, but Zenobia didn't add to them. "Is that what Wolfram did—wave his gun around?"

"Yes."

Her eyes closed. "Idiot."

So Yasmeen had often said, but his sister should know the rest of it. "Stupid, yes. But also exhausted. He returned a week late, and Venice wouldn't have given him time to rest or eat." A month spent in the ruined city with too many zombies and too few hiding places. "When he climbed up to the airship, he ordered my crew to set a heading for the Ivory Market. I refused and told him to sleep it off before making demands. That's when he drew his gun and—"

She broke off. Zenobia was shaking her head, a look of disbelief on her face. "You *waited* for him?"

Yasmeen had. Blissed on opium and wondering why the hell she was still floating over a rotten city. But she'd known. She'd read through each damn story of his, each impossible escape, and she'd known he'd make it out of Venice, too. So she'd waited. And when he'd finally returned to her ship, she'd had to toss him back— believing he might still make it.

But after he'd tried to take her ship, she wouldn't wait for him again.

"I waited," she finally answered. "He still owed me half of his fee."

Zenobia studied her expression before slowly nodding. "I see."

Yasmeen didn't know what the woman thought she saw—and didn't care, either. She was more interested in the reason Archimedes had been late. "He couldn't have known I'd wait," she said. "And the sketch wouldn't have been worth anything to him if he died there."

Zenobia's chin tilted up at an unmistakable angle, a combination of defiance and pride—as if she felt the need to defend her brother. "Perhaps he was late for the same reason you stayed: money."

Yes, Yasmeen believed that. If she had followed Archimedes' orders and flown directly to the Ivory Market, he could have quickly sold the sketch. Which suggested that he'd risked his life because if he'd left Venice without the sketch, he'd have been dead anyway.

He'd owed someone, and whoever it was intended to collect. Few debts would need a da Vinci sketch to cover them, though. Even small salvaged items like those Archimedes usually collected sold high at auction. Of the baubles in Zenobia's parlor, the miniature alone would purchase a luxury steamcoach.

"Does he really owe so much?"

"Yes."

"So you changed your names and went into hiding." Not that Archimedes Fox had done a good job of hiding, traipsing all over the world as he did.

"Yes." Zenobia's sigh seemed to hang in the air. They'd almost reached the Rose & Thorn before she spoke again. "Is there anything else? For Lady Lynx," she added, when Yasmeen raised a brow.

"Yes." The walk here had reminded her of one rule that she'd been fortunate to have learned before Archimedes Fox had boarded her airship. "Don't let her go soft for a man."

Zenobia stopped, looking dismayed. "A romance adds excitement."

"With a man who tries to take over everything? Who wants to be master of her ship, or wants the crew to acknowledge that she's his little woman?" Yasmeen sneered. God, but she imagined it all too easily. "What man can tolerate *his* woman holding a position superior to him?"

Zenobia apparently couldn't name one. She grimaced and

pulled out her notes. "Not even a mysterious man in the background? More interest from the readers means more money."

Yasmeen wasn't always for sale, and in this matter, the promise of extra royalties couldn't sway her. "Don't let her go soft. Give her a heart of steel."

"A heart of steel," Zenobia repeated, scribbling. She looked up. "But . . . why?"

Why? Shaking her head, Yasmeen signaled for the rope ladder, which would take her back to her lady. Zenobia had begun that morning tied up and gagged, then had a gun shoved against her throat and her body used as a shield—and yet she had to ask *Why?*

The answer was obvious. "Because there's no other way to survive."

Yasmeen flew into Port Fallow from the east, high enough that the Horde's combines were visible in the distance. After their war machines had driven the European population away and the zombies had infected those remaining, the Horde had used the Continent as their breadbasket. They'd dug mines and stripped the forests. Machines performed most of the work—and what the machines couldn't do was done by Horde workers living in enormous walled outposts scattered across Europe. Soldiers within those compounds protected the laborers from zombies and crushed any New Worlder's attempt to reclaim the land.

But thirty years before, Port Fallow had been established as a small hideaway for pirates and smugglers on the ruins of Amsterdam, and had boomed into a small city when the Horde hadn't bothered to crush it. Either they hadn't considered the city a threat or they hadn't been able to afford the effort. Yasmeen suspected it was the latter.

Two generations ago, a plague had decimated the Horde population, including those living in the walled compounds. A rebellion within the Horde had been gaining in popularity for years, and after the plague, had increased in strength from one end of the empire to the other. Now, the Horde was simply holding on to what they still had, not reclaiming what they'd lost—whether that loss was a small piece of land like Port Fallow or the entire British isle. No doubt that in the coming years, more pieces would fight their way out from under Horde control.

Just as well. A five-hundred-year reign was long enough for any empire. Yasmeen would be glad to see them gone. But then, she'd be glad to see a lot of people gone—and currently, Franz Kessler was at the top of her list.

It wouldn't be difficult to find him. Port Fallow contained three distinct sections between the harbor and the city wall, arranged in increasing semicircles and divided by old Amsterdam's canals: the docks and warehouses between the harbor and the first canal, with the necessary taverns, inns, and bawdyrooms; the large residences between the first and second canals, where the established "families" of Port Fallow made their homes; and beyond the second and third canals, the small flats and shacks where everyone else lived. Kessler's home lay in the second, wealthy ring of residences, and he sometimes ventured into the first ring—but he'd never run toward the shacks, and only an idiot would try to climb the wall. Few zombies stumbled up to Fladstrand, but not so here. The plains beyond the town teemed with the ravenous creatures, and gunmen continually monitored the city's high walls. Kessler couldn't run that way. The harbor offered the only possibility for escape, but Yasmeen wasn't concerned. Though dozens of boats and airships were anchored at Port Fallow, not a single one could outrun *Lady Corsair*.

And of those ships, only one made her glad to see it: *Vesuvius*. Mad Machen's blackwood pirate ship had been anchored apart from the others, floating in the harbor near the south dock. Yasmeen ordered *Lady Corsair* to be tethered nearby. She leaned over the airship's railing, hoping to see Mad Machen on his decks. A giant of a man, he was always easy to spot—but he wasn't in sight. She caught the attention of his quartermaster, instead, which suited her just as well. Yasmeen liked Obadiah Barker almost as much as she liked his captain.

With a few signals, she arranged to meet with him and descended into the madness of Port Fallow's busy dockside. Men loaded lorries that waited with idling engines and rattling frames. Small carts puttered by, the drivers ceaselessly honking a warning to move out of their way, and rickshaws weaved between the foot traffic. A messenger on an autogyro landed lightly beside a stack of crates, huffing from the exertion of spinning the rotor pedals. Travelers waiting for their boarding calls huddled together around their baggage, while sailors and urchins watched them for a drop in their guard and an opportunity to snatch a purse or a trunk. Food peddlers rolled squeaky wagons, shouting their prices and wares.

Yasmeen lit a cigarillo to combat the ever-present stink of fish and oil, and waited for Barker to row in from *Vesuvius*. His launch cut through the yellow scum that foamed on the water and clung to the dock posts.

Disgusting, but at least the scum kept the megalodons away. In many harbors in the North Sea, a sailor couldn't risk manning such a small boat—barely more than a mouthful to the giant sharks.

His black hair contained beneath a woolen cap, Barker tied off the launch and leapt onto the dock, approaching her with a wide grin. "Captain Corsair! Just the woman I'd hoped to see. You owe me a drink."

Possibly. Yasmeen made so many bets with him, she couldn't keep track. "Why?"

"You said that if I ever lost a finger, I'd cry like a baby. But I didn't. I cried like a *man*."

Yasmeen frowned and glanced at his hands. Obligingly, he pulled off his left glove, revealing a shining, mechanical pinky finger. The brown skin around the prosthetic had a reddish hue to it. Still healing.

She met his eyes again. "How?"

"Slavers, two days out. I caught a bullet." He paused, and his quick smile appeared. "Literally."

"And the slavers?"

"Dead."

Of course they were. Mad Machen wouldn't have returned to port otherwise. He'd have chased them down.

She looked at the prosthetic again. Embedded in his flesh, the shape of it was all but indistinguishable from a real pinky, the knuckle joints smooth—and, as Barker demonstrated by wiggling his fingers—perfectly functional. Incredible work.

"Your ship's blacksmith is skilled." So skilled that Yasmeen would have lured her away from *Vesuvius* if the idiot girl hadn't been soft on Mad Machen.

"She's brilliant," Barker said. He replaced the glove and glanced up at *Lady Corsair*. "None of your aviators have come down. Is this just a stopover?"

"Yes." Even if it hadn't been, she wouldn't leave the airship unmanned while the sketch was aboard. "I'm only here long enough to have a word with someone. We'll fly out in the morning."

"A word with someone?" Barker had known her long enough to guess exactly what that meant. "Would you like me to come along?"

She didn't need the help, but she wouldn't mind the company. "If you like."

"I would. I'll fetch a cab. Where to?"

His brows lifted when she told him their destination, but he didn't say anything until they'd climbed into the small steamcoach.

He had to raise his voice over the noise of the engine. "Why Kessler?"

"He talked when he wasn't supposed to."

"Is anyone dead?"

"Miracle Mattson. Kessler gave information to him."

Barker's frown said that he was having the same thought Yasmeen had: Men like Kessler and Mattson didn't usually do business together. Though plenty of art was smuggled into the New World, it wasn't something Mattson ever handled. If Kessler needed weapons, yes. Not a sketch.

The coach slowed over the bridge across the first canal, crowded with laborers passing from the third rings to the docks. Three ladies wearing narrow lace ruffs around their necks and dresses of embroidered linen over corsets and crinolines stood at the other end, as if waiting for the bridge to clear of rabble before they crossed it. Yasmeen watched them, amused. Five years ago, the residents of the second circle had tried building bridges that were only for their use. That arrangement hadn't lasted beyond the first week.

By the time the bridge was out of Yasmeen's sight, the ladies still hadn't crossed it. She looked forward again. Kessler's home lay around the next corner.

"Do you want me to go in with you?" Barker asked.

"Just wait in the cab. I doubt I'll be long."

"What do you plan to do?"

The same that she'd done to Mattson. "Make certain he won't talk again."

The cab rounded the corner and slowed. Yasmeen frowned, rising from the bench for a better look. Wagons and carts blocked the street ahead, each one loaded with furniture and clothes. Men and women worked in pairs and small teams, hauling items from Kessler's house.

Barker whistled between his teeth. "I don't think he's talking now."

Barker was right, damn it. The households in Port Fallow operated in the same way as a pirate ship. When the head of the business household died, the household's members voted in a new leader who took over the family. But Kessler's business was in knowing people, and keeping those names to himself. No one could carry on in his profession, and his blood family had no claim—and so everyone who worked for him, from his clerk to his scullery maid, would split his possessions and sell them for what they could.

Seething, Yasmeen leaned out of the coach and snagged the first person who passed by. "What happened to Kessler?"

The woman, staggering under the weight of a ceramic vase, kept it short. "Maid found him in bed. Throat slit. No one knows who."

He'd probably flapped his lips about someone else's business. Yasmeen let the woman go.

"So we turn around, then?" the driver called back.

If he could. Carts, wagons, and people were in motion all around them, crowding the narrow street. Several more had already parked at their rear. A steamcart in front of them honked, and earned a shouted curse in response. Beside them, a wagon piled high with mattresses lurched ahead, giving them more visibility but nowhere to move.

The cart that took its place didn't block Yasmeen's view. Her gaze swept the walkway across the street—and froze on one figure. *Oh, hell.* Her muscles tensed, ready to fight . . . or flee.

Dressed in a simple black robe, the woman stood facing Kessler's house. Unlike everyone else, she wasn't in hurried motion. She watched the activity with her hands demurely folded at her stomach and her head slightly bowed. Gray threaded her long brown hair. She'd plaited two sections in the front, drawing them back . . . hiding the tips of her ears.

As if sensing Yasmeen's gaze, she looked away from Kessler's home. Her stillness didn't change; only her eyes moved.

Yasmeen had been taught to stand like that—to hold herself

silent and watchful, her weight perfectly balanced, her hands clasped. She'd been taught duty and honor. She'd been taught to fight . . . but not like this woman did. Yasmeen knew that under the woman's robes was a body more metal than flesh. Designed to protect. Designed to kill.

It was difficult not to appreciate the deadly beauty of it—and hard not to pity her. Yasmeen couldn't see the chains of honor, loyalty, and duty that bound the woman, but she knew they were there.

And she knew with a single look that the woman pitied her in return. That she saw Yasmeen as a woman adrift and without purpose—a victim of those who'd failed to properly train and care for her.

Yasmeen lowered her gaze first; not out of cowardice, but a message that she wouldn't interfere with the woman's business here—and she certainly wasn't stupid enough to challenge her.

Next to Yasmeen, Barker eyed the woman with a different sort of appreciation. Of course he did. She'd been designed to provoke that response.

"Don't try," Yasmeen warned him.

"She's a little older, but I like the mature—"

"She's *gan tsetseg*, one of the elite guard who serves the Horde royalty and the favored governors."

Barker didn't hide his surprise—or his doubt. He studied the woman again, as if trying to see beneath the demure posture and discover what had earned the elite guard their terrifying reputation.

He wouldn't see it. The elite guard earned that reputation when they dropped that modest posture, not when they wore it.

He shook his head. "She's not Horde."

"She's not a Mongol," Yasmeen corrected. The Horde weren't a single race. In five hundred years, their seed and the empire had spread too far for every member of the Horde to be Mongols. Only

royalty and the officials from the heart of the empire were still relatively unmixed, but since they provided the face of the Horde to
New Worlders and the occupied territories, the assumption that
everyone in the empire were Mongols had been carried along with
it. "Just as not every man and woman of African descent born on
the southern American continent is a Liberé spy . . . or a cart-puller."

His face tightened. "Cart-puller?"

"I am saying that you are *not*. You cannot even hear it without
being ready to go to war again?"

"Because you haven't been called one," he said, before adding,
"I wasn't a spy."

Yasmeen snorted her response.

He grinned and glanced over at the woman again. "Why is she
here? No one in Port Fallow is Horde royalty."

"Then she's here to kill someone, or to take them back to her
khanate." Obviously not Yasmeen, or she'd already be dead. Instead,
she was forgotten. The woman was watching the house again . . .
waiting. "Whatever her purpose, don't get in her way."

"All right." Barker leaned forward and tapped on the cab driver's shoulder before dropping a few deniers into his palm. "Shall
we walk? By the time we return to the docks, I'll be ready for that
drink."

Yasmeen would be ready for three.

Yasmeen drank three, but not quickly. Barker took his leave
after finishing the one she owed him, but Yasmeen stayed on, nurs-
ing hers until they were warm. Some nights in a tavern were meant
for drinking, and others were meant for listening. Fortunately,
nothing she heard suggested that word of the sketch had gone
beyond Mattson and Kessler. She turned down one job—a run to

the Ivory Market along the Gold Coast of Africa. Lucrative, but he hadn't been willing to wait until she returned from England, and she wasn't inviting anyone onto her airship before the sketch was in the Iron Duke's fortress.

She hadn't always been able to turn down jobs. Now she had enough money that she could be choosy. Even without the fortune that would come after selling the sketch, she could retire in luxury at any time—as could her entire crew.

She never would.

Midnight had come and gone when Yasmeen decided she'd heard enough. She emerged from the dim tavern into the dark and paused to light a cigarillo, studying the boardwalk along the docks. It was just as busy at night as during the day, but the crowd was comprised of more drunks. Some slumped against the buildings or slept beside crates. Groups of sailors laughed and pounded their chests at the aviators—some of them women, Yasmeen noted, and not one of them alone. The shopgirls and lamplighters walked in pairs, and most of the whores did, too.

Yasmeen sighed. Undoubtedly, she'd soon be teaching some drunken buck a lesson about making assumptions when women walked alone.

She started toward the south dock, picking out *Lady Corsair*'s sleek silhouette over the harbor. Familiar pride filled her chest. God, her lady was such a beauty—one of the finest skyrunners ever made, and she'd been Yasmeen's for almost thirteen years now. She knew captains who didn't last a month—some who weren't generous toward their crew or not strict enough to control them. Some were too careful to make any money or too careless to live through a job.

She'd made money, and she'd lived through hundreds of jobs during the French war with the Liberé: scouting, privateering, moving weapons or personnel through enemy territory, destroying a specified target. Both the French and the Liberé officers sneered when she'd claimed that her only loyalties were to her crew and the gold, but they used her when they didn't have anyone good enough or fast enough to do what she could.

Then the war had ended—fizzled out, with the Liberé possessing the most territory and thereby considered the victor. All of the same animosities still simmered, but there wasn't enough gold left in the treasuries to pay for more fighting. So Yasmeen had left the New World, returned back across the Atlantic, and carved out her niche by taking almost any job for the right money.

Lately, that meant ferrying passengers over Horde territory in Europe and Africa—a route that most airships-for-hire would never take. Sometimes she acted as a courier, or she partnered with *Vesuvius* when Mad Machen carried cargo that needed airship support, fighting off anyone who tried to steal it from them.

A routine life, but still an exciting one—and the only kind of settling down that she would ever do.

Yasmeen flicked away her cigarillo, smiling at her own fancy. *Routines, excitement, and a particular version of settling down.* She'd have to record that thought and send it to Zenobia—along with an account of the little excitement that was about to take place.

Someone was following her.

A man had been trailing her since she'd left the tavern. Not some drunken idiot stumbling into a woman walking alone, but someone who'd deliberately picked her out—and if he'd seen her in the tavern, he must know who she was.

But he must not be interested in killing her. Anyone could have shot her from this distance. Instead, he tried to move in closer, using the shadows for cover. He needed lessons in stalking. Her pursuer paused when she did, and though he tried for stealth by tiptoeing, his attempts only made him more obvious. Of course, he couldn't know that Yasmeen was at her best during the night—and that she had more in common with the cats slinking through the alleys than the lumbering ape that had obviously birthed him.

She'd only taken a few more steps when he finally found his balls and called her name.

"Captain Corsair!"

The voice was young and quivering with bravado. He'd either taken a bet at the tavern or was going to ask for a position on her ship. Amused, Yasmeen faced him. A dark-haired boy wearing an aviator's goggles and short jacket and stood quivering in the middle of the—

Pain stabbed the back of her leg. Even as she whipped around, her thigh went numb. An opium dart. *Oh, fuck.* She ripped it out, too late. Pumped with this amount, her mind was already spinning. Hallucinating. A drunkard rose from a pile of rags, wearing the gaunt face of a dead man.

No, not a drunkard. A handsome liar.

Archimedes Fox.

Yasmeen fumbled for her guns. Her fingers were enormous. He moved fast—or she was slow. Within a blink, he caught her hands, restrained her with barely any effort.

She'd kill him for that.

"Again?" he asked, so smooth and amused. "You'll have to try harder."

The bastard. She hadn't tried at all. And though she tried now, she sagged against him, instead—and for a brief moment, wondered if she'd fallen against a zombie. Each of his ribs felt distinct beneath her hands.

But zombies didn't swing women up into their arms. And they didn't talk.

"My sister sends her regards," he said against her cheek. "And I want my sketch."

"I'd have let you have it." She couldn't keep her eyes open. Her words slurred. "You just had to ask."

"Liar," he said softly. "You'd never have given it back."

Ah, well. He was right about that. But he might have been able to talk her down to forty percent. She began to make the offer, but couldn't form the words.

Blissful darkness swirled in and carried her away.

Chapter Three

Perhaps drugging the woman he intended to fall in love with wasn't the accepted method of kindling a passionate romance, yet Archimedes considered it the most sensible way to proceed. If Captain Corsair had killed him immediately, their relationship would have been just as tumultuous as he could have hoped, but much too short.

As it was, she'd hung on to consciousness longer than he'd expected. Infected with nanoagents, she should have dropped when the opium dart hit her, but she'd managed to reach for her guns. Another second or two, and she could have shot him. Death had galloped close. His heart still pounded from how near it had come.

All in all, a good start.

With a grin, he looked to Sven, whose wary gaze had locked on the captain's face as if he expected her to wake at any moment. "You'd be wise to return to Fladstrand tonight."

The young aviator nodded. "Any message for your sister?"

"Confirm that I received her express. I'll reply to her letter within a few days."

"I'll tell her." He pulled on the woolen cap that would keep his ears from freezing in the open seat of his skipper balloon. "I don't envy you when she wakes up."

Archimedes doubted that. Any boy who built his own flyer and regularly raced it around the North Sea had a taste for danger. Even if that taste wasn't as well-developed as Archimedes', any man who held this woman should be envied, no matter what she did upon waking.

Which might be sooner than he'd anticipated. The long muscles of her back flexed against his forearm as she stirred, turning her cheek away from his shoulder. A line formed between her dark brows. Even unconscious, she was aware that something was wrong. Perhaps dreaming of gutting him—except she'd probably be smiling, if that was the case.

He'd have liked to see her delectable lips curve when she opened her eyes, but he'd work for her smiles later. For now, he needed the sketch, and he'd risk her anger to recover it.

He wouldn't risk her reputation. A few of the drunks stumbling along the walk or rutting between the crates might have heard her name called or seen her fall into his arms, but they probably hadn't glimpsed the dart—and most of them probably wouldn't remember tomorrow, anyway. Those that did would assume she'd taken a man for a night's sport. When he carried her to the room he'd rented, however, Archimedes had to be more careful. There'd be others about in the boardinghouse, and not all of them would be sloshing stupid with rum. Captain Corsair might forgive him for the opium dart, but wouldn't forgive a rumor that she'd been taken to his bed, unconscious and completely at his mercy.

Her long coat concealed her distinctive tall boots and black breeches, but the blue kerchief might as well have been a signal flag. He tugged at the silk tails tangled in her braids until the kerchief slipped from her head, then lifted her higher against his chest.

Her face tipped back toward his shoulder, obscuring her angular features. The dark and a quick step should prevent anyone from realizing exactly who he held.

A damn quick step. He started into it as she stirred again—his heart still pounding, but feather-light against his ribs.

He'd known that she'd be in his arms one day. And he wasn't the least bit surprised that he hadn't gone about it in the usual way.

In the garret that served as his room, Archimedes changed out of the drunkard's rags and turned to find Captain Corsair awake and regarding him with narrowed eyes. His fingers stilled on the buckles of his emerald waistcoat.

She hadn't stirred again on the way to his room, hadn't made a single noise after he'd laid her on the narrow bed. Now she stared at him, her gaze a whetted blade. No confusion or uncertainty clouded her eyes. Only the thin ring of green around her dilated pupils told him that she was still blissed on opium.

"Captain," he greeted her. Unwilling to take his attention from her again, he left his boots lying on the floor and finished buckling his waistcoat. The emerald silk matched his eyes, and he was certain she'd notice. By the time he'd taken the two short steps to the side of the bed, he was certain she'd noticed everything—particularly the contraption locked around her left wrist and the pile of weapons on the bureau.

He glanced toward the knives and pistols. "How does your airship fly with you aboard? You've tucked enough steel and iron into your pockets to weigh down Father Calvin the Blowhard."

She smiled, and the curve of a soft mouth never seemed to have so many sharp edges. Archimedes knew that if he'd been a sensible man, he'd have run to the nearest priest—blowhard or not—fallen to his knees, and prayed that she wouldn't come after him. He'd heard of men who'd boldly hunted boilerworms across the Australian deserts freezing in terror at the sight of Captain Corsair's smile, but the shiver it gave Archimedes had nothing to do with fear.

Instead, he thrilled to the realization he hadn't had to work very hard for her smile after all.

As there was room on the mattress next to her hip, he sat. Her smile vanished. He suspected that if he'd run his fingers the length of her thigh, tension would have hardened her muscles to stone.

But although he wasn't always a sensible man, Archimedes didn't touch her. He *hadn't* touched her beyond the brisk, necessary search for weapons. And though it had killed him, he hadn't even touched her warm skin during that brief exploration, not even when he'd spotted the small key on the silver chain around her waist. Some actions crossed a boundary into unforgivable. Captain Corsair was uncharted territory, but he didn't think he'd crossed the line yet.

No need to mention that he'd sniffed her hair while searching through the thick strands for pins that she could use to stab him. *Tobacco and coconut.* He'd never smell either again without remembering the silken plaits that weaved the intricate crown, usually hidden beneath her kerchief. Without wondering whether she braided them herself, arms lifted like a dancer's and her neck arched.

And absolutely no need to mention the short black tufts at the tips of her ears. She'd purposely concealed them under her braids and kerchief, and he suspected that admitting the inadvertent discovery would leave her feeling as violated as shoving his hand between her legs.

She could keep her secrets. One day, when he nibbled on her ears, perhaps she'd reveal them.

"No doubt I missed a few weapons," he told her. "You've likely tucked some away in places that no man would search—at least, no man who intended to live."

Her eyes narrowed farther, but her gaze turned inward, as if searching out the truth of his statement. When she focused on him again, he saw anger and irritation, but nothing like his sister's description of the biting cold that had come over the captain's face before she'd shot Miracle Mattson.

If she hadn't believed that he'd kept her clothes on and his hands to himself, Archimedes knew he'd already be dead.

"Do you intend to live, Mr. Fox?" Blissed, her accent was strong, but she didn't slur the words.

"I always intend to live, Captain."

"You have a stupid way of going about it."

He grinned. "Not too stupid, as I'm still alive. Would I have been if I hadn't dosed you with the opium? You'd have seen me rise up out of those crates, assumed I was a threat, and shot me."

"I wouldn't have considered you a threat if you hadn't ambushed me."

True. "But it wouldn't have been as exciting."

This time, her smile didn't show the edge of her teeth, but he wasn't fool enough to consider himself safe. "Are you threatening me now, Mr. Fox?"

Until he'd turned around and found her watching him, Archimedes had considered it. The threat would have been simple: If she didn't turn the sketch over to him, he'd invite half of Port Fallow up to see her on his bed, wearing a slave bracelet. He wouldn't have made good on the threat, of course. No one else would ever see her like this. But the moment Archimedes had met her eyes, he'd realized that she'd never forgive him for simply speaking that threat.

Threatening her life was another matter entirely.

"Of course I am." He gestured to the room's single window, which offered a moonlit view of her airship hovering over the water. "You're going to invite me up to *Lady Corsair* and hand over the da Vinci."

"Or . . . ?"

His gaze flicked to the bracelet. Constructed of copper, the segmented casing concealed the delicate clockworks and springs inside, as well as a dozen small needles that pierced skin and injected a deadly dose of poison. A terrible device, it had been outlawed in most of the New World—and in Port Fallow, was ridiculously easy to obtain. The bracelet could only be removed if the segments were rotated in the correct order; the wrong sequence activated the springs, injecting the poison.

Of course, a bracelet that could be worn without fear wasn't enough—a slave could run away and live, as long as he took care not to twist the segments. Something had to guarantee the property would come back.

She sat up, running her fingers over the hairline joints in the copper casing. "Did you set the timer?"

"For one hour."

"These contraptions are notoriously unreliable."

"So am I." He rose, ducking his head beneath the steeply sloped roof. "The bracelet flatters you. I wouldn't bother to take these precautions with anyone else, but I know very well how quick you are."

After boarding her airship in Venice, he'd stood with his back to the rope ladder, pulled out his gun—useless though it was, the gunpowder soaked through—and aimed it at her. A moment later, Captain Corsair simply hadn't been standing in that spot anymore. She hadn't been anywhere on the deck. He'd barely had time to draw a breath before she'd come up behind him—*up the outside hull of her ship*—and dragged him over the gunwale.

Her lips pursed. "So the bracelet is your revenge, then."

"Revenge because you threw me off your ship?" Did she think he blamed her for that? Surprised, he shook his head. Someone would have to wrong him before he'd ever take revenge. "You were justified. No, that bracelet is only to make certain that you don't throw me off it again before you give me the sketch."

"I might still—and I'll make certain to drop you to the ground rather than the water this time."

"Ah!" Elation lifted through him. He braced his hands against the sloping roof and leaned in close. "I knew you spared me. Shall I tell you what I thought as you dangled me over the mob of zombies?"

"Return the favor and spare me whatever idiot thought it was."

"No, not idiotic." He waited until she looked up from the bracelet and met his eyes. "I thought, Finally, the mysterious and beautiful Captain Corsair is holding me in her arms. And I swore that you would again."

Her brows rose. "And what part of that *isn't* idiotic?"

"You'll see. I have a collection of fine waistcoats and a handsome face." He stepped back to let her take in the full effect of both, and her smile spread to the edge of a laugh. Perfect. "You've already proven susceptible to them, and refrained from killing me at least twice: when you discovered who my father was after I first boarded your airship, and again when you threw me from it. I'm certain that means we're destined to be together."

"That it does, but only until our business concludes—and I still want fifty percent."

If Archimedes could, he'd have given it to her. "You'll only get the standard twenty-five."

"I prefer your sister's offer."

"Mine isn't negotiable."

"Isn't it?"

"No."

She regarded him for a long moment before shrugging. "I suppose twenty-five percent is still a goodly sum," she said. "Can you give me any assurance that I'll receive it after the auction?"

"Do you trust my word?"

"No." Despite her smile, her eyes were hard as polished agates. "I'll take you to the Ivory Market on my lady."

"Can you give me any assurance that I'll reach the market alive?"

"Do you trust my word?"

He grinned. "No."

"Then we don't—"

"I'll see that you get your share," he said. "Because if you don't, I know you'll find me—and I'm tired of being chased down for money. So I'll find you instead."

"You won't need to find me. I'll meet you at the market."

Of course she would. He expected to see *Lady Corsair* riding the tailwind of his hired airship from the moment they flew out of Port Fallow. *The Swan*'s captain would probably arrive in Africa with a few new gray hairs, but with Yasmeen as an escort, no doubt it would be the safest route he'd ever flown.

"Then I'll buy you a drink when I see you there," he promised before warning her, "I'll begin courting you then, too."

Her laugh was soft and low. With a movement that seemed to exist between a lazy stretch and an acrobatic flip, she swung her legs off the mattress and rose from the bed. Ah, God. Had she any idea how watching her affected him? Graceful, lithe, strong—and deadly. Her every step seemed to contain a threat. Unhurried, she crossed the small room toward the bureau topped with pistols and knives, and despite the bracelet she wore, every moment he expected to feel her foot smashing in his skull, her fingers crushing his throat.

She only retrieved a silver case from the pile of weapons and slipped a cigarillo between her lips. He reached for the spark lighter before she did, and the captain had no objection when he came close enough to hold the flame to the cigarillo's tip. She regarded him over his clasped hands. When the tip glowed orange, he stepped back and lit his own.

The captain looked pointedly at his cigarillo. "You court your sister's wrath. You're a brave man."

Not that brave. "I don't smoke them near her. Only with you."

"Why is that?"

"They're expensive, and although a bulging purse in my pants might appeal to you, it also attracts the wrong sort of attention."

"So they boast that you're wealthy?" Her eyes were bright with amusement or opium. Perhaps both. "But not rich enough, if you need the sketch so badly."

"True," he said. "But that will change after I sell it."

If he had any money left over after he settled his debt, that was. He felt her assessing stare as he sank into the chair and began pulling on his boots.

Her expression thoughtful, she tapped ash into her palm. "If you sell it quickly at auction in the Ivory Market, you won't receive as much from the sale as you could from a private collector. You probably won't even receive as much as the sketch is worth—and my twenty-five percent won't amount to as much as it could be."

"It won't, but I don't have the luxury of time."

"I propose a deal, then. I'll hold on to the sketch—or we can ask a third party whom we both trust to keep it for us."

Who did a woman like Yasmeen trust? "Is there such a person?"

"The Iron Duke."

Archimedes laughed. Almost ten years ago, when the Iron Duke had only been known as the pirate captain Rhys Trahaearn and Archimedes had still been smuggling weapons as Wolfram Gunther-Baptiste, he'd provided Trahaearn with enough explosives to destroy the Horde's controlling tower in London. After Archimedes delivered the bombs to *Marco's Terror*, however, Trahaearn hadn't trusted him enough to sail with them—and into the ocean he'd gone.

"He threw me over the side of his ship, too."

"Yet you aren't destined to court *him*?"

He flattened his hand over his heart, fluttered his lashes. "Alas, the sight of his face does not make me catch my breath."

"And Scarsdale?"

"Your lover?" Or friend. During the journey to Venice they'd all shared dinner in her cabin, and Archimedes hadn't been able to determine exactly what the relationship between the mercenary captain and the Earl of Scarsdale was. But whatever the nature of it, Scarsdale posed no threat. The man was terrified of heights, and Captain Corsair would never abandon her airship.

"Yes." She turned to the bureau and began sheathing knives, tucking away pistols. "You get along well with him."

"But do I trust him to hold the sketch? He might use it to tempt you into running away with him and making you his countess."

She snorted, a half-laugh that emerged on a puff of smoke.

That response was good enough for Archimedes. "But suppose I did trust them. What would you propose?"

"Take the cash I have aboard my lady. If that isn't enough, I'll withdraw the money I keep in trust for the aviators' families. You pay off your debt, and we sell the sketch at our leisure . . . each receiving fifty percent."

A fine proposal, but with one flaw. "You have ten thousand livre?"

Her ragged gasp cut off mid-inhalation. She choked, coughing on smoke and astonishment. She pounded her fist against her chest, stared at him with wide, watering eyes.

"Ten *thousand*?"

"Yes."

"By the lady's shining teeth," she breathed. "Little wonder you changed your name. Altogether, I only have a fifth of that."

A significant fortune by any standard, but still not enough. Archimedes stood and stomped his feet more snugly into the tall leather boots, ignoring the shouted curse from the room below.

"We need to be aboard your airship before the hour is up," he reminded her.

He half-expected her to kill him now, but she only shook her head, muttered "Ten thousand," and started for the door. On the stairs, she tied the kerchief over her hair, but waited until they were outside before speaking again.

"How the hell did you stack up ten thousand in debt?"

"I lost a shipment."

"One shipment worth that?"

"Yes." He tossed the stub of his cigarillo into the water sloshing against the dock. "My supplier was unhappy."

"If you'd lost ten thousand of mine, I'd have killed you for it, too."

But she wouldn't kill him for a sketch worth more? He didn't ask, though. No need to encourage her. "Zenobia told me what you did to Mattson. Thank you for that."

"You can thank me with fifty percent." She arched her brow at him when he laughed. "No? Don't give me your gratitude, then. It was never for her. Mattson tried to cheat me with an actress. Did he believe I'd be so stupid and not see through it?"

"The actress tried to cheat you, too. She's still alive."

"And she was as much of a threat to me as you are: none. Unless, of course, you manage to make a fool of me. She didn't."

But he had. Archimedes fought the sinking sensation in his gut. "How many men have ever managed to make a fool of you?"

She offered her hard-edged smile and glanced down at the bracelet. "The better question is: How many are still alive?"

"One," he guessed.

"And if you'd like to keep it that way, Mr. Fox, make certain not to do it again." She smoothed her woolen cuff down her wrist, hiding the bracelet. "If you even *suggest* to my crew that you've threatened your way aboard my lady, I'll rip out your spine."

He could see she meant it. God. "That's unbearably arousing."

She swept a considering look the length of his body, pausing once. Her gaze lifted to his again. "Your purse is bulging, Mr. Fox. Tuck it away before you board."

There wasn't any room in his breeches to tuck it, but a walk to the end of the docks and the breeze carrying the harbor's stench into his face did the trick. Yasmeen stopped beside *Lady Corsair*'s steel tethering cable and gave it three hard strikes with the flat of a blade. Above, a woman's head popped over the side, her pale blond hair washed in gold by the light of the deck lanterns. Ms. Pegg, Archimedes remembered from the journey to Venice. After the captain had taken her knife from his throat and allowed him on board, Pegg had shown him to his cabin, shaking her head all the way as if he'd been headed to the gallows rather than a finely appointed stateroom.

Silently, Yasmeen held up her fist. Pegg nodded and disappeared. A loud *clank* sounded. A moment later, the cargo platform unfolded from the side of the wooden ship and lowered on rattling chains. When it reached a few feet above the docks, the captain leapt to the metal platform and struck one of the chains. It jolted to a halt, and Archimedes climbed up before it reversed direction. She looked him over, cool amusement settling into her expression.

Ah. So his presence would be played as a joke in front of her crew. That suited Archimedes. If no one took him seriously, no one would consider him a threat—and they'd ask fewer questions when he left.

The platform rose, and the loud continuous clink of the chains being winched into the windlass prevented any further conversation until the platform clanged into place against the rail.

Yasmeen hopped to the deck. "Thank you, Ms. Pegg."

Pegg's hand remained frozen on the windlass's lever, her eyes wide and fixed on Archimedes' face. After a sharp look from the captain, the aviator managed to stammer a reply. Yasmeen nodded briskly and started for the quarterdeck. Archimedes followed, aware of the nudges and whispers moving from aviator to aviator, the surprise and the disbelief. Several crossed themselves—they must have been Castilian, Lusitanian, or hedging their bets.

And amusement was exactly the right way to play his return from the dead, Archimedes realized. It was as if the captain had never expected any other outcome after she'd thrown him from the ship.

Rousseau waited amidships, near the ladder that led to the lower decks. The quartermaster had been with *Lady Corsair* since the war, but whether he'd fought for the French or Liberé, Archimedes hadn't been able to guess. Aside from the lift of impressive black brows, the man didn't comment on his miraculous reappearance.

Formally, he stepped to the side as Yasmeen approached, deferring to her lead. "Your ship, Captain," he said.

"Thank you, Mr. Rousseau." She crushed out her cigarillo. "You remember Mr. Fox, of course, and how our last meeting concluded with me dropping him into a canal to see whether he could swim."

The quartermaster's mouth twitched. "Yes, Captain."

"It turns out that he can. So I've lost that bet, and now I'll feature in his newest adventure."

"As a villain, of course," Archimedes said. No need to tarnish her reputation.

"Of course, sir." Rousseau looked him over. "How far did you have to swim?"

"Only to the door I'd been using as a raft. From there, I rowed to sea."

Rousseau nodded. "A boat picked you up?"

"Yes." And a boat in the Adriatic meant either smugglers or Horde fishermen. "But if I tell you about it now, you won't have reason to buy copies of the serial adventure."

The amusement in Yasmeen's eyes warmed to something genuine. She continued on to the ladder. "Mr. Rousseau, please inform Ginger that I'll be in my cabin. I won't need dinner, but she can bring mine for Mr. Fox."

"Right away, Captain." Rousseau turned toward the bank of

copper pipes that ran throughout the ship and allowed the aviators to communicate between decks.

Archimedes followed Yasmeen down the ladder and into a dimly lit passageway. Ropes and gliders hung from bulkheads. At the end of the corridor, the captain's quarters occupied almost a full third of the deck, with the passenger cabins directly below. Narrow doors along the passageway led to locked storerooms and berths for the senior crew members.

A sturdy, dark-haired girl of twelve or thirteen in a cobalt tunic and loose trousers emerged from a small cabin near the entrance to the captain's quarters. Archimedes had a glimpse of bunks filled with two more girls before she slid the door closed. The girl turned to the side to let them pass, standing tall with her shoulders pressed against the wooden bulkhead.

"Only one dinner, Captain?"

"Yes, Ginger." She hauled off her long coat and handed it over to the girl. "Tea for me."

As soon as they were past, the girl took off at a run, her bare feet slapping the boards. Though Archimedes wasn't hungry, he wouldn't refuse food from *Lady Corsair*'s galley. Fragrant and delicious, the dinner he'd taken here had rivaled any other meal that he'd ever eaten. The same couldn't be said of the fare on many airships.

Still, he had to wonder about the offer. "Should I check for poison?"

"I can fit my fist between your stomach and the buckles of your waistcoat, Mr. Fox. How long were you at sea?"

Long enough. The whole ordeal had stripped every pound of extra weight from his body and then some. But if his appearance made her imagine putting her hands under his clothes, it was worth the hunger he'd suffered. "As I'm still alive, it obviously wasn't *too* long."

"And what sort of boat rescued you?" She glanced back at him. "As you are still alive, it obviously wasn't a smuggler's."

"No, but I'll ask Zenobia to tell it that way."

"And what would be the true route?"

"A fisherman's boat to Pflaum. From there, I decided between walking north along the top of the Hapsburg Wall, or taking a grain barge to Cairo."

"Zombies or a city full of Horde soldiers," she said. "What did you choose?"

"In summer, I'd have chosen the wall. Winter, the only choice is Cairo." Where there hadn't been nearly as many soldiers as he'd expected; they'd been replaced by rumors—the most popular that they'd been ordered east to defend the heart of the empire. "From there, I boarded an airship to the Ivory Market, and then a ship to Port Fallow."

"All without your purse?"

"I stowed away and stole what I needed to. And I still had my guns."

"You threatened your way aboard? That didn't work so well the last time."

Archimedes disagreed. She'd thrown him overboard but he'd ended up on her lady again, so it had worked perfectly well. He didn't mind taking a roundabout way. "I traded the guns. Horde rebels are always looking for weapons."

"That they are, though the rebels are also difficult to find." Yasmeen lifted her cabin's door latch and led the way inside. "Interesting that you knew where to look for them."

He bowed before stepping through the entrance. "I have many talents, Captain."

With a roll of her eyes, she shook her head and crossed her quarters toward the writing desk bolted to the starboard bulkhead. He watched the pull of her tight breeches across her luscious bottom before glancing around her quarters—the same quarters his father had once occupied. Gone were the shelves of leather-bound books, the unforgivably firm bunk, the straight-backed chairs, and the solemn table as simply made as the sparse fare that had topped it. Emmerich Gunther-Baptiste had been a lean, hard man, and his cabin had been the same.

Though also lean and hard, Yasmeen had filled her quarters with softness and color. His boots sank into thickly woven rugs. Bright silk cushions surrounded a low mahogany table; carved grapevines and leaves created an intricate pattern in the wood. In the recessed berth, red curtains formed a tent over her mattress, which appeared to be little more than an enormous pillow. The cabin's two portholes had been enlarged to let in more light, and between them hung a large metal cage. Inside, two lovebirds flitted and chirped.

Yasmeen sank to her heels beside the desk, where a steel strongbox squatted on wide feet—though not quite like any strongbox he'd seen before. Shaped like a fat egg standing on end, the smooth casing possessed no hinges, and he couldn't determine the location of a lid or a door. Curious, he joined her.

She didn't attempt to conceal the movement of her fingers across its face. This close, he could see the thin seams joining the steel, but he still couldn't make out the pattern of a door. She rotated one section clockwise. At the front of the strongbox, a steel panel the size of his palm lifted a few inches, parallel to the casing. Not much room. Archimedes had to lay his cheek against the strongbox to peer beneath the panel to see the twelve flat metal dials, each resembling the face of a clock, and each of them blank except for a faint, raised dot.

"Based on the al-Jazari locks," she said, sliding her hand under the panel. "But with improvements."

A combination lock, like the slave bracelet. "You can't see the dials."

"No." She grinned. "And neither can you."

No numbers to memorize, just the position of the dots—and she had to do it blind. "And if you mistake the sequence?"

"Then I'll need to ask my blacksmith to make me a new hand. But not this time."

She sat back. A series of hollow clangs sounded from deep within, like knocks from inside a tomb. The rounded top slowly unscrewed, widening the gap in the midline seam and revealing the six inches of steel that formed the housing. Christ. When closed, a firebomb could hit it and wouldn't do any more damage than a few scratches and a smear of smoke.

The top finished spinning. With another hollow *thump*, the belly of the strongbox opened like a drawbridge, pivoting on an interior steel rod. Coin bags were stacked neatly inside. She reached in, withdrew a leather portfolio cover, and held it out to him.

"Your sketch, Mr. Fox."

She'd transferred the sketch from his protective satchel to this? Dear God. He hadn't trusted the satchel to be watertight, but he also hadn't exposed the paper to air and moisture again. Had it been damaged? Heart pounding, he untied the strings and lifted the cover. Two plates of tempered Rupert glass shielded the delicate paper, yellowed with age. Ink had faded to brown, but the elegant lines of the glider and the distinctive backward handwriting were unmistakably da Vinci's.

Or rather, an incredibly well-rendered copy of his work. He closed the portfolio. "Where's the original?"

She bristled. "The *what*?"

"I don't traipse through zombie-infested cities to be fooled by a fake, Captain." He tossed the portfolio back into her strongbox. "You should sell that. Scholars will be clamoring for a look at the sketch, and a replica will be as close to it as most of them will ever get."

Her hand dropped to the knife at her thigh. "Mr. Fox—"

"I wondered why you agreed to hand it over so easily. It's a clever ruse. Had someone held a knife to your throat, you could have given them the fake and they wouldn't have known the difference. I do."

Silence reigned for a moment. Even the lovebirds quieted, as if aware of the tension. Finally, Yasmeen relented and shook her head.

"Very well." Her smile held no apology as she rose to her feet. "You understand I had to try."

He'd have been disappointed if she hadn't. A da Vinci sketch falling into the hands of someone unprepared to protect it would only end in tragedy.

Ducking his head, he looked into the strongbox. "Is it hidden in here?"

"Feel around inside and find out."

Even without the wicked edge of her voice to serve as a warning, he wouldn't have. "Does it close on a timer, too?"

"Yes."

Clever and useful—his favorite sort of device. Curious, he looked up at her. "What would you have done if I'd left with the forgery?"

"Laughed. Then I'd have sold it for no less than fifteen thousand, and kept a portion."

Only a portion? Yet she said it so easily that he believed that had truly been her plan. "And what of the rest?"

"I'd have given you your ten thousand." Her cool smile appeared again in response to his surprise. "If I possess five thousand livre, Mr. Fox, then adding another ten thousand means nothing. It is like having two hundred puddings. It doesn't matter if I give away half, because it's impossible to eat the hundred that remain, anyway."

A scratch at the door prevented his reply. He stood as Ginger rushed in. She wound through the cushions scattered around the table and set down a covered tray. As she straightened, her gaze darted from the open strongbox to Yasmeen's face.

"Will there be anything else, Captain?"

"No. I'm to be left alone until I call for you." When the door closed behind the girl, Yasmeen glanced at him. "She'll be upset when she hears that the forgery didn't fool you. But if scholars will buy copies, she won't be too disappointed."

"*She* created that?" Incredible. "Where did you find her?"

"Oyapock." She named the Liberé capital on the coast of the southern American continent. "But to hear the rest, you'll have to buy the first Lady Lynx serial adventure."

Archimedes almost laughed, but the same instinct that often saved him from stumbling into a room full of zombies stopped the sound in his throat. If he'd taken the forgery, she'd claimed her response would have been laughter, too. But she wasn't laughing. Instead, she regarded him with the same cool amusement that she'd used with her crew—the amusement that said everything was happening exactly as she'd anticipated. And it was, in one way: When he sold the sketch, she'd still be receiving a ridiculous fortune. Perhaps not five thousand, but even two thousand was the equivalent of having more puddings than could ever be eaten.

Apparently the money wasn't the issue at all. If he'd taken the forgery, she wouldn't have laughed because she'd gotten away with the fortune—she'd have laughed because she'd gotten away with the sketch . . . and made a fool of *him*. Instead, he'd thwarted her at every turn.

He was treading close to the unforgivable, he realized. His captain possessed a heart of steel, but he'd managed to wound her pride.

God help him when that bracelet came off.

"Zenobia still intends to write those," he told her. "All of England loves Mina Wentworth. They want more adventures featuring women hunting kraken on airships, and my sister is nothing but practical. *I* am the romantic."

"The fool."

"I'm a man of sense and restraint." To prove it, he walked to the table and lifted the silver dome from the plate. God, a man could weep. Cubes of seasoned lamb on skewers lay atop fluffy yellow rice. The scent of saffron and garlic wafted upward on a cloud of steam. Archimedes prayed he'd be alive long enough to eat a few bites. For now, he only plucked a swollen purple grape from the cluster beside the plate. He turned to Yasmeen and approached her with slow steps. "My sense tells me that I could derive no greater pleasure than to feed you grapes and lick the sweet juice from your lips. A rational man needs only to take one look at your delicate fingers to know that heaven could be found in the scratches across his back, and then to wake you the next morning with a kiss to your mouth . . . and then I'd kiss you everywhere else."

She watched him come, heat burning through the cold amusement. "This is sense?"

"*And* restraint. Because I also know that if I tried to kiss you now, you'd kill me." Stopping an arm's length away, he popped the grape into his mouth, and triumphed when she laughed. "Don't pretend that I'm the only fool in these quarters, Captain. My father's cabin spat in the face of love and companionship. Yours invites it in. And he certainly didn't keep a pair of lovebirds."

"This cabin merely invites my own comfort. The birds remind me of the difference between caged and free—and that cage might free me, one day." She tilted her head and studied his features, her gaze caressing his face like the flat side of a razor. "Do you love me, Archimedes?"

He couldn't have mistaken the calculation in her eyes. If he loved her, she was already deciding how to use that emotion against him. God, what a woman. Never accepting defeat, and using any means necessary to win.

When he *did* fall in love with her, he'd fall painfully hard. It would be as inevitable as death . . . but he hadn't yet dug his grave.

"Not yet," he said. "I'll need encouragement first."

"Encouragement from me?" She laughed when he nodded. "Then we're both safe—and you should be relieved. Two men have said they loved me. You've probably heard stories of what happened to them."

He had. One gutted, the other stripped naked and hung from her ship, his ass bared to his own city when she'd flown into the Castilian port. "Loving you would be worth it."

Her laugh seemed to catch on a bitter note. Perhaps some man had said those words to her before?

Perhaps they hadn't.

Unfortunately, he didn't have time to prove that he meant it. "Our hour is almost past. I need the sketch."

"I don't have it aboard—"

"Use the key around your waist." He regretted the hardening in her eyes, but it couldn't be helped. "These were my father's quarters—and my sister reminded me of the hideaway behind the wardrobe."

Archimedes preferred to forget the hideaway behind the wardrobe. Their father had used it to hide them away whenever they'd spoken out of turn—or simply spoken.

"Goddammit." She turned toward the wardrobe with a growl of frustration. Her fingers dipped beneath the sash at her waist, withdrew the silver key. "You and your sister. Wily foxes, the both of you. You chose your name well."

"It was a toss between that and the equally apt 'Archimedes Stallion.' But Zenobia won."

"Yet she still calls you Wolfram."

"To her, Archimedes Fox is a character, or a disguise I wear."

"And you? Do you still think of yourself as Wolfram?"

"Only when I've done something foolish or I'm about to die."

"And who are you now?"

"The man who plans to fall in love with you."

"Wolfram, then."

"No," he said, and the gravity in his voice must have surprised her. She paused, looked back at him. "With you, I am always Archimedes."

Her lips parted, but she didn't immediately respond—perhaps she couldn't decide *how* to respond. Her gaze searched his features for a long moment.

"Archimedes Fox," she mused. The corners of her mouth tilted gently. "With balls of iron and a silver tongue. I admire both in a man."

His heart almost stopped. Then it began to race, his body tensing—his instincts screaming at him to flee. Captain Corsair would never soften so easily. He was in trouble.

"You're dangerously close to encouragement," he warned her.

"I forgot to mention your thick head."

She reached beneath the wardrobe, pulled on some hidden lever, and stepped back. The large cabinet swung open like a door, revealing the small keyhole in the bulkhead behind it.

"My father always had to shove the wardrobe aside." And then shove it back into place until he was ready to let them out.

"And the scratches in the boards gave away the location," she said. "So I improved it. I can move the wardrobe from inside the hideaway, too, so that no one can trap me within."

Archimedes couldn't respond.

"There were scratches inside, too." She didn't glance back at him as she inserted the key. "All around the lock and in a few places on the walls. Tally marks, as if counting off days. And the name *Geraldine*, written beneath a bawdy little poem."

Their father had beaten her for that. "She's always been a writer."

"And what have you always been?"

"Lucky."

"So it would seem. You are not still in there, after all."

"Oh, he always let us out in time for the sermon on Sunday. In truth, that was crueler than leaving us inside."

"After hearing a few of those sermons, I have to agree." She opened the panels and stepped inside the shadowed closet. For a moment, Archimedes wondered whether to worry that she'd stowed weapons inside—but of course she had. And it hardly mattered, because she'd been armed the entire time.

When she emerged, he immediately recognized the converted glider in her hands. *His* glider, transformed into a reinforced satchel that he'd designed to carry delicate paper artifacts. "You didn't open it?"

"Of course not. Only a look through the glass as we left Venice, and again when Ginger created the forgery. I have not even smoked in my quarters since I've had it aboard."

Oh, his captain was simply amazing. "I could kiss you."

"I'll bare my ass for your lips later."

He laughed and took the contraption, not bothering to hide the shaking of his hands—excitement and relief, a powerful combination. He flicked open the satchel's cover and the familiar pain lodged near his heart, the incredible sensation of beholding something beyond price, beyond beauty. How could she *not* kill him for this?

Intending to ask her, he glanced up, but the words caught in his throat, his voice arrested by her expression. Lips softly parted and eyes bright, her face echoed his emotions as she looked at the sketch, but with something more: *longing*. Then she blinked, and the familiar hardness appeared. Her gaze met his.

"Why?" he asked hoarsely.

Though he'd only managed to speak part of the question, she understood him perfectly.

"For the same reason you don't seek revenge. Just as throwing you overboard was completely justified by your stupid attempt to take my ship, so is your desire to reclaim this sketch. It *is* yours—

and I've been a thief, but I prefer to steal only when necessary. And then there is this." She rolled her sleeve back over the bracelet. "Remove it now, please."

"Of course." He set the glider contraption aside. Her fingers were warm and callused, the skin of her inner wrist smooth, her nails strong and curved like claws. He rotated the first copper segment. "You'll follow me to the Ivory Market?"

"Yes. And when our business is settled, perhaps we'll make time for something more."

Her voice was low, throaty. His heart began to pound. Carefully, he turned the next segment. A brief touch against the side of his neck almost made him jump.

The fingers of her right hand slid along his jaw. Her slow smile exposed sharp teeth. "Careful, Mr. Fox. I'd hate to be poisoned."

Sweat dampened his heated skin. His blood raced. "Only one more segment."

Her hand drifted across his shoulder, down his left arm. He twisted the copper once . . . then again. The bracelet *click*ed.

Yasmeen stiffened. Anger and disbelief flashed over her expression, followed by terror. "You fucking bast—"

Her eyes rolled back. He caught her when she dropped.

"Opium," he said urgently against her ear, hoping she was still conscious enough to understand. "Not poison. Never poison for you."

Her head lolled forward, her muscles went lax. Copper glinted as an object fell from her right hand and *thunk*ed against the boards.

Archimedes stared at it in astonishment. Another slave bracelet—larger than the one still around her wrist. *Good God.* When had she palmed it? Only a few seconds ago, she'd been running her fingers over his skin.

He'd known he was in trouble. He hadn't realized just how close she'd come to turning the tables on him.

Thankfully, the opium had acted more quickly this time. He'd expected to dive into the hideaway until the drug had taken her down, but apparently even Captain Corsair didn't have much resistance against a second dose. Was it too much?

No. Her breathing and pulse were both strong. She simply needed to sleep it off. He glanced at the bed but immediately recognized the folly of it. She might forgive him the trickery, but she wouldn't if any of her crew came in and saw her drugged in bed, fully dressed.

She also wouldn't forgive him if he stripped her naked.

Damn it all. He looked to the hideaway—and hoped she could forgive him this, too.

He didn't risk the food, no matter how tempting. And if, during the ride down to the docks on the cargo platform, he entertained the fantasy of wearing only a slave bracelet in Yasmeen's bed and feeding her tender morsels on command, at least none of the crew could discern his thoughts.

That probably wasn't what *she'd* had in mind for him. Ah, well. She'd be after him soon enough, and he looked forward to the chase.

With the satchel strapped to his back, he hopped off the platform to the dock. Though the night was in the wee hours, there were still a few handfuls of sailors and aviators about, most of them staggering. The only person not in motion was a robed figure at the west end of the docks—

Oh, Christ save him. Archimedes almost stumbled over his own feet when his heart burst into a rapid pace and his gut urged him to run, then forced himself to continue walking as if nothing were amiss.

Cold sweat gathered along his spine. A man with a taste for danger, he embraced the sweet excitement and challenge of it, but even standing a hundred yards from that woman was nothing like the delicious thrill of being next to Yasmeen. With the captain, there always existed the hope of success.

If the woman at the end of the docks spotted him, there would be no hope at all.

Archimedes walked almost forty yards before casually turning toward the wooden crates stacked along the boarded walk. They'd hid him well before, and they could do the same now. He hunkered down next to a sailor passed out and his clothes soaked in urine—if he was lucky, his own.

Breathing through his mouth, Archimedes forced a crate forward a few inches and created a narrow opening through which he could watch the woman. Judging by the angle of her body, she didn't appear to be looking his way, though he couldn't be certain. From this distance, he couldn't even be certain that she was Temür Agha's assassin—but the rebel's personal guard had stood exactly as this woman did now: quiet and watchful, as if nothing escaped her notice.

Hopefully, Archimedes had.

Minutes passed. The awkward crouch cramped the muscles in his thighs, but he'd sat through worse for longer. The woman didn't move. What was she looking at? Perhaps the harbor itself, studying the boats and airships. He glanced back at *Lady Corsair*. Like the other airships, her balloon shone like a pearl in the moonlight, and the deck lamps emitted a soft glow.

Or perhaps the woman was simply watching the aerial acrobats.

He saw them now, swooping their gliders around *The Grecian Queen*. Two of the four broke their arrow formation and spiraled upward, before dipping back around the *Queen* in a long, looping dive. Late for practice, but some of the troupes that traveled the North Sea guarded new maneuvers as carefully as state secrets, to build anticipation for their shows.

As skilled as they were, these acrobats would be nothing compared to some of the spectacles the woman saw in Temür Agha's court.

He looked toward the west end of the docks. She wasn't there. His heart seized, but he didn't dare poke his head up over the crates. He waited, stiff with tension. Footsteps approached on the boards. Not the assassin. He wouldn't hear her.

A sailor swaggered into view, with a satisfied puff to his chest that told Archimedes he'd spent time in the bawdyhouse or a serving girl's bed.

Archimedes cleared his throat as the sailor passed. "Do you see a woman in a black *djellaba*? A Musulman's robe," he clarified when the sailor simply looked at him.

Recognition lit the man's eyes. "I saw her. A pretty little raven. She turned onto the north dock."

Away from them. Thank God. Archimedes tossed the sailor a gold sous and took off at a run.

That silver-tongued bastard.

Blissed and spinning, Yasmeen kicked out four times before her foot connected with the wardrobe lever. She felt total shit: cotton-mouthed, feverish as hell, her lungs aching. She didn't trust her legs to stand. Opium had never affected her like this before—and it wasn't the first time she'd taken two darts in less than an hour. But her head wouldn't clear. Her eyes burned. She smelled smoke.

Smoke?

"Captain?"

The voice echoed in her head. Yasmeen struggled to her knees, fell against the hideaway doors. They slid open, vomiting her onto the cabin floor. The pattern on the rug beneath her cheek blurred. The edges of her vision narrowed, darkened.

"Captain! You have to come!"

Strong hands grabbed her wrists. Wool burned across her back, and Yasmeen recognized Ginger, blood dripping from a gash on her forehead, cheeks wet with tears.

Dragging her toward the door . . . because there'd been smoke. *Oh, Lady. No.*

Viciously, Yasmeen bit her own tongue. Blood flooded her mouth. Clarity flooded her mind. She pushed her feet under her. Ginger hauled her up.

"I'm up." And steady enough. "To the bell, girl. Wake the crew!"

The girl shook her head, more tears spilling. Her tunic was soaked in blood, Yasmeen realized. Too much to only come from the cut on her head. "They're dead, Captain. They're all dead."

"What? How?" Had the boiler exploded? Without waiting for an answer, she raced for the corridor. Her feet slipped just outside her cabin door. Her hands slapped against the bulkhead, and she caught herself before—

Oh, God. Sarah. Thema. The two girls lay in the passageway, throats slit.

Yasmeen stared, horror and disbelief filling her stomach with bile. Behind her, Ginger's chest heaved on a wretched sob.

Hardening herself against the sight, the sound, Yasmeen drew her pistols. "Who did it?"

"I didn't see. I ran to your quarters. They hit me coming through."

They. Yasmeen stopped breathing and listened. No steps. No sounds but a deep crackling. "Are they still here?"

"I don't think so. I closed the ladders to the lower decks, Captain, and cut off the air. But she's burning down below."

Burning. The word slashed across Yasmeen's heart, but she forced herself not to feel it. "Take a glider, Ginger. Go to *Vesuvius.* Tell Mad Machen everything you know."

"But—"

Yasmeen turned, looked at the girl.

Ginger's mouth snapped closed, and she nodded. "Yes, Captain."

By the time the girl unhooked the glider from the bulkhead, Yasmeen had searched the remaining cabins on the deck. Not one of her aviators had been caught in bed. Though some were in their smallclothes, each had daggers in their hands or guns at their sides.

They were all dead.

The iron covers over the hatchways to the lower decks blazed hot as a stove. She'd have risked a burn to save her crew, but she didn't dare open them. The rush of air would blow any fire into a conflagration and kill anyone left alive. The only hope for *Lady Corsair*'s crew was to drown her.

She met Ginger at the ladder leading topside. Yasmeen climbed to the weather deck first, but it was impossible to shield the girl from the carnage. Steeling herself, Yasmeen moved carefully through the bodies to the tether line anchoring the airship to the dock. She hauled back the capstan's lever. Her lady gave a great shudder as the machine began to wind the tether cable, dragging her down to the water.

Ginger came up out the hatchway and unfolded the glider. "Are you coming, Captain?"

Yasmeen didn't know. "Go, Ginger. Now."

The girl ran for the side and jumped. A heated updraft lifted her, and the glider wobbled, but she quickly gained control.

One made it off alive, then. It could never be enough.

Yasmeen turned back to her crew. Anger and desolation followed her around the deck. Pegg, blond hair matted with blood. Pegg the Mister, his staring eyes fixed in his wife's direction. Bebé Laverne, who'd once saved the entire crew with a derringer she'd hidden between her ample ass cheeks. Rousseau.

Oh, sweet lady, Rousseau. She knelt beside him, closed his eyes, smoothed her fingers over his wonderful, bushy brows. If only she'd been here to fight beside him.

His stomach had been opened. All of the aviators had been killed with blades—quietly and quickly. As soon as her crew had become aware of the danger, they'd been able to reach their weapons, but most hadn't had time to use them.

Whoever had done this, Yasmeen would do the same to them—but she wouldn't promise quiet or quick.

The sound of grinding metal stopped her heart. *No.* Yasmeen raced to the capstan. The tether line vibrated with tension. The air around her wavered with heat. Gritting her teeth, she braced her feet against the deck, threw her weight against the capstan's steel spokes, adding her strength to the machine's.

It wouldn't matter. She knew it wouldn't. The capstan was strong enough to pull the airship down, but not when a fire was heating the hydrogen in the balloon's envelope, expanding the gas. The capstan couldn't become any stronger—but her lady would become lighter and lighter. Eventually the tether line would snap.

But more likely, her lady would explode first.

Already stretched tight as a drum, the balloon appeared ready to burst at the seams. It would only take a tiny leak, enough air to fill a sigh.

Or a scream. Yasmeen let hers loose, pushing against the spoke with all her might, her muscles shaking with effort. It didn't move.

Her lady shuddered again. Yasmeen's feet skidded out from beneath her. Her knees crashed into the deck. Spikes of pain shot up her thighs.

The deep rumble from below became a roar.

Yasmeen's throat closed, and she listened to the sound of fire tearing through the lower decks. Her lady's belly had burned through. Perhaps only a small hole in the hull, but now air was rushing in . . . and there was no hope of saving her now.

A spark landed near her knee. Another. Yasmeen forced herself to her feet. Fire climbed the ropes toward the envelope. Not much time—and there was one thing left to save.

She dropped down through the hatchway into a corridor of smoke and flame. The door to her quarters was burning. She slammed through.

The steel strongbox was closed. That was all she'd needed to know—but she couldn't return the way she'd come. Flames rolled across the ceiling of her cabin.

Left alone since they'd wound down during Archimedes' visit, the mechanical lovebirds were still quiet. She ripped the bottom of the cage away, fitted it into the starboard porthole, twisted until the escape mechanism engaged. Glass shattered and wood shredded as the porthole rotated open, doubling in size. With another twist, she could create a standing autogyro from the two portholes, but she had no time, and the turbulence from the fire would likely tip it over, throwing her into the spinning blades. Better to dive into the harbor, and swim for the docks.

Yasmeen hauled herself up to the porthole's steel ring—and paused to look back once, like a sentimental fool.

The moment she turned away, her lady exploded.

If not for his sister, Archimedes would have abandoned everything at the boardinghouse and kept running. But there were letters in his belongings that connected Zenobia to him, the directions to her home written clearly—and Temür Agha's guard wasn't anything like the bumbling assassins he'd sent before.

Everything he needed fit into a single sack. He lay the converted glider on the bed and scribbled a letter to his sister. They'd already determined the safest location if she needed to flee. As soon as he was able—*if* he was able—he'd contact her there.

With luck, he'd be able to board *The Swan* tonight and convince the captain to leave immediately. After selling the sketch at the Ivory Market, he'd sail to Morocco and satisfy his debt with Temür.

With enough luck, that would be the end of this, and the rebel would call off his assassin.

Archimedes extinguished the lamp and moved to the window, his gaze searching the docks below. He didn't see the woman, but there were too many shadows to be certain.

He looked to the harbor. *The Swan*'s deck lamps were lit. Probably best to run to the airship now rather than to wait—and if *The Swan* had an early start, Yasmeen's anger might have cooled by the time she caught up to him.

Perhaps she was already looking. *Lady Corsair*'s decks were ablaze with light, as if she'd woken the entire crew and planned to—

No. His heart skidded to a stop. Not ablaze with light. Just ablaze . . . and he'd left Yasmeen drugged and hidden in a closet.

Dear God.

The explosion came in a great flare of light. Archimedes shouted, shielding his eyes. The window cracked. The walls shuddered. And then he was flying down the stairs, onto the docks, joined by men, women, all running, half of them still pulling on their clothes. Even in Port Fallow, an airship catching fire was a disaster that brought help, not the vultures. On the water, ships unfurled their canvas sails, moving away from the burning, floating debris that had once been the finest skyrunner on the seven seas. Above, airship engines started, huffing great bellows of steam, dropping their tethers and fleeing the heat and sparks.

Pieces of burning envelope fluttered through the air like confetti. The south dock was ablaze. Archimedes raced down the flaming boards, eyes watering from the intensity of the heat and smoke and *he'd left her drugged and helpless.*

"Yasmeen!" He shouted over the noise of the engines and cries for help, but the sound was lost beneath the roar of the burning ship. Desperately, he searched the glowing water. *"Yasmeen!"*

The end of the dock collapsed. Hands gripped Archimedes' shoulders in an unbreakable hold, yanked him backward, then dragged him when he struggled. He froze when a burning timber crashed into the boards where he'd been standing. He looked back, recognized the giant man.

"Eben Machen?" His voice was hoarse from screaming her name.

The mad pirate's fingers hardened painfully on his shoulders. "Wolfram Gunther-Baptiste."

"Yes." A fool, about to die, but he still had hope. This man was a friend to her. "Yasmeen. Oh, God. She was—Did she survive? *Did you see her?"*

Hope vanished when Mad Machen shook his head. Archimedes couldn't mistake the despair in the pirate's eyes when he looked at the burning ship. It quickly hardened into a mad resolve. He let go of Archimedes' shoulders, slapped his arm.

"We'll haul out the boats and search the water. We'll find her."

They didn't find her. They found bodies, so many bodies— all burned beyond recognition but for scraps of cloth, prosthetic limbs, a few gold teeth. No one that fit Yasmeen's size and shape.

The ship was still burning when it sank beneath the surface. Archimedes dove again and again into the water, trying to fight his way inside before it sank too deep. He tried past the rising of the sun, until his hands shook and his teeth chattered, and Mad Machen threatened to break his neck rather than let him go down again. He attempted to drink the coffee they brought him, but vomited it back up when he imagined her at the bottom of the harbor, still trapped in the hideaway.

A boiler explosion, everyone said. It happened all the time.

And every time it was repeated, Captain Machen got a mad look in his eyes. Only after the man finally called him Archimedes did he realize what the pirate had been thinking when they'd met on the docks: Wolfram Gunther-Baptiste provided weapons and explosives.

But Archimedes Fox hadn't done this.

He'd killed Yasmeen, though. The knowledge crushed every other thought, every other care. He didn't remember making his way back to the boardinghouse, or climbing the stairs to his room, but his legs were still trembling from the effort when he opened the door.

The *unlocked* door.

He stared at the empty bed. The glider contraption was gone. They hadn't taken anything else, but that was enough. Too much. He dropped his head to his hands, slid to the floor.

And knew his luck had finally run out.

Chapter Four

Eventually, Archimedes crawled to the bed. Fever set in. For three days, he tossed in his sheets, and woke shivering in clothes drenched with sweat. When the boardinghouse matron came round, he discovered that during his delirium, he'd somehow had sense enough to post the letter to Zenobia. As arranged, she didn't reply. He didn't send another message telling her the sketch had been taken. When he could manage the stairs without tumbling down, he took a meal and a pint at the nearest tavern. Around him, everyone spoke of where they'd been when *Lady Corsair*'s boiler had blown; no one mentioned a da Vinci sketch or a satchel that could convert into a glider. The next day, he chose another tavern, bought a meal and several pints, drinking as he listened to the talk around him. By the next week, he rarely bothered with the meals. He drank and listened, and then drank more.

Two months after *Lady Corsair* had burned, Archimedes woke with a pounding in his head and a knife at his throat.

A low voice purred in his ear. "What will you call this adventure? *Archimedes Fox and the Drunkard's Filthy Stench*?"

Yasmeen? Archimedes opened his eyes to a coal dark room, not daring to hope. Dreams of her had come before. He'd always woken, cold and shaking, his face wet—but it wasn't wet now, and he wasn't shaking. A weight pushed on his chest until he could hardly breathe. Was she sitting on him?

"You're heavier than you look, Captain," he said on a wheeze.

She hissed. Pain bit his neck with the edge of her blade. Ah, sweet bliss. Not dreaming at all.

And she was alive.

Without any air to laugh, Archimedes grinned as elation poured through him. It didn't matter if she killed him now. Focusing on the feel of her, he realized that she'd straddled his chest, her knees and shins pinning his shoulders and upper arms to the mattress—but he could bend his elbows. He could lift his hands. He could reach her waist. She stiffened when his fingers slid over her hips.

Solid. Real. Warm.

He felt the trickle of blood down his throat. Her breath skimmed over his jaw. Her hair tickled his face. Was she close enough to kiss him?

Oh, God. Please.

Her voice was soft. "Tell me the truth and I'll make it quick: Did you set fire to my ship?"

What the hell? *No.*

But he could only mouth the word—and it was too dark for her to see. Goddammit. He shoved his hands beneath her ass. As if prodded, she jolted forward, her weight shifting long enough for him to breathe.

Long enough for him to bite out, "I *never* would!"

"So you already said." She settled back down, trapping his hands, but this time allowing him room for shallow inhalations. "I can see, you idiot. Why would I ask if I couldn't?"

"Why say you'd make it quick if you wouldn't?"

Her dark laugh filled the room. "That's true enough. I'd have flayed you alive."

Why say it—and why ask? Suspicion crawled into his mind. "Is there someone who needs to be flayed?"

"Yes. It wasn't a boiler explosion." A sharp claw scraped down his jaw. "And you don't have my twenty-five percent, do you? Do you even have the sketch?"

Could she see the flush of his skin? He wasn't often ashamed or embarrassed, but admitting that someone had stolen the sketch was pure humiliation. "I've been searching for it."

"At the bottom of a pint?"

"I've found treasures in odder locations." He'd found one sitting on his chest.

"Who took it?"

"I wish to God I knew. But if the idiot thief didn't use the sketch for privy paper, he'll try to sell it. So I'll hear word of it soon."

"Find me when you do. Goodbye, Mr. Fox."

Her weight lifted suddenly, and he sat up, blindly trying to follow her. His searching hands caught her thigh before she could move away, and he snaked his arms around her hips. Her fingers fisted in his hair, but she didn't rip his head off.

"Yasmeen. I'm sorry for the hideaway. And I'm so very, very—" He cut himself off, recognizing the swelling through his chest, the choking grief that would come, now overwhelmed by incredible joy. He finished in a rough voice, "*Very* moved by your survival."

He released her. She didn't let go of his hair. "Because of you, Mr. Fox, I couldn't protect my crew. Instead of fighting when my lady was boarded, I was lying in that closet."

God. Archimedes closed his eyes.

Pain tore through his scalp as she yanked his head back, forcing him to look up at her. "But I also suspect that if I hadn't been in that damn hideaway, I'd be dead, and no one would be left to avenge them."

He would have. If he'd known, he'd have hunted them to the ends of the earth.

If he'd known . . . and now he knew.

Determination filled him. "Who are they?"

"I don't know. Yet."

Abruptly, she let him go. A spark lighter scraped. The flickering glow illuminated her face. She drew on the cigarillo, the tip burning orange. He stared at her, all but overwhelmed again by the beautiful angles of her cheekbones, the point of her chin, the fullness of her lips.

Icy amusement curled her mouth as her gaze ran from his head to his toes. "Did you have company?"

He looked down at himself. Naked. Ah, yes. It had been snowing when he'd stumbled home. He'd slipped into a garbage heap, and the matron hadn't allowed the stink to enter her house. Walking up three flights of stairs without a stitch of clothing obviously hadn't offended her, however. She'd watched him the entire way.

Lying back, he folded his arms behind his head and offered Yasmeen a more flattering view. "My only companions have been my dreams of you."

She snorted and turned for the door. Terror ripped through to his bones. No, he couldn't lose her this quickly again. He reared up out of bed, but stopped in surprise when she said, "Zenobia sends her greetings from London. You ought to let her know that you're not dead."

Greetings from—"What? When?"

Yasmeen grinned over her shoulder. "Take a bath, Mr. Fox. Then come find me at dawn. Perhaps I can think of a use for a man with balls of iron and a silver tongue."

He *was* dreaming. "Find you where?"

"If you can't figure that out, you're of no use to me after all."

By the time the door closed behind her, leaving him in the dark again, he'd already figured it out. *Vesuvius* had sailed into Port Fallow that evening. He'd find her on Mad Machen's ship. But that was the easy one—because if an exploding boiler hadn't destroyed *Lady Corsair,* then who the hell had attacked her? He'd need to figure that out, too . . . but the *why* was all too obvious.

They'd been looking for the sketch.

Yasmeen's knees always ached in the mornings now, as if during the short hours of sleep, her body returned to the three weeks she'd spent in bed, healing her shattered legs. Upon every waking, she stared up at the deckhead over her narrow berth, thinking that she ought to have just let Mad Machen cut them off after his men dragged her out of the water. His blacksmith could have given her better legs. Stronger. Faster. Impervious to pain. Maybe with a few concealed weapons that let her shoot bullets from her toes.

And perhaps Yasmeen would take to wearing a robe and demurely folding her hands, too.

Gritting her teeth, she pushed down the worsted wool blanket and swung her legs around. A film of ice covered the water in the washbowl. She shivered through her quick bath, and dressed in the new clothes that felt as stiff as her body. They'd wear in, eventually. Within a half hour, her damn knees would loosen up, too.

Rubbing warmth into her hands, she paced her tiny cabin, listening to *Vesuvius*'s crew go about their duties on the deck above. When the ship's bell rang the hour and she could walk without shuffling like an old woman, she joined Barker and Jannsen, the ship's surgeon, in the wardroom for breakfast.

Jannsen looked up from his book when she entered, and

watched her over his reading spectacles as she crossed to her chair and sat. "You look well."

"I slept well."

"Did you use the sleeping draught?"

"No." She preferred to smoke her opium—and she preferred to wake up aching rather than to wake up needing more. She knew better than to take a draught every evening; too many people went straight from a surgeon's tender care to the bowels of an opium den. She glanced at Barker and narrowed her eyes. "Why the fool's grin?"

"You owe me a drink. Tenner saw you leave the ship."

Ah, her midnight excursion. When they'd been sailing out of London, she'd bet the quartermaster that she could slip away from *Vesuvius* without being noticed. Last night, she hadn't even tried to be furtive; she'd asked Tenner to help her lower a dinghy to the water.

But she'd pay up, simply because of how good it had felt to be out and about again—almost as good as it had felt to straddle a naked Archimedes Fox's chest. She hadn't expected to take such pleasure in meeting with him. Even now, she couldn't fathom how the anger that she'd carefully nurtured for months had been disarmed. Perhaps it had been his unabashed joy upon seeing her alive, and his earnest apology for his part in it. Perhaps it had been the dangerous stillness that had overtaken him when he'd determined to avenge her crew. Perhaps it had been the rough shadow on his jaw, the laughter in his emerald eyes, his easy grin.

Perhaps it was the fire that spread through her veins, kindled by every ridiculous word he said. If he hadn't smelled like a bilgewater trout, she'd have stayed a bit longer and burned it out. No reason not to. They'd played a short game of chase through obstacles of his identity and the sketch, but Yasmeen wasn't playing anymore. She had a single purpose now: to find the pig bastards who'd attacked her lady. It would take time and money, but she'd happily spend both.

Outside the wardroom's porthole, the sky was dark, with only a faint lightening in the eastern sky. Work would begin soon. If today's salvage expedition went well, she'd have reason to celebrate. There were worse ways to go about it than riding the sheets on a handsome man with a lean body and a silver tongue.

Not *many* worse ways, but still tempting enough to try it out once or twice.

Because the thought of that silver tongue made her feel generous, she said, "After I have my strongbox, I'll buy you a drink *and* a pound of Guajaca coffee."

Barker's eyelids became heavy, as if his latest ladylove had just whispered into his ear. A weak version of the brew was a sailor's staple, but as Barker often rapturously described it, the difference between the strong Guajaca blend and the drink aboard *Vesuvius* was akin to the difference between cream and whey.

Yasmeen rarely drank either, though the beans had once lined her strongbox with gold. To her mind, coffee was simply proof that civilization still existed in the New World after the Europeans and Africans had fled the Horde, whose khans and generals had believed that everyone beyond the Ural Mountains was a soulless barbarian. Yasmeen wasn't inclined to agree with that belief, except for when she drank the barbaric piss that New Worlders called tea. But coffee was *supposed* to taste like barbaric piss, and the French and Liberé had fought a war over the ownership and taxing of it.

War and taxes. The Horde and the New World were separated by oceans, but in Yasmeen's experience, all civilizations were the same in essentials.

But because she was feeling generous, she wouldn't disrupt their quiet breakfast by saying so.

*   *   *

Dawn had filled the clouded sky with a faint light when Yasmeen emerged onto the weather deck. The chill wind slapped her face. She folded her heavy collar up, tugged her woolen scarf in place over her nose and mouth. *Vesuvius* had anchored near the north dock. Her gaze searched the busy boardwalk, the dinghies cutting across the water, the rowboats-for-hire.

A flash of bright color near a tinker's cart caught her attention—a tall man wearing lime-green breeches. Though he faced away from her and a hat concealed his hair, that couldn't be anyone but Archimedes.

So he'd come.

She reached for her silver cigarillo case. Tucked into her belt, it had been one of the few things that had survived the explosion and her fall into the harbor. Her gloves made her fingers thick, and she fumbled the catch before sliding it open. Only a few cigarillos remained inside. No matter. When Ivy Blacksmith retrieved the strongbox from beneath the water, she'd buy more.

The cigarillo calmed her jumping nerves. On the docks, Archimedes weaved through the carts and coaches, passing the boats-for-hire. Was he light on coins? If the sketch had been stolen, maybe his purse had been, too.

But, no. He stopped by a messenger in an autogyro, and a coin passed between them. Perhaps sending the message that he couldn't join her?

Footsteps approached across the boards. Yasmeen recognized Ivy's quick stride and turned to greet the blacksmith. Her copper hair tucked beneath a wool cap and her freckled cheeks red from the cold, the woman usually wore a smile that was sweet to behold.

But now she was grinning, all but vibrating with excitement.

"It's ready as soon as you are. We only need to sail closer to the south dock before we launch."

Yasmeen glanced around the decks. Though she had no doubt that Ivy's submersible had been brilliantly designed and perfectly constructed, the diving machine hadn't been tested before. If the blacksmith went into the water and anything were to happen to her, Mad Machen would likely go truly mad, and strangle Yasmeen for not stopping her. But if he were here from the outset, he'd only blame himself.

"Where's Captain Machen?"

Ivy's grin became a laugh. "There." With a hand made of mechanical flesh, she pointed to an old herring buss floating nearby, its sails furled. "It's Big Thom's salvage ship. Eben's borrowing his diving suit so that he can keep an eye on me while I'm down there."

Madness. The whole point of the submersible was that it would be safer than a suit, but Eben had a reputation to uphold. A feared pirate couldn't also be a softhearted sap who desperately loved a sweet blacksmith, so he'd worry about her below the water, where there wouldn't be any witnesses to it—and probably claim that he only wanted to prevent Ivy from using the submersible to escape him.

Still, those dive suits were a death trap. Love made idiots of everyone. "A gold sous says that you end up rescuing him," she said.

"I'd be a fool to bet against that." Ivy's gray, ungloved fingers curled over the edge of the gunwale as she leaned forward, eyes widening. "Is that man attacking the messenger?"

Yasmeen looked to the docks, where the autogyro was hovering above the boards, the young messenger's legs spinning full tilt, the long blades a blur overhead. Beneath it, Archimedes had hold of the horizontal steel bar that served as the bottom of the boy's seat frame. He began to run, pushing the autogyro to the edge of the dock, the unbuckled sides of his overcoat flapping open like wings and revealing an orange waistcoat.

"Oh, blue heavens!" Ivy cried out as man and autogyro dropped from the dock, wobbling wildly. His boots splashed in the water before the machine leveled out and began to gain altitude. Archimedes whooped, and his familiar deep laughter carried across the harbor.

Yasmeen had to laugh, too. He just couldn't take the easy route, could he?

The worried furrows in the blacksmith's brow smoothed, and she watched them approach *Vesuvius* with an expression that seemed at once distracted and intensely focused. "With this much wind, I wouldn't ever climb on one of those. But do you see how his weight stabilizes it? It's because he's so low. I'd have to figure out a way to land despite some heavy object hanging below—or design them not to land at all. For an airship, perhaps. And with that much weight, two to spin. That boy is sweating already. And by the blessed stars, those breeches are something else."

"So is Archimedes Fox," Yasmeen said.

"The adventurer?" Ivy glanced at Yasmeen for confirmation. After a moment of disbelief, her eyes softened and she looked to the man hanging beneath the autogyro again. "In London, the girls in our house who knew their letters would read his stories aloud to the rest of us. We'd pool our pennies when a new copy of the *Gazette* was printed, though sometimes it meant going without a supper. It was worth it, though. No matter how terrible the danger, he always escaped. *Always*. Even when it seemed impossible." She smiled with the memory. "We listened to them so often, I knew chapters by heart."

So did Yasmeen. Perhaps that was why she'd found it so difficult to hold on to her anger—not because of his lean body or charming grin, but because in a sense, Archimedes Fox had been one of her closest companions for almost a decade.

And now, he made her laugh when she had little reason to.

"I heard he was someone else," Ivy said quietly.

Of course she had. Mad Machen wouldn't have known any better, not immediately. "It's funny, the things you hear on these seas. About ten years ago, I heard a story about a weapons smuggler who was betrayed by the Lusitanian mercenary he'd hired to carry his cargo from Reval to Copenhagen. Santos Silva was the mercenary's name—have you ever heard of him?"

"No."

"That's because Silva and his men put a gun on the smuggler, and promised to leave him alive if he handed over the crate of weapons. Of course they wouldn't have, so the smuggler dove behind the crate for cover and shot all of Silva's men except for two seamen and the cook—he's the one I heard the story from. But a smuggler who can kill eight men and then sail their bodies across the Baltic Sea so that his remaining associates will know better than to betray him doesn't sound like the sort of man who'd laugh his way across a harbor beneath an autogyro, does he?"

"No, he doesn't," Ivy agreed, smiling. "That sort of man sounds like Archimedes Fox."

Clever girl. "So he does."

Flying near enough now that Yasmeen could see the buckles of his waistcoat and the diamond pattern in the orange brocade, Archimedes called out, "Permission to board, Captain?"

"It's not my ship!" she called back. "You'll have to wait for your welcome!"

"Wait? Well, that's a fine way to ruin my entrance!"

Grinning, he tilted his head back and said something to the messenger above him. Their direction veered slightly, carrying Archimedes to *Vesuvius*'s tall poop deck, where the autogyro's blades were less likely to catch on the rigging.

"I have to talk to him for a bit," she told the blacksmith. "Then

I'll bring him over to meet you. He'll probably try to persuade you to take him under."

"Not today, not until I've tested her. But give me ten minutes to polish her guts, and I'll let him crawl around inside."

"He's charming," Yasmeen warned her.

"Yes, but I can't try to escape Mad Machen with a passenger in my boat, can I?"

"If you escape with my strongbox, I'll quarter you."

Ivy heaved a great, theatrical sigh. "And now fear for my life forces me to come back."

Yasmeen shook her head. She'd once paid the girl a fortune to leave Eben alone; Ivy had used the money to set up a blacksmith's shop on *Vesuvius* instead. But Yasmeen supposed that it had worked out in the end: Ivy had also used a portion of that fortune to build the submersible for her, and it hadn't cost Yasmeen a bit.

The autogyro flew up over the stern, blades whirring. Lines of sand provided traction on the icy boards as Yasmeen made her way aft, where Archimedes landed lightly on the deck, his face flushed with exertion and laughter. Around them, *Vesuvius*'s crew gave him a hearty cheer, and he bowed, sweeping lower when he caught sight of Yasmeen.

"Not their captain, but *my* captain," he said.

"I wouldn't have you. Within a day, you'd be strapped to a whipping post for disregarding my orders."

"That's true enough," he said, straightening. Heat flared in his emerald eyes as he looked her over, and Yasmeen stiffened. Oh, he'd ruin everything. From his silver tongue would come a suggestion of *where* she could whip him and order him about, the crew would hear it, and then she'd have to string him up naked from the side of Mad Machen's ship.

His gaze caught on her face. Relief slipped through her when he said, "I have followed one of your orders, however."

So he had. He'd bathed—and shaved, though he hadn't needed to exert himself to that degree. She liked a rough jaw.

"And here I am, at your disposal," he continued. "What do you require?"

She turned toward the stairs and gestured for him to follow. "Only a conversation, Mr. Fox. And I hope to soon have a gift for you."

Ivy Blacksmith hadn't yet named her submersible, but Yasmeen had heard the crew members call it *The Copper Prick*. Yasmeen could see a faint resemblance in the cylindrical body and the rounded head, but she thought the name was wishful thinking on their part—the width of the capsule was as tall as a man, and in length was three times a man's height. From there, the resemblance in shape ended. The tail tapered off into a propeller set over a pair of flat rudders, and she'd never encountered a prick with a raised bump on the shaft similar to Ivy's glass observation dome in the capsule's hatch.

Perhaps she was more selective in her pricks than Mad Machen's crew.

She led Archimedes amidships and stopped near the port rail, where they could watch the activity around the copper submersible without standing in the crew's way—and where they could speak in relative privacy.

"Is this my gift?" He gestured to the submersible. "I already have my own, you realize."

God's truth, men were all the same. But he also appeared suitably impressed by the machine—as any man ought to be. "Your gift is the copy of your sketch, if all goes well. Depending upon the sort of person you'll have to steal the original back from, you'd be wise to put distance between you before she has a chance to realize it's missing."

His gaze snapped to hers. *"She?"*

He knew, Yasmeen saw immediately. His expression resembled that of a man who faced an oncoming battalion of war machines, with a mob of zombies closing in from behind. For all of his frivolity, for all of his charm, this man was also deeply aware of the dangers the world threw at them.

"I can't be certain," Yasmeen said. And it seemed strange that the elite guard would steal such an item—they didn't steal anything, unless it were necessary. But who could say what another person considered necessary? "But Miracle Mattson learned about the sketch from Franz Kessler. You've heard what happened to him?"

"His throat slit. That wasn't you? In her express, Zenobia said you were coming to speak with him."

"I didn't arrive in Port Fallow until after it happened. But a woman was there, watching the house. I had no reason to think she knew anything of the sketch at the time—not until I heard from one of Mad Machen's men that you were hiding in a crate, and paid him a sous to look for a woman in a robe. Were you truly hiding?"

"Wouldn't you?"

"If I thought I was her target. So you knew what she was. How?" Not many New Worlders recognized a *gan tsetseg* woman.

"I've seen Temür Agha's guard."

Temür Agha. Fifteen years ago, the general had crushed the rebellion in Constantinople by razing the city to the ground. Of royal blood, cunning and ruthless, his name inspired terror across the empire—including the ruling houses in Xanadu. Even the Khan hadn't dared an assassination, and instead had named him the governor of the Moroccan occupied territories, sending Temür to the farthest edge of the empire.

Even that meant risking an insult: officials and *dargas* were assigned to the territories outside of Asia as a punishment, not reward. Temür hadn't retaliated, but from the beginning of his governorship, rumors had been swirling that he was amassing great power in Morocco and would soon try to march across the empire. Ten years had passed, and he hadn't yet—but Yasmeen wouldn't place bets against it happening, eventually.

She didn't care one way or another. In the meantime, she avoided Morocco as much as possible. Archimedes apparently hadn't had the sense to, and the idea that he'd hidden from the woman amused Yasmeen; obviously, someone had explained what the elite guards were capable of, but hadn't mentioned that they weren't rabid murderers who gutted everyone who passed them. Only loyalty and duty were more sacred to the guard than self-control and compassion. If the woman had found him huddling near a crate, she'd have probably given him a blanket or a coin.

Unless Archimedes had reason to think the woman had targeted him.

Yasmeen froze with her cigarillo halfway to her lips. "Your debt," she said. "Is it to Temür Agha?"

"Yes."

Her stomach rolled into a hard knot. "And that woman was his guard?"

"I don't know. I didn't see her clearly. I didn't want to take the risk."

Only an idiot would. "I saw her clearly. What did Temür Agha's guard look like?"

"Long black hair, braided here." His fingers met at the center of his forehead and dragged back over his ears. "Beautiful. Skin like teak on her face, but gray hands."

Yasmeen pursed her lips. He'd just described half of the elite guard after the women had been altered with mechanical flesh. "Anything helpful? Was she tall? Full-lipped, thin-nosed, curly-haired, round-faced? Did her features give any hint of her ancestry? Did you hear her speak?"

"Straight hair. She didn't speak. She was as tall as that black-smith." He indicated Ivy. "A Turk, perhaps. Or Hindustani."

A better description, but it was still impossible to be certain. "Perhaps the woman I saw was Temür's guard, then. But as two months have passed and you aren't dead, I suspect not."

Yasmeen *hoped* not. If she discovered that the woman had boarded her lady, Yasmeen wouldn't be able to avenge her crew alone; she'd need to hire a group of mercenaries and assassins. If the woman was Temür Agha's guard, however, it hardly mattered whether Yasmeen went by herself or with a small army; either would turn into a suicide mission.

"Franz Kessler and her presence on the docks might be a coincidence," Archimedes said softly. "But not likely. If Kessler had told her of the sketch, she might have guessed it was aboard *Lady Corsair*. Were all of your crew killed before the explosion?"

Yasmeen nodded. He'd put it together exactly as she had. "They barely had time to draw their weapons."

"That sounds like the elite guard. What I've heard they can do."

"What they *can* do, yes." But not what they *would* do—and that was where Yasmeen became uncertain again. "But if she was only after the sketch, she could have stolen it without killing any-one, and without anyone aboard seeing her."

"And if she couldn't open your strongbox?"

Would she rage through the airship, taking out her frustration on the crew? Yasmeen didn't think so. But perhaps the woman hadn't been alone. Though Ginger had never seen who'd attacked her, she'd had an impression of "they." Yet at such a moment, in the dark, one quick person could have seemed like many.

Yasmeen simply didn't know. "Whatever happened, when she didn't find the sketch, she might have realized that you'd had it when you left my lady."

"*If* she saw me," Archimedes said.

"She saw you."

"But—"

"She saw you." Suddenly amused, Yasmeen caught his gaze. He'd managed to surprise her by hiding beside a crate in a pile of rags, but he wouldn't have escaped the attention of that woman. "Even if we're wrong and she was only strolling along the docks for her own pleasure, she saw you."

His eyes searched her face. "How do you know so much about them?"

"Don't be dense, Mr. Fox. And don't tell your sister, either. I'm waiting until her curiosity about my background is on the verge of killing her—and then I'll negotiate a better royalty in exchange for each new crumb." She appreciated the deep laugh that served as his response, the squint of his eyes as it shook through him. "Was seeing this woman your reason for sending Zenobia to London?"

His laugh faded. "Yes."

"To the Iron Duke, no less. I thought you didn't trust him?"

"I wouldn't trust him to protect *me*. But who's more capable of protecting her?"

Yasmeen could only think of a few names, but none who had incurred the same sort of debt to Archimedes that Rhys Trahaearn had. The Iron Duke had thrown him from his pirate ship, but Wolfram Gunther-Baptiste *had* boarded that ship in good faith and fulfilled the job asked of him. Trahaearn considered anyone who served his ship under his protection—which meant providing help when needed. When Archimedes asked for something of this nature, there was no question that the Iron Duke would do it.

But Archimedes probably didn't understand that—most likely, he'd just rolled the dice.

"And if the Iron Duke is reluctant, who more likely to talk him into it than Scarsdale?"

He grinned. "Did he need to?"

"No. But you're right. How could Scarsdale resist the author of the Archimedes Fox adventures? He and your sister have been inseparable since she arrived." And because she couldn't resist, either, "Perhaps Zenobia will soon be a countess."

Archimedes' grin fixed to his face, and he gave his head a hard shake, as if to clear it. "Eh?"

She flicked her cigarillo over the side of the ship. "She's a practical woman. It'd be a good fit—and perfect timing. He's searching for a wife. Duty calls, and he needs the heir and spare."

He stared at her, as if trying to read the truth from her face. Yasmeen smiled, showing her teeth. An expression of relief slipped over his features, then worry, then relief again. Finally, he said, "I can't decide if you're serious. I think I ought to write her."

"Perhaps you should," Yasmeen agreed.

The wind picked up, chopping the harbor's surface into rough waves, but making for a quick sail to the south docks. Mad Machen ordered the anchor dropped near the site where her lady had crashed into the water and returned to the main deck, where Big Thom ran a test of the dive suit's air pump, checking the flow through the long, coiled tube. The hand-cranked device forced air to circulate through the waterproofed leather hose and into the diver's brass helmet—which meant the diver relied on someone else simply to *breathe*.

Madness. Even the tiny enclosed space in Ivy's submersible would be preferable, and Yasmeen wouldn't take money to dive underwater in *that*.

No doubt Archimedes would do it for free. Yasmeen looked starboard, where a hoist suspended the submersible over *Vesuvius*'s side, copper skin gleaming in the dull sunlight. From inside the capsule, Archimedes' exclamations of awe and questions to Ivy had echoed hollowly through the open hatch for the past twenty minutes, but his voice had smoothed out now, hints of flattery and teasing slipping through.

Trying to charm her into taking him down, no doubt. Good luck to him.

She made her way across the deck toward Mad Machen, who was holding the full-length canvas suit at arm's length, a frown darkening his scarred face.

"How does a man get into this blasted thing?"

"There's a double-flap fastening in the back," Yasmeen said, but his question sparked a note of alarm in her head. "You've done this before, haven't you?"

"I've dived before. This looks to be a hell of a lot easier. You don't even have to hold your breath."

Yasmeen looked to Big Thom, who rose from his crouch next to the air pump, shaking his head. The man lived up to his name, with broad shoulders made wider by the pneumatic braces across his back and chest. Combined with his steel prosthetic arms, the apparatus gave him tremendous hauling power—and during the Horde's occupation in England, he'd hauled fish. He ran a salvaging boat now, though by the looks of it, he hadn't been hauling up much treasure.

"No," Big Thom said. "It's not easier. When you told me you'd dived, I thought you understood that. But you're not going down. Not in my suit."

Big balls, too. Not many men would say "no" so baldly to Mad Machen's face.

Quiet fell over the main deck. The crew wasn't used to hearing that word said to him, either.

"She's not going down alone. Not on this first run."

"That's your business," Big Thom said, as if he didn't see the pulse throbbing in Mad Machen's temples and the tension whiten-

ing the pirate's knuckles and lips. "Unless you've practiced swimming with the brass guards over that canvas, weighing you down,
you aren't any good to her anyway—and I'll probably be hauling
up your dead body."

"Then I won't use the guards."

Ivy's voice called from starboard, "And lose your *other* leg to a
shark?"

Yasmeen glanced over her shoulder, where the blacksmith was
climbing out of the submersible's hatch, her eyebrows drawn and
mouth tight. She leapt to the deck, followed by Archimedes.

"There's more than that," Big Thom added. "You've got to know
to keep your hose from kinking. You've got to know how fast you
can come up. Give me a few hours and I'll find a diver who can go
down with her. You can't."

"I can," Archimedes said.

Yasmeen huffed out a laugh. Of course he could. And was idiot
enough to offer.

Mad Machen's wild gaze landed on her face. Ah, softhearted
Eben. She'd have blamed love for this, but he'd already been a bit
mad before he'd met Ivy.

She shrugged. "He made it through the Underwater Perils of
Porto."

The pirate looked to Archimedes. "You go down, then. If she
doesn't come back up, I'll kill you."

That wouldn't do at all. Yasmeen said, "But before he kills you,
make sure to hook that hoist chain to my strongbox."

Archimedes grinned. "I'll do that."

He shrugged out of his coat, Mad Machen handed the canvas
suit to her as he crossed the deck to meet Ivy—and that quickly,
Yasmeen became an idiot's valet. Facing her, only a foot away,
Archimedes held her gaze while he shed his waistcoat.

"Will you fear for me, Captain?"

"No. You have a fool's luck."

"It does seem to be returning." He sat back against a tackle chest and hauled off his boots. "Perhaps because you came back to me. My favorite mercenary."

That nonsense didn't even warrant a response. He stepped into the diving suit and she fastened the back, checking the edges for a watertight seal. The water would be cold. Wet and cold could be disastrous.

"I think Big Thom's half in love with her," Archimedes said. "I probably ought to warn him about Mad Machen."

Yasmeen looked around his shoulder to where Mad Machen and Ivy stood with the salvager. The blacksmith was showing him the submersible's air pump, which operated in the same way as the diving suit's pump, but was cranked by a windup mechanism instead of by hand. Big Thom did appear stricken with longing, yet not by Ivy herself.

"It's her *arms*, you idiot." When the Horde grafted tools onto the laborers in the occupied territories, it cared about function, not appearance. The skeletal prosthetics beneath the salvager's heavy coat sleeves and gloves probably looked more like thin steel bones than limbs. "He's likely never seen mechanical flesh before."

"And couldn't afford it even if he had?"

"Yes." The only person outside of Xanadu who could manipulate the nanoagents necessary to create mechanical flesh was the Blacksmith in London, but his work didn't come cheap. And though Big Thom could buy a pair of arms on credit, few people risked owing a debt that large to the Blacksmith—especially if they couldn't be certain of making every payment. She gestured to the quartermaster, standing near the main mast. "Barker will be paying off his leg for a decade."

Archimedes whistled softly. "That's a heavy weight."

"Not as heavy as ten thousand livre."

"That only weighs as much as a stolen da Vinci sketch." He smiled faintly when she snorted, his gaze on Ivy and Big Thom again. "What of the other sort? Your Pegg had a foot that looked like a foot, even if it was metal. One of your gunners had arms of the same type. I forgot his name."

Yasmeen ignored the ache in her throat, the sudden tightness around her lungs. "Mr. Pessinger," she supplied. "That was Ivy's work, too."

"Ah. Why am I not surprised? I thought they were mechanical flesh until Pegg let me have a closer look. But her prosthetic was an actual machine, not metal made flesh and shaped by the nanoagents. I've never seen such intricate gearwork and hydraulics before. Incredible."

"Yes."

She couldn't keep the thickness out of her voice. Archimedes' head swung round, his gaze sharpening. Avoiding his eyes, she handed him the first of the brass guards that buckled around his lower leg—he could put these on himself.

"Won't you go down with us?" he asked softly.

"To see my lady broken and to pick at her shattered bones?" She'd do better stabbing herself through the heart. "No, thank you, Mr. Fox. I'll leave the traipsing through ruins to you."

His eyes searched her face for a long moment before he nodded and stooped to fasten the guards at his lower legs and thighs. She buckled more plates over his chest, back, and arms, until he resembled an invading crusader from the centuries before the Horde's invasions.

She hefted the domed helmet over his head and fastened the bolts, then tapped the round glass plate over his face. "You ought to have had one of these in Venice! I couldn't have lifted you to toss you over!"

His muffled laugh fogged the small window. She smiled in

response, and his splayed, awkward walk across the boards continued to improve her mood. Big Thom verified the air flow in the
domed helmet. The crew rolled back the net stretched across the
gangway so that he wouldn't have to climb over the side of the ship.

He dropped into the water a few minutes later, followed by the
submersible. Mad Machen stood at *Vesuvius*'s starboard bulwark,
his fingers clenched on the gunwale as the capsule sank beneath
the surface. Yasmeen paced the decks and smoked the last of the
cigarillos in her case.

Eleven hundred livre sat at the bottom of the harbor. That money
was a skyrunner, swift and sleek. A full complement of arms and
cannons. A seasoned crew, supplies. She'd buy mercenaries, information, loyalty. If necessary, she'd purchase a war and bring it to the
doorstep of those who'd dared to hurt those under her protection.

They'd pay. Oh, how they'd pay.

A shout hailed from starboard. Heart pounding, Yasmeen ran
to the side. The water alongside the ship seemed to boil, and the
submersible suddenly emerged through the roiling surface—with
Archimedes riding astride the large capsule. Hoots of laughter and
lewd shouts joined the cheers of the crew, and this time Yasmeen
was inclined to agree with them: The man did have enormous balls.

Mad Machen ordered his men to the hoist. Below, Ivy threw
her hatch open and poked her head out. Her gaze locked with the
pirate's before she searched out Yasmeen's.

Her grin almost split her pale cheeks. "We got it!"

They had it, but forever seemed to pass before she *saw* it.
The submersible's cable winch had to be wound by hand, and even
after Big Thom replaced the straining crew, the going was slow.
Brought in too fast on a rocking ship and swinging cable, the
strongbox could smash like a cannonball against the hull.

Yasmeen distracted herself by helping Archimedes out of his suit, and shouted for coffee and a blanket when she saw the chattering of his teeth, discovered the icy cold of his hands. When she rubbed his fingers between her own, a man had never seemed so pleased with himself.

But, hell—she was pleased with him, too. She was pleased with the whole damn world.

The strongbox finally lifted out of the water, the casing dull but undamaged. Archimedes stood beside her, a wool blanket clutched over his shoulders, as Big Thom carefully brought the strongbox around over the side and lowered it to the deck. Yasmeen sank to her heels in front of it.

"Captain Corsair!" Ivy called her name before she could touch the casing. "That's one of the Blacksmith's, yes? A blind-dial combination?"

"Yes." No doubt the girl had constructed a few when she'd worked in the Blacksmith's shop. "Why?"

Ivy crouched beside her. "They're strong, but sometimes the dial mechanisms are knocked out of alignment if they're hit hard. That explosion shattered your legs. A force like that might have been enough."

Enough to change the combination? "So what do you propose?"

"I'll open it for you."

Unease flittered through her. "*You* can open my strongbox."

Could the *gan tsetseg*?

The blacksmith wiggled her gray fingers. "I can touch your skin and feel your nanoagents moving. Sensing the tumblers falling into place . . ." She trailed off, as if unable to think of a comparison to anything as easy. "It'll be safer for you."

And Yasmeen preferred not to spend her first coins on a prosthetic hand. She gestured for Ivy to proceed. The girl did so quickly, and if Yasmeen jumped a little when the steel panel snapped closed on Ivy's wrist, she wasn't alone. But the mechanical flesh was unharmed, and a moment later, Ivy smiled and sat back. The top unscrewed and the belly opened.

An empty belly. No sacks of gold coins. No leather portfolio.

"Oh!" Ivy said. Her brow furrowed. "But I thought—I . . . *Oh*."

"Yasmeen," Archimedes said quietly.

Her hands shook. She reached for a cigarillo, then remembered she didn't have any more. Her stomach formed a sick, aching knot.

I have nothing.

Not even a way to avenge her crew. Panic began to build, shortening her breath. She fought it back, fought the terror.

This was what a heart of steel was for—and she'd crawled out of *nothing* before.

"I'm sorry, Mr. Fox. I don't seem to have your forgery, after all." She rose to her feet, ignoring him when he repeated her name. "Thank you, Ivy, for all of your help. Mr. Barker? I believe I owe you a drink. I'd like to pay up now."

While she still could.

Chapter Five

Of all the rough taverns near the docks, the Charging Bull was arguably the worst of the lot. Archimedes didn't expect to find Yasmeen there, but after a tour through half of Port Fallow's rum dives, he realized that was *exactly* where to find her. There was no counting the number of tales he'd heard about Captain Corsair in a tavern brawl, tearing through the other patrons like paper. Not so many stories lately, but the captain had been gutted by that empty strongbox. If she was looking to take out that pain on someone, there was no better place to look than the Charging Bull.

Approaching the entrance, he thought the brawl had already started. A crowd shouted encouragement inside—chanting *Henri! Henri! Henri!* above the noise of the musicians. A glass shattered against the floor as he walked in, followed by the crash of a chair and two swearing sailors. The scent of stale sweat and tobacco filled the air. Every table was occupied, all looking to the middle of the room, where a boy of about fourteen lay on a table with his trousers around his ankles. A woman straddled his narrow hips, her bodice down and skirt up. A crowd of aviators chanted in time with the whore's bouncing breasts. Someone had paid to make the boy a man, apparently.

Automaton musicians dressed in French navy uniforms played a jolly tune on the harpsichord and violin. No live musician would play here; too many had been knifed through the ribs for an off-key tune or in simple drunken bad temper. Archimedes found Yasmeen sitting at a table in the back corner, watching the boy's deflowering with a mildly amused expression. Her seat was situated in the only relatively quiet part of the tavern, given that those around her sat askew to their tables, hunched over their drinks as if they didn't dare turn their backs on her but also weren't going to risk looking her in the eyes.

A half-finished pint waited in front of her, a smaller glass empty beside it. Her brows lifted when she saw him, and she pushed out a chair with the toe of her boot. An invitation. More than he'd hoped for, but as she didn't immediately speak, Archimedes wouldn't assume that conversation was included with it. He ordered a round for them both when the barmaid appeared, sweating from the heat of the room.

From the center of the tavern came a chorus of cheers. Only the boy's feet were visible, his toes spreading wide, ankles stiff, and legs jerking as he orgasmed. Yasmeen picked up her pint, raised it with the rest of the room. Her gaze met his.

"To young love," she said.

Archimedes grinned. "May it always be so innocent."

"And as lucrative for at least one partner." She downed the pint in a few swallows. The table shivered as she slammed the glass back down. "What brings you to the Bull, Mr. Fox? Looking for sport on a table?"

"Looking for you."

Her knuckles rapped the tabletop. "Then climb on up."

Another invitation? And one that he could imagine, all too easily: wood at his back, and Yasmeen riding him. His hands filled with her soft breasts. Her claws digging into his shoulders. Wet heat surrounding his prick, taking him deep. Archimedes shifted in his seat, his body hardening. Not tonight. By God, he wanted to—but he'd wait until he *needed* to.

Yasmeen leaned forward, looking intently into his face. He could have distilled a potent liqueur from her breath. Too drunk for any sport, though he wouldn't have known just watching her, listening to her. The woman could hold her drink.

He wasn't a bit surprised by that fact.

"I believe I've done the impossible and rendered you speechless." She sat back. "I don't like it. I never thought to choose between your iron balls and your silver tongue."

"They're both at your disposal."

"That's much better. Ah, so is this." She accepted a foaming pint from the barmaid. "Thank you, Mr. Fox. Now, then. What brings you here?"

"You brought me here. I remembered tales of Captain Corsair and tavern brawls."

She laughed into her glass, lowered it. "You've heard those?"

"After you shot my father, I listened for any news of you." He lifted his drink to her. "I ought to have bought you one thirteen years ago."

In truth, he ought to have just killed the old man himself, but he'd still had some vision of proving him wrong. Now, he knew: If a job needed doing, then best just to get it done.

"I was glad to oblige. I've never had ambition of being roasted alive."

"So you had ambition of being bloodied and drunk in tavern brawls. Such honorable pursuits, Captain."

"Quite honorable." As if to prove it, she took another drink. Her tongue swiped the foam from her upper lip, and she used the tip of her middle finger to catch the bit left at the corners of her mouth. "I'd made a name for myself in the New World, but I couldn't get a job in Port Fallow. I offered to go into England—this was still when the Horde's tower was up, controlling everyone infected by the right nanoagents, and no one else dared to fly in. I lowered my rates to a pittance. But the only offer I got was from a sailor, for that sort of work."

With a lift of her chin, she indicated the woman who'd just climbed off the boy and was sidling up between twin brothers.

"The offer came with a grab to my tits, so I broke his arms. Then his mates decided to show me that I was nothing but a whore." Brimming with amusement, her gaze met his again. "I was the only one left standing—and afterward, I picked up a job from someone who'd seen the fight. So I fought until I made a name for myself again. I suppose that was around the same time you were making a name for yourself, too."

A new name. "Mine came later. About six months after you gutted Bloody Bartholomew."

"Ah, Bart." Eyes narrowing, she reached into her red sash and withdrew her cigarillo case. "You had a partner, too, didn't you? Besson, Barson—"

"Bilson."

"Yes. And he's dead?"

"So the story goes."

"I see—" She broke off, frowned. The expression disappeared in a blink. Without opening the silver case, she slipped it back into her sash. "In truth, he ran from Temür Agha."

"Yes. He stayed for a while. After the first assassin came, though . . ." Archimedes shook his head. "Last I heard, he took an airship to the heart of the northern American continent and leased a farm from one of the native confederacies."

"You never thought of doing the same?"

"Staying in one place? I'd be better off dead."

She nodded. "And so it is with me, too. I also feared that without an airship, I'd have more trouble. But you get around well enough without one."

"I'm an outstanding example," he said.

"Oh, yes. Only two months after the Iron Duke threw you off the *Terror* near England, you were making an enemy of Temür Agha in Morocco. Getting around quite well, and making an outstanding example, indeed."

Her eyes shone with laughter, another invitation to join in, and he did easily. A crash near the bar silenced them both, their hands dropping to their weapons. Only the twins, wrestling over who'd be the first to have a go. He turned again to Yasmeen, who was watching the fight, her fingers tapping against her glass.

"I would bet on one, but there is not even a scar for difference."

If she bet on one, Archimedes would put a coin on the other. "We could call them the red shirt and the blue."

"If they end this fight without the both of them losing their shirts, it's not worth the wager." She looked to him. "And what did you think of Ivy's submersible?"

"Astonishingly brilliant." He'd seen submersibles before, but none so nimble. "Did she build it for you?"

With her drink to her lips, she nodded.

And that was perhaps even more astonishing. "How is it that you are friends with Mad Machen, Scarsdale, and the Iron Duke?" The *Terror*'s surgeon, navigator, and captain. "As you said, you'd barely made a name for yourself here by the time Trahaearn blew up the Horde's tower in London. Yet you seem to know a good number of men who were aboard his ship."

"You've heard that story, too."

"No." He was certain.

"Yes. You just haven't heard all of it." She angled toward him in her chair, hooking her arm over the back. "It was Bart. So dangerous and handsome. Older, with silver at his temples and scars in all the right places, and tales of when he'd sailed his own mercenary ship. I was twenty years old, and couldn't have fallen faster if I'd jumped from my lady."

"In love with him." Not so innocent, but still young.

"Oh, yes. That wasn't all, of course. He knew Europe, knew the locations of the Horde outposts. He taught me well and took only a reasonable percentage. Soon enough, I let him move into my cabin. I got pregnant." Her eyes glittered. "I told him."

She reached for her sash again. Archimedes pulled out his cigarillo case first, flipping it open. She selected one, holding it to her lips while he lit the end.

"Thank you." Her exhalation of smoke sounded like a grateful sigh. "I hadn't planned on a baby, but I liked the thought well enough. I'd raise her on my lady, free to go wherever we wished. Bart, however, decided that he'd rather just have my ship. We went to bed the night I told him, celebrating. As soon as I was asleep he stabbed me through the belly."

Christ. "So you gutted him."

"And then some. I don't often lose control, but . . ." She shrugged. "I had reason. I didn't have a surgeon aboard my lady, though. I wasn't healing well and fever was setting in. After two days, I took a risk and hailed the nearest ship."

"The *Terror*?" A hell of a risk.

"Yes. Mad Machen cut me open, sewed me up, and kept me aboard for two weeks. Afterward, when the Iron Duke asked me to scout the coast ahead for them, I did. It's still the only job I've ever done for free."

"And so your heart of steel was born."

She snorted. "No. I was still young. More wary, but not wary enough yet—and Bloody Bartholomew wasn't the only man who has wanted my ship."

And damn them all. "The comte, too?"

"No. By that time, I'd learned. But he didn't want my ship, he wanted adventure. He paid for passage to Egypt, the Hapsburg Wall, the ruins of Greece. And he was charming, handsome, rich."

"Nothing at all like me, thank God." Archimedes couldn't claim to be rich.

Her laugh was warm and low. "Not as entertaining, at least. But fun. I took him to my bed."

"Yet you strung him up?"

"He pinched my ass."

"A bedding usually involves a hell of a lot more than that." Done well, at least. "I never took you for a prude."

"He did it in front of my crew." The humor left her face. "I could have an orgy in my cabin and my crew wouldn't care. But if I allow a man to pinch my ass while I'm treading my lady's decks, there's no reason the crew couldn't, either."

A severe punishment for the offense, however—unless that offense wasn't accidental. "Did the comte know?"

"I warned him. He'd made comments before, innuendos that I told him would undermine my authority. But his pride couldn't accept that I ranked above him on my ship, that I was master and commander. He had to show my crew that I was under him, in some manner." She suddenly shifted to the side as a mug flew past her head, shattering against the wall—half the tavern had joined in with the brothers. "And that was the end of my association with the comte."

"Rich, handsome, charming. As is Scarsdale."

Sharp amusement curved her mouth. "Yes, he is. Would you like to hear that I recently spent three weeks in his bed?"

No, he wouldn't. Not out of jealousy that she'd gone to Scarsdale's bed—though he felt the swift pain of that—but the jealousy that Yasmeen had gone to Scarsdale when she'd been hurt. After hearing Ivy mention shattered legs that morning, he knew there was more to this story than she suggested.

"Recovering?" At her nod, he asked, "Do you love him?"

"Yes."

And more pain sliced near his heart. God. Was he so far along already? This was more unsettling—more terrifying—than he'd expected. "Yet you hand him over to my sister."

"If she's truly a practical woman, it would be a good match. She couldn't ask for a more dedicated companion."

Yet Scarsdale would never love Zenobia as she deserved, because he was pining for the heart of another.

But, no. The amusement in Yasmeen's eyes didn't match that of a woman who was longing for an impossible love.

"He's your friend," Archimedes realized.

Now a full smile shaped her lips. "Yes. We did try the bed once. But we were both laughing so hard by the middle that we couldn't make it to the end."

He couldn't imagine. Laughing with her, yes. Not being able to finish? What kind of man would look at her, touch her, and not be . . .

"Ah," he said. "He's a—"

Archimedes cut himself off before disaster struck.

Her brows lifted. "A what?"

He knew many words for men who swived other men, but not a single one that wouldn't insult the man she loved. "A friend."

She offered him an appreciative nod. "You're a clever man, Mr. Fox."

"I thought I was. But although I believed that I was taking clever advantage of your drunkenness to discover so much about you, I'm coming to realize that nothing you've said has been anything you didn't intend to say. And I wonder why."

She hesitated. The sounds of the brawl intruded, a nearby table collapsing beneath the weight of tussling men, but he didn't think that was why she waited. She was gathering herself.

Finally, she said, "After I swam to *Vesuvius*, I spent those first three weeks in bed. The next weeks, I spent writing letters and talking to solicitors. I had money in trust for my crew, you remember. A significant amount."

"Yes."

"I've used it often. When an eye is lost, a leg, a hand—I'll pay for the replacement or give them a retirement. A true retirement. With the amount I gave, combined with what they earned on my ship, they wouldn't need to work again. And those who died in service to my lady . . . my crew made a prince's wages, but dead, their families lived like kings. I didn't expect to pay it all out at once, however."

Twenty-five crew members and a king's sum to the families of each. "So it's all gone."

"Yes. But it shouldn't have mattered."

Because of the strongbox. God.

She must have seen the realization in his face. "Yes. And if I correctly interpreted a few things that your sister said while we were in London, I believe we are in the same situation, Mr. Fox—though yours not as dire."

It was true. "I haven't had a significant find in some time."

A laugh slipped from her. "No?"

"No. Enough for room, board, a few extras." He lifted his cigarillo case as an example, then understood why she was laughing. He *had* made a significant find. "And the sketch, of course."

"Yes, the sketch. Though now there are two sketches of interest to us: the forgery, because whoever possesses that must have taken it from my lady and killed my crew. And the original, because whoever has it stole a significant sum from us both—and stole your freedom from Temür Agha. So I'm proposing an arrangement between us."

"To find the sketches."

"Yes. You know people. I know other people. Between the both of us, we will hear word of at least one sketch. Perhaps we'll be lucky and find the original and the forgery in one person's hand." She sat back. "The arrangement I propose is to share information and retrieve the sketches together. No trickery. No slave bracelets."

"And not much money." Not that it mattered. If she hadn't proposed this, he would have.

"No. Do you find that a significant obstacle, Mr. Fox?"

"It never has been before."

Satisfaction and determination set her expression like stone. "Good. I have a few items to sell. They won't amount to much, however, so I doubt we'll be buying information. Your charm and my blades will have to do."

Fascinating. She was friend to the richest man in London, yet relied on her blade? "You won't borrow it from the Iron Duke?"

"A debt has more weight than the coin that pays it," she said. "I don't like to owe anyone. Especially friends. Why do you not borrow from your sister?"

"Oh, no. I've heard that story before: To support the needs of her wastrel brother, a sister shackles herself to a leering, dissolute rake who beats her every night and brings diseases home from a whorehouse every morning." He shook a clenched fist. "I vow I will *starve* and throw myself at my own leering rake before I subject Zenobia to that."

Laughing so hard that tears formed in her eyes, almost a minute passed before Yasmeen caught her breath. She wiped her cheeks. "You're the most absurd romantic. She'd leave you to rot first."

"That's true enough." Both statements were. "So do we have an agreement, then?"

All trace of laughter faded. "As long as we both understand: We are partners. I will not give you orders, and even if I take you to my bed, you will do nothing to undermine me or assume supe-riority. If you betray me, I will gut you."

If I take you to my bed. This was one of the finest moments of his life. "I understand."

"You don't have anything to add? No stipulations of your own? Warnings?"

"I've already given warning that I intend to fall in love with you."

Her gaze hardened. "The time for games is past, Mr. Fox."

"It's not a game." He matched the gravity of her tone. "Not for lack of trying, I've never been in love. I desperately want to be. And I've come to realize that you've been in my thoughts so long, you're the only one for me."

"I won't encourage you."

"It's too late for that. You encourage me with the way you blow the smoke from between your teeth when you're frustrated. You encourage me with every quick thought and irritated glance. The flick of your eyelashes, the fullness of your lips." He let his gaze slip over her features, worshiping each one. "Your sneer."

Her lips smashed together, and she seemed to fight another laugh before finally relaxing into a smile. "Very well. Fall in love with me, if you like. But don't expect me to do the same."

"I don't."

"All right, then." She leaned forward, green eyes locked on his. "Shall we seal our agreement in blood?"

"I've already promised you my heart."

"Not *our* blood." She tossed a glance to the next table, where a tangle of men beat each other senseless. At the bar, a whore had her legs locked around a sailor's thick neck and her hands over his eyes while a female aviator pummeled his stomach. The other end of the tavern was a mass of shouting and punching, tables tipping and glass breaking. "Theirs. And we'll see how well we watch each other's backs."

Archimedes grinned and shrugged out of his jacket. Far quicker than he, she was already across the room before he stood—and he took a few seconds to watch Yasmeen's very delectable back before a burly woman picked up a chair to swing at it. With a whoop, he dove in.

His head throbbed again, but not with drink—and instead of Yasmeen's knife at his throat, her arm supported his waist. She hadn't stopped laughing since pulling him up from the tavern floor and half-carrying him out to the docks. Her arms were warm and strong, and Archimedes thought that he'd let himself be coshed over the head more often.

Which might, he realized, be the sort of thought only a coshed brain would have.

Her feet slid on the icy boards. Archimedes braced his own, caught her against him, his arm hooked around her waist. *Heaven.* Swearing, she steadied herself and lifted her hand, signaling for a steamcoach idling near a cabstand. As soon as it began puttering toward them, she looked up into his face. Her fingers touched his forehead and came away with a bit of blood.

She shook her head. "I yelled a warning that she was behind you."

He'd heard, he'd looked. "She winked at me."

"Idiot," she said, with no real bite to it. "Barmaids live to smash brawlers over their heads and steal their purses. You're lucky she only got away with your waistcoat."

He sighed. "My favorite, too."

"I like the blue best."

"Then it's not such a loss, after all."

They both backed up a few steps as the rattling coach slid to a stop next to them. Yasmeen called the direction of his boarding-house up to the driver. *Then to the docks, where she'd row out to Vesuvius?* Archimedes didn't ask, didn't dare presume. He opened the carriage door, and though she rolled her eyes when he held out his hand, her fingers folded over his as she climbed aboard.

He'd barely seated himself before she climbed aboard *him*.

His breathing stopped. She straddled his legs, the inner muscles of her thighs taut. His hands caught her waist. The coach lurched into motion. She fell against him and he felt the press of her breasts into his chest, the play of her fingers through the back of his hair. In the dark, he couldn't see her expression, but there was no mistaking the warm purr in her voice when she said, "Perhaps we ought to seal our agreement in another way, Mr. Fox."

A devil's choice. Archimedes clenched his teeth against the answer his body demanded him to give. She was still drunk. This would just be a fuck—for her. He wanted more.

But he didn't want to reject her. Her pride was an enormous thing, and even his tongue might not be able to soothe this wound.

Her hot mouth found his neck. A tortured groan welled up from his chest, and she laughed softly. Sharp teeth grazed his jaw before her lips tugged on his earlobe.

"You hold my waist, yet you're all but holding me away," she said into his ear. "Is this a no?"

God help him. "Yes."

"A pity. You'd fall in love with me *much* faster."

No doubt. "I don't want to fall in love too quickly and miss every emotion along the way—even if it leads to frustration and pain."

"Truly?" Though unable to see her, he sensed that she was studying his expression. "You're an unusual man, Mr. Fox."

Then her weight and warmth were gone, his body left aching. A spark lighter flared in the seat opposite; he saw her face, the amused smile, and his cigarillo case—he hadn't even felt her lift it—before the light died.

"Stay with me anyway," he said. "Don't row out to *Vesuvius* this late. Sleep in my room."

"I don't *sleep* in the same bed as a man."

Of course she wouldn't. Not after Bloody Bartholomew. "I'll use the floor."

"Uncomfortable for you."

Better than fishing her body out of the harbor. "There's an empty room next to mine," he said. "Sleep there tonight, and I'll explain it to the house matron in the morning."

Her pause told him she was considering it. "All right. I'll need a room soon, anyway."

"When does *Vesuvius* sail out?"

"In a few more days."

The coach shuddered to a halt. Yasmeen didn't wait for him to open the door. Hopping out, she flicked a coin to the driver. So he *had* hurt her pride, and now she was stabbing at his—but he'd known she was a difficult woman.

That didn't make her paying for the cab sting less, especially now that he knew how little money she had. Gritting his teeth, Archimedes followed her through the boardinghouse entrance. A small lamp offered feeble light in the foyer. A boy in tweed trousers, coat, and hat slept on a bench against the wall. Probably some urchin who'd sneaked in from the cold. When Archimedes closed the door, he jerked awake and blinked owlishly.

"Stay there if you like," Archimedes told him as he passed the bench. "I won't alert the matron."

"She knows I'm here, sir." The boy rubbed his face. "Mr. Gunther-Baptiste?"

Archimedes froze. Ahead, Yasmeen turned smoothly, as if she'd never been headed in the opposite direction. Her gaze found his before she glanced past him, peering into the next room as if searching the darkened parlor for more visitors.

He faced the boy. "I am."

"A message, sir." The boy offered him a letter, the paper rolled and tied with a string rather than folded and sealed. "He told me to wait for you. He said if you couldn't come tonight, to please send a reply that you will come tomorrow morning."

Dread clutched at Archimedes' throat, but he took the message and moved closer to the lamp. The Arabic script was small, neat.

Wolfram,

An opportunity for true freedom has arisen, and your assistance would be appreciated. I will explain all when I see you. Please accept my apologies for the abrupt notice and the hasty summons. I depart from Port Fallow tomorrow.

Hassan

Archimedes glanced up at the boy. "Hail that cab again. Tell him to wait for me."

The boy darted for the door.

"Shall I come?" Yasmeen said. Her fingers rested lightly on the knives sheathed at her thighs.

"No." He wouldn't risk her. "It's only an old friend, but I don't know when I'll return. Take my room tonight; I'll take the other if I need it."

"Are you certain?" Her gaze slipped over his face as if searching out the truth.

God. He should have kissed her in the cab. But if he kissed her in desperation now, no doubt she'd follow him. "I'm certain," he said. "Sleep well, Captain."

She smiled and turned for the stairs. "Beware the barmaids, Mr. Fox."

Hopefully, that would be *all* that he had to beware.

Chapter Six

Hassan's lodgings lay beyond the first canal, in the heart of Port Fallow's wealthy ring of residences. Archimedes knew the location; when his purse had been heavier, he'd spent several nights in a suite of well-appointed rooms. But although they were larger and more comfortable than in Archimedes' current boarding-house, they hardly befitted Temür Agha's prime counselor.

So did the lack of guards and attention that Archimedes received upon his arrival. A liveried house porter showed him inside, led him up the stairs. The door of Hassan's suite opened to the porter's quiet tapping.

Opened by Hassan himself. A grin widened his bearded cheeks. He spread his arms in welcome, the loose sleeves of his knee-length tunic billowing with the movement. A rectangular bulge beneath the linen was the only remaining evidence of the apparatus that had once been grafted to his chest, designed for labor in the Rabat salt factories. The lung tanks had allowed him to remain beneath the surface of the salinity pools while he cleaned the crystallization from the filters— and now, lent a deep metallic resonance to his every breath and word.

"Wolfram!" He came forward, clasping Archimedes' hand between his. "It is very good to see you."

A warmer greeting than Archimedes anticipated—or deserved, perhaps. Hassan couldn't have known that Archimedes had deliberately sunk the barge that carried Temür Agha's war machines rather than simply losing the shipment, but the counselor might have guessed.

"As it is to see you, Hassan," he replied. "Though unexpected."

"Yes, well—Come. Come inside. I will explain all."

Archimedes followed, disconcerted by the counselor's ebullience. Though he knew the cause of the difference—Hassan was far enough from the Horde's control tower in Rabat that the radio signal couldn't suppress his emotions—in every previous meeting, the counselor had been reserved, choosing each word thoughtfully.

Archimedes was glad for the man, though if Hassan hadn't had much time to adjust to the change, the counselor might be hoping for a swift return to Morocco. Archimedes had once experienced the tower's dampening effect, and the terrifying inability to feel what he'd *known* he ought to feel still lingered like a cancer in his mind. Yet Hassan had lived his entire life under its influence. It was possible that the strength of the man's emotions would be more frightening than the lack of them.

For now, however, Hassan only seemed filled with pleasure at seeing him.

A parlor decorated in pale blues lay to the left. Though three men—two in French naval uniforms, and another as simply dressed as Hassan—were standing around a card table with a large map spread between them, Hassan led him to a sitting room. More rolled letters lay atop a writing desk. A window looked over the tree-lined canal, the bare branches flocked with ice and snow. Hassan gestured to two armchairs flanking the open fireplace.

The counselor settled into the chair nearest the flames. "You'll forgive me. I feel the cold to my bones here. Do you see the gray?" He lifted his chin, stroked his fingers through his curly black beard. "I grow old. Has it been ten years since I saw you last?"

"Not quite nine," Archimedes said.

"Ah, yes. Yes." A faint smile touched the man's mouth. "I can still hear Temür's rage echoing through the *kasbah* when word of the barge's destruction came. Much has changed since that day. But not *enough* has changed."

And with that single statement, the counselor's reserve returned—but it wasn't completely familiar. Weariness accompanied it now, the sort that Archimedes usually saw in soldiers who'd been at war for too long, and with no end to the fighting in sight.

"What would you change?"

"We have long been under the foot of the Horde, Wolfram, and Temür has sacrificed much to lift it. But now the heel is his."

From rebel to dictator. "I'm sorry to hear that."

But not completely surprised. A man with as much power as Temür would not give it up easily, no matter his intentions at the beginning.

The man nodded once, an understated gesture that said Archimedes' sorrow was nothing to his. A deep sigh resonated from his chest. "You have always been a friend to the Horde rebels, Wolfram. I wonder now if you will be a friend to the rebels in Rabat."

"I didn't know there *were* rebels in Rabat."

"A growing number, led by Kareem al-Amazigh." He tilted his head toward the door, as if indicating the man Archimedes had seen in the parlor. "He inspires many of us and reminds our people of the old ways, but we are a people who have not fought for centuries. We need to light a fire beneath them—as was done in England, when the fall of the tower sparked the revolution and drove the Horde out."

"But you want to drive Temür out," Archimedes guessed.

"Yes. And if God wishes it, to put a new man in his place—to create a hero, as the Iron Duke became when he destroyed the tower in London."

"For this, you want my help?" Archimedes grinned. "I *do* have the looks of a hero."

"You have never been serious. It is fortunate that I know you, or I would believe you mock our struggle."

"Never that."

"Which is why I met with you alone. Kareem does not know your heart. Please consider that when you speak with him." Hassan leaned forward, holding his hands to the fire. "You provided the Iron Duke with explosives."

Was this the help that he wanted Archimedes to give? Shaking his head, Archimedes said, "I procured those through Temür. I can't find more for you, not quickly."

And his obligation to Yasmeen came first.

But Hassan made a sweeping motion, as if to return his response. "No, this is not what I hope for. We have a man to supply the weapons, but we do not have the money. This is why we turn to you."

For money? Archimedes had to laugh. "My purse is light, old friend."

"You misunderstand me. I know your life has moved away from smuggling. It is your new occupation that interests us. We will not plunder our own people, but there are treasures of value to the north, and they all belong to no one. Treasures like the da Vinci sketch you discovered."

Archimedes' heart gave a heavy thump. "Where did you hear of the sketch?"

"It is known that Temür possesses it." A frown creased the counselor's brow. "Did you not pay your debt to him?"

Did he? Christ. Did the man have the forgery or the original— or both?

He realized Hassan waited for an answer, and though it felt as if he were speaking after a blow to his stomach, he managed, "I did."

The counselor nodded. "Then you see how such treasures might help us, though you are not Kareem's first choice because of your former association with Temür. We've secured the services of another man, Vincent Ollivier, from the university in Martinique. Are you acquainted?"

He'd never heard of him. Archimedes shook his head.

"He has many maps, diaries. He has studied da Vinci's movements during the Fifty-Years' Siege of the Hapsburg Wall. He believes he can find the location of the clockwork army."

For God's sake. "He's a fraud. I can't tell you how many times I've—"

"Fraud or not, we *are* funding the expedition. I am certain that even if such a rare find eludes us, God willing, we might collect enough smaller items to pay our supplier. But Ollivier lacks practical experience, so I've persuaded Kareem that your participation is necessary . . . and that your loyalty isn't misplaced."

It wasn't. His loyalty lay with Yasmeen, but this expedition might solve several of their problems. "Will you be aboard?"

"Yes, if God wills it. Kareem leaves tomorrow for the New World, hoping to win support and allies there. I will oversee the expedition."

"Do you return to Rabat afterward?"

"That is my intention."

"Will I be able to return with you?"

"Ah, now I see." A chuckle resonated in the counselor's chest. "Your debt is paid, but you wonder if you'll be shackled the moment you step off the airship. I can promise you safe entry if God wishes you the same."

Perfect. "I'll want the same for my partner—and I'll be going as Archimedes Fox. Wolfram Gunther-Baptiste is dead."

"Of course. Are you still partnered with Bilson? I heard a rumor he was also dead, but I hoped it was not true."

"It is. Zombies took him in Paris. The woman I'm partnered with now has ten years' experience flying over Europe, however. There's no question of her skill or trustworthiness."

"If you say that, I believe you." But doubt or worry entered the man's eyes. "A woman?"

A step near the door prevented Archimedes from replying. Kareem al-Amazigh entered. Archimedes stood and took the measure of the future hero of Rabat. Tall and wiry, he gave the impression of strength without the added bulk of overindulgence. Soft brown eyes, a firm mouth, and a full beard suggested compassion and maturity—and a handsome face didn't hurt his cause.

"Mr. Gunther-Baptiste." Kareem smiled with warmth, but Archimedes could see the sharp scrutiny the man gave him, pausing briefly on his bruised jaw and rumpled clothing. "Did you win?"

"I was on my feet when I left." No need to mention that Yasmeen had supported him. "In some fights, that's as close to a win as a man can hope for."

"True words, Mr. Gunther-Baptiste. I trust Hassan has relayed our needs to you?"

"He has. I need to confirm with my partner, but I'm confident we'll be joining the expedition."

"Excellent. We've secured the airship *Ceres*. If God wills it, she leaves tomorrow at noon."

A pit formed in Archimedes' stomach. With effort, he maintained his pleasant expression. "*Ceres*? Under Captain Guillouet?"

"You know the captain? That is good. It is always best not to begin important endeavors with surprises." With a sweep of his hand, Kareem gestured for Archimedes to precede him to the parlor. "We searched for some time before finding an airship that didn't include females on the crew. I believe that is one of the great tragedies the Horde has forced upon us all: our unmarried women pressed into labor, rather than protected and supported by their fathers and brothers."

"A great tragedy," Archimedes echoed gravely.

The resounding noise behind him might have been a groan.

Yasmeen woke, aware that she wasn't alone in the room. Hopefully it was only Archimedes. Her knees hurt too much to relish a fight with anyone else.

Her eyes immediately adjusted to the dark. Archimedes sat slumped in the chair opposite the bed, wearing a linen shirt with tails pulled free of his lime breeches, legs extended and crossed at the ankles. Even relaxed, the muscles of his calves were strongly defined. A dusting of hair covered his skin, and his feet were heavily callused. When they'd met, the sun had burnished the hair on his head with streaks of gold, but winter had darkened it. The same shade roughened his jaw.

She wanted to rub her cheek against that dark stubble. To climb into his lap and feel his body hard against hers. He'd burned like a furnace. He'd probably keep her warmer than the bed, and as long as he was that, she wouldn't care if he didn't touch her again.

For a while, anyway. She liked to be touched, loved the slow curl of sensation over her skin that followed a hand smoothing over her stomach, the flex of fingers down her spine. She trusted very few men to do it, however—and now one of them was holding back while he fell in love with her.

Foolish man. No good could come of it. Sense told her to stop him. But she suspected that if she tried, Archimedes would only be encouraged. He wasn't a man who took the easy path. No, he *sought* the more difficult ones.

Which meant there was nothing to be done. The only way to

discourage him would be to make herself easy—and a woman didn't come any easier than she'd been last night.

Perhaps he heard her stifled laugh, or saw the gleam of her grin in the dark. His head lifted. "Are you awake?" he asked softly.

She came up onto her elbow. "Awake, and wondering why you aren't in Iceland, trying to pry apart the frozen thighs of the virgin cults. They pose much more of a challenge than I do."

"If all I wanted was to fuck, yes. But I've lusted before, and that's not what I desire now." He reached for the lamp, filled the room with a soft yellow glow. She watched as his gaze slid over her. She'd slept in one of his long shirts, and the untied neckline had slipped down her arm. Unbound for the night, her hair curled over her bare shoulder. He paused only briefly on her ears before meeting her eyes again. "I also want to be certain that I'm not confusing lust with love."

Yasmeen had done that before. "Perhaps there's no difference. Or perhaps you can only know if you've satisfied one, and the other remains."

"Then I will soon be a very frustrated man." He drew a deep breath. "Also, we are married."

Yasmeen grinned. She hadn't been *that* drunk last night. "Caught by the boardinghouse matron, were you?"

"I know where a sketch is."

Her humor vanished. She jolted up to sitting. "What? Where?"

"With Temür Agha in Rabat. There is also a rumor that my debt is settled."

Oh . . . oh, fuck. She did not care for money *that* much. Vengeance was another matter. "Is it the forgery?"

"I don't know. I hope it is not. If Temür discovered that the debt was settled by a fake . . ." He drifted into a laugh, shaking his head.

Temür would be enraged. But it wouldn't matter, because if he had the forgery Yasmeen would kill him. "We have to see it."

Archimedes nodded. "To that end, we are to join an airship

expedition that will eventually take us to Rabat, and my friend Hassan will help us past the trading gates."

Ah, good. That would have been the most difficult part. Though the Horde-occupied territories traded with the New World, few merchants and officials were invited past the port gates and into the cities—and Rabat wasn't easily approached from another direction like England, which was shielded from zombies by the surrounding water and often cloudy enough to fly an airship over, unseen. Yasmeen and Archimedes could have sneaked past Rabat's heavily guarded gates, but it was far simpler to walk through.

"Hassan," she said. "Who is he?"

"One of Temür Agha's advisors. His prime counselor, though he has retired from the position, and gives quiet support to Temür's opposition. He enjoys more freedom than most in Rabat, and that retirement is how he traveled here without question—he has been taking small tours, so that his absence would be unremarkable."

Yasmeen doubted that. Any man who did not note the comings and goings of a close advisor was a fool, and Temür Agha was not. But she cared little about politics; if Hassan could grant them entry to the city, she would take it. "Who is he to you?"

"When I was smuggling, he was Temür's right hand. I often negotiated and secured weapons from him when Temür wasn't available, sent messages through him. He's a good man."

Now he made no sense. "Weapons *from* Temür Agha? I thought he was buying them from you—that you got the weapons from the rebels."

"He *is* a rebel."

"No."

"Yes," he insisted quietly.

"He burned Constantinople to the ground to destroy a rebellion. Do not tell me I am wrong; I was there. I heard the screaming as the firebombs dropped and the war machines rolled over homes.

I smelled the bodies roasting and left to rot." She would *never* forget that smell. "Do not say he is a rebel."

His face dark and eyes haunted, Archimedes nodded. "You aren't wrong. But I have heard another story—though probably only bits of it. Hassan can tell you."

Perhaps he could, but it didn't matter. Rebel or not, the only thing to know was that Temür Agha was a ruthless man, not to be crossed lightly.

"So tell me about this expedition—and why we are married."

Archimedes closed his eyes. "It's aboard *Ceres*."

"*Ceres?*" Her laugh started, and she couldn't hold it back. "Guillouet will never let me aboard."

"He will, because you won't be crew, but part of the expedition."

Would money outweigh Guillouet's self-righteous loathing toward her? Oh, but that would be fascinating to see. "Then why are we married?"

"Because Kareem al-Amazigh, who is paying for the expedition, doesn't believe that unmarried women should be flying around without the protection of their brothers and fathers. So we'll be married and sharing a cabin."

She laughed again, loving the absurdity of it. Though the protection of a loved one was a noble sentiment, most of the women in Rabat didn't even know who their fathers and brothers were. In the occupied territories, the Horde's practice of taking laborers' children from their parents and raising them in a crèche erased all familial ties.

Finally able to breathe, she wiped her eyes. "So he has found religion, then? He sounds much like your father."

"Even my father hired you."

"Yes, but I wasn't a woman. I was foreign." She grinned when he tilted his head back, groaning as if in memory of his father's speeches. "But don't worry—I won't shoot Kareem al-Amazigh. Hopefully."

"He won't be aboard." He met her eyes again, and the sudden seriousness of his expression stopped her response. "I have to warn you now. Perhaps I should have spoken up when we made our agreement, but before I spoke to Hassan, I'd still hoped that the woman we saw wouldn't be Temür Agha's guard and we wouldn't have to travel to Rabat to find the sketch. It's a long story, but I was shot, and Hassan gave me a transfusion of his blood—infecting me with his nanoagents so that they could heal me."

"I see." Each occupied territory had a different tower, operating on a slightly different frequency. An infected Englishman could travel to Morocco without being affected by the signal. But a man infected by someone susceptible to the tower would be, too—even if the infection were passed on far away from the occupied territories. As soon as he traveled within the tower's range, it would affect him. "Will you be useless to me in the city?"

His skin had drawn tight, paling over his cheekbones and jaw. "I can follow orders, carry out instructions. I can act of my free will, but there's no driving emotion, no need, no fear. I wouldn't react to danger or respond to a threat in the same way."

"So you'd lose your balls of iron and silver tongue."

"Yes."

And that terrified him, she realized. Yet he wasn't backing out of this arrangement. He still planned to help her . . . if he could.

"We will see what happens," she said. "Perhaps it will not matter at all. And as long as we are discussing possible shortcomings—"

She swung her legs over the side of the bed. The crack of her knees sounded like muffled gunshots.

"Mornings are difficult," she said. "They loosen up, but I don't know how quickly I can move before they do. If we're ever attacked, I'll probably just stay in bed and shoot whoever comes through the door."

Gaze locked on her knees, Archimedes slipped out of his chair, knelt in front of her. Fingers hovering an inch above her skin, he traced the path of the still-fading scars.

"The ones on the right leg are cleaner," she said. "Those were Jannsen's—the surgeon on Mad Machen's ship. Ivy tells me that Eben's hands were shaking a bit on the left leg, because he'd just spent most of the night in the harbor looking for me, but he wouldn't let her take over. There are about thirty screws still in the bones. Sometimes I think I should have just let Eben cut them off, but they are fine legs, aren't they?"

He looked quickly up into her face, brows drawing together as if not quite believing her wicked tone. When he saw the grin that matched it, he gave a smile of his own.

"Very fine legs. But I'm still waiting."

"Why? We're married now."

"I will not even kiss you until my heart is so full of longing that I cannot help myself. And if you initiate a kiss, I'll consider it a sign that you've fallen madly in love with me, too."

He was serious, she realized. "I'll *say* I love you in bed, if that's what you want to hear."

His brows rose. "Would you truly?"

Would she? If he came to love her, could she tell him the same? Yasmeen had no compunction about lying, but she'd been on the receiving end of such a lie before, and the knife to her belly had hurt less. She wouldn't do that to him.

"No." She shook her head. "I wouldn't."

"Thank God," he said. "Because I'm not ready for you to break my heart."

"But if you fall in love with me, I *will*."

"I know. But try not to break it in Rabat, where I wouldn't feel the anguish properly." He stood and held out his hand. "Now, then. Shall I help you loosen up? *Ceres* awaits us . . . Mrs. Fox."

"Captain Fox," she said, clenching her teeth as he pulled her to her feet and slid his arm around her waist. "And now I'm doubly glad you didn't call yourself 'Stallion.' "

"That will be your secret name for me. I hope you tell everyone."

She laughed through her first step, gritted her teeth again. But with every step, anticipation built. They'd soon be en route to the sketch.

And she was going to completely ruin Captain Guillouet's day.

Chapter Seven

They found *Ceres* tethered on the main dock, spars extended and sails furled. Constructed in the fashion of a sugar sloop, a fat balloon held up her heavy-bellied ship, and two propellers flanked a tapered tail. Well made, and although not as sleek or as swift as her lady, *Ceres* would have been fine to look upon if she hadn't been decorated to advertise Guillouet's loyalties. A Huguenot cross was emblazoned across both sides of the balloon in gold and blue, shouting his allegiance to the French king.

Yasmeen hopped out of the steamcoach, and held open the carriage door while Archimedes dragged out their trunk and hefted it onto his shoulder. They didn't have to walk far, though they missed the cargo lift's current run. Four marines and their equipment were already ten feet into the air when she and Archimedes reached the loading platform. *Marsouins*, by the regimented look of them, skilled in aerial and underwater combat—and as they weren't wearing uniforms, probably turned soldiers-for-hire. If Kareem al-Amazigh had secured them for this expedition, he must be expecting Archimedes to find a significant amount of treasure. Al-Amazigh would need at least ten livre just to recoup the cost of the mercenaries.

Archimedes set the trunk by his feet. "Aside from his famous opinion that women shouldn't be serving aboard airships, what have you heard of Captain Guillouet?"

"That opinion is not just his, but famously a navy opinion," Yasmeen said.

No matter the New World nation, very few sailing ships allowed females to join their crews. Guillouet had simply carried on the tradition after he'd been decommissioned and purchased *Ceres*.

"So the makeup of his crew isn't cause for concern, then."

"Don't mistake me, Mr. Fox: I don't have much confidence in any ship that doesn't include women. It means that either the captain doesn't trust his crew to follow his rules, or he doesn't trust his own ability to keep them in line."

"Or he thinks women have no place aboard an airship."

For Guillouet, it was probably a bit of both. "I think *sailors* have no place aboard an airship—and Guillouet is still a sailor. He has no business in the air."

"Is captaining a boat so different from captaining an airship?"

"You truly ask? I'd hate to kill you on our first day of marriage." When he grinned, Yasmeen looked up at *Ceres* with a sigh. "See how he's dressed her up? Guillouet treats her like a whore, parading her around and pandering to patriotism simply to secure a few more rides and a few more coins."

"Forgive me, but—you hired out your lady for men to ride."

She turned narrowed eyes on him. "I didn't say she wasn't a whore. I said he *treats* her like one."

His brows rose. "And that makes all the difference?"

"If ever you'd been treated like a whore, you'd know it does." His lack of reply felt like a brief, angry silence. On her behalf? It was kind of him, but she was sorrier for the airship. "Guillouet was also a cousin to Rousseau."

"*Your* Rousseau?"

"Yes. They both served the French in the war—Guillouet with the navy, Rousseau with the aeronauts. When the treasuries ran low, they were among the first to go. But Guillouet still claims that the continued Liberé Obligation was justified."

"I see," Archimedes said.

Probably better than Yasmeen did. She hadn't arrived in the New World until a few years before the end of the decade-long war, which had been brewing for centuries. Every person gave a different reason for it, but almost everyone agreed that the root of the conflict lay in the sixteenth century, when the zombie infection began to spread west across Africa. The Huguenots, who'd already established settlements in the Caribbean and plantations in the southern American continent, had sent fleets of ships to the west coast of Africa on a mission of mercy. Full kingdoms were given passage across the Atlantic and resettled on Huguenot territory north of the Great Cinnamon River, their only obligation to pay for the use of the land with gold or labor.

Of the next hundred years or so, Yasmeen knew little—until the French, embroiled in a war for territory with the Catholic Lusitanians to the north, offered to release any Africans of their Obligation if they joined the French armies. Thousands went, but Castile and the native confederacies put their weight behind Lusitania, and the French gained little territory north of the Caribbean Sea. The war over, thousands of families who'd fought for the French—now calling themselves the Liberé—found few places to settle and work, and many were told they weren't fit for anything better than pulling carts. Some returned south, but many more moved north, where trade and land agreements with the native confederacies made for more factories and fields offering pay equal to skill.

Archimedes' sister had overstated when she'd claimed that every family in the New World had Liberé and native relations. Many did now, it was true. But if she'd said "neighbors," it would not have been an exaggeration at all.

In the southern American territories, still owned by the king, the Liberé name slowly spread—even among the French nobles and officials who governed the territories. Resistance began with the refusal to acknowledge the longstanding Obligation taxes, still imposed on anyone of African descent. French troops moved south, squashing rebellions as they flared up. Governors and officials were assassinated or replaced, and nobles fled. Overt resistance faded, and began to gain strength in parlors, instead. Supported by the king, churches in the French islands spoke eloquently of duty and obligation—and cart-pulling families like Rousseau's and Guillouet's spent more time in churches than in parlors. When the king promised full citizenship for those who fought for him, they both answered the call.

When the war fizzled, the French began to cut costs. In the first order, twenty thousand commissioned and warrant officers were pared away—the majority of them Liberé. Though the government claimed the decision of whom to let go had been based on officer seniority, Rousseau had said he'd finally seen the truth of where he stood with his countrymen, and would stand with them no longer. Guillouet had accepted the promised citizenship.

But now he was here, because there'd been little opportunity for him in the remaining French territories following the war.

"And what do you think?" Archimedes said.

"Of the war?" At his nod, Yasmeen laughed. Oh, but she'd started many entertaining tavern brawls this way. "I think that the French kings owned the land, and that taxes are the way of the world." When his face darkened and his mouth opened, she grinned and continued, "I also think that, for hundreds of years, it was in the Huguenots' best interests to think of the Liberé as cart-pullers, and so they justified their every action with the original obligation so that they could continue believing they were right—and continue filling their treasury."

The thunderous expression lightened. "I can still fall in love with you, then."

He would do well to wait until she was done.

"I also know that the Liberé are burning down villages and massacring natives to clear land and grow more coffee. The Lusitanians supported the Liberé in the war, but they smuggle in slaves from the Horde-occupied territories to work their mines. The Castilian queen and her court eat from plates of gold while her people starve in the streets and call for her head."

"And Johannesland?" His eyes were bright with amusement. "My mother's people are not so terrible."

"Their princes squabble among themselves, and they supported the French simply because the king is not Catholic. They are not terrible, but they are stupid, and that is almost as bad." She looked up as the cargo lift began to descend. "The French are no better or worse than all of them, because everyone serves their own interests. And that is why I prefer Port Fallow and the Ivory Market to all the rest of the world: No one pretends they are doing anything else."

"Including you . . . even though it would serve your interests to reach Rabat more quickly aboard Mad Machen's ship."

Damn him for picking at nits. Of course she'd thought of that, and rejected it. "It serves my interests *not* to have my friends killed while helping me." She gave him a smile that showed the sharp edges of her teeth. "A husband, however . . . it will be quicker than divorce."

His laugh was loud and full, and continued over the clank of the lift coming to a rest on the platform. He dragged their trunk aboard—filled primarily with his weapons and contraptions, and the warmest of their clothes. For Yasmeen, that meant *all* of her clothes, and the few heavy woolen and fur pieces she'd traded for her silver cigarillo case that morning.

She braced her feet when the lift began to rise. "Did you bring any cigarillos?"

"A few, but not many. I only smoke them with you."

Because they were so expensive. Yasmeen sighed. "I'll probably become irritable."

"Do you think I'll notice the difference?"

The look she gave him would have cowed a lesser man, but nothing of Archimedes Fox was less, including the width of his grin. She could not help but laugh, and it was still in her mouth when the lift locked into place against *Ceres'* side. Waiting to welcome them aboard, Captain Guillouet stood a few feet away, looking so much like his cousin Rousseau that pain stabbed her chest.

His gaze landed on her, and his face contorted with disbelief and anger, erasing all resemblance to his cousin. He turned to the man waiting next to him, who by description Yasmeen guessed was Hassan.

"*That* is the wife?"

Every aviator on deck turned to look. Clearly taken aback by Guillouet's tone, Hassan only nodded.

"She is not welcome on this vessel!"

Guillouet bellowed the declaration so that everyone would hear—and would know him for a fool when he was overruled on his own ship. Yasmeen barely contained her amusement; that would not go over well with the crew, either. No need to antagonize the only people who could make this trip unbearable.

Hassan looked bewildered. "Explain, Captain."

"Corsair. She calls herself Lady Corsair. It means she was a privateer—a friend to the French, you understand? But she was no friend to us."

She'd done every single job well. Yasmeen reached for her cigarillo case, but it wasn't there.

When Hassan looked to her, she said, "The French newssheets gave me the name."

"Newssheets." Guillouet spat. "Misguided fools, supported by the nobles. You took our money *and* Liberé money that rightly belonged to our king."

Already, the irritation began to set in. "Then it seems I only took French money," she said.

Understanding finally came to Hassan's face, and Yasmeen realized that he hadn't been lost, only having difficulty with the language. "A mercenary?"

"Yes," Yasmeen said.

Though there was no visible hardening of Hassan's expression, though he didn't stand any straighter or raise his voice, he suddenly gave the impression of quiet strength and authority. He looked to Guillouet. "Does her presence mean you will not take *my* money, Captain?"

The threat was clear. Guillouet's jaw tightened, the struggle visible on his face. An airship captain who stood on principles over money soon had no ship to stand on. "I will not allow her to share meals in my cabin. You cannot ask that insult of me."

"You will insult her, too?"

"It's no insult," Yasmeen said. She didn't want to eat with him, either. "The wardroom will do."

Faint apology entered Hassan's voice. "The wardroom is taken by the *marsouin*s. I have already displaced several of the captain's men."

"We can eat with the crew," Archimedes suggested. "We've made the acquaintance of several, and enjoyed their company before."

They had?

"Very well, then." With a sharp nod, Guillouet pivoted on his heel, began shouting orders.

With the only threat to her diminished, Yasmeen finally looked away from Guillouet and glanced over the aviators on deck. Her gaze stopped on one large man who sported a puffy bruise over his left eye and a split lip. The red-shirted twin. She couldn't suppress her grin when the recently deflowered Henri raced toward them, offering to show them to their cabin. The boy reached for the trunk but was stopped by Archimedes.

"I've got that, young Henri," Archimedes said. "It's heavier than it appears."

The trunk wasn't at all heavy for a man infected by nanoagents, but it did look impressive when he so easily hefted it over his shoulder and turned to Hassan.

"Hassan, allow me to introduce my wife—Captain Yasmeen Fox."

He took far too much pleasure in saying that. She returned Hassan's greeting, adding in Arabic, "Thank you for handling that so well. Though I am not surprised by your diplomacy, given all that my husband has told me of your association with him."

His eyes widened slightly, and his gaze ran over her face, as if trying to place her appearance and dialect. Yasmeen wondered what his reaction would be when she removed the warm hat with the Arctic fox-fur flaps that covered her braids—and her ears.

"It is sometimes the nature of business, unfortunately," he said. "And now I see that it was wise to bring your husband on as Archimedes Fox. We will hope that Captain Guillouet doesn't realize who Wolfram was selling those weapons to."

When her brows rose, Archimedes supplied under his breath, "Primarily, the Liberé."

Yasmeen laughed, and was favored by a grin from the older man.

"It *is* very good to meet you, Captain. I hope you will come speak with me later, after you've settled—and I have had my midday rest. I am but a frail old man."

He continued smiling as he spoke, but Yasmeen couldn't miss the weariness behind the good humor. She nodded and looked to Henri, who had been waiting, listening, and clearly not understanding a word.

"Well, Henri. Show us the way, then."

Their cabin was tiny, housing two stacked bunks with barely space enough to walk beside. Brass hooks screwed into the bulkhead offered a place to hang their clothing, and their trunk slid below the bottom bunk. A washstand stood in the corner. A porthole offered just enough sunlight to see.

It was perfect.

"Top or bottom?" Archimedes said, indicating the bunks.

"Bottom." Her knees wouldn't allow anything else. "That went well with Guillouet, didn't it?"

"Very. And now it will be easy to avoid him."

"Yes." Seeing the man would be inevitable, especially on the main deck, but no one would expect them to exchange any words. "I'd like to go above before we start out."

"And see how a sailor's crew handles her?" Archimedes guessed correctly. He retrieved his fur hat and their aviator goggles. "I'll accompany you, and count the number of faults you add to Captain Guillouet's character."

"We will see if they ever equal yours." Tugging on her own hat, she stepped into the corridor and almost collided with a portly man, face long and belly ample. Receding brown hair had been combed back from his pale features, and he wore a mustache and beard in the current French fashion, with chin and jaw shaven, and whiskers sweeping to his ears like a walrus's.

Recognition hit her. "Why, it's Mr. Ollivier!"

"Lady Corsair." His eyes darted from her face to Archimedes', then down the passageway as if looking for an escape. "I didn't realize you were aboard."

"Oh, yes. With my husband, Archimedes Fox. You've heard of him?"

"Yes." Surprise brought his focus back to Archimedes, and curiosity slipped through his panic. "Yes, of course. I follow your adventures with interest, Mr. Fox."

"Of course you do," Yasmeen said. "Tell me, will you be eating at the captain's table?"

"Yes."

"Wonderful." She grinned. "I have heard we will speak to you about the expedition when our friend Hassan awakes. I look forward to seeing your maps. Until then, Mr. Ollivier!"

She had to give Archimedes credit—he waited until they were up on the main deck before asking, "What was all that?"

"I will tell you." The engines started, a familiar thrum beneath her feet. *Oh.* Her heart hitched painfully. On earth or in sky, there was no sweeter sound than a well-tended propulsion engine. "Come with me aft!" she called to Archimedes over the noise. "There's no net across her bow—we don't want to be killed by a bird!"

A few aviators heard her. Yasmeen didn't care. A captain took care of their safety, or he didn't deserve the title. She led Archimedes to the stern, where the engines spewed clouds of smoke and steam into the air.

He turned his back to the rail. "Also, because it's loud!" he shouted. "You won't be overheard!"

"Yes!" she called out and leaned closer. "Do not eat or drink anything without letting me taste it first. *Anything.* Even something from your trunk, if you keep a flask."

Suddenly serious, his green eyes met hers. "Why?"

"Ollivier's an assassin. Or he was, during the war. A Liberé sympathizer. He'd pose as an academic—in truth, he *is* an academic—and make his way into important households. He uses poisons." A cowardly way to go about it, in Yasmeen's opinion, but Ollivier considered poison a more refined method of assassination than knives or guns. "Guillouet probably doesn't know. He calls me a traitor, but Ollivier *is* a traitor."

"Do you think he would poison us, then?"

"I don't know. The war is long over, but he might fear that I'll say something—or hold it over his head. So we'll be careful."

Archimedes nodded. The engines directly below their feet were huffing hard now. With the propellers beginning to spin, even shouts were difficult to hear. She held up her goggles and gestured to the pair around his neck. When the wind started, he'd want to put them on.

The crew hauled in the canvas sails that had taken them out of the harbor. *Ceres* skimmed over the snow-covered plain south of Port Fallow, beyond the high wall, where the bodies of zombies lay piled against the base. The sugar sloop wouldn't gain as much speed as Yasmeen's skyrunner, perhaps forty-five knots at her best, but even at that speed the wind tangled her hair and the icy cold burned her face. Yasmeen pushed the goggles up to her forehead. Archimedes might wonder if her tears were from the wind or the joy of flying again—but there was no difference. She looked over at him, found him watching her through the smoked lenses of his goggles.

"Do you see how she can make you feel?" she shouted. "And if you care for her, there's nowhere she can't take you. So it doesn't matter how she earns her money. If she can make you feel like this, you treat her like a lady."

But, oh *how* she missed hers.

*   *   *

Archimedes remained with her above decks for hours, watching the plains run up into the great forests. Enormous sections had been cut through them, swaths of tree stumps with seedlings growing between. Knowing that stripping the land would leave it useless to future generations, the Horde had established a regulated system of harvesting and replanting over the centuries.

Yasmeen leaned in, called over the wind. "Does it seem that we're heading toward Vienna?"

He hoped not. Nothing was there. But he couldn't confirm it; Hassan hadn't woken from his rest, after which they'd meet with Ollivier.

Shielding her eyes against the setting sun, she pointed west. In the distance, a Horde outpost rose out of the trees like a giant stone citadel.

"They are flying dangerously close," Yasmeen said. "Who is their navigator?"

He shook his head. They hadn't had a moment to talk to any of the crew, though several were on deck. Beneath the watchful eye of Captain Guillouet, they probably didn't dare. Initially, Archimedes had wondered if Yasmeen remained above decks just to piss the man off, but no—she simply couldn't bear to go below.

A large stand of old forest appeared below them. Archimedes pointed to a path cutting through it. "Is that a road?"

Yasmeen frowned. "I can't recall seeing it before. Do you have a pair of biperspic lenses?"

She wouldn't ask the captain or helmsmen for the spyglass, of course. "I do," he said. "But they're in my trunk."

A bell rang. Yasmeen's head jerked around, and she opened her mouth before snapping it closed. She caught his gaze, sighed. "It's not my ship."

He didn't need to ask how difficult this was for her. She'd remarked many times on what the crew did right and what could be improved. Other times, she simply watched with frustration tugging at her lips, her fingers twitching and reaching for her belt. If he went below for the lenses, he'd probably serve her better by bringing a cigarillo—though she'd have a difficult time keeping one lit when she wasn't behind the helm's shield on the quarter-deck. That might irritate her more than the lack of smoke.

She turned her back on the deck to look over the side, as if determined not to be interested in the goings-on. The slowing of the propellers turned her back round.

"Are we stopping?"

Yasmeen looked to him as if he might have seen something while her back was turned, but he shook his head. The aviators had suddenly become more active, and the captain gave orders from the quarterdeck, but Archimedes couldn't make out the words.

The engines quieted, blowing only steam now, venting the boilers with no propulsion. The aviators extended the spars in preparation for unfurling the sails.

"Oh, look at that." Yasmeen's amused voice brought him to the side again. She was looking over into a clearing below. "It's Jasper Evans's harvester. I can't believe he made it all the way here."

Archimedes believed it. Shaped like a combination of an armored coach and a scorpion, the machine rolled on tracks of steel plates rather than segmented legs, with giant shears in the front and shredders behind. Whether it met a forest or a mob of zombies, the harvester would tear through it . . . and must have torn through almost two hundred miles.

Five months ago, Jasper Evans had famously escaped the English navy, who had been firebombing his underground compound in Calais. He'd taken with him his ladylove, Dame Sawtooth—an airship pirate who was everything that her name suggested. Unlike the laborers in the occupied territories who had tools grafted to their bodies by the Horde, the Dame was a New Worlder who'd chosen her augmentation: a jaw full of sawblades instead of teeth.

He glanced back at the crew. Captain Guillouet had disappeared from the quarterdeck, probably gone below. Most of the aviators on deck were at the side of the ship, looking down at the harvester.

A light dusting of snow covered the machine. The round hatch at the top had been left open. Though Archimedes couldn't believe that the two fugitives would be hiding inside, Yasmeen knew them better than he. He'd heard tales of Scarsdale and Captain Corsair drinking them under the table in the Port Fallow taverns, simply for the fun of listening to Evans's soused ramblings.

"Would Evans and the Dame be in there?" he asked.

"No. But if he is, we're complete fools to be hovering over the clearing like this. Jasper is cracked but he isn't harmless." Her gaze swept the edges of the clearing. "No zombies yet."

"No. But they'll come." Archimedes nodded toward the four marines who'd climbed up to the main deck and were setting their rapid-fire guns near the bow. "Especially if they begin shooting."

Zombies were attracted to noise and movement. When Archimedes was on the ground, he couldn't always avoid moving, especially if he needed to get around. But avoiding any noise was critical to survival.

Unless he was running for his life. Then noise became optional and better than dying.

Hassan climbed out of the hatchway and onto the deck, rubbing the sleep from his face. He joined Archimedes and Yasmeen at the side and looked over. "Captain Guillouet tells me that this man and woman have a large reward on their capture, whether dead or alive."

"That's true," Archimedes said. The English navy had sent notice to almost every town on the North Sea, spurring too many unprepared excursions into zombie-infested Europe. "It's fifty livre each."

"Shall we attempt it, then? I know it is not the sort of treasure we intended to find."

Not a clockwork army, but still lucrative. He looked to Yasmeen, who was shaking her head.

"The Dame was barely alive when they escaped. She might have died during their journey, but he loves her. He wouldn't leave her body down there to rot. And leaving the hatch open . . . if he's alive, he wouldn't have. If he died inside, he wouldn't have."

"He might have left it open while he was gathering provisions." Archimedes was familiar with that tactic. "If he's chased, he doesn't have to take time to open it again."

"But that also means that he hasn't returned—so he'd be a zombie or lying dead out there somewhere." She indicated the dense forest with a sweep of her hand. "But there's also the way he left the harvester out in the open like this. It's not like him. After the navy stole the steelcoat suits from him, he guards his inventions."

Hassan nodded thoughtfully. "I agree, it sounds unlikely that either is inside. But would you be willing to take a closer look to be certain?"

Fifty or a hundred livre was a lot to pass up. "I'll go down," Archimedes said.

"Then I will, too." Yasmeen met his eyes. "At least if Dame Sawtooth's body is there, she's easy to identify."

Archimedes saw the crew moving toward the cargo lift and stopped them. "That makes too much noise. We'll take the rope ladder."

They unrolled it quickly. He glanced at Yasmeen, who was slipping off her long coat and heavy hat.

"I'll go down first," she said.

"But—"

"I'm faster. If any zombies do come, I can kill them before you do." She glanced at the marines. "Tell them to hold off shooting."

Almost faster than he could track, she went over the side. Not bothering with the rungs, she slid quickly down the ropes. Near the bottom, she flipped her legs out, spun through the air like an acrobat, and landed silently in a crouch. God, what an incredible woman. His own descent was embarrassingly slow by comparison.

He reached the ground. Snow crunched softly under his feet. The light was fading quickly, the edges of the clearing lost in shadows.

"Do you see anything?"

"No." Her voice was as quiet as his. "Let's go."

She ran toward the machine. God, she was quick and light on her feet. She rounded the machine and paused. The oval door-sized hatch on this side was also open.

Unease slipped through him. Leaving the hatch open on top made sense—zombies didn't climb. But they could walk right through the main hatch. "Would he do *this*?"

"No." She studied the dark interior. "But I would wager anything that he's set it to blow."

"When's the last time it snowed?" He judged the snow around them. "Two, three days ago? But there's barely any on the machine, and no tracks. The wind might have cleaned it off, but either way, it hasn't been sitting long."

"He's probably hiding around here somewhere and this is his warning system." She met his eyes. "What do you think?"

"I trust my gut. If we go in there, we're dead."

Yasmeen agreed. They ran back to the ladder, climbed up.

Hassan met them at the top. "You didn't go inside?"

"She's rigged to blow," Archimedes said.

One of the marines stepped forward. The leader of the group, Archimedes guessed. His boots polished to a high shine, each buckle of his jacket in a straight line, his brown beard precisely trimmed, he looked the sort that lived by details and never let imperfections pass by without correcting them—or destroying them.

"What sort of explosive? We're trained to defuse several types of devices."

"Including Jasper Evans's devices?" He looked to Hassan. "You know me well. If there's a chance to survive, there's nothing I won't try. I don't believe there's much of a chance here."

After a brief moment, Hassan nodded. "All right, then. We will let it be."

"But you didn't *see* the device, Mr. Fox?" This from Captain Guillouet. "You only *think* that it's there."

"I didn't see it," Yasmeen said. "But I know Evans well enough to say he'd rather destroy the machine than let someone else have it."

Archimedes gritted his teeth when the captain didn't acknowledge her answer with so much as a glance. Christ. She had more experience and knowledge than half the men on that deck put together.

Guillouet continued, "Mr. Hassan, if you've passed on this opportunity to collect the reward, I hope you'll forgive the small delay as I allow my crew to try?"

"Yes, but I counsel against it."

"And pass up a possible fifty livre reward?" Guillouet smiled. "If I split it equally between my men, that's two each. That's more than they make in a year. I believe they'll take that risk."

Several of the aviators nodded, eyes widening at the mention of such a sum. Yasmeen's mouth tightened.

Guillouet turned to the marine. "Mr. Bigor, please lead your men down. Be quick, before you lose the light."

"Yes, sir." Bigor jerked his head at his men, and they moved in step to the rope ladder.

Anger was one of the few emotions that Archimedes never deliberately stoked, and he was slow to rise to a temper. But it could happen, now and again.

"Mr. Bigor, a moment!" he called out. When the man paused at the side of the ship, Archimedes joined him and said, "Have you encountered many zombies before?"

The man gave a stiff nod, eyes hard. "A few."

Only a few? Archimedes wasn't surprised. The four men were skilled, no doubt, though he'd have wagered they hadn't been long on this side of the Atlantic.

A moan sounded from below, barely audible above the creak of the ship and the flap of canvas. But of course there was—Archimedes had just yelled the man's name, hadn't he? And no one had called him an idiot.

From the corner of his eye, he saw Yasmeen lean over the side and scan the tree line. Apparently she'd been listening for the moan, too.

"Then you probably know to destroy the brain, or take off the head," Archimedes said. "But there's more to know."

He drew his revolver. The other man tensed, but Archimedes was already turning away from him, looking toward the harvester. He tipped the bullets out of the chamber. Picking up one, he flung it at the machine. The bullet struck the top with a faint *ping*!

"They're fast," he said as one burst from the shadows and raced across the clearing, hissing. With matted hair and sunken features, the zombie was too emaciated and filthy to determine gender—or perhaps all indications had been eaten or rotted off.

Many of the aviators recoiled in instinctive repulsion. Bigor didn't flinch. He raised his hand, stopping his comrade when the other marine aimed his rifle.

"They'll investigate any noise." Archimedes threw another bullet. *Ping!* The zombie was growling now, a rasping, ravenous sound. "And if they encounter a structure, they'll search for a way in."

The zombie disappeared around the side. Archimedes waited.

The explosion rocked the harvester back, flipping the shredder's tail up like a scorpion readying to strike. Metal shrieked. Smoke boiled from the top hatch.

"And that's all there is to know." Archimedes clapped the man on the back. "You can go down and look for the Dame and Evans now, Mr. Bigor, but you'd best hurry. I can already hear more of them coming."

Yasmeen wouldn't have handled that half as well. Too used to giving orders, she'd have insisted that Guillouet retract the order he'd given the marines, and probably would have ended up shooting someone—or at least throwing punches. She'd never have considered throwing bullets.

She followed Archimedes down the ladder from the main deck, and was halfway to their cabin before she realized that he was furious. He stalked into the small room, throwing his hat and coat over his bunk. Two paces brought him to the washstand. He whipped around, almost paced into her.

Taking a quick step back, she flattened her hand against his solid chest. His heart pounded. His jaw had set like stone, his emerald eyes were bright. Her breath seemed to slip away. Oh, he was magnificent when roused. She could have looked at him for hours, but she settled for the time it took to breathe again.

"You're an impressive specimen of a man, Mr. Fox," she finally said.

His gaze narrowed, fell to her lips. The pace of his heart quickened. Then he all but wrecked her when he stroked the back of his fingers down her cheek.

Pleasure streaked through her, the urge to lift into his touch and purr. She contained her shudder, remained still as he covered her hand with his, holding it to his chest. His eyes closed, and she was never more grateful for a moment alone.

She pressed the tips of her fingers to her cheek, steadied herself. He didn't even know what he'd done to her—and how rarely she felt a sweet touch that asked for absolutely nothing. Swallowing, she said, "You averted that disaster up there perfectly. Of course, Guillouet will hate you now, too."

"It can't be helped. He's a shit captain." He expelled a hard sigh. "It's not just that he's a sailor."

Perhaps not. There were many reasons that men unsuitable to be captains were put in the position. "Well, I'm beginning to believe I was wrong about why the French cut him from their ranks. It's not because of ancestry or money at all. He's a blind ass."

A smile finally lifted the corners of his handsome mouth. His eyes opened—not angry now, but not amused either. He regarded her thoughtfully. "There are few things my father said that I've ever agreed with, but one of them was: There are men who give orders, and men who take them. Captains, they often seem like they give them, but there's always a superior officer somewhere that he answers to, and an admiral that answers to a king or a parliament, who answer to their people. But a man making his living out here—or a mercenary—answers to no one. So a man fit to be captain in a war might not be fit to captain his own ship, because there's no one thinking for him anymore and telling him what to do, how to act."

Though Yasmeen didn't disagree, she couldn't help but be amused. "I remember this from a sermon. I believe your father's point was that we are all deceived about our place, and we all take orders from God."

He grinned. "I just take the bits I want to."

"And what are you, Mr. Fox?" Yasmeen knew what she was. "Do you give orders, or take them?"

"I'm the type to get the damn job done myself." He lifted her hand, pressed a warm kiss to the backs of her fingers. "Now, let's find out where this job is taking us."

Chapter Eight

Featuring a private privy and wardrobe, a writing desk and a berth that was wider than a plank, Hassan's stateroom was larger than their cabin by far. A small table allowed him to eat in privacy, if he preferred—now, it was spread with a large map. Hassan settled into the table's cushioned chair, quietly sipping his tea and leaving Yasmeen and Archimedes to discuss their route with Ollivier, who didn't speak Arabic. On the desk, Ollivier had piled several books, sheaves of notes, and old maps.

The first city he pointed to made Archimedes groan. "No," he said. "Vienna is picked clean. I myself have been there seven times, a total of four months on the ground. There's simply nothing left."

Yasmeen said, "All of the men I've carried there have said the same. There's nothing to be found. It's been abandoned the longest, so it's been picked over the longest."

"I am not interested in Vienna, but just outside of it. I had opportunity to study Prince Albert the Fair's archives," Ollivier said, as if in explanation. "His many-times great-grandmother was one of the Fleeing Hapsburgs."

A member of the ruling family in Vienna and the surrounding principalities during the Horde's advancement into Europe, the Hapsburgs had fought to the bitter end—and in the New World, were as celebrated as da Vinci. But a few of the Hapsburg family had fled; they had not been looked upon kindly, and were often portrayed as villains and cowards in the theatrical plays and histories.

From beneath his notes, Ollivier brought forth a colored woodcut print protected beneath a glass plate. Faded greens and browns depicted rolling hills behind a walled city, with a river and swimming swans in the foreground. The peaked roofs of the city were all in orange and blue, and the buildings stood tall, with several ornate spires reaching into the pale sky.

"The old man was the last of his line before his demise, so I was able to acquire this woodcut from his collection, which is a faithful reproduction of a painting made by the Hapsburg grandmother."

Yasmeen looked up at Archimedes. No doubt "acquiring" meant stealing after he'd poisoned the man. Lovely.

Ollivier continued, "Her painting of the city was the latest one that I've seen created by someone actually *in* Vienna. Many others are based upon older artworks or drawn from memory. Do you see this?" He pointed to a stout stone structure in the background, almost hidden in the rolling hills. "I've never seen it in any other depiction."

Eyes narrowing, Archimedes leaned close to study the woodcut. "That's true. I haven't seen it before, either. But I also haven't seen anything like this ruin when I was in the city."

"But it is up in the hills, do you see? If the forest had grown up around it, the view might have been obstructed."

Archimedes nodded. "All right. What do you think it is?"

The assassin hauled out another map of Vienna and the surrounding area. "A possible place to build the clockwork army. Its position is perfect: near enough to the Hapsburg Wall that if the Horde were to break through, the soldiers would be readily available to stop them—but also far enough away to allow time to mount a defense."

"The Hapsburgs had da Vinci's machines on this side of the wall."

"But they were created to defend the wall and to halt the Horde's machines, not to stop troops of mounted soldiers from coming through. A clockwork army could slow them."

Though clearly doubtful of that possibility, Archimedes peered at the woodcut again, asking Ollivier about dates, verifying the history of the piece. Yasmeen only half-listened, watching him, admiring the line of his jaw, his careful study of the items Ollivier had brought. She'd never given much thought to how he'd prepared for his adventures, but he'd obviously done something similar to this: poring over old maps, reading through letters, comparing different accounts of the Horde advance and Europe's retreat.

Finally, he nodded. "Clockwork army or not, if the structure was newly built before the zombie infection came through the city, then it's worth looking for—and hopefully it was built solid enough that it's more than a pile of rubble."

Ollivier beamed. Encouraged, he selected more maps. "If we find nothing there, our next location is Brenner's Pass."

Brenner's Pass? Yasmeen shook her head. She easily found the pass on Ollivier's map. She placed her finger directly beside it. "There is a Horde outpost right here."

"And that only supports my theory. This has long been recorded as an important pass. If the Horde broke through the wall, they would have needed to come through the pass to the Italian peninsula. And we know from the letters of generals and merchants that there were supplies being sent up to the pass, along with engineers and laborers. They were building something there."

"Da Vinci's machines," Archimedes said.

"Those, too. But even if we do not find the clockwork soldiers, this location isn't picked over. We'll find something in the fortress they constructed there. And in the deep snow, the zombies won't be such a threat."

Archimedes gave him a long, unreadable look before glancing at Yasmeen. She grinned, showing him the tip of her tongue caught between her teeth. His shoulders shook in a silent laugh, and the exaggerated lift of his brows said he was astonished that she'd managed to remain silent.

Ollivier might know his way around a map, but he clearly hadn't spent any time on the ground. Although severe cold could freeze a zombie, it didn't kill them, and they were mobile again as soon as they thawed. A very cold zombie was sluggish; because of that, many people thought that if one of the creatures was surrounded by snow, it posed less of a threat. But the worst danger came from deep snow, with zombies under it, and not quite cold enough to slow them down.

"What of the outpost?" Yasmeen said. "If *Ceres* is spotted, the Horde will come and look."

"We could hike in to the fortress or drop in on gliders at night, and arrange for pickup after a few days," Archimedes said. "As long as *Ceres* doesn't hover during the day, it won't draw attention to us."

Ollivier nodded, and seemed to breathe a sigh of relief. "From there we move around the Adriatic Sea," he said. "I've picked out a few locations to search, all based on their tactical position."

Archimedes frowned. "Tactical position for what?"

"You recall the fragment of the correspondence between da Vinci and Luca Pacioli? They were discussing Hannibal marching on Rome."

Shaking his head, Archimedes said, "Rome has been picked

through like Vienna. The Church has been sending salvagers for hundreds of years."

"Oh, no—I was thinking not of Rome itself, but the strategy. The Hapsburg Wall had already been constructed. If da Vinci and the generals wanted to send an army east, they'd have to get over their own wall first. But if they go about it as Hannibal did, and come from an unexpected direction . . ." He pointed to the boot of the Italian peninsula. "Launching from here, perhaps, and attacking the Horde from the south. And they'd have kept it quiet, so that the Horde wouldn't know they were coming."

Again, Archimedes didn't appear convinced, but he nodded. "All right. It's worth a look. May I study your notes?"

Obviously pleased by the request, Ollivier nodded and began gathering his papers. "Yes, of course. Let me put them in order, and I will have them brought to you."

Arms full, he left the stateroom. Archimedes looked to Hassan. "He knows what he's about. He has unique sources. He's put the information together in unusual ways, but it's good information."

"Good. We'll be in Vienna tomorrow morning; you can start your work then, God willing." With effort, the older man stood, his heavy breath resonating deeply in his chest. "Forgive me. I'd hoped to have more opportunity to sit with you before I joined the captain for dinner, but the business with the reward has cut into that time. Perhaps tomorrow, you will take the midday meal here with me."

"We will," Archimedes said.

Hassan's gaze moved to Yasmeen, then to the kerchief over her hair. Though the tips of her ears were concealed beneath the blue silk, she had no doubt that he'd recognized what she was.

He smiled faintly. "You are a surprise to me, Captain Fox. I am tempted to throw diplomacy away and miss dinner in the captain's cabin simply so that I can discover more about you."

Miss the captain's dinner the first night aboard *Ceres*, after he'd brought an insult to the captain aboard, and allowed Archimedes to destroy a possible hundred-livre reward? "You flatter me," she said. "But you are too wise to be tempted at all."

Hassan's smile broadened. "There are times I wish I could be the fool—especially when I face a night spent soothing ruffled feathers."

"It is too late. *I* have taken the part of the fool," Archimedes said, coming around the table and sliding his hand into hers. "I have already succumbed to temptation and will spend the night basking in her presence. Come, my wife. A fine meal awaits us."

It had been some time since Yasmeen had eaten with an aviator crew, but the messes on an airship's berth deck were all the same. Long tables ran down the center of the deck. Benches on either side provided seats. Farther aft, beyond a set of paneled partitions that provided little privacy, rows of bunks lined the sides of the deck.

Silence fell when Archimedes and Yasmeen climbed down the ladder, though the aviators must have known they were coming; word of the altercation with Guillouet as they'd boarded would have swept through the crew before she and Archimedes had settled in their cabin. Eighteen men sat at the table—only the deck crew on watch was missing. She saw curiosity, irritation, a refusal to meet her eyes. All right. She wasn't sure whether each of those reactions was because she was a woman or because she was Captain Corsair, but she'd figure it out soon enough.

But whether these men considered themselves her enemy, it was always best not to make an enemy of a cook. Though the stew slopped onto her tin plate wouldn't have been fed to her crew, Yasmeen smiled and said thank you.

Archimedes walked with her to the table. She'd already told him who to sit by, if possible—the first mate had influence over the other aviators, and they'd already made his acquaintance. With his charming grin in place, Archimedes stopped beside the big man with the bruise over his eye.

"Last night, I thought you hit me so hard I saw double. Now I know it's not true."

The first mate laughed and made room on the bench. Across from him, his twin did the same. "I wish I'd known I was fighting Archimedes Fox. I'd have shined my knuckles up a bit."

Yasmeen took the seat next to him as Archimedes rounded the table. The first mate glanced at her, but though she'd taken twice as many men down in the brawl, he didn't invite her into the joke as he had Archimedes. That was all right. They didn't have to feel comfortable with her. She was here to observe and listen, not to make friends.

She picked up a powder biscuit, broke it in half, and stared. It was wormy.

The mutter came from farther down the table. "Captain thinks she's too good for us."

No, worms didn't bother her—she simply didn't understand why an airship carried infested supplies. Unlike a ship that spent weeks between ports, an airship could refill their stores easily.

She bit off a chunk, searching for any unusual flavors. The barley and salted-beef stew had already begun to congeal. The watered-down grog tasted like shit, but it was all safe to eat—and all from the same source. She met Archimedes' eyes, gave a small nod.

A thin aviator on Archimedes' right cleared his throat. "I was sorry to hear about *Lady Corsair*, Captain. A fine ship, she was. It was always a pleasure to see her fly."

"She's not a captain." This came from the other end of the

table. "She has no ship, no crew, no commission. She's not a captain."

"She's my captain," Archimedes said.

Yasmeen smiled and waited for it.

"*Mon capitaine?*" The first mate's brother lifted his head. "On this ship, there's 'my arse' and 'my God,' but no 'my captain.'"

Cheers sounded up and down the table, the men laughing. Archimedes' brows rose. She shook her head. It wasn't mocking, and their reactions told her what she'd hoped to discover: A good portion of these men had once been sailors, but they weren't tied to the navy with bonds so tight that good-natured humor couldn't slip in between.

"You're still mine," Archimedes said, holding her gaze.

Yasmeen's lips parted. How did he do that? It was a personal, possessive claim, stated in front of a crew, but it was clearly supportive rather than undermining her.

Flustered, she looked to the thin aviator beside him, the one who'd complimented her lady. "Thank you, Mr. . . . ?"

A blush darkened his cheeks. "Leroy, ma'am."

"Thank you, Mr. Leroy. It was a pleasure to fly her."

The first mate leaned forward, stuck his hand over the table. "Vashon, here. Peter. That's Paul."

"Vashon," Archimedes repeated. "Of the Flying Vashons?"

Yasmeen's brows rose. The Vashons were a famous French aviator family whose generations of military honors and aerostat inventions had built them into a legend.

"Cousins, but they don't claim us," Peter said. "We ran into a bit of trouble when we were younger, flying off in airships that didn't belong to us."

"Vashon airships," Paul added.

"We'd probably still be welcomed in the fold if they'd been anyone else's. And if we hadn't tried to race to the Arctic Circle, deflated the balloons in an ice storm, and ended up making a boat of the ships. Have you ever seen a great white bear? Me, either. One day, though." He shook his head and continued the introductions, gesturing toward the quiet man on Yasmeen's left. "The shy one there is Cassel. He talked to a woman once—then his mother put her tit back into his mouth to shut him up. The raggedy one next to him is Simon. That bitter one next to him is Mr. Engels, our navigator's mate." He indicated the man who'd said she wasn't a captain. "He never left the war."

"There are a lot of men that haven't got out." Engels didn't glance at her. "My brother Vincent, who was killed by a firebomb in Bonaire after she scouted out his garrison for the Liberé. You're licking the ass of that woman, Vashon. Even the captain thought it was an insult to eat with her."

"Yet the captain thought it appropriate for me to eat with you," Yasmeen said. "Either I'm an insult he's passed on to his crew instead of bearing the burden of my presence himself, or he decided that my company is tolerable, after all. Which do you think it is, Mr. Engels?"

Engels's mouth shut. He gave a sharp nod and looked down at his plate.

He'd hate her still. That was just fine. She'd made her point. If he continued tearing her down, he'd be calling out his own captain with every word.

"I think the captain wanted to give us something more pleasant to look at than our first mate's ugly face," Paul said, and grinned when chuckles started around the table.

"That's very kind, Mr. Vashon." Yasmeen met Archimedes' eyes across the table. "I'm pleased that you find my husband as handsome as I do."

The first mate laughed outright before he settled back, gave her a thoughtful look. "Your crew had women."

"About half of them were."

"Don't you worry about fornication?"

He said the word as if he'd suffered through a few too many sermons.

"No," Yasmeen said. "They're welcome to do whatever they like, as long as it doesn't interfere with their duties or disrupt my crew's ability to work."

"But aren't women always falling pregnant? Aren't you always losing crew members?"

"It takes two to make a baby, Mr. Vashon," she said dryly. "So I let them know that if a pregnancy occurs, it won't just be the woman going. I've found it makes the both of them more willing to use sheaths."

"Sheaths?" Peter looked to his twin. "How do you suspect Guillouet would respond to that suggestion if we offered it to him?"

"Maybe as well as the other suggestions we've given him." Paul glanced at Yasmeen, then to Archimedes. His voice lowered. "Captain believes that women only serve one function, and it's not aboard a ship. But he thinks the whorehouses are just fine—and I'll say that I do, too. There's no one looking at you with big eyes in the morning."

"Whorehouses are damn fine, I agree." Peter sighed. "I'd still prefer the women and the sheaths."

Yasmeen preferred women and sheaths on a ship, too—especially when they were aboard *her* ship. The familiar ache of losing her lady started up halfway through dinner, and while she remained quiet, Archimedes entertained them all with stories of his adventures. She excused herself early, and was cleaning her guns when Archimedes came into the cabin almost an hour later, his hands empty.

"No notes?" she asked.

"Ollivier is still in the captain's cabin. It'll wait until morning." He looked her over, sitting on the bunk in her breeches and shirt. "How modest are we, Mrs. Fox?"

"Not very."

"Good."

Turning his back to her, he shrugged out of his jacket and hung it on a hook. Yasmeen tucked a pistol beneath her pillow and the other between the frame and mattress over her head. She moved to the washstand, poured water from the ewer into the bowl.

She heard Archimedes' breath catch when she stripped off her shirt. Without turning, she pushed her breeches and small pants to her ankles, kicked them to the side. The water was cold, her soap slippery. Goose pimples raised under her fingers as she began to wash. Her nipples hardened. She didn't pretend it was the cold. Knowing that he watched her was almost as pleasing as a touch.

The scent of resin filled the air with every stroke of her hand over her skin. His rough voice came from behind her. "What's that fragrance?"

"Olibanum," she said. More subtle than a flowery perfume—and to her nose, warmer and more luxurious. Too expensive for her now, the soap had been a gift from Scarsdale before leaving England. "My favorite."

"It was coconut the night I shot you with the dart."

"That was oil for my hair."

She glanced over her shoulder. Archimedes wore only his drawers, the drawstring tied at the waist, the linen stretched over an impressive erection. The glow of the lamp cast gold over the hardened muscles of his chest, the ripple of his abdomen. Watching her, his emerald eyes burned with a hot light.

By the lady, she wanted him.

How long had it been since she'd wanted a specific man? Forever, it seemed. She'd wanted the sport and pleasure of the bed. If she found someone attractive, she'd take them for one night, have a quick tussle, and leave with her need satisfied. It had little to do with wanting them, and everything to do with finding release.

But after all this time, she wanted him. Archimedes Fox.

She reached for the small towel folded beside the bowl, but stopped her hand when she heard the pad of his feet, coming closer.

"Allow me, Yasmeen," he said. "Please."

Please. She felt like saying it instead, but she only nodded. Standing behind her, he took the towel, unfolded it over his palm. The rough caress of cotton began at her shoulders, drying the length of her back in long sweeps. Yasmeen clenched her teeth, her head falling forward. She wanted him inside her—but this was even better. Though he practiced restraint, allowing himself only this, such a caress was her sweetest pleasure. Only his bare hands would have been more welcome.

The stroke of the towel slowed over the curve of her ass. Oh, sweet lady. The men she was with were rarely patient. And those who took their time still never moved beyond a squeeze of her tits, a grab of her ass.

Not that she'd have wanted them to. Those men served a purpose, but she didn't look to them for this, wouldn't trust them to touch her with such intimacy. She trusted Scarsdale, and his caress had been pleasurable—but never combined with this exquisite ache, the wetness gathering between her legs.

The rough towel slipped around her waist. He pulled her closer, her back to his chest, thin linen doing nothing to shield her from the press of his erection between her cheeks and against her lower back. His free hand flattened across her belly, the towel sweeping slowly beneath her breasts. From deep in her chest, her purr vibrated against his hand, his stomach.

His low voice reverberated against her ear. "You won't try to seduce me into bed?"

"I don't need to." Her head fell back against his shoulder. "This is just as good."

"It is," he said, and she heard his surprise. Boldly, he slipped his hand between her legs. She lifted her foot to the washstand, and he swept slowly down her thigh. "I thought it would be torture, but no."

"You would do that to yourself?"

"Yes. I'd enjoy it."

She laughed. "Come, Mr. Fox. I will do the torturing for you."

She slipped into the shirt he'd discarded—God, but she liked his smell. Many in the Horde believed a person's essence could be trapped in clothes worn so close to the skin. Yasmeen only knew that he was pleasant to look upon and delicious to her senses.

She tugged at his drawers. "Do you truly want to sleep in damp clothes?"

"No."

The hoarseness of his voice said that *this* would be torture. Pleasurable, but not as she experienced it. He untied the waist, and they slipped down his muscled legs. The defined ridge over his hips told her he still hadn't completely gained the weight he'd lost after Venice, but although he'd drunk his meals for two months, it hadn't softened him. He carried no extra flesh anywhere.

"You keep yourself strong."

"If I lie around for two months and try to run from zombies, I can't run very quickly."

"No, I imagine not." She rolled the soap between her fingers. "What did you do in Port Fallow? Not running through the streets."

"I went to the pugilist's club." Though his response came easily, his muscles were rigid, his head bent. Waiting for her.

"As your face is still handsome, you must not have fought too many men."

"They've installed the weaving machines. Trying to punch

those bags of sand takes more of an effort than fighting." He closed his eyes. "It's not half the effort of holding still for this."

She smiled up at him, then moved around to his back as he'd been to her. Fingers slippery with soap and water, she slid them over his shoulders, washing in a long swathe. His muscles clenched, his buttocks like rocks. Soapy water dripped down his spine to the cleft between. She washed her way down his biceps, his forearm, to his hand. She worked lather into his palm.

"If you wish to wash yourself, Mr. Fox, I will pretend not to notice."

A hoarse laugh escaped him, and was strangled when her hand slipped around, soaping those delicious ridges at his hip.

"Be practical in this matter, Mr. Fox. We will wake up in Vienna, where we might be chased by zombies. You can try to run after staying awake half the night with a stiff cock, or try to hide what you are doing in your bunk—or you can take care of it now."

"Ever so practical." His hand slipped forward. "Sensible."

Not at all—this was madness for her, too. She listened to his harsh breathing, watched the long stroke of his hand. She could not see anything of what he did but the movement of his arm, but she knew what it would be to bed him. He would be slow. She would scream.

But for now, she wrapped her arms around him from behind and used both hands to soap his heaving chest. His free hand clutched at hers.

"Yasmeen." He groaned her name.

She slid her inner thigh up the outside of his. She was wrapped almost completely around him now, his shirt wet between them. He stiffened, shook. His back bowed. He brought her hand to his lips and pressed his open mouth hard against her palm. His tongue tasted her flesh as he came.

His breathing slowed again. Reluctantly, she unwound and found a handkerchief to wipe his palm. "Wash this when you've finished," she said. "I recommend doing it last."

He nodded, gaze roaming all over her face. She rinsed his body with handfuls of clean water, wiped him with the towel. After taking off his shirt, she hung it on the hook to dry and climbed into her bunk.

A few moments later, wearing only his drawers again, Archimedes crouched next to her with a cigarillo between his lips. He lit the end and passed it to her. His emerald eyes regarded her, and for the first time, she could not discern his thoughts from his expression.

Between them, they'd smoked almost to the end of the cigarillo before he said, "Was it all practical?"

Yasmeen smiled. "No."

"You also don't like to owe."

"No, I don't."

"It wouldn't have been a debt. I enjoyed touching you, too."

"As much as touching yourself?"

"No, touching you was . . . different. More pleasurable than orgasm. And even stroking myself, I felt more than I usually . . ." He trailed off, his gaze caressing her face. "How goes your heart? Still of steel?"

Like a strongbox, battered on all sides. She took a final drag, passed the stub back to him. "I have not kissed you yet, Mr. Fox. Is your longing strong enough to initiate it, instead?"

His serious gaze never left hers. "I think my longing will be much, much greater than I thought."

"You *mean* to break your heart against mine," she realized, and understanding slid through her. He'd been terrified of the Horde tower's dampening effect on his emotions. "You want to feel as much as you can, even if it hurts. You never want to feel anything so shallowly again."

"Yes."

So he planned to have her break his heart. "And what will you do if I fall in love with you, instead?"

He grinned. "Then God help us both."

Chapter Nine

The forest had reclaimed most of Vienna. The old walls marked out a rough perimeter of the city, and ruins were marked by sparser growth, long grasses upon heaps of stone. To the east, the twisting branches of the Danube flowed in a meandering path. When the initial wave of zombies had spread west from the Hapsburg Wall, that river had helped slow the zombies' progress and saved many of Vienna's residents . . . for a time.

Vienna had been one of the first cities affected, and the number of zombies had still been relatively few. The river, city wall, and a garrison of soldiers had served as adequate defense, giving the Hapsburgs and their generals opportunity to study the creatures—and, when it became clear that the zombies' numbers were growing and that the infection spread so easily that one loose zombie could destroy a city, to plan an evacuation. It had been similar to a story repeated across Europe: At the first sign of the zombie mobs, the populations of many great cities had used the rivers to protect them, rushing in a panic to the opposite bank. Once there, they destroyed the bridges and executed or confined anyone discovered with a bite. The water only held the zombies off for a while, however—if only one bite was overlooked, or concealed by someone still hoping to find a cure, the infection spread.

The stories had taught Archimedes well, though. From the airship, he scouted the locations of the nearest water—even if it was nothing more than a big puddle. Aside from the river, however, he wouldn't find much water in the snow-covered landscape, so he took other precautions.

He'd traded the bright waistcoat and breeches for heavier, darker clothing that wouldn't shout his presence to the zombies. Leather guards buckled over his neck, his arms and legs—if he went down under a zombie, the guards might save him from a bite long enough to get back up. His shoulder harness carried his grapnel and pneumatic launcher, rope, a hand-winch, a miners' drip lamp for underground and darkened chambers, extra ammunition, a prybar, and machetes. Though revolvers were holstered at his hips, he preferred blades when fighting zombies: they were quiet and never needed to be reloaded. He kept several strapped to his thighs and sheathed in his boots, and two foot-long blades in the spring-loaded mechanisms embedded in his leather forearm guards.

Guillouet cut *Ceres*' engines as they passed over the city, allowing them to sail in silence toward the foothills. Archimedes saw Ollivier's confusion when he came up to the deck and looked out, and remembered his own disorientation upon his first visit. Almost every painting of Vienna showed the hills close in the background, but in truth, they were still some distance away.

The quietness of the engines was welcome after a full day and night of huffing and vibrations, and the look on Yasmeen's features even more so. Her expression was pure pleasure as she lifted her face to the wind, her heavy lashes lowered against the morning sun as if she were soaking up the warmth through her skin.

Had she looked half so satisfied last night? Unable to see her face as he'd dried her body, he didn't know—and he hadn't seen her expression when she'd wrapped herself around him, either.

She'd been so hot against him, so sleek. He still reeled from the memory of how she'd purred against him, then so easily offered the means of his release without touching him.

He had few inhibitions, but he'd never pictured stroking himself off while a woman washed him like . . . a wife? He didn't know; he'd never imagined having a wife at all. She'd washed him as if she were completely content to do only that, though he knew she wanted him in the bed. More like a mistress, or a concubine, though Yasmeen fit neither. He didn't keep her.

Perhaps it was the opposite. Perhaps *he* was to be the concubine, serving her every need.

A tempting thought.

Almost an hour later, a signal from one of the marines at the bow pushed him out of those imaginings. Amid the first rise, within a stand of tall trees, stood a stone tower—round and solid, and more like the cylindrical Rouen keep than the arches and peaks of the contemporary Viennese buildings. Snow topped a conical roof— parts of it had collapsed, though not badly, as if the roof structure was well-supported beneath. A pass overhead didn't reveal any gaping holes that would allow Archimedes to rappel directly into the keep. Only narrow arrow slits opened the stone walls.

Archimedes circled the deck as the airship began to turn for another pass, taking a layout of the surrounding area. Trees made the zombies more difficult to spot, but if he and Yasmeen were quiet, it meant any zombie would have more difficulty spotting them, too. Still, in a forest it often seemed as if the creatures sprang from nowhere—many lay motionless and mindless until something caught their attention. Archimedes had been surprised more than once, saved only by his reflexes, leather guards, and luck.

He glanced at Yasmeen and his heart constricted.

God. The mere thought of her hurt down there destroyed him—a fear that stabbed at his chest, just as painful as he could have hoped. This was part of love, to suffer. He'd planned to do it in silence, to experience the beautiful agony of the great romantics.

Faced with it, however, beautiful agony was shit. He'd crow if it meant she was never in pain. Quickly, he made his way back to her side.

"I ought to go alone," he said.

She narrowed her eyes at him.

"One person makes less noise. And—"

"I'm coming," she said.

He reached for the buckles on his arm. "Take my guards, then."

"They'll only slow me down."

Panic caught in his chest. He stepped close, spoke so only she could hear. "Watching *Lady Corsair* burn was hell. But I think now, it would kill me. And if you were bit by the zombies . . ."

No, he could not even *think* it. His breathing stopped when she pushed her face close to his, looked into his eyes with an expression that was almost gentle.

"Stop letting yourself fall for me, Archimedes. Anything that makes you worry for someone else's ass over your own does you no favors, and I like you too well to see you die."

He couldn't have stopped now if he tried. "I'd die to protect you."

"Idiot."

Why, when he *knew* she'd have done the same? "Don't tell me that you wouldn't have risked your life for your crew."

"That is duty, loyalty. Not a foolish reaction based on unsupported fears." She studied him. "Did I tell you of Constantinople? I was raised within walls, and only allowed out into the city on rare occasions."

"A crèche."

Many cities within the empire had them. Not to the extent that the outlying territories did, where almost all of the children were raised in them until they were sent into labor. Within the empire, the crèches functioned more like orphanages, the children educated and given assistance in finding a suitable position afterward.

"No, not a crèche. More like a palace, where I was given the best food and education—and trained to fight. I fought every day of my life until I was fifteen, beginning in the morning and then again at night. When Temür destroyed the city and I escaped, I could count on my fingers the number of full days I'd been outside those walls. Yet I journeyed on foot alone across Greece, armed only with two knives and my wits. I am not like a crèche baby, born, fed, and then changed into a laborer. I was *bred* to be fast and strong. I was bred to be quiet. And I was bred to kill. You want to protect me, but in truth, I'll protect you. It was what I was made for. So let me do it."

That was incredible. *She* was incredible. And yet . . . His jaw clenched, despair tugging at his heart.

How was he to do anything for her?

"Ah," she said, watching his face. Her sneer mocked him. "It is easy to fall in love with a woman who is always making you feel more of a big, powerful man. You ought not have picked me, after all."

"That isn't it." He didn't question his abilities. "It is simply difficult to know that I offer nothing at all to the woman I'm falling in love with."

Her expression lightened. "You offer me nothing? Stupid man. You already give me what few men could. It is rare the man who has the confidence to let me be what I am, whether it is captaining an airship, climbing atop you in a steamcoach, or brawling in a tavern."

She thought she wouldn't make him feel a bigger man? Hearing this from her, it was all he could do not to swagger around with a puffed chest.

But it was a chest that deserved deflating. "I haven't always let you be," he reminded her. "I tried to take your ship in Venice."

"With a gun that didn't work." She surprised him by knowing. "It was the stupidest thing I've ever seen. Still, I admired your balls."

"You knew the gunpowder was wet?"

"I didn't know if it was wet or if you were out of bullets. But we found you on a raft in the middle of the canal, safe from zombies, and yet you were shouting across a pile of ruins to our ship in the middle of the night. If you could have, you'd have signaled with a gun—either then or earlier."

He would have. For a week, he'd been praying for the airship to notice him, but by that time, dirty and starving, he'd resembled the zombies more than a man. He'd have given anything simply for a bright waistcoat to wave on a stick.

"Would you have still forgiven me if it was properly loaded?"

"No, Mr. Fox. If you'd aimed a properly loaded gun at me, I'd have shot you dead. I threw you over the side for being an idiot, pulling it on me in front of my crew and then ordering me about."

Had there ever been such a woman? "The idiots are all of the men who want you to be something else."

"Ah, well. Quite a few of them are dead now." She grinned at him. "I'll help you not to join their number."

Until Bigor and his marines met them at the rope ladder, Archimedes hadn't known that Guillouet had told the men to accompany them on the ground—but as long as they could be quiet, Archimedes didn't care. He shook his head when the man drew a gun, as if in preparation to go down.

"Try to be silent. If one or two come at us, kill them with your machetes or crossbows. One shot will bring the others, and they'll be a little slower in the cold and snow—but against a mob, that won't matter."

The man gave a short nod. While the other marines holstered their guns and readied their weapons, Bigor pointed to each. "Dubois, Durand, and Laurent—representing a combined forty years serving our king, and one year in Europe. Your assistance yesterday was appreciated."

"My pleasure. The worst way to begin an expedition is by dying in an exploding tree harvester."

"I believe you are correct, Mr. Fox." Bigor's flat gaze moved to Yasmeen, then back to Archimedes. "Shall we precede you?"

"No."

Archimedes stepped to the side, and though she didn't need the support, took Yasmeen's hand in his, helping her over the gunwale and onto the ladder. Her eyes met his briefly. He let go.

She slid down. Quiet, so quiet. On the ground, she remained crouched and listening, looking into the trees as they followed her down. Archimedes led them across the snow to the keep. Behind him, three of the marines spread out, keeping watch in all directions. Yasmeen at his side, Archimedes moved around the tower. Halfway around, they located the arched doorway—the entrance sealed up with stone blocks.

Moving almost as quietly as Yasmeen had, Bigor joined them. His voice was low. "Protecting something inside?"

Probably. He'd seen the same in other cities, other villages. Many strongholds became depositories for treasures that the fleeing citizens couldn't carry with them—and everyone assumed they would eventually return. Archimedes' first find had been something similar, a journey begun after months of sifting through fragments of letters and cryptic references.

He retrieved his iron prybar, fitted the end between the blocks. The stones didn't shift. Christ.

"Anything we use will make noise," Yasmeen whispered.

Archimedes nodded, studying her face. She already had a solution, he knew, but she wouldn't like depending on Guillouet to carry it out. "A distraction?"

Her teeth clenched. She tilted her head back and looked up the side of the tower, then at the surrounding terrain. Weighing her options, he thought. Finally, she nodded and turned to Bigor.

"We need Guillouet to fly *Ceres* to that stand of trees, so he has a clear shot at this door. His boilers need to be at full steam before he starts her engines up, and run half power into the electrical generator. He'll use the rail cannon to take out these blocks." She took a deep breath. "The zombies *will* come. So as soon as he fires on the keep, he needs to kick in the propellers and take *Ceres* at least two or three hundred yards off. Once there, that crew needs to shoot their rifles, drawing the zombies to that location while we head inside the tower—and once we're in, even two of your men guarding the entrance can handle any strays. When we signal, *Ceres* can pick us up."

Bigor nodded. "All right. What signal?"

She glanced up. "We'll be on the roof. Even if the zombies follow *Ceres* back, we're out of reach."

"They won't climb up?"

"They don't climb," Archimedes said. "They'll go up an incline or stairs, so they might follow you up onto a pile of ruins, but they don't have the brains for vertical."

"All right." With another sharp nod, Bigor ran for the rope ladder.

Archimedes followed Yasmeen away from the keep. The rail gun's accuracy meant they didn't have to go far, and they waited, back to back, watching the trees. A soft moan came from the west; Durand took the zombie down with a crossbow bolt shot through its eye.

Bigor returned to the ground. Above, steam boiled from *Ceres*' tail as she sailed into position in line with the tower's entrance. So far, Guillouet was following Yasmeen's instructions.

She turned her head to whisper, "Shall we make a wager? What do you think might be inside? Gold, jewels? If I'm very lucky, cigarillos?"

He grinned but shook his head. It was impossible to know, and depended upon the manner the zombie infection spread, and whether the population had time to gather more than a few items before they fled. Some cities had time to contain the infection and to prepare—and until the very end, Vienna had been one of them. Blocking the entrance to this tower could have been to protect something inside, or simply to keep the zombies out until they returned.

"Don't bet on the last. There was no tobacco in Europe," he said.

"No tobacco, no opium; no wonder the Horde thought they were barbarians."

A high-pitched whine suddenly ripped through the air as the engines started, firing the electrical generator. Yasmeen tensed, watching the woods. The rail cannon fired, silent until the ball rammed into the blocks, blowing through the entrance in a shower of shattered stone. The marines moved toward the entrance to search out any zombies inside—just in case.

The whine faded. *Ceres*' propellers began to spin, the engines huffing. The airship retreated west, the crew already shouting, shooting, making noise. Yasmeen ripped off her hat, angling her head as if trying to listen for moans over the ruckus.

She suddenly stilled. "I hear them. A *lot* of them."

Archimedes took her hand, started toward the keep. "Let's get inside."

"No." She set her feet, eyes wide. "Oh, by the lady. Run, Archimedes! Bigor!" she shouted. "Come away from the keep! Run! To the ship!"

The marines were already backing away from the keep—and now Archimedes could hear them, too: moans and growls, all coming from inside, nearing the shattered entrance.

When the zombies burst through, he was already turning to run.

Yasmeen kept pace with him, suddenly sprinting ahead to meet a zombie that darted from between the trees in front of them. Her machete chopped through the zombie's neck, its head flying. The moans behind them became louder, more, closer. He heard the marines shout, the cracks of their guns. Ahead, Yasmeen whirled, revolver in hand, aimed at Archimedes. Her weapon sounded, again and again, each bullet whizzing past him, striking flesh.

He didn't want to know how close the zombies had been. His boots crunched through the snow, and he couldn't think about slipping—only about running and making sure they both made it back to the airship. When he caught up, Yasmeen traded her gun for her machetes and ran with him.

"She's coming back around!" Yasmeen shouted.

Someone on the airship must have seen the mob and alerted the captain. Above the bare trees, *Ceres* was making a slow turn, the crew's rifles picking off zombies below. Oh, Jesus. Their distraction had worked too well. Even if they outran the mob behind them, the noise of the airship drew more from all directions, too many for the crew to shoot. The rope ladder dropped, and Yasmeen's scream of *"No!"* was lost in the moans and the huff of the engines. Zombies attacked the swinging ladder, emaciated hands gripping the ropes, pulling—cutting off their easiest escape.

Movement from the corner of his eye warned him. Archimedes pulled his gun, fired. The zombie dropped. They were almost to the airship but more were racing toward them, some abandoning the ladder, others coming in from the forest.

Machetes flashing, Yasmeen sped ahead and killed three with astonishing efficiency. She whipped around, shot another. "Tree?"

Not good enough. Archimedes reached back, gripped his pneumatic launcher. He aimed for the airship, fired. The grapnel arced upward over the side, the long rope trailing behind. Steel hooks caught the gunwale, held fast.

He heard Yasmeen's wild laugh. She leapt for the rope, began climbing. Archimedes waited for her to climb high enough, three zombies falling to his bullets before he followed her up. Clawing hands grasped his boot, almost yanked him down. A crack sounded from above; the zombie's head exploded. He looked up. Holding herself steady with the rope between her thighs, Yasmeen hung upside down, the barrel of her gun smoking. She grinned before rocking back up, hauling herself upward with astonishing speed.

The rattle of the cargo lift joined the moans and gunshots. The crew dragged the rope ladder up halfway, shooting a path clear for the marines. They dropped it again as Bigor reached the airship. The four marines began climbing all at once, as if this weren't the first time they'd had to share a single ladder in a rush.

Yasmeen reached the deck. She leaned over the side, hauled Archimedes over. Chest heaving, laughing, Archimedes turned to look below. Jesus. The zombies were *still* coming out of the keep.

"Well—" He had to stop, catch his breath. "Now we know where they confined the infected."

Yasmeen laughed. Her bright eyes met his, her smile brilliant. He watched it die as her gaze lit on something beyond him.

"Oh, fuck," she said softly.

He looked around. Near the rope ladder, the marines were huddled over one of their men. Bigor had torn away Durand's sleeve. The bloody marks couldn't be anything but a bite.

The crew hushed.

Without turning his head, Bigor asked, "Mr. Fox, how long?"

A ball of lead settled in Archimedes' gut. "If he has nanoagents, a few days. If he doesn't, a few hours."

Durand closed his eyes. Bigor bent his head toward the other man's, said something too low to hear. A moment later, he stood and faced Captain Guillouet. "Will you please clear the deck, sir? We would like to say our farewells."

Though his expression looked suddenly weary, Guillouet's shoulders straightened. "I have to stand witness."

"He's our brother, sir."

"That's why I have to stand, marine."

Bigor's face tightened, but he nodded.

Yasmeen tugged on Archimedes' hand. "Come."

He followed her to the hatchway, where the deck crew was gathering, waiting their turns on the ladder. Softly, he said, "Should we say something to him before we go?"

"What can we say?" She slid down the ladder and waited for him below before starting along the passageway to their cabin. "He asked to have the deck cleared. That was his request. So we honor it."

"And the captain?"

"Too many people try to hide their loved ones after a bite." The weariness on her face matched the captain's. "Guillouet standing witness isn't personal, it isn't an insult. It simply says: The crew comes first."

And her crew had also always come first, Archimedes knew. "You've done the same?"

"Too many times. And too many times, I've been the one pulling the trigger." She stopped as a gunshot sounded above. Her eyes closed. After a long moment, she looked up at him. "If I'm ever bit, please do the same for me. Don't make me do it myself."

"I will." It was the most difficult promise he'd ever made. "I'd ask the same, but there's no question that you'll shoot me—even if I wasn't infected."

A smile touched her mouth, but her eyes remained serious. "It might take more for me to shoot you than you think. I suppose that means I'm not as dangerous to you. Is that disappointing?"

Was it? He recalled the pounding of his heart as he'd shot her with the opium dart, the delicious fear that had accompanied him back to *Lady Corsair*, certain she'd try to kill him at any moment. That fear *had* gone, but it wasn't a loss: every moment with her was more thrilling, more fulfilling, even if she wasn't trying to shoot him.

And he had more fears now to replace it: fear for her life, fear that when this expedition was over and her vengeance satisfied, he'd never see her again. And though he knew her heart was steel, though he looked forward to the longing of an unrequited love, he also knew the fear that she'd never feel the same in return.

She might not kill him, but he was still on a path that didn't lack for danger. It lurked behind her every touch, her every smile, her every word. With each one, he fell a little more—but instead of hope, his shattered heart waited below.

"I'm not disappointed," he said.

He was terrified.

Unsurprisingly, the airship's galley provided Hassan's table with marginally better food and the luxury of wine—which, Yasmeen noted, Hassan didn't touch. Conversation was subdued. She and Archimedes barely mentioned the morning's adventure, though she knew if there'd been any other outcome with Durand, neither one of them could have resisted upstaging the other.

Instead, she refilled her wine and listened as Archimedes told Hassan of an island in Venice that had been used in the same way as the keep, then of another island on the Seine. He mentioned dates and names with no effort, no pausing to recall details—as if history were as familiar as his own family.

In the serial adventures, Archimedes Fox never studied. He never sought mysteries; they simply fell into his lap. But in truth, Archimedes Fox was a scholar with a gun, a grapnel, and a need to fling himself into danger.

That made the real man infinitely more fascinating.

Not to Hassan, however—or because he'd known the real man for longer. And though he was subtle, steering the discussion to Venice and Archimedes' recent journey aboard *Lady Corsair*, she could see that his route would take him to her. Archimedes must have seen it as well, and—perhaps protecting her from questions she might not want to answer—not-so-subtly turned the conversation back around. Amused, Yasmeen watched their back-and-forth until she sensed a hint of frustration in Archimedes' reply. Their maneuverings had been entertaining, but not worth hard feelings.

At a pause in their exchange, Yasmeen met Hassan's eyes and said, "I won't think it rude if you ask."

The man colored slightly. Archimedes lifted his wine to her.

"Then tell us all, my wife."

She narrowed her eyes at him, but Hassan didn't waste any time. Shaking his head, he said, "Not all, please. I merely wondered if you were from the same house as Nasrin."

Nasrin, the wild rose. "Temür Agha's guard?" she guessed.

Hassan nodded. Archimedes had gone utterly still, his gaze fixed on her face as if not to miss a word. Because she'd mentioned the guard, or because he was learning more about her, information that didn't come from stories or rumors?

The idiot. If he wanted to know, he only had to say so. She would tell him.

Not here, however. No, there was another story that she wanted to hear, and it wasn't her own. She needed a full picture of the man who might be responsible for the death of her crew, not rumors and stories. She wanted to hear it from a man who knew him.

"I knew of several *gan tsetseg* by that name," she said, "but there are also many I don't know. I was raised in Constantinople."

"It is unlikely you know her, then. Nasrin was from the Punjaab, but was raised by the house in Daidu." Then, in a careful tone, "Constantinople?"

"Yes." She held his gaze. "I escaped while Temür Agha razed the city."

He gave a deep, resonating sigh. "You must have been young. That is why you were not altered."

"Yes." The mechanical flesh and weapons weren't grafted on until after they were fully grown. It had been near that time for Yasmeen—but this was also not what she wanted to hear, and she didn't care to be subtle when she steered. "Archimedes told me that I was wrong about Temür—that he hadn't been the one to burn the city."

"No," Archimedes jumped in immediately. "He did burn it. I only said he was a Horde rebel."

"He was *destroying* the rebellion."

"You are both correct," Hassan said. His hand shook slightly as he reached for the teapot, but Yasmeen couldn't determine whether it was with emotion or age. He paused before refilling his cup, as if noticing that she'd finished her glass of wine. "Shall I pour some for you?"

"Is it from the New World?"

Humor brightened his face. "Yes."

"No, thank you. Drinking nothing is better than that."

"I must disagree; even this tea is better than nothing." He grimaced slightly as he took a sip. "Though I wish I had thought to stock my own supply. Captain Guillouet does not trust any foods or drink that do not come from the Americas. He fears infection."

So that was why nothing was fresh. Centuries before, the Horde had concealed the nanoagents in the tea and sugar they'd traded in

Europe and northern Africa. By the time they activated their controlling signals, much of the population was infected and helpless
to fight back, making their invasions as painless as slipping a
greased finger into the barrel of a gun that didn't hold any bullets.

Setting his cup down, Hassan continued. "There are those in
the empire who would not blame him for his fear. When word of
the occupations in England and Africa reached Xanadu, it made
many uneasy—as uneasy as news of the zombies had a century
before. What if the creatures crossed the empire's walls and great
rivers? What if the Great Khan set up towers to control his people
instead of the barbarians? Few would speak out against Argon
Khan, however, under whose rule the occupations were ordered—
but it was then that the rebellion began to form."

Yasmeen hadn't known that. She'd been taught that Argon
Khan had been as wise as Munduhai Khatun, as generous as
Toqta Khan. To learn differently didn't surprise her, however—
every Khan was powerful enough to write his own history.

But it also meant there was only one way that Hassan had
heard differently. "Temür Agha told you this?"

"Yes. Perhaps it is true; perhaps it is not. Perhaps it is only what
he was told by others in the rebellion. But it is important to know
that there was also *another* rebellion, though the roots of that go
deeper, and was one that challenged the seat of the Great Khan."

Yasmeen knew of this one—the heirs of Ögedei, the youngest
son of Genghis Khan, could not have been more reviled in the histories. When the great general Batu, son of Genghis Khan's eldest
son, had been named his grandfather's successor, Ögedei's sup-
porters had called Batu's legitimacy into question, reminding all
that Genghis Khan's wife had been raped in captivity before the
birth of Batu's father. Though Batu had crushed the opposition, he
allowed his uncle Ögedei to live, sending him to secure the peninsula ruled by the Goryeo emperors.

Ögedei's descendants did not forget the question of legitimacy, however—and the blame for many assassinations within the royal line were laid at their feet. Yasmeen didn't know if that were true, or if Ögedei's heirs were simply a convenient scapegoat.

"Twenty-five years ago," Hassan said, "Kuyuk the Pretender began amassing an army in the White Mountains east of the Black Sea, claiming to be Ögedei's heir. The Horde's generals searched for him, but even though a generation had passed since the great plague, they had too few soldiers to be thorough, and for a decade Kuyuk remained well hidden—then the Great Khan sent Temür to flush him out. Kuyuk ran northwest, around the sea, then southeast."

"On a route to Constantinople," Yasmeen murmured.

"Even Temür doesn't know whether that was the Pretender's intention, or if it simply lay in his path as he returned east. His army must have been exhausted by the flight, low on supplies and starving—perhaps he only attacked the city to replenish his provisions. But Kuyuk claimed that he would prove to Xanadu his royal blood, a direct line from Genghis Khan, by sacking a city in the same way. Temür was not far behind him."

The man paused, sipped his tea. Though he gave little indication of it, Yasmeen sensed that his thoughts were troubled, his emotions suppressed.

"Temür had long been embroiled in another battle, though it was one that took more care and diplomacy—to convince the Great Khan to strike down the towers in the occupied territories. But the territories are lucrative, so the Khan would not. Temür requested the governorship of the northern African territories, but the Khan wanted to keep him close. But the Pretender's sacking of Constantinople posed a real threat to him—not that he feared Kuyuk would march on Xanadu, but that the people's confidence in him would be further damaged, and support for the rebellion—

the *true* rebellion—would grow. So the Khan made the promise that if Temür stopped the Pretender, he would have Morocco."

"But he didn't just stop Kuyuk," Yasmeen said. "Temür *obliterated* him, along with the city. There were still citizens there—citizens of the empire."

"Yes," Hassan said. Though he said it unflinchingly, a deep weariness seemed to settle over him. "He wanted to make certain that the Khan feared him enough never to go back on his promise. Then he sent Nasrin to destroy the Khan's stable."

"*What?*" Still trying to take in the implications of Temür's actions, trying to decide the sort of man they made, the shock of that statement sent her reeling. "Did she succeed?"

Hassan nodded. "Almost completely."

"The stable?" Archimedes leaned forward, frowning. "For his ponies? I haven't heard this."

"Mongols don't put their ponies in stables. It was a prison, a workhouse for the European mathematicians and philosophers that the Polo brothers and the fool Marco introduced to Toqta Khan." Feeling light-headed, Yasmeen reached for her cigarillo case. *Damn it.* She clenched her fist, took a breath. "But they are all dead, of course, replaced by those from within the empire. They are called the Khan's magicians. But that word is wrong—there is no magic; it is only superstition. They are his inventors. The cleverest children are picked from the crèches and the villages, and brought to Xanadu—and of those, the cleverest are chosen for the stable." A golden cage, much like the houses of the *gan tsetseng,* and those chosen were never allowed to leave. "The stable has been available to the royals, *only* the royals, for centuries. Their technologies are guarded like no other secret, though of course we *see* what they have created every day. But how does it work? So it is magic to many of those in the empire."

"The nanoagents," Archimedes realized.

"Those," Hassan said. "But it began earlier: the war machines that were sent west."

"The kraken, the megalodons, the giant eels," Yasmeen put in. "All created when the European navies began to put steam engines in their ships, the better to take the war to the Horde empire—so the Horde created monsters drawn to the engine vibrations. The *gan tsetseg*, the mechanical flesh, the towers, the boilerworms . . . There is too much to name, and I'm certain that even I have not heard of it all. But all of it was theirs, all of it designed to strengthen the empire and protect the royal family." She turned to Hassan, still disbelieving. "She destroyed the stable? She killed them all?"

"Yes. Perhaps a few were left. It's impossible to be certain."

All of that knowledge, the brilliance, the centuries of work . . . but Yasmeen couldn't be sorry. That was too much power in the hands of one man.

"But of course, the truth is hidden," Hassan said. "Temür has made certain the rebels know, but to most of the empire, the Khan's magicians were only a story to begin with, so the tale of their destruction makes no difference. The truth about the Pretender and the sack of Constantinople has been squashed as well, and instead, Temür Agha crushed a rebellion."

"And now you hope to crush him," Archimedes said.

"I don't hope for that, no." Hassan shook his head. "If God wills it, Temür will understand that it is best for all if he steps down. For as long as he governs, the people of Rabat will not *see* the difference between his rule and the Horde's—and they will always fear. But if one of our own governs in his stead . . . ? They will have hope."

"And if he's killed?" Yasmeen asked.

Hassan closed his eyes. "I cannot think of that. I pray that when the tower comes down, he will see that Rabat cannot be truly free until he has gone."

Until he has gone. If he had the wrong sketch, then Yasmeen would help him along.

The older man sighed again, and Archimedes met Yasmeen's eyes. She nodded. Yes, they had almost stayed too long—and Hassan was likely looking forward to his midday rest. She'd discovered almost everything she wished to know, anyway.

Almost. "Why don't you drink the wine? Do you fear poison?" The corners of Hassan's eyes creased with his smile. "No. It is because the sin is greater than the benefit."

Yasmeen recognized those words. "So you have also taken up the old religion—as Kareem al-Amazigh has."

"As Temür Agha did," he corrected gently. "When trying to restore a city after two hundred years of occupation, one can't simply erase everything the Horde has put into place—there would be chaos. The Horde's support will be gone, and so we searched for new rules of governing, new policies . . . and the economic rules from the Qur'an were very good, very fair. They resonated with us, as they do the people—as does the faith. But I will admit, we are feeling our way. Much of the scholarship was lost, and there is still conflict in our hearts."

"You could appeal to the scholars in the Far Maghreb," Archimedes suggested.

"We have. They will not return from the New World as long as Temür is still governor." He smiled again. "Until then, I will follow my conscience—and drink tea fit for camels rather than wine."

Chapter Ten

Archimedes followed Yasmeen out of Hassan's stateroom, before spinning around and entering again. Curious, she stopped to wait for him, then had to laugh when he came back out with the bottle of wine in hand.

Yes, they could put it to much better use. His grin wide, his long stride carried him close, but she didn't back away. She loved to look at him—his wicked smile, his active expressions, his handsome features. She *wanted* him close.

If only his longing would grow deep enough to kiss her.

She felt his breath instead, the dip of his head as he bent to her ear. "Did you find out everything you wanted to know about Temür Agha?"

"Mostly, yes."

"Good."

He didn't move. She was listening for others; so was he. His gaze roamed her face, fell to her lips. "When I kiss you, I don't know if I'll stop."

She didn't want him to. Her heart pounded as his mouth moved across her cheek, hovered over her lips.

"Now, I breathe your breath, and it's sweeter than any kiss I've ever had." His thumb dragged over her bottom lip. "When I'm finally inside you . . ."

He trailed off, his eyes glazing as if imagining it. Yasmeen did, too—the heavy thrust, the slide of sweaty limbs. Opening her mouth, she bit the tip of his thumb, and with a flick of her tongue, tasted the salt of his skin. His eyes met hers, and the world stilled.

A door opened farther down the passageway.

He drew back, pushed his fingers through his hair. His breathing wasn't steady. "I'll see if Ollivier has those notes ready."

"Don't drink anything."

"I won't."

She looked down the passageway. "If Bigor's in the wardroom, I'll talk to him about tomorrow."

"We'll go in before dawn?"

"Yes." They'd reach the pass by the middle of the night. Using the darkness for cover, they could slip in—or they could wait a day. She didn't want to wait. The more quickly this expedition finished, the more quickly they'd fly to Rabat.

Archimedes stopped at the next cabin, knocked. Yasmeen continued aft. Amidships, she met Deflowered Henri, who paused and fidgeted, mouth flapping like a fish as she passed. She'd seen that look before on young aviators: anxious to speak with her, but lacking the position to address her without being acknowledged first.

Because she could still remember his feet twitching on a tavern table, his stiffened toes spreading wide—and because the memory still amused her to no end—she stopped. "Yes?"

Bright red, he said, "Is it true you only gave your crew fifty percent, ma'am?"

It was true. "Why?"

"Last year, your girl Ginger said she earned three livre. But the engine stoker's boy says he's heard only a fifty percent split between *Lady Corsair*'s crew. Even Guillouet gives us seventy, so I told him that couldn't be true. And as she's dead, I won't stand for him calling her a liar."

The boy was defending Ginger's honor. That was sweet. "Ginger's still alive, Henri. She's with a friend of mine in London. If you like, I can pass on a message for you."

"No." His blush deepened. "Thank you, ma'am. I just wanted to know, so I can tell the stoker what you said."

Was it so important? Interesting. In Yasmeen's experience, if the boys on a ship were discussing earnings and percentages, then the rest of the crew was, too. She might as well set straight whatever rumor was flying around.

"I gave them fifty percent," she said and watched his face droop. "But she did earn three livre last year. Most of my crew earned five each."

"Truly?" His eyes widened. "And Ginger said that if they lost a hand or an eye, you paid for a replacement, too."

"Yes."

"I *told* him that. He said: But she can't replace their lives."

Yasmeen hoped she didn't run into this stoker's boy anytime soon. "That's also true. Now go on, before the captain finds you talking with me and thinks you're staging a mutiny."

Face suddenly pale, he ran off. Yasmeen grinned. Young boys were so serious. It was only a bit of humor at her own expense, but he must have taken her at her word.

She continued down the passageway. The wardroom lay all the way aft, two decks above the engines. Already huffing along, it wouldn't be long before *Ceres* arrived at Brenner's Pass. She hoped Guillouet had experience with the mountain winds.

Before she had a chance to knock, Laurent opened the door, obviously on the way out. He stopped suddenly, brows lifting.

"Is Mr. Bigor in?"

Stepping back, he gave a little jerk of his chin, inviting her in. A man of few words, apparently. He held the door open for her, then Dubois followed him out.

A designated cabin for officers to dine and take their leisure— or on a private ship, the senior crew, purser, and surgeon—the wardroom was larger and better appointed than the berth deck and mess. A small shelf held a selection of leather-bound books. Several comfortable chairs and a writing desk sat on one side of the room; the dining table filled the other.

All of them had been pushed aside to make space for the marines' equipment. Yasmeen's throat tightened. Eleven, twelve years ago, *Lady Corsair*'s stateroom had often looked the same.

Though they'd been hired for defense on this expedition, *marsouin*s had specialized in aerial and water infiltrations during the war. Brass diving suits were mounted along one wall. Collapsible gliders were folded next to them. Crates held other gear, weapons. They'd carried their own arsenal and equipment, not relying on the airship's—apparently, that still held true.

Bigor sat at the table, a small chest open in front of him. He stood as she entered, gestured for her to sit.

A stack of personal effects lay next to the chest, and one by one, Bigor packed them inside. Letters, a rag doll, a ferrotype photograph of a woman and a baby . . . the chest was full of Durand's belongings, she realized. Bigor was preparing to send them off— probably to the woman in the photograph.

"I'm sorry about your man," she said softly.

Jaw hard, he nodded. "It's not often we have a chance to say good-bye."

"I know." And that was better than nothing.

"We might have all been the same if not for your bullets. Thank you."

She nodded her own acknowledgment. There was nothing to say. It hadn't ended up being enough—but he was likely counting his every shot, too. Wondering if he'd just pulled the trigger one more time, maybe he'd have killed the zombie who bit Durand.

"Only one letter left to add now—mine." He closed the chest, but didn't lock it. "He has a wife in the Antilles."

"You'll send her a good story, I hope."

"He has many worth telling. But today, I'll probably put his name on a few of your bullets."

So that his wife could hear that Durand had died after saving his comrades; that they only lived because of him. "That's fine."

He gave another sharp nod, but this time, it seemed rough around the edges. "You don't expect it to be this. The war, yes. You fight for a reason and shoulder a burden of responsibility, duty—and of doing things I'd never want my wife and children to know. In the war, they send a letter home that only tells the family that he fought with honor, he fulfilled his duty—and it's truth. But I'm still doing things I don't want to describe in a letter, and when I go, a good story is all I can hope for. And like Durand's, it will probably be sprinkled with lies."

The lies didn't matter to Yasmeen; she'd built her reputation on bits of truth she'd chosen other people to know, and that would be all anyone knew of her when she died. But responsibility and duty . . .

Only a few months ago, she'd looked at Nasrin and pitied the *gan tsetseg* for the chains that bound her. But Yasmeen had her own; her airship gave her freedom but had bound Yasmeen with duty and loyalty to the men and women that served it. She'd willingly borne those chains—and when the links snapped, it had been a physical pain.

Yet to never feel their burden again was unimaginable. To never feel the wind in her face, *her* wind. To never feel her engines beneath her feet. To never feel pride in her aviators, to know a job well done. She would be willing to bear those chains and risk the pain again—for the right ship, the right crew.

She thought of Archimedes, and an unfamiliar ache bloomed in her chest. Would she be willing to risk the same for the right man? One who knew her now, better than anyone else ever had. But that wouldn't be risking pain; it would be risking her heart, exposing her belly. Yasmeen didn't know if she could do that—even if, like Archimedes, she wanted to.

And she didn't.

Bigor locked the chest. "But you aren't here for Durand."

"No. It's about tomorrow, and the pass. Mr. Fox and I have been discussing strategy—and we agree that our first priority is avoiding notice from the Horde outpost."

He nodded once—his default response for any statement, apparently. "And you need me to put it forth to Guillouet."

"Yes. Hassan has already heard and approved it, but the captain might want another opinion."

Bigor undoubtedly understood the rest: Another opinion, as long as it wasn't hers or Archimedes'. He nodded.

"The Horde outpost is directly across the valley from the old fortress. We plan to come in the early morning, before dawn—sailing straight through, and using the gliders so that *Ceres* doesn't have to stop and hover. But once we're in the fortress, we won't be able to see if the Horde has noticed and if they're coming."

"So you want us to stay on *Ceres* and keep watch."

"Yes." If the Horde came, it wouldn't matter if two were at the fortress, or five. But three skilled men on *Ceres* might make all the difference. "If she sails farther down the valley, she can hide out of the Horde's line of sight, but you'll still be able to see if they begin to cross the valley. If they do, *Ceres* can fire her engines and reach us before the Horde. With the three of you on watch, Mr. Fox and I won't have to keep looking out the windows—and we'll go through the fortress more quickly. We'll be picked up after nightfall on the second day. The new moon will help conceal the balloon—and if we need the cargo lift, it'll be there."

He nodded. "And so will we."

She went above decks, where the wind cleared her head, allowed her to think of absolutely nothing but the mountains passing beneath her feet, the route they were taking south. *Ceres* was a good ship, bucking the wind with barely a sway. Nothing like her lady had been, but solid. When Guillouet was finished flying or dead, she would serve another captain, and perhaps another. Hopefully, she'd be treated well, loved, and serve many more.

Near the end of the afternoon watch, she reluctantly started for the ladder. She couldn't remain up on deck all day. She passed one of the Vashons—with his black eye hidden under his goggles, she couldn't tell if it was Peter or Paul—and acknowledged him with a nod.

"How goes the sky, Captain?"

Yasmeen almost missed a step, so great was her shock. Even on a mercenary ship, his familiar address was a severe break of protocol. But she'd sensed no enmity from either twin the evening before; he might have simply been pushing to see her reaction. She wouldn't give him one—and he wasn't hers to discipline. Smoothly, she turned her stumble into a pause, and responded as if he'd addressed her formally. "Very well, Mr. Vashon."

She continued on and had to stifle her groan when Guillouet abandoned the quarterdeck and intercepted her near the ladder.

Quietly, he said, "You will not speak with my crew, Mrs. Fox."

Her brows lifted. Ordering her about was the surest way to make her do the opposite.

His jaw was tight. "I'd heard rumor that you've been stirring up my men with talk of low wages."

Was that what this was about? Fuck. Though it rasped against her pride to do it, she said, "If there is any talk, Captain, it was in your favor. In conversation, they asked what percentage I gave. I told them fifty percent. Less than you."

Satisfaction briefly loosened the tension in his features. He had his own pride, and discovering that he paid a higher percentage than *Lady Corsair*'s captain obviously soothed it. "This was conversation in the mess?"

"Yes." No need to point a finger at Henri. "I haven't spoken with your crew outside of it."

Some of the tension returned, but this time, Yasmeen sensed that it wasn't directed toward her. Holding her gaze, he said, "Beginning this evening, I would like for you to take your meals in your cabin, and to remain there as much as possible."

This was also an order, but Yasmeen's instincts didn't immediately rise against it. Though he didn't explain it, Captain Guillouet's concern was clear—and a mutiny could be dangerous for anyone who wasn't a mutineer. "And my husband?"

"Can eat where he chooses."

She nodded. Whatever rumors had reached his ears, Guillouet obviously believed they'd been sparked by her presence, even if she hadn't sparked them herself. "We will be away from the ship for two days, Captain, beginning tomorrow."

"Yes," he said, and she saw relief lighten some of his tension. And it might be true: The talk might settle without her presence to prompt it. Crews often grumbled, and rarely did it escalate into something more—but whether it did would depend on Captain Guillouet.

And in this instance, at least, he'd done exactly what Yasmeen would have. So she returned below, prepared to keep her mouth shut, her eyes open . . . and her gun within reach.

In the cabin, Archimedes was in his bunk, lying on his side with elbow propped as he paged through Ollivier's notes. Ah, but he truly was a fine specimen of a man. He looked up, met her eyes. His smile faded. "What is it?"

Yasmeen held up a finger. She didn't want to talk with him from across the cabin, even as small as it was. With the pipes running through the ship, sometimes voices carried over the engines, and she wasn't familiar enough with *Ceres* to know where the dangerous spots were.

After shedding her coat and hat, she went to the side of the bunk, crossing her forearms on his mattress. He leaned forward, and she said softly, "Captain Guillouet fears a mutiny."

His brows shot up. He drew back to study her face, as if to determine whether she was serious. "We are but two days out."

"*We* are," she said. "They left the New World many weeks ago. If there was already dissatisfaction, then seeing Guillouet's reaction to my coming aboard and the insult of him sending me down might have sparked more."

"But they didn't seem insulted by you. Well, not all of them."

"That doesn't matter so much, does it? The grumblings would not truly be about me. But, regardless—I am confined to our cabin until we leave tomorrow morning."

He stared at her. "And you agreed to that?"

"Mutiny is never to be taken lightly. Even if this is not a navy ship, the crew would fear anyone witnessing what happened. Perhaps we'd be safe simply by staying out of the way, but it's impossible to know. So we ought to ready our packs and gliders for tomorrow, but *keep* them ready, even after we return."

She'd rather take her chances in the wilds of Europe than stay aboard a mutinous ship.

Archimedes seemed to agree. He nodded. "All right."

"When you go to dinner, bring back my plate first so I can taste it." It all came from the same pots; he should be all right to eat his afterward. "When you eat with them, listen—especially to what isn't being said. Last night, I didn't sense anything of this sort, but most mutinies are whispers in the dark, not out in the open."

"I'll do that," he said.

She sighed. "And then I will be glad we are not on this ship the next two days."

"And Hassan?"

"If it does happen, tell him to stay in his room, to be quiet, and if they come for him, to offer money—and to give them all the wine."

"And remind them he is a friend to Temür Agha."

His gaze was flat and hard, reminding her that a dangerous, clever mind lay behind those emerald eyes. Archimedes wasn't thinking of what Temür might do; he was thinking of what *he* would do if Hassan were harmed.

"Yes," she said.

"And the marines?"

"If the crew is riled to the point of mutiny, the marines' presence alone might be enough to suppress it. But I will add that they rarely are riled to that point, no matter their complaints. Your father was *much* worse than Guillouet, and though we hated him, we'd never have attempted mutiny. Even the man your father tried to roast had only been overheard complaining—he could have been set down instead with strong discipline. If the example needed to be made, maybe a whipping." And though Yasmeen didn't hesitate to kill when necessary, the entire situation had been horrifying. First the roasted mutineer, and then the number of men she'd shot just to stay alive . . .

She couldn't regret it, but there was nothing good in it, either. "Even if he'd ordered a whipping for *me* after I'd shot the roasting man, I wouldn't have mutinied. If *Ceres'* crew rises up because of wormy bread and a lack of women, they are not much of a crew at all."

Mouth firmly set, Archimedes shook his head. "And hearing all that only makes me more glad that you killed him."

"Then why didn't you? And how is it that an educated son of a fanatical mercenary became a weapons smuggler with the Horde rebellion?"

"Why not kill him? I thought I'd eventually prove him wrong. And as the war heated up, he was home less often, and left us there. I don't doubt that if he'd gone back for good while Geraldine—Zenobia—was still living there, I would have." He swung his legs over the side of the bunk, dropped to the floor. "As to the rest, I was just trying to get away from my father as much as possible. That meant supporting whoever he didn't."

"The Liberé?"

"Yes."

Going down on his heels, he dragged their trunk from under the bed—intending to start on their packs as they talked, she realized. Not yet. When he stood and reached into his watch pocket for the key, she hooked her foot behind his knee and pushed against his chest. Unbalanced, he sat down hard on the trunk's lid and almost tipped over backward, stopping when he braced his hands against the bunk behind him. She straddled his hips, smiling, looking down at his face as his expression moved from surprised to amused . . . and then, with a subtle shift, gained a wicked edge.

"I think you like this position, Mrs. Fox."

She rasped her claw across the rough stubble beneath his jaw, marveling at how easily he lifted his chin, exposing his throat. He wasn't stupid, so that had to be trust.

"With you between my legs, at my mercy?" She squeezed him

with her thighs. "Yes, I like this position very much. So do you, I think."

His cock was already rigid beneath her. She rocked forward, loving the way his eyes closed, his teeth clenched. He shifted his feet, widened his legs. Yasmeen's breath caught as she settled more firmly against him.

"I like it," he said. "Very much. Now hold still."

"I don't take orders well."

"For this, you will." He sat up. At her back, his hands slipped beneath her shirt. His strong fingers began slow circles up the length of her spine.

"Oh, yes." Yasmeen's eyelids seemed suddenly heavy, weighed down by the pleasure sliding across her skin with each circular stroke. She all but melted against his chest, slipping her arms around his back to hold herself against him, and let him do as he willed. "But tell me about the smuggling."

"There's little to tell. Bilson was a friend from university. We both supported the Liberé, and he knew someone who needed men to bring weapons in from Horde territory. So we did."

But that wasn't all, Yasmeen wagered. "And it was dangerous."

"You have me down, don't you?" His mouth curved into a wry smile. "Yes. Almost all of the meet-ups with suppliers were at the Hapsburg Wall, or at the edges of the empire. The first was on the southern coast of the Baltic Sea. I saw my first megalodon, my first zombies, spent the whole journey with my heart pounding, certain I would die. And the moment we were done, I couldn't wait to return."

She laid her cheek onto his shoulder. "According to the stories, you were good at it."

"I was."

"Until you lost your cargo." The smooth motion of his hands faltered slightly, and made her wonder— "*Did* you lose it? Did you sell it to someone else? What did you do with the money?"

"I didn't sell it. I sank the barge." His voice was low. "This was not long after I was shot, after I was infected by nanoagents, was affected by the tower. My emotions were a wreck—and Temür was shipping war machines to the Liberé."

She opened her eyes, stared blindly past his neck to the porthole. That sort of power would have ended the conflict quickly. But, no—he'd changed his name six months after Bart had stabbed her, she remembered. "But the war was over by then—the Liberé had already won."

"Aside from a few skirmishes, yes. The Liberé said they wanted to have the machines, just to make certain the French weren't a threat again. But I was convinced they'd use them, and war machines on any side tipped the scales too far. So I sank them."

While his emotions had been in turmoil. "And now what do you feel?"

His hands lazily stroked up to her shoulders. "I don't regret it."

"Despite all of this trouble now with your debt, the search for the sketch."

"Yes."

"My crew is dead, my ship gone."

His hands froze. Obviously, he'd never put it together like that. "God, Yasmeen. I can't . . ."

Lifting her cheek from his shoulder, she shook her head. "I don't blame anyone but the person responsible—and the person who gave the order."

Fingers gliding down her sides, he asked softly, "And if it's Nasrin, how will we kill her?"

We. She liked the sound of that too well. "We don't have to kill her. If we kill Temür, she'll die. Of course, getting past her to Temür is another problem entirely." She smiled when his brow furrowed in confusion. "You cannot release a weapon like Nasrin without some tether. When she was altered and the royal she served was chosen, her nanoagents were aligned to his. Even if duty failed, she would save his life simply because hers is also at stake."

"So if he dies, she dies."

"Yes."

"That's . . . barbaric."

Perhaps. "But to her, it's beautiful."

"And to you?"

"It's both." To the *gan tsetseg*, whose very existence was created to honor an act of love and protection, those bonds of loyalty and duty *were* life—and there was nothing else. Yasmeen couldn't believe the same, not anymore, but she couldn't shed everything from her upbringing, and there were memories and stories that she held close. So, too, would the other women. "I'd never wish it for myself. I'd have hated it. But I've also recently thought that there are some bonds that I do welcome, because I receive something that makes the burden worth bearing in return. So I understand her a little better."

"Perhaps you do. But even if you loved me, I wouldn't want you to do that. I would rather you never loved me at all than to know my death killed you."

Such a romantic. Sitting up, she cupped his strong jaw. His gaze locked with hers. She lowered her head, breathing his breath. *Yes.* He was right: This was almost better than a kiss. When he whispered her name, she pressed her face into his neck, smelled his incredible scent.

How could she know what this bond between them was? Friendship, yes. A common purpose. Perhaps the rest was only lust. Perhaps it was more.

Right now, lust was enough.

Dropping her right hand between them, she loosened her breeches, slipped her fingers inside. By the lady, he made her so wet.

"Yasmeen."

She loved the sound of his voice, the need in it as he rasped her name. She loved the boldness of his fingers replacing hers. She loved his heavy groan when he found her, slick and hot, loved the tension in his lean body. Purring when his fingers pushed deeper, she rose and fell against him, and he shook with agonized restraint.

"You torture yourself so well." Panting, she licked his throat, felt him shiver. "Come, Archimedes Fox. Torture me, too. Make me scream."

But the only real torture would have been stopping. He explored instead, discovering what gave her the most pleasure, his fingers clever and adventurous. He learned her quickly. Writhing against his hand, Yasmeen hovered over him, lips all but touching his, breathing his breath—until she did finally scream, muffling her cries against his neck.

Chapter Eleven

Archimedes forced himself out of bed when the soft knock came at the door, hoping it didn't wake Yasmeen. He loved how irritable she was when her knees hurt, but couldn't love the reason for it—and at least he could support her through it. In just a few days, their mornings had become ritual: a quick wash, followed by pacing. Today, that ritual had to begin earlier, but they'd start with a meal.

As Archimedes had requested the night before, a galley assistant brought their breakfast to them—two bowls of oat porridge and black coffee. Yasmeen hated the coffee, but Archimedes would drink hers, too. She lifted her head from her pillow when he pulled the trunk from beneath her bunk—God, what she'd done to him on it yesterday—and used it as their table. Eyes still heavy, she began pacing right after eating, hobbling along. She didn't seem to have slept any better than he had—wondering half the night if they would be under a mutiny, perhaps.

Finally, she dressed in extra layers, strapped on her weapons, and gathered their packs: food in both, a bedroll to share in his, a change of clothes for each of them in hers, in case those they were wearing became wet. Not much, but the packs had to be light, especially with the excuses for gliders that were aboard *Ceres*. All airships carried them for emergencies, but hers must have been purchased at the start of the war twenty years prior.

Yasmeen would take the lead when they jumped from the airship. With no light from the moon and the deck lanterns extinguished, Archimedes could only make out the shadows of the peaks rising around them, the faint lights from the Horde outpost—he wouldn't have been able to spot the fortress against the opposite mountainside. The ship sailed silently, the wind biting his cheeks. Bigor met them on the main deck, looking as straight and fresh as if he never needed sleep. He held up two folded batwing gliders, and Archimedes saw Yasmeen's relief.

"Thank you, Mr. Bigor."

He nodded. "You'll probably hit crosswinds. Not strong, but enough to toss those older ones over. These were made to maneuver in inclement weather, and the wing size can be adjusted. You're both familiar with them?"

"Yes," Archimedes said. Uneasily familiar with them. These gliders maneuvered so well, even acrobats used them—and the *marsouin*s were trained for aerial infiltration.

Yasmeen joined him at the side of the ship. Her eyes narrowed when she saw his face. "What is it?"

He shook his head and slipped on his goggles. Now wasn't the time to tell her of his sudden suspicions, but they nagged at him, dimming his usual thrill when they jumped from the airship, caught the wind.

Though he couldn't see the fortress, Ollivier's notes had included drawings and floor plans. Designed with the simplicity of a monastery and the strength of a citadel, high stone walls formed three sides of a rectangle, with the mountainside serving as the fourth. At the corners and at the main gate, crenellated towers overlooked the valley. Instead of a keep, a two-level stone barracks supported the interior base of the curtain wall, strengthening the defenses and providing chambers for storage, quarters for the soldiers, engineers, and laborers, a foundry to produce the steel needed for da Vinci's machines, and a smithy to shape the parts. The walls and barracks surrounded the enormous courtyard, where the machines were constructed before they rolled out of the main gate.

Yasmeen banked as she approached the southwest tower, aligning herself over the curtain wall and extending the glider's wings, allowing the greater surface area to catch the air and slow her down. Skimming over the crenels, she landed atop the wall and ran along its wide surface, folding the wings back as she came to a stop. Archimedes came in right after her, snow hardened by wind and sun crunching beneath his boots. Yasmeen was a dark silhouette against all the white; over the side of the wall, the courtyard lay in dense shadow.

"There are footprints," she said quietly.

Zombies, then, somewhere. The fortress wouldn't have been constructed with defense against them in mind; it had been built before the zombie infection. He followed her to the southwest tower, where an arched doorway led to a spiral stair, the wooden door long rotted away. All was darkness inside, but Archimedes didn't dare light the drip lamp until they were behind the curtain walls.

"I can see," Yasmeen said. Drawing her machetes, she entered the twisting stairwell. Snow covered the first steps, but the stone was bare past the turn. His palm against the rough block wall, Archimedes felt his way in the dark, and almost bumped into Yasmeen when she stopped.

Her whisper was irritated. "It's too dark for me now, too."

With a silent laugh, he opened the valve to start the gas and lit the lamp. The reflector bowl cast a wide, bright light, revealing granite blocks and steps. A few more turns, and the stair opened to the barracks' second level.

Yasmeen hesitated briefly. "This one first?"

He nodded. Better not to have a zombie at their backs.

They stepped out into the corner chamber. The barracks ran north into the side of the mountain and east along the face of the wall toward the main gate, a long series of chambers connected by doors. To the north, the chambers were all but empty. Either the departing soldiers had taken everything with them, or the Horde outpost had done some scavenging of its own. A few tables remained—perhaps too big to take down the stairs. Arched openings in the stone walls served as windows overlooking the dark courtyard, and small mounds of snow piled on the sills and the stone floor.

No zombies.

They returned to the tower and started east. Debris on the floor gave Archimedes some hope of a find, but he'd sift through it after they secured the fortress. They reached the gate, where the fortifications were twice as thick and separated the barracks that ran along the curtain wall. Another twisting stairwell led below, and with the top level cleared, they didn't have to fear zombies coming at them from above.

"Shall we make a stand here?" Yasmeen murmured. "We can escape through the stairs if we're overwhelmed."

By all appearances, they wouldn't be. There were fewer zombies in this region to begin with, and only one set of footprints above. Though they might simply be lying quiet, as they had been in the Vienna keep, it was more likely that only a few were here.

He nodded. "Yes."

They dropped their packs, readied their weapons. After a glance confirming that she was ready, he gave a whoop that echoed through the chambers. Removing her hat, she exposed her softly pointed, tufted ears. She turned her head, listening.

"Anything?" He didn't need to whisper now.

"Not yet." She drummed her machetes against the stone wall, making racket enough to wake the dead. "Hiyoooooo, *zombieeees*!"

When the echoes and his laughter faded, she shook her head. "I don't hear anything."

"All right. Let's move on."

They cleared more chambers, arriving at the southwest tower again, then heading north toward the mountainside. The snow outside had piled higher than the window openings, drifts spilling into the chambers in large mounds. In the courtyard, dark machinery jutted up through the white, huge and indistinct—war machines abandoned in the middle of construction, or simply the scrap heap from what was left. Yasmeen stopped at one of the windows, peering out, her head tilting back as her gaze continued upward.

Her lips parted. "There's snow all over so I can't see what it is . . . but it's huge. Not like one of da Vinci's. More like one of the Horde's early war machines, the domed clambering ones that looked like turtles."

Unease rippled through him. That didn't make sense. How could something that big get into the fortress—or out? It would have to crash through the walls, and they were intact.

A rumble sounded from the courtyard. Yasmeen froze, eyes wide. Archimedes doused the light, heart pounding. That hadn't been zombies.

That had been a steam engine.

The clank of metal against stone echoed through the chambers, followed by a huffing snort. Then more clanks, in a recognizable rhythm: walking on four feet. A wolf, a horse, a cat. God knew. Maybe something like the ratcatchers in London, cats changed by the Horde into large, vicious hunters with steel armor, razored teeth and claws . . . only by the sound of it, much bigger.

Archimedes stared through the dark, listening to the clanging echo. He couldn't get a fix, though it had to be in one of the barracks. The snow in the courtyard would have muffled those steps. "Which direction is it coming from?"

"South." The way they'd come. Her hand grasped his as an orange glow appeared in the farthest chamber, near the tower. "Let's go. We can cut through the courtyard to the barracks on the opposite side."

She led him to the window. They scrambled up the mound of snow, slipped down the drift pile into the courtyard. They went quickly, knee-deep in the snow, Archimedes praying that zombies weren't under it. The mountainside lay to their left. Machinery rose through the snow on their right, dark amid all the white. Good. Lots of places to hide.

The huffing of the engine quickened, the clank coming faster— galloping. Then suddenly, not clanking. Archimedes' heart raced. It was in the courtyard. Yasmeen suddenly darted to the side, pulled him down next to a piece of machinery. Another snort sounded. Closer. Crouching, they felt their way along the machine, searching for the end, a corner to go around, something to hide behind. The orange glow suddenly offered more light, and Archimedes saw: There was no end to the machine until it reached the other side of the courtyard.

That meant as soon as the thing following them entered the corridor created between the mountain and the machine, it would have them in a direct line of sight.

"Fuck." On a desperate breath, Yasmeen pulled him down again. She sheathed her machetes, drew her guns. "Whatever it is, I'll distract it. You run to the barracks, to the southeast tower. I'll meet you there."

No goddamn chance in hell. He'd run out there naked before he let Yasmeen use herself as bait. But as a sensible man, even when stalked by a giant huffing animal, he put it to her in the least likely way to piss her off.

"No," he said simply.

"Archimedes—"

"Let's see what it is first. If it's faster than you, running out there would be suicide."

She nodded and stood. Archimedes rose with her, his hands searching the side of the machine. He found pipes, riveted panels. Plenty to grab on to. They could climb, and—

Oh, Good God.

A giant mechanical horse galloped toward them, but it was a horse made in hell. Eyes glowed with orange. Steel spikes jutted from its chest and neck. Two rapid-fire guns were bolted to its sides, both aimed forward. Fifteen yards away, it came to a sudden stop on legs made from thick pistons. Iron plates formed the skin. At least ten feet tall at the withers, its barrel-shaped body was big enough to hold the devoured remains of twenty men.

Or just a few men, if they were driving it. But how would they see? In the orange glow and changing shadows, Archimedes spotted the narrow vertical slots on its chest.

"Eye slits," he said. "Between the spikes."

Someone was in that thing and looking back at them.

The rapid-fire barrels spun.

"Oh, you fucking bastard." Yasmeen swore at the machine and grabbed his hand. They raced, and it came after them, pounding and snorting. Yasmeen whirled, whipping a knife through the air. The blade slammed into the center eye slit, stopped only by the hilt.

Then she was simply gone.

Archimedes stopped, turned. She was running straight at the giant machine, her long silk kerchief in hand.

He sprinted after her. "Yasmeen!"

She impaled the scarf over the chest spikes, covering the eye slits. With a leap, she was up on its neck, scrambling across the back. Looking for an entrance, he realized. The horse reared, huffing steam from its nose—and from its ass.

Suddenly laughing wildly, Archimedes raced toward it, straight on as she had, out of the firing line of the two guns. The barrels spun. No ammunition. Faintly, he heard shouting from inside, muffled by steel and drowned out by the engine. The horse came down from its rear in a hard stomp. The ground shuddered. Rattled by the impact, Yasmeen fell over its head, thumping to the snow at its front feet. Archimedes dove for her, rolled away as the steel hooves stamped again.

A long piece of wire stabbed through the eye slits, dislodging the scarf. Yasmeen crouched beside him, both motionless, waiting to see the direction the horse moved before they sprang.

The machine quieted, instead. A panel opened in its belly. Guns aimed, they waited.

A young man tumbled out and fell to his knees beneath the mechanical beast, hands outspread as if to show he had no weapons. His face downturned, he was almost crying, Archimedes realized—and his mouth was moving. Over the rumble of the engine, he heard the apology in the Horde language: "I didn't know it was you, *gan tsetseg*, but thought one of the soulless had come. Forgive me, lady."

Gan tsetseg. A flower of steel—the same thing Yasmeen had called herself and Nasrin.

Yasmeen stood stiffly, gun still pointed. Archimedes holstered his.

"He says he's sorry, steel flower," he told her in French. "He thought we were zombies."

Yasmeen blinked. "I couldn't make it all out. His accent is strong." She lowered her gun and spoke in Mongolian. "Stand up now."

Her accent was strong, more like Temür's than the common Horde rebels that Archimedes had met, but the young man immediately complied. About eighteen or twenty, with rounded face and teary brown eyes, he stood in long quilted tunic split up the middle and belted with a sash. Boots of leather and fur protected his feet.

Yasmeen holstered her weapon. "How many are in the fortress?"

"Only me and no one."

"Where is no one, then?"

A name, Archimedes realized. Nergüi.

"In our chamber. She sleeps heavy with opium."

"She?"

"My grandmother."

Yasmeen nodded. "And you are?"

"Terbish." *That one.*

She smiled faintly. "Your family had bad luck come calling for you before, yes?"

Though his mouth didn't curve, Terbish's eyes crinkled at the corners. Both tears and fear vanished from his face. "Yes."

She gestured to the horse, quietly rumbling behind him. "Did you build this?"

"Yes."

"It's incredible. Will you let us look inside?"

His eyes widened, and he stepped back, arm extended. "Please, lady."

Terbish and Nergüi had taken one of the chambers near the foundry. To keep the heat from escaping, they'd covered the windows with thick wooden planks from the tables and the entrances with heavily woven curtains. Two pallets lay close to a hearth built from stone and steel, making an efficient oven. A gray-haired woman snored lightly on one.

Terbish bent to wake her. "It will be a few minutes before she rouses. Please, sit."

Yasmeen glanced at the woven mats beside the pallets and sank down, crossing her legs. Archimedes crouched, and she had to smile. He wouldn't relax yet. She could move quickly enough it didn't worry her.

The older woman stirred. Not blissed on opium, Yasmeen saw, but probably drinking a medicine before she slept. The stiffness of her movements suggested arthritis. Nergüi's eyes widened, then she stilled when she saw Yasmeen's ears. Quick fear appeared, and then she was up, pushing Terbish off to collect food from their stores. She stoked the fire, and poured fermented milk from a horsehide bag hanging nearby.

Yasmeen accepted the small bowl. After the snow outside, the thick drink was pleasantly warm, slightly sweet and pungent. She passed the bowl to Archimedes.

"I didn't hear ponies," she said. Aside from the terrifyingly huge mechanical one. "Do you keep them here?"

"Across the valley." Nergüi settled onto her mat, crossing her legs as Yasmeen had. "We return to the outpost each week to replenish our supplies."

"You don't live there?"

"We do. But what is there to do in the winter? There is nothing to harvest, everyone only sits and waits for something to happen. The soldiers are gone, so all of us that are left have only our own families to feed."

And so it was with all of the outposts: the workers allowed outside the walls, but locked in by zombies and their duties. "The soldiers are gone? Where?"

"To Xanadu, to defend against the rebellion, though the news we receive from outside says there is no rebellion to crush." Nergüi grinned and clicked her tongue, obviously not fooled by the official statements. "Perhaps they have flung the rebels all away."

To the Horde outposts. Just as governing an outlying territory was a punishment, so too was this. With many soldiers about, the outposts effectively became a work prison for entire families. "And what will you do with no soldiers about?"

"Me? I only cook. The boy only builds."

Ah. She was being careful with Yasmeen about—not a soldier, but uncertain why a *gan tsetseg* and Archimedes were here. Yasmeen gave the old woman a quick explanation, saying that they'd only come to collect some of the barbarians' equipment, before suspicion led her to ask:

"Did Terbish build his machine from the parts that were left here?"

"Yes."

So they might not find much at all. But why the horse? If they were rebels, did they plan to use it? It did seem the sort of fanciful machine a young man would make. "And one day, will he ride his pony across the empire?"

"No, no." Nergüi's smile bunched cheeks as round as Terbish's. "That is just to cross the valley."

When the sun rose, Terbish showed them the courtyard. Five airships could have been tethered comfortably within its walls, and it was taken up with a dark machine. Yasmeen stared up at it. Roughly shaped as if someone had chopped off the top of a mountain and placed it in the courtyard—but it was a mountain made of propellers and pistons, valves and pipes—too large to be anything but awe-inspiring. She couldn't make sense of its purpose. Propellers might have been for direction, but couldn't provide propulsion—not for something this massive.

"What is it?" Archimedes said, and Yasmeen was thankful she was not the only one who hadn't yet figured it out.

"A flying machine. Of course it is not finished. But in another five years, it will rise."

Oh. How to say this without offending? Yasmeen settled for "It's very heavy."

Terbish stared at her. Then a bright smile widened his mouth. "No. This is only the shape. Come."

He raced around the machine.

Archimedes grinned and walked with her—neither one in such a hurry.

"This is a surprising find," he said, and she knew he was not speaking of the machine, but Nergüi and Terbish.

"That is the very best kind."

"Yes. We won't find much here. Nergüi says the fortress is almost picked clean."

"Then we'll enjoy two days of food that doesn't crawl with worms."

"Will they have enough?"

"Will you offend them by asking?" She lifted her brows. "Me neither. It sounds as if they replenish often, but we'll give them what we have in our packs, too."

And try not to be embarrassed by the offering. The mare's milk alone had been richer in flavor and more satisfying than anything she'd had aboard *Ceres*. Still, Nergüi and Terbish might enjoy the novelty of barbarian food at its worst.

The young man waited for them near a small ledge jutting out from the machine, and hauled himself up. "Come inside!"

He led them to an opening of a large pipe. More tubes lined the interior. Bent over at the waist, she followed Terbish inside. The pipe narrowed until they were crawling across the metal. Feeling squeezed from the outside in, Yasmeen forced herself to keep following the young man, and when there was no more light, following the sound of him.

"I think God is angry with me," Archimedes grumbled in

French. "My face is all but buried in your delectable ass, and I can't see to enjoy a moment of it."

Yasmeen laughed, then her palm encountered more metal— smooth, slightly warm. Unsettled by the unexpected texture, she yanked her hand back. Ahead, Terbish lit a lamp, and she found herself at the entrance to a small, spherical chamber, without enough room to stand. The walls were gray and looked softer than they felt.

Mechanical flesh.

Terbish ran his hand along the curving wall. "It has to grow, and it will cover all of the iron and steel like a skin, using what it needs from them and discarding the rest. It will be light"—he tilted his head, as if considering—"Light*er*. Much lighter. And it will be able to lift itself."

Yasmeen had no idea if that were true. But how could he have this? The Khan's stable had been destroyed. She looked to Archimedes, who was also taking in the chamber with an astonished expression.

"Where did you find the mechanical flesh?"

"It was given to me." He stroked the wall again, and Yasmeen thought that it responded—a slight flexing, like a muscle tensing beneath skin. "One summer when I was still a boy, a man came through the pass. He met with my mother, who was alive, and grandmother while they worked in the valley. He spent the night in the fortress, and my mother, grandmother, and I avoided the soldiers that evening and brought food to him, and we ate with him. They knew he was a magician, and asked him to take me on his journey, so that I could leave this place. They brought a toy that I had built, to prove that I was clever enough to join him—but the magician said he did not know where the road would take him, and to wait, and to build a machine made of my changing dreams, and he would return and help me leave."

Obviously not recognizing this for a well-told story, and a family favorite at that, Archimedes interrupted the young man's telling of it. "How did they know he was a magician?"

"Because he was made from this. Very big, all gray, no hair."

Yasmeen laughed in surprise, and looked to Archimedes. He wore an expression of disbelief. "The Blacksmith?"

She couldn't be certain, but the magician's description resembled his. The Blacksmith of London was the only man she'd ever known made almost entirely out of mechanical flesh.

Terbish shook his head. "I don't know that name. He said he was also Nergüi. He left, and I began to make the biggest, grandest machine that I could think of. My first was the pony, as strong as any that Genghis Khan used to ride across the steppes. Then my grandmother pointed to the mountain peaks, so near to the Eternal Sky, and I began to build that, instead. A year ago, the magician returned. He gave to me a piece of mechanical flesh no bigger than this"—he held his hands cupped together—"and told me to put it in the heart of my machine, and she would grow. And she has."

Astonishing. Yasmeen could not stop grinning, imagining it. "And what will you do with your flying machine?"

"I will take my grandmother, and we will either travel everywhere in the world or return and lead the rebellion. Perhaps both."

"The Blacksmith didn't tell you what to do with it?"

"He said it was mine. He said it was for kindness." Terbish stroked the metal again. "And that I only have to keep my heart big enough to match it."

Chapter Twelve

After crawling out into the sunlight and dropping into the courtyard's deep snow, Archimedes turned to her. "Are you as certain as I am that this thing will eventually fly?"

"I don't know." But he could see that she did. She was certain it would.

"I feel like I should be terrified. Can you imagine this in the sky?" He shook his head. "But I'm . . ."

"Overwhelmed."

"Yes."

"It's a good story. Let's hope Terbish doesn't grow up to be a dictator."

He looked to her. "And when will you tell me your story, steel flower?"

"Tonight. It isn't something to tell by sunlight, but with firelight and food and wine . . . or mare's milk." She smiled. "Should we begin our search? Perhaps we will find something."

They didn't, but it was still incredible to walk through the fortress, to feel the size and strength of it. With the soldiers gone from

the outpost, the worry of discovery was all but gone. That afternoon, he and Yasmeen added their supplies to the food stores, and
though Nergüi looked doubtful as she sniffed the dried meats, she
cooked a thick stew from it, made hearty with roots and onions and
seasoned with herbs. With more fermented mare's milk, he finished
the day pleasantly full and warm. Terbish brought out an opium
pipe, and for long, quiet moments, Yasmeen shared it with Archimedes. When she returned the pipe, she looked as fully relaxed as
he felt, sitting cross-legged on the bedroll with Archimedes stretched
out behind her, up on his elbow and his knee cocked, giving light
support to her back. Terbish lay similarly stretched out on his pal-
let, and the older woman sat on her mat, taking her draught.

Archimedes wondered, "Do you have nanoagents, Nergüi?"

She gave an amused cackle. "So that the Great Khan might
control us, too?"

"Rebels have much in common with the New World," Yasmeen
said in French. "But I would never tell either of them that."

Archimedes laughed, and watched as she seemed to settle in
without moving much at all—just a sigh, and a slight pressure
against his leg as she rested more fully against him. "So what sort
of story are you telling us?"

"A tragic one," she said. "It began with love, as tragedies
always do."

"If that is your opinion, no wonder your heart is of steel."

A sharp *shht!* from Nergüi. Archimedes stifled his laugh. It had
been some time since he'd been hushed, but he settled in, too,
watching Yasmeen's face as she began.

"There was a warrior queen, clever and strong, who held
together the empire through turbulent times. Manduhai the Wise,
wife to the Khan and Khatun herself after he died of long sickness,
she ruled and all of the empire loved her, but for the heirs of Ögedei, who wanted to tear her throne away."

This was not her story, he realized. At least, not as Terbish's had been, but something she must have heard again and again. Blissed, her voice had taken on the cadence of a poem in the Horde language that her heavy accent seemed to emphasize, lift.

"She bore many sons and daughters, and taught them all in the ways of the Eternal Sky and the Earth Mother, and taught them to love the mountains that brought men close to the sky, and the rivers that were the mother's blood. All her children were favored, but none more than her son Barsu Bolod, the Steel Tiger, who everyone agreed would be Khan when her eyes had closed. She told him that he must find a wife, but only to marry one who was as strong and as fierce, as noble and as wise as she. Barsu Bolod searched the empire, looking for such a woman, when he was beset upon by bandits trying to take his gold. He fought, but there were too many. But his warrior's cries were heard in a nearby village, where there lived a maiden of beauty and boldness. Taking up her spear, Khojen slew the bandits, and their blood spewed into the earth like a thunderstorm. Barsu Bolod saw her, and loved her, and knew that she would stand beside him when he was Khan, and if ever he fell too early, she would defend their people with the ferocity of a tiger. He brought her back to Xanadu, and presented her to the wise queen, who saw that Khojen's soul was a mirror to her own. They were married, and in their happiness, they agreed to the queen's wise advice to travel around the empire, so that the people would know them both."

She paused. Not to wet her lips, Archimedes saw with astonishment, but because she was overcome with feeling. Her eyes glistened and her throat worked. Perhaps it was only the opium—but whatever she claimed of her heart of steel, she burned with deep emotion.

What would it be to be loved by her? God, he would give anything to know.

"They traveled to the lands of Goryeo and read the carved blocks. They walked through the flowered temples of Khmer. They bathed in the sacred river, and floated lamps filled with oil across her waters. They reached for the Eternal Sky upon the highest mountains. They crossed the deserts and walked three times around the house of God.

"Everywhere, they were welcomed and showered with gifts. But although Lady Khojen was given gems and gold, treasures uncounted, she would not be parted from the gift of the Persian lynx, the caracal with the tufted ears and golden fur. It sat upon her lap, always, purring as she stroked its soft side, and would not allow anyone but Lady Khojen and Barsu Bolod to caress it. Like Lady Khojen, it hunted with ferocity and defended its mistress from those who might come near. But as they traveled, the wise queen grew old. Her heart and her eyes began to fail. When the happy pair heard news of the wise queen's illness, they returned across the empire, full of all they had seen and heard, their own hearts wise and good. But the heirs of Ögedei had news of their route, and while they rested at a trusted house, they were set upon by the traitorous dogs."

Tears gathered in her eyes, began to slip down her cheeks. Her voice never faltered, her breath never sobbed. Nergüi sat across from her, weeping softly. She knew this story, too, Archimedes realized. Perhaps all of the Horde knew it.

"Warriors in full, they fought, but Barsu Bolod fell. Lady Khojen, the mirror of his mother's soul, threw herself upon him and took a blade meant for his heart, but it could not save them. Impaled together, they breathed their last, and the heirs of Ögedei raised their knives to desecrate the bodies. But the caracal, who knew by the scent of blood that her mistress had fallen, would not let them touch the once-happy couple. With teeth and claws, it defended them. When friends of the wise queen came to the house, they found the caracal had slain all that attacked her beloved son and his fierce wife. When Manduhai the Wise heard this, she knew the animal would always be friend to the Khan and to the empire, and ordered her magicians to create a woman who would never falter in her guard, a woman of teeth and claws, a woman as beautiful as a flower and as strong as steel, with the loyal heart of the caracal. And so it was done—and the *gan tsetseg* have served the true house of royal blood from that day."

Silence fell. The fire crackled. Yasmeen stared into it, pupils dilated, cheeks wet. After what seemed an endless time, Nergüi gave a snore. Terbish lay with his back to them—sleeping or quiet.

Yasmeen looked to him and said softly in French, "Except for me. I don't serve anyone but myself."

"And Lady Lynx was more accurate than Zenobia knew."

Smiling, she lay down beside him. "Yes."

He thought of the rumors that the Horde bred animals with people. He'd never believed it, discarding the talk as the vicious sort that people spoke of their enemies. But there was some truth in it, bits and pieces. Not that women had lain with apes, but they *had* been mixed, in some way. "Is it through the nanoagents?"

"Yes. The inventors at the stable combined the essence of the caracal with that of our mothers. I don't know how. And I don't know who she is," Yasmeen added. "The mothers are chosen through the crèches, and we never see them."

"And when the *gan tsetseg* have children? Are they still like you?"

"I don't know. I never will have my own—after Bart stabbed me, it was too much for my nanoagents to heal, though they worked so hard they began killing me with the fever. Eben also tried to repair my womb in surgery, but . . . he could not, though he fixed what he could. I would kill Bart again, just for that loss. And the others cannot—they are metal all below. But there must be some in the houses that can't be altered now that the Khan's stable is gone, and they will bear children. Perhaps then we will see."

All metal below. "Can the others . . . ?"

She grinned. "Your brain works exactly as every other man's. Of course they can."

"But they don't have to serve that way, too?"

"No. If she's treated like a whore, she can crush them. Quite literally, in every way." She turned her head, looked into the fire again. "Doesn't it bother you to know?"

"What?"

To his surprise, she flicked her ear. But they were not even so very different: the same shell as any person's, though slightly tapered at the tip and topped by that short tuft.

"No." He reached out to trace the curved edge, and she drew away, smiling.

"Not here, Mr. Fox."

"Why?" He knew she loved it when he stroked her—and he had scratched a cat's ears before, had seen the reaction. He lowered his voice. "Are they sensitive? If I stroke them, will you embarrass yourself in front of our hosts?"

"No, Mr. Fox." She rolled to face him and came up on her elbow, her mouth almost to his. "It's just that they're very, very . . . ticklish."

He squeezed his eyes shut, stifling his laugh.

Her fingers stroked the side of his jaw. "Do you stay awake first, or do I?"

"I will." Though they didn't have to worry about the soldiers, it was still best to keep watch. "Five hours?"

"Yes." Softly, she pressed her lips to his neck. He heard her deep inhalation, as if drawing in his scent. "Do you know that I have read all of your stories?"

He didn't. But now his mind sifted frantically through them, trying to remember what Zenobia had included, what was fact—and what he might hate to have Yasmeen know. Carefully, he asked, "What did you think?"

"Archimedes Fox did some very stupid things."

Ah, yes. Some of those were fact, too. God. Gritting his teeth, he said, "You think so?"

"Yes." She sighed against his throat. "And yet, I could never get enough of him."

And while he was still trying to find the words to reply, she climbed into the bedroll and closed her eyes.

Yasmeen would be sorry to leave. The freezing cold, empty fortress, and the two days spent walking through it with Archimedes Fox had been perfect in every way. Yet as they climbed to the southeast tower after saying their farewells to Nergüi and Terbish, his expression was thoughtful, maybe troubled.

He doused the light at the top of the tower, and they waited atop the wall. Fresh snow covered the flying machine in the courtyard, making it difficult to see even with her eyes. Terbish and Nergüi had agreed to their request to meet the airship alone; knowing that she and Archimedes had been friendly with two members of the Horde might raise suspicions against them, and she didn't want to add to the crew's tension.

Farther up the valley, *Ceres* approached under full sail, her deck lanterns dark. Apparently they hadn't mutinied yet.

And Archimedes had nothing to show for this expedition thus far.

"Are you worried because there was nothing to find?" she wondered.

He shook his head. She couldn't read him—only that something was wrong.

"Have I already broken your heart?" She hoped not. She hoped she never did. She hoped that if he loved her, that he would go on, content to love her.

"Not yet." His gaze softened. He stroked his hand down her cheek, then suddenly cupped her jaw in both hands and his head fell, hovering, hovering just above her mouth. His ragged breath across her lips seemed to echo the shaking of her body.

Her heart pounded. "Kiss me."

"Kiss *me*," he said.

Damn him. Why did he never follow orders? "I can't. But I want to finish this, and I *need* you in my bed. How can your longing *not* be great enough, when I want you so much without love? When will you love me, long for me enough to kiss me?"

"When will *you*?"

Her chest ached suddenly, painful, deep. "That was not part of this. You know I cannot."

"I don't know that anymore. Ah, God. And that makes the pain worse. If you *can* love me but *won't* . . ."

Torment filled his eyes, his voice. He clutched her against his lean body, face buried in her hair. She kissed his neck, jaw, wrapped her arms around his shoulders, holding him tight.

And he said softly against her ear, "I saw gliders that night."

"What?" She drew back, looked up into his face. "What night?"

"Just after I left you on *Lady Corsair*, while I was hiding from Nasrin behind the crates. I thought they were acrobats, practicing— as they sometimes do late."

"So?" They did practice late.

He looked to the batwing gliders that Bigor had lent. "There were four of them."

Her stomach suddenly seemed filled with hot coals. He thought Bigor and his men had boarded her lady? But that was exactly the type of work they did in the war. Quiet, quick, and then erase the evidence.

She remembered Bigor's voice. *Doing things I'd never want my wife and children to know.* Had that been an apology? An explanation? An excuse?

Just something said from one person who'd lost their brother to someone who'd lost their crew?

"How can we know?" she whispered. "What happens if we ask them?"

"I think they could very easily kill us."

"Not *easily.*"

"No—the decision would be easy for them."

And so it would be. They didn't leave evidence. "Who hired them before al-Amazigh did? Does Hassan know who recommended them, what contact they used? You can't find a team like that in a tavern."

He nodded. "We'll ask him."

"Yes." By the lady, she could not imagine . . . And now she was sorry she'd saved any of them from the zombies.

No. She was still glad she'd saved three of them. Not just because they might be innocent.

But she'd rather kill them with full knowledge if they weren't.

Suspicion was like a toothed saw through her heart, rasping away. *Ceres* came in over the wall, dropped the rope ladder. Yasmeen reached for it, then glanced back, over the dark courtyard.

"I think I will come back in five years, just to see whether it flies."

"And I will come with you."

Together? She held his gaze long enough to say it, but didn't say it aloud. Turning away, she started up the ladder.

No sign of Bigor and his marines on deck—just Captain Guillouet. Definitely no mutiny, then, but it had been a rough few days for some. Hassan stood next to the captain, face slightly pale, weary. "Did you find anything? Do we need to lower the cargo lift?"

Archimedes came up behind her. "Those at the Horde outpost must have taken everything. There's nothing left."

The old man gave a resounding sigh and nodded. "We will go south, then. It will be warmer, if nothing else." He looked to Captain Guillouet. "We go to Italy."

The captain moved off to give the necessary orders, and Yasmeen was left, feeling more stupid than she'd ever felt. It was warmer on the boot of the Italian peninsula, though not significantly at this time of year and on an airship. Hassan might feel better.

But he shouldn't have been feeling poorly at all. Older men and women felt their age, just as Nergüi did . . . unless they were infected with nanoagents. Except for a fever now and again as the nanoagents fought off severe sickness or attempted to heal a badly injured body, the infected were almost always healthy. Thousands of people in England had lived their lives without so much as a sniffle, and Yasmeen would have wagered anything that the same was true in Morocco.

Yet if it was poison, no one else was suffering from it. The other men who'd been eating at the captain's table showed no sign of sickness . . . and they would have exhibited symptoms faster, because they weren't infected. But Hassan consumed one thing that no one else did.

"Hassan," she said quietly. "No more tea. Drinking nothing is better than that."

He frowned, and then understanding came over his features. "Who?"

"We will speak in your—"

Near the rail behind her, one of the crew called out, "Zombie on the tower wall, Captain! May I fire?"

Her breath caught. There were no zombies in the fortress. *Oh, no.*

"No!" Yasmeen said sharply. "Hold your fire."

Quiet fell over the ship. Guillouet stared at her, face darkening in fury.

Oh, by the lady. She had not even thought—hadn't checked herself. Opening her mouth was the hardest damn thing she'd ever done. "My apologies, Captain, but—"

"You're giving orders on my ship? Fire, Mr. Simon."

Yasmeen turned, but Archimedes had already whipped around. His foot struck the back of Simon's knee as he pulled the trigger. The gun bucked upward, bullet whizzing past the envelope.

Yasmeen faced Guillouet again, hands outspread to placate. "Please understand, Captain. It's not a zombie. It's a boy."

Shock registered on his features. "A *boy?*"

"From the outpost."

"From the Horde?" Shock became distaste. "And yet you stopped my man from shooting it."

It? Rage swept through her. Archimedes tackled her from behind, wrapped his arms around her stomach, pinning her hands to her sides. Quickly, he said, "Apologies, Captain. I'm sure this is only a misunderstanding."

"Captain," Hassan said easily. "The shot might have alerted the outpost."

A shout came from the starboard side. "They're lighting up across the valley, Captain!"

"Fire the engines!" Guillouet called out, and stepped forward. "Mr. Fox. You will keep your wife in her place and her mouth closed or I will do it for you."

Yasmeen felt Archimedes' nod.

"She's to be confined to your cabin. She is not to speak to any man aboard this ship. When her meals are brought to her, she will face away from the door so that my men do not even *look* upon her."

"I'll beat her, too," Archimedes said.

Guillouet was not amused. "Frankly, Mr. Fox, it would not be amiss."

"A war machine, Captain!" The shout sent a hail of responding cries through the crew, panic as sails were drawn in, orders yelled down brass tubes. "They've lit it up! One of the tentacle machines that rip airships from the sky!"

The captain gave a final look to Yasmeen. "Get her below."

Then he was off, and over the starboard side Yasmeen caught a glimpse of the gigantic machine, body rising like a cone as high as the citadel, illuminated by the tall acetylene lamps that lit the outpost walls.

"Should we tell them that there aren't any soldiers to man it?" Archimedes said against her ear, and without waiting for her to answer, "No, I don't think so, either."

Still holding in her fury, Yasmeen shook her head—and walked quietly to the ladder while the crew panicked around them.

Keep your wife in her place.

It echoed in Yasmeen's head until she couldn't shake the rage. Not at Archimedes—she knew it wasn't at him. But as soon as they entered their cabin, she couldn't keep herself from rounding on him with a snarl. "You stopped me!"

His eyes were suddenly bright, hard emerald. "And you let me! I couldn't have held you back if you hadn't allowed it—and that couldn't have ended until one of you was dead."

"It would have been him!"

"I know."

Her teeth clenched. That wasn't enough. She screamed, whipped

toward the bunk. The upper mattress shredded to pieces under her
claws. It still wasn't enough. She whirled back to Archimedes, who
watched her with lifted brows.

"Now we both have to sleep on yours."

Yes. That would be enough.

"Come on," she said, chest heaving. "Now. No more nonsense
about kissing. I want to be fucked."

His gaze flattened at *nonsense.* "Not like this, Yasmeen."

"This is how I want it. Angry, hard, rough. If you can't do it,
I'll find someone else. On a ship full of men, it'll be no problem."

His jaw hardened. "You will *not.*"

"Why? Will it hurt you? Oh, tenderhearted Archimedes Fox."
Mouth curling into a sneer, she put her face to his. "You say you
want to feel everything. Do you want to feel what it's like to watch
me fuck someone else?"

"Do it, then," he said through clenched teeth. "Do it."

Idiot. Did he think he was calling her bluff? She didn't want
anyone else, but she'd fucked without caring about the man she
was with before. Did he truly think she couldn't do it again? Just
bodies fucking, it didn't matter.

And she could end all of this now, she realized. This nonsense
about falling in love with her, about longing and waiting to break
his heart. She could do it now, and no matter what else Archimedes was, no matter what foolish ideas he had about feeling everything, she knew he *wouldn't* keep on this path after she went to
someone else. Hell, she wouldn't even have to fuck anyone to do it.
She could leave, wait, make him think she had. She'd break his
heart, and that would be the end of it. He wouldn't try to win her
love or even a kiss after that.

Two steps carried her to the cabin door. She opened it.

And like a fool, looked back.

Archimedes wasn't angry anymore. His face had whitened,

skin taut with shock and hurt, eyes bleak as if he were already watching her with another man. Pain slashed across her chest. She'd done that. She'd *deliberately* done that to him, hacking away at the bond that had formed between them. And if she stepped out of the cabin, she'd break it. Maybe she already had.

That wasn't what she wanted. That was not what she *needed*. Bodies fucking didn't matter . . . and Archimedes Fox did.

Yasmeen closed the door. "I can't," she said. "I'm confined."

She smiled, and his laugh sounded, short with disbelief and relief. She went to him, slipped her arms around his waist. His hands were shaking as he pushed them into her hair, but so was she. She recalled his face as she'd opened the door. His pain. Tears started to her eyes, the ache growing inside her chest, as if it were about to rip apart.

Closing her eyes, she pressed her face into his neck. "Lady Lynx also does some *very* stupid things."

"I won't tell Zenobia," he said, his voice rough. "And I can't seem to get enough, either."

"Then take more," she said. "Please."

Still holding her against him, he backed to the bunk. Her fingers found the buckles of his shoulder harness. He shrugged it off, then reached for her heavy coat. Her hat. She unfastened the leather guard around his neck. The knives at her thighs. His holsters. The guns at her belt. She began to laugh when she started on the guards at his forearms at the same time he dropped to his knee, fingers searching out the fastenings to her boots.

He looked up at her, pressed a kiss to her inner thigh. The warmth of his lips penetrated through to her skin, and she shuddered, her laugh dying.

"You can take the top, Yasmeen," he said. "I'll take the bottom."

By the lady. She ripped her shirt over her head, stood bare before he'd unbuckled her right boot down to her knee. Biting her bottom lip, she watched him, the cold frame of the upper bunk pressing into her back. Her dark nipples hardened to small bullets, and to make him hurry, she cupped her breasts, fingers playing with their stiffened tips, craving his fingers, his mouth.

Oh, but it only slowed him. He watched her hands instead of his own, and when she slipped her hand into her breeches, his fingers fumbled on the buckle at her ankle. He groaned.

Yasmeen slid her hand deeper, lightly pinched her clitoris and imagined his lips, his teeth. Her knees almost folded. She gripped the bunk for support. "Hurry, Mr. Fox. I'd hate to do the job myself."

With a sound almost like a growl, he gripped her hips, tipped her back onto the lower bunk, ass barely supported by the edge of the mattress.

"Now, *wait*." He finally pulled off her right boot, pressed a hot kiss to her ankle. His jaw rasped up the length of her calf. His fingers tugged the waist of her breeches.

She laughed. "My boot—"

"I don't care." He stripped her breeches fully down her right leg, lifting her knee to maneuver them off. The left leg, he simply pulled down as far as he could. "My God, I forgot there's more."

Just the small, loose pants that fell to mid-thigh—and then she'd be open to him. Yasmeen lifted her hips, pushing them down, the same way he had her breeches: off her right leg, just as far as she could on her left. "Hurry."

"Oh, no. None of that here." Still fully clothed, he pushed her legs apart, strong fingers pressing into her thighs. "You like to be tortured, Mrs. Fox. You like to be stroked, to go slow."

She loved all of that. Anticipation wound through her, tightening her muscles, building the hollow ache at her core into agony. He wasn't going to fill that completely, she realized. Not tonight.

"This isn't the kiss I expected," she panted. Though she wasn't about to complain.

His handsome features stark with need, Archimedes bent his head. "I've wanted this almost as long."

And he definitely wasn't in a hurry now. He began with a slow, broad lick up her center. Yasmeen gasped, her back arching. Another slow lick, his tongue spreading her slick folds, the tip flicking against her clit. She cried out, and barely had time to catch her breath before he was there again, his tongue pushing into her with a leisurely thrust and then sliding up, slow, thorough. He didn't stop, didn't stop, thrusting and licking so slowly, her clit aching for release but he kept that slow, even pace, lapping at her until she was so wet that even with his continual licking she could feel the slickness on her inner thighs, sliding along the curve of her ass. Her body writhed, as she tried to find another angle, another pressure, but his tongue swept through again, that devastating flick at the end that brought her so close, so close. She screamed his name, begged. His tongue came up and swirled, and she bucked against his mouth, sobbing. His long fingers pressed into her, and she couldn't take any more. His lips closed over her clit and his tongue ran over her like a succulent kiss and she was over, broken. Her body clenched, again, again.

She finally fell back, sweating, her body still shuddering. Then Archimedes climbed into the bunk, and she was wrecked.

Lying on his back, he hauled her over his chest, her limp legs straddling his thighs. His hand swept her body, soothing, pleasing. He kissed the wet from her eyes, but he didn't kiss her mouth, didn't fuck her, he simply stroked her skin until sweet lethargy weighed her down like opium.

"You're an idiot to love me," she whispered.

"Am I?" He didn't sound convinced.

"Yes." She drew in his scent, so strong and warm. "But, still—it is a fine thing, to be loved."

And tucking her face against his shoulder, she slept.

* * *

Yes. It would be a fine thing, to be loved.

When they'd made their agreement in the Charging Bull, Archimedes hadn't lied when he'd told Yasmeen that falling in love with her wasn't a game. But until now, he didn't know how wrong he'd been.

He *had* been playing a game. A game of luck, a game of chance, with his heart as the stakes, deep emotion and heartbreak the prize—and he hadn't known what any of that meant. But he'd had the smallest taste of it when she'd opened that door, and he never, *ever* wanted to feel like that again. So he could continue on, trying to feel every single emotion, and finish the game broken and poor.

But now that he was in love with her, Archimedes simply wasn't playing anymore.

Chapter Thirteen

Yasmeen stirred when Archimedes slipped out of bed, but she didn't lift her head. He didn't bother with his boots or a jacket, and picked up his dagger from the cabin floor. Silently, he made his way to Ollivier's door and inside.

With a single bunk and room for a small desk, Ollivier's cabin was more spacious than theirs. The man slept on his side, facing away from the door. Archimedes slid his dagger against the man's neck, nudged him awake. Ollivier opened his eyes, his hand moving beneath his pillow. Archimedes let him feel the blade. He froze.

"Put your hands on your head, Mr. Ollivier. Very good. Now, stand up—Nuh-uh! Hands still on your head. There you go. Let's take a walk, have a little drink together."

In a nightdress that came to his knees, Ollivier was silent until they reached the door. Then he tried for outrage. "This is an affront to my dignity, Mr. Fox. If you don't want to share the credit of the find—"

"There's no find yet, Mr. Ollivier. Now close your mouth until we reach the stateroom, or I'll cut out your tongue."

Archimedes wouldn't, actually; the whole point of this was for the man to talk. A toe would do just as well. A finger. The head of his prick—which, apparently, had begun dribbling piss during the short walk to Hassan's stateroom.

On second thought, the tongue would be fine. Ollivier could write his answers.

He wasn't surprised to find Yasmeen already in Hassan's cabin, heating a pot of tea over the small gas burner. How had she fastened her boots so damn quickly? Obviously Archimedes would have to practice.

"Sit here, Mr. Ollivier," Hassan said, gesturing to the chair opposite his. "I thought we might have some tea."

Shaking, Ollivier sat.

Hassan poured his cup. "You'll forgive me if I only watch. My French is poor."

"A scream for mercy sounds the same in any language," Yasmeen said, sliding the teacup across the table. "Did you make it strong, Mr. Ollivier? His nanoagents fought off the poisons, but what about you? What would a sip of this do?"

"I don't know what you're speaking of."

Yasmeen smiled.

"Very well." Ollivier wiped his sleeve across his forehead. "What is it you want to know?"

Archimedes took the chair next to him. "We want to know why."

"Because I was hired to."

"By *whom*, Mr. Ollivier?"

The man was breathing hard, sweating. "I was given orders by the *marsouins*. But al-Amazigh is paying me."

Hassan's expression didn't change. "Kareem al-Amazigh?"

"Yes."

"Why?" Yasmeen asked.

"He doesn't trust Mr. Hassan. Your association to Temür Agha is too close." He spoke directly to Hassan. "He believes you will eventually betray him."

God. Then al-Amazigh didn't know Hassan at all. Archimedes shook his head. "Then why this expedition? Why not a more direct assassination?"

"Temür Agha is a powerful man, Mr. Fox. Al-Amazigh wanted the death to appear natural, the result of sickness, so that there would be no retaliation."

"But he also needs the money," Hassan said. "Is that right?"

"Yes. So he hired me to look for the treasures."

Archimedes leaned forward. "Al-Amazigh didn't want me included on the expedition, initially, because of my association with Temür. Are you supposed to kill me, too?"

"No." He shook his head. "That is not mine to do."

Yasmeen hissed. "Whose is it?"

"The *marsouins*'. After the expedition is over."

Archimedes looked to Hassan. The man showed little, but he'd had years of practice concealing his emotions.

"Al-Amazigh must desperately want that money," Yasmeen said.

"I do not know," Ollivier said. "I was not told more."

A feral expression slipped over her face, lips drawing back over sharp teeth. "And what of *Lady Corsair*?"

"I don't . . . What of her?"

"Two months ago, she was boarded in Port Fallow and my crew slaughtered. Do you know anything of that, Mr. Ollivier?"

"No." He shook his head emphatically. "No. Two months past, I was in Martinique. I did not even speak to Bigor until six weeks ago."

"Why you?" Archimedes said. "You have no name for yourself in this field. You sympathized with the Liberé. How did they know to choose you for the expedition?"

"Bigor discovered me dosing the coffee in a noble's house. He was there for another reason, and couldn't risk the questions raised by my disappearance if he had killed me. But he has known of me since then. He remembered." His hands clenched on the table, tears filling his eyes. "I was done with this! For ten years, I have only studied, taught. I wanted my name to be spoken in the same breath as da Vinci—but not like this!"

"Come now," Archimedes said. "You wouldn't have minded that so much."

Ollivier wiped his eyes. "No. In truth, no. It would be worth it. Or even to have it spoken in the same breath as Archimedes Fox."

Yasmeen grinned, leaned across the table, raised the teacup to his lips. "How about, 'Vincent Ollivier, slain by Archimedes Fox's wife'?"

"Oh, God, please no—"

"Stop." She pulled back, her eyes hard, no humor left. "Understand this, Mr. Ollivier: You are leaving this cabin alive tonight. You are to give no indication that we've spoken of this. If you must, poison yourself to give the appearance of sickness, and remain in your bunk for the remainder of the expedition. Can you do that?"

"Yes. Yes, yes."

"Wonderful." She stood, gestured to the door. "Go now. And sleep well, Mr. Ollivier."

After the smile she gave him, Archimedes would be surprised if the man ever slept again. He waited at the door, watched Ollivier enter his cabin before turning back to the others.

"So, al-Amazigh has arranged to kill us all," he said, and looked to Hassan. "Why? Do you think Ollivier knew the truth of it?"

Tiredly, the old man shook his head. "I could not say. It is true that he worried about your association to Temür, but of mine? He must know I would not compromise the freedom of our people. Perhaps it was to keep some other truth from me."

"And what of the *marsouins*?" Yasmeen asked. "Do you know how or when he became acquainted with them?"

"Yes. There is a man—a weapons smuggler, the one who will

provide the explosives for the tower. He told Kareem of the *marsouins*, and said that if ever he needed to complete a job, they were the men to contact. This was several months ago. Kareem has contacted them several times, I believe."

"What is the smuggler's name? Do you recall?"

"Of course. He is called Mattson."

Miracle Mattson, who Yasmeen had shot in his sister's home. He watched her eyes close as the full realization swept over her. Mattson had known of the da Vinci sketch, and must have told Bigor and his men—or perhaps he'd told al-Amazigh, and the rebel had sent in the marines to collect the sketch. They must have reached her strongbox before the timer closed, then attempted to erase the evidence by blowing her ship.

A short expedition, and much more lucrative than the current one. Though the sketch was a fake, Yasmeen's gold had not been.

Had al-Amazigh discovered that he possessed a forgery? Had he heard of the sketch that Temür Agha had now . . . or, even if he had heard, did he think Archimedes had found two?

"Hassan," she said, and he heard the roughness in her voice, the pain that must be lodged deep within. "How did al-Amazigh pay for this expedition? How did he pay for the *marsouin*s?"

"He went to Port Fallow three months ago to sell the jewelry that I gave to him. Temür has been generous to me these many years. I had a small collection."

A small collection wouldn't amount to much—and probably not enough to fund an expedition. But the final connection slid into place. "Did he sell the jewelry through Franz Kessler?"

"That I do not know."

"How long was he in Port Fallow?"

"A month or so." Clearly troubled, he glanced from Archimedes to Yasmeen. "There is something here you have not said. Is this what you asked of Ollivier—about *Lady Corsair*?"

Her mouth tight, Yasmeen nodded.

"You believe al-Amazigh ordered it? That Bigor's men carried it out?"

"Yes," she said. "It begins to seem that way."

He tapped the ends of his broad fingers together, his face thoughtful. "Will you kill them tonight?"

"I haven't decided." She banged her fist on the table. "*Goddammit.* If we were not aboard this ship, I wouldn't hesitate."

Because of the precarious tension within the crew, Archimedes realized—surprised, he had to admit, that it was even a consideration for her.

"I understand that this is not my place," Hassan said carefully. "But I would ask that you wait. If they have no plans to kill you and your husband until after some treasure is secured, then you are safe until then. Perhaps, in the meantime, I can discover more about why Kareem has chosen this route."

Archimedes wasn't so certain. He cared much less about al-Amazigh's plans than he did Yasmeen's life. "And what if Ollivier gives us away?"

"Then I suspect Bigor will be surprised by your wife's capabilities. You probably ought not to be with them by yourselves, however. Tomorrow morning, we will be over Brindisi."

The site of their next search. "We'll go down alone," Archimedes said.

In their cabin, Yasmeen lit one of their few remaining cigarillos and paced while Archimedes settled onto the bottom bunk. Sleeping together now. That was all right. That was good. *That was the only damn thing that was good—*

Pain struck at her chest. She paced faster, but couldn't outrun it. She dug her fingers into her hair, tried to stop it, but the agony only settled in her throat, welled tears in her eyes. Instead of stand-ing there, shaking, she crushed out the cigarillo and slid in next to Archimedes, and he wrapped her in his arms as she cried silently against his throat.

He kissed the top of her head, simply held her until she stopped. "You wanted to kill them tonight."

She wanted her *crew* back tonight. But she'd have settled for ripping out throats, tasting their blood and pain.

"Yes," she said, and rolled onto her back, relit the cigarillo. She passed it to him when he came up on his elbow. "But I can be patient."

Though he didn't make a sound, she felt his laugh against her side. She narrowed her eyes at him.

"You doubt me?"

"Yes."

"You're wrong." She plucked the cigarillo from his lips. "And you also take a very long time to pass this back."

He grinned.

"I said that to make you laugh," she told him. "You didn't get the better of me."

His smile became tender, and he brushed a stray hair from her forehead. "No. You have definitely gotten the better of me. This might be the wrong time to tell you, I don't know."

"Tell me what?"

He took a deep breath. "I love you."

Oh. Her lips parted. He slipped the cigarillo from between her teeth, bent his head. His mouth brushed hers, so sweet. When she lifted to deepen the kiss, he drew back.

That was it? Yet, in its perfect way, enough.

Smiling, she lay her head on the pillow again. Despite every-thing, she felt almost settled now. She *would* be patient. She *would* avenge her crew.

And she would hold the heart of Archimedes Fox very, very close.

"Not the wrong time at all," she said.

Why had he never been to Brindisi before? Aside from the zombies, it was a near-perfect city, full of churches and forts and castles whose thick walls stood for hundreds of years without crumbling to ruins. Clear turquoise waters filled the harbor, and on one of the islands—free of zombies—sat an enormous red structure that had been called only "Sea Fort" in Ollivier's notes.

It was far more than that—it was a hoard of relics worth salvaging. Archimedes only picked a few to take back to *Ceres*; finding nothing at all would raise suspicions, and too many would be a treasure and a signal for Bigor to kill him. So he found small painted icons in the chapel, and would return later for the altarpiece. He found a faded tapestry, and left a sundial in the shape of a lute.

But although Hassan might have been satisfied by the few things he'd brought back to the ship, Archimedes knew not to stop there. They had discussed Brindisi with Bigor before they'd learned of his connection to Mattson, so the marine was aware that several locations in the port city were to be explored. He and Yasmeen dutifully crept through a church, and he found a diptych of an archangel and the Virgin, and a lead bowl plated with gold.

If it had been solid gold, he'd have left it.

He could have easily spent weeks here, but he settled on two days. They remained out until after midnight the first day, and almost immediately dropped into sleep on return to *Ceres*. He woke to the cracking of Yasmeen's knees. As soon as she loosened up, they scouted a new building from the airship and went down again, lowering the rope ladder to the roof. After a cursory search, they climbed back up, scouted another building, then a castle overlooking the harbor. A number of zombies milled around in the courtyard, so many that it took Archimedes a few moments to recognize what they were milling *around*. His heart thumped against his chest, and his head swam.

Yasmeen caught his arm. "Archimedes?"

He forced the excitement from his expression, though he wanted to shout and laugh. In a low voice, he said, "It is his *crane*."

"What?"

"The pile of rotted wood below. Do you see the shape of the iron that used to bind it, the giant wheel, the long arm? It's a machine for lifting. I saw a replica of da Vinci's sketch once. This is his crane, almost exactly."

"Ah." She studied the shattered remains. "So what was he lifting?"

Archimedes almost didn't care. He wanted to slide down into the courtyard, simply *touch* the iron. But the number of zombies made that impossible, at least until he returned. He judged the length of the crane arm, followed the arc of it in his mind.

"There." He pointed to the curtain wall nearest to the harbor. "Something could be lifted to the top of the wall and taken into that tower."

"All right." She met his eyes. "There's a lot of stairs."

She was right. The castle didn't possess a regular, symmetrical structure, but sprawled across different levels of walls, towers, halls, and courtyards. Stairs running up the side of the curtain walls gave zombies easy access to the tower—there were already several stumbling along the stone walkway atop the wall.

"We kill those, then we make certain we're quiet," he said.

They did, and even better, the tower had a door—partially rotted, but intact, so that if any more zombies climbed up to the wall, they wouldn't see Archimedes and Yasmeen moving around inside. So long as they were quiet, they shouldn't capture the zombies' attention.

They waved the airship away and went inside. The tower had been designed for defense. The chamber was round, with only a few small openings set at an angle high in the thick stone walls—shafts for ventilation, perhaps, or to let the light in. Dust and stone debris covered a slate floor. Feathers were scattered about, the remains of nests visible in the ventilation shafts and the rafters. Heaps of old cloth had molded in piles and gave home to mice that scattered when he lifted one dark, stiff edge. A bed had collapsed on itself—and on the far side of it, lying on the floor, he found the clockwork man.

"Yasmeen," he whispered, and slipped to his knees.

He felt her fingers against his shoulder, heard her sharp breath.

Shoulders of iron and the gear guts had rusted. A copper pendulum at the heart had tarnished and warped. The fingers were nothing but steel tubes, the arms a system of pulleys whose ropes had long disintegrated. It had no legs and no head. Just a torso with arms, partially finished and abandoned—it was the most wonderful thing he'd ever seen.

And they had to leave it here.

"Ah, God," he said. "Ah, God."

She crouched beside him, her arms wrapping around his shoulders. "We'll come back for it."

He slipped out of her arms and lay on the floor. "I'll stay and guard it."

Yasmeen snorted softly, her half laugh quickly muffled. "You don't even—"

The crack of a gunshot sounded outside. Archimedes sat up, pulse racing. He stared into Yasmeen's eyes, saw the same shock and surprise.

"Was that from the airship?" she whispered.

The airship that was hovering over the harbor, not far from the tower—and the curtain wall lay in a direct line between *Ceres* and the zombies that would be rushing to investigate the sound.

Over the pounding of his heart came the pounding of feet, the moans and growls. Jesus. He raced for the door. *Thank God, thank God*, it opened inward—though chunks were missing in the rotted wood, big enough to shove hands through. With enough pressure, those holes would likely become bigger.

It couldn't be helped. He braced the door with his weight, set his feet. "Is there another way out?"

But Yasmeen was already racing through the room, feeling along the walls, looking for one. She turned back to him, eyes wide. "No."

"Take my grap—"

The first zombie hit. The thud reverberated through his back, but he held fast. Yasmeen shoved her palms against the door beside his shoulders, adding her weight.

"My grapnel," he said, and two more rammed into the door. Or the same one, with a friend. His boots skidded, just a tiny bit— and he could hear more coming over the ravenous growls. "The ventilation shafts. We'll climb out."

Maybe. The openings weren't big.

"All right. Go," she said. "Shoot it."

No, no. She hadn't—

"Archimedes." She met his eyes. "You've practiced shooting that launcher; I haven't. I'll hold the door. You'll need to go up first, anyway, because the second person is going to have to sprint and climb—and I'm faster."

"I'm stronger." And the zombies weren't hitting the door now, but piling against it—pushing, pushing.

"Yes. So you'll need to be fast," she said.

Goddamn it. But he nodded. "On three, we switch."

At her nod, he counted. She slipped smoothly into his place, feet braced, jaw clenched with effort. An emaciated arm snaked through a hole, grasping hand waving near her leg.

"Hurry," she said.

He raced to the nearest ventilation shaft, took a second to breathe, to steady his arm. The grapnel launched, hitting the ceiling of the shaft but bouncing through. Behind him, Yasmeen laughed with relief.

"Go up!"

He dropped his shoulder harness—no chance he'd make it through with it. He climbed, digging his toes into the wall to go more quickly. He pushed his head into the shaft, felt the sun, the breeze.

His shoulders didn't fit.

He tried again, another angle this time, diagonally in the square shaft. His hands were sweating on the rope, his arms aching. Every second was another that Yasmeen was holding the door. No matter how he squeezed, his shoulders didn't fit through.

Chest heavy, he dropped back to the floor.

"No," she said. "Don't you—*No!*"

"Yes." He braced his hands against the door beside her—*Thank God*—slimmer shoulders, and smashed the heel of his boot onto a hand groping along the floor. "It has to be this way. My manly physique is simply too powerful."

Her eyes filled. "No."

"Yes. Now, on three—we switch."

He began to count, and *God*, he wished he'd kissed her properly first. He wished he'd made love to her as she'd wanted. Hard, fast, angry, slow . . . it didn't matter now.

"Three," he said and took her place, feeling the hammering against the wood, the reverberating growls. "Now shoot me and go."

Her gaze lifted to his. The tears were gone, he saw. Her eyes were clear, and hard, and cold. Her killing look, he knew—that heart of steel wrapping completely around her.

And then she kissed him.

Warm, firm, his mouth was everything she wanted, needed. But the zombies were growling behind him, and she couldn't linger. She didn't have much time, not if she wanted to save him.

She *had* to save him.

Yasmeen drew away, and saw his astonishment, his agony, his hope. It changed to flat denial as she said, "I'm coming back for you."

"No—"

"Don't you *dare* die," she said. "I'm coming. And if you're not here, you're going to break my heart, Archimedes Fox. So hold that door."

She sprinted for the rope. Seconds later, she stuck her head out of the shaft, looked up. *Ceres* hovered above—coming to rescue them, after some fucking idiot had nearly killed them.

Her shout was met with several from the decks. The rope ladder spilled over—out of reach, but she leapt for it, swinging above the harbor cliff.

On the deck, she ignored everything but the man she wanted.

"Bigor! I need your diving suit. Now, now, *now*!"

With a sharp nod, the marine ran for the ladder. Yasmeen stripped off her jacket, her boots. "Captain! Bring that rope ladder right to the tower door!"

He stiffened like she'd shoved a burning rod up his ass. "Mrs. Fox, you don't—"

"Some bastard on your ship fired a gun and *he's going to die down there*! Give me the fucking ladder!"

Though Guillouet shook with rage, he nodded to the mate. Good. If he hadn't, Yasmeen would have killed him.

Bigor returned, carrying half the suit. The two other marines carried the rest. With amazing speed, they helped her into the thick canvas, fastened and buckled the brass over her limbs. The zombies might get a bite in between the brass plates, but wouldn't break through the canvas. The brass helmet reduced her sight to nothing, but it didn't matter: If it moved, she was going to kill it.

The canvas gloves were too heavy for a gun, but machetes were just fine. She gripped the handles. The suit felt like moving with chains tied to her ankles, her elbows. Bigor yanked the hose out of the top of the helmet, and fresh air came in.

She clanked over to the rope ladder, grabbed on, and dove in. *So heavy.* She fell to one knee on the stone wall as she landed, and they were on her, but Archimedes was waiting. Her blades hacked and chopped. The zombies growled and moaned, and there were so many but she would not stop, *she'd never stop—*

A crack sounded, the snap of wood. The tower door. Oh, by the lady—the door. She whipped around, and through the tiny, blood-streaked window of her helmet, she saw the zombies pushing against it, she saw the door shatter.

Her heart shattered with it.

I'm coming back for you.

Archimedes held on to that. He held and held—the door didn't. Wood shattered. Hands grabbed at him. He raced across the chamber, heading for the grapnel rope. His shoulders were too wide, but *by God*, he could hold on until she arrived.

Boots digging into the wall, he hauled himself out of reach. He heard a sound like a muffled scream of rage and pain. *Yasmeen.* She'd seen the door go down.

So he'd let her know he was still inside. His revolvers were in his holsters. Gripping the rope with one hand, Archimedes aimed, fired. God, how many were in here? Thirty or forty? He'd take a good number down, but prayed for a reload to drop out of the sky.

Or for a woman with a brass suit and machetes. He laughed as she came through the door, mobbed by zombies but slashing them down with brutal efficiency. There was nothing elegant about her movements now, just vicious hacks of her blades that sent heads and arms thudding to the floor. The brass plates were covered in gore.

"I love you!" he called out, then shot a zombie coming at Yasmeen from behind, and another trampling the clockwork man. He heard more shots now, too—and there were fewer new zombies racing in. The crew on the airship must have been clearing off the wall leading to the tower. He fired until he was out. Only a few zombies left in the chamber. He dropped, triggered the springs at his forearms, and hacked the blade through the zombie that came running at him. Yasmeen finished off the last.

He heard her laugh, muffled by the helmet. The chamber floor was an inch deep in blood, deeper in twitching body parts. He wiped off the blades usually hidden in his forearm guards and pushed them back in. His shoulder harness dripped; he didn't think about it, just slung it over his arm.

The cargo lift waited outside. They stepped aboard, and Archimedes unbolted her helmet, lifted it off, tossed it aside. Her face was streaked with sweat—and tears? Her chest hit his with a clank, and she was laughing again when he kissed her, so deep, unable to stop until they were almost at the deck. He unbuckled the blood-streaked plates, the soaked canvas. Her breeches and shirt were clean, her calves and feet bare.

When the lift clanked into place, they faced Captain Guillouet's loaded gun.

Yasmeen stilled, her hand tightening on his. Archimedes waited, then realized—she didn't have a gun, and his revolvers were empty.

"Mr. Bigor, please escort Mr. Fox to the wardroom, and guard him while I speak with his wife. Keep a gun on him at all times, so that she knows not to step out of place."

Bigor hesitated for only the briefest moment. Then he drew his weapon, aimed it at Archimedes. "Mr. Fox."

"If you hear any kind of commotion from Mrs. Fox, shoot him."

"Yes, sir."

"Take him below."

With her gaze locked on Guillouet's gun, Yasmeen let go of his hand. As Archimedes stepped from the cargo lift to the deck, he said softly, "I'll be coming for you."

Then he saw her eyes, and *now* he knew cold. Now he knew hard.

"You'd better hurry," she said.

No commotion. Yasmeen could have disarmed Guillouet and taken him down with barely a sound, but she couldn't halt a commotion if everyone saw her do it. So she would be patient.

Obviously feeling bold with his pistol aimed at her face, Guillouet stepped close. "Come to my cabin, Mrs. Fox."

Wrapping his fist in the hair at her nape, he shoved her in front of him, tucked the gun barrel behind her ear. She walked obediently, noting the expressions of the crew around them. Vashon with jaw set and a disapproving glower, and the twin with an angrier match. Some shock. Some who wouldn't look her way. Guilt? Uncomfortable?

As they should be. When a man forced a woman into his cabin, it usually only meant one thing.

"Who shot the gun?" she wondered aloud. Their quick glances and the pain lancing through her scalp told her without a word. "*You*, Captain?"

"Twenty years on a ship and I have *never* had to shout over my own men," he said. "And I will not talk over you. Do not speak again until I tell you to, Mrs. Fox."

So he'd had to shoot his gun to get the attention of his crew. What had they been arguing over? Wages? Women? Did it even matter?

Not really. Captain Guillouet wouldn't be a captain much longer.

He held the gun on her as they went down the ladder. He pushed her past a staring, wide-eyed Henri.

"Even the boy paid for his," Yasmeen said.

Pain exploded in the back of her head. She stumbled, and black spots danced in her vision. Her claws dug into her palms. He'd whipped her with the gun butt.

Now, she might not even make it quick.

He shoved her through the cabin door, locked it behind him. "Stand next to the table, Mrs. Fox, and turn around."

With her back to him, her hands flat on the surface. She complied, then watched him over her shoulder. "Will raping me truly make your crew behave, Captain?"

"I don't want to do this. I don't want to touch you." His hand tugged at his breeches. "But they will see you put in your proper place."

"My proper place?" She laughed. "And so this is why you won't have women on the crew. You can't stop yourself from raping them after they dared to climb out of bed."

"You've brought this on yourself."

"Oh, yes? Well I must say, for someone who doesn't want to touch me, your prick seems eager."

"Eyes forward!" He moved in behind her, pressed the gun to her shoulder. "You're fortunate I did not do this in front of my crew and then toss you to them!"

She was fortunate? No. That might have saved *him*.

His hand curved up her ass. Yasmeen whipped around, dropping her shoulder. His pistol fired, the bullet digging into the table, wood chips striking her cheek. Her elbow smashed into his ear.

He staggered back. Her foot struck his hand. The gun went flying. He turned to run, and she caught him before he made another step, bringing him to his knees with her forearm locked against his throat and her hand in his hair.

"Alive," he wheezed. "You need me alive. Or they'll kill him."

"Maybe. But I think I'll get them first."

She twisted past the crack. He dropped to the floor.

A sudden commotion of running feet sounded down the passageway. The door crashed open. Archimedes burst through, the long blades at his forearms dripping with blood, eyes wildly searching the cabin. They stopped on her.

She arched her brows.

His gaze dropped to Guillouet. "Goddammit. Can't I save you just *once*?"

"You've already saved me twice, just using your grapnel." She lifted her gaze to the bruise forming on his cheekbone. "Who was that?"

"Bigor." His fingers gently traced her jaw. "He's still alive, but tied."

"Good." She'd deal with him in a bit.

He held up his hands, showed her the bloody blades extending from his wrist guards. "And I'm sorry, I surprised and killed the other two marines while getting away. Are you all right?"

"Just a headache. Why are you sorry?"

"They murdered your crew."

Oh. She shook her head. "I don't *like* killing. But I'll do it if it needs to be done. I'm just glad it's done."

He glanced down at Guillouet and sheathed his blades. "So am I. Now what?"

"Do you want her?"

His brows drew together. "Do I want who?"

"The ship. *Ceres*. Do you want control of her?"

"No."

"Then she's mine."

For now. *Ceres* was a lady, but would never be *her* lady.

Archimedes followed her as she started for the door. "All right. And then?"

"And then . . . I'm ready to head to Rabat."

Chapter Fourteen

By the lady, she hated leaving Archimedes this quickly. There was much to say—but there was also now a ship to manage.

His voice caught her in the passageway. "Yasmeen."

She turned, caught sight of Guillouet's body in the cabin before the door closed. That would need to be removed, the wardroom cleaned. "Yes, Mr. Fox?"

"I kissed you on the cargo lift. Do you need to hang me over the side of the ship?"

Her gaze snapped to his. His emerald eyes were steady on hers, his features set with determination.

He would let her, she realized. If it meant making certain her position was secure, he would let her strip him naked and humiliate him.

Such a man, to let her be, to give her so much. Why had it taken her so long to see?

She shook her head. "No. That kiss was personal, and nothing to do with rank or our relative positions. All who saw would know that."

"All right." His grin held more than a hint of relief. "I'm glad to hear it."

But because he also needed to know, she said, "But now, there is a line, and it will end at that cabin door. When I tread her decks, I am captain. When we're alone, we can do whatever we like."

"Or when we've just been saved from zombies."

"Yes." She approached him, took his hand in hers. "And even in that cabin, I will not kiss you while we stand over a dead body. I will not kiss you when there is work that *must* be done. I want nothing more than to kiss you now, as I desperately need to."

"But you won't."

"I can't." She sighed. "And I can't order you to do the same, because you are not part of my crew—but I ask the same of you."

"You will have it." His fingers squeezed hers. His gaze didn't waver. "And I am not crew, but I would like to stand behind you. Not above, not below. To back you up, should ever you need it."

Her heart filled, and she nodded. "Thank you, Mr. Fox."

"Always, Captain—" He paused. "Are we still married?"

She laughed. There was no need to be; they no longer relied on al-Amazigh for their passage to Rabat. But, in truth, Yasmeen had come to enjoy it. What did it matter that these bonds were not official? She liked to bear them.

"I think we must be," she said. "I don't know an institution in the world that would grant a divorce to us."

"True." With a grin, he bowed over her hand, pressed a kiss to her palm before letting her go. "Then we are well and truly stuck, Captain Fox."

Unsurprisingly, she encountered a mix of emotions and shouted questions when she went above and called for all hands on deck. Though some were dismayed when Yasmeen succinctly laid out that she'd killed Guillouet while he attempted to rape her, she didn't see blame. That, more than anything, gave her hope for this crew.

For almost an hour, she fielded questions about wages. *I will split between you whatever the captain held in his strongbox, minus* Ceres' *costs. The purser will verify my numbers.* About their destination: *We will continue our expedition to Rabat, and deliver Mr. Hassan home.* About taking women into the crew: *I will be here, but I do not intend to stay aboard long enough to hire new crew.* How long would she stay? *We will return to Port Fallow, where Mr. Fox and I will depart and leave the airship in your hands.*

The last surprised them. The speculation about who would become captain then overtook the decks. Yasmeen held up her hand. When they quieted, she gave them the only advice she could: "Choose a captain who knows that he serves the ship and the crew, first. You will be taking orders from this person; choose someone that you trust will have your interests at heart, as well as his own, every time he makes a decision—even if those decisions are not what you want to hear."

She looked to the Vashons. Her gut told her that one of them—or both—would be Ceres' captain. That could be either a brilliant arrangement, or a disaster. "And if it is between the two of you, do not treat her like a whore, fighting over who will have a first go."

They both grinned.

Probably a disaster. "Now, there are bodies on this ship that will be cared for and given proper send-offs, and a wardroom to clean. Aviators on watch duty, attend to your posts; all others report to the first mate for your details. In an hour, I want to see all mates and masters in the wardroom with their ledgers. Heave around, then."

They broke up and headed to their posts, a few muttering . . . but fewer than she expected. Not a bad crew at all.

She didn't know what the hell Guillouet had gotten so wrong with them.

She was incredible. Archimedes watched Yasmeen take over the ship, and by mid-afternoon, all was running smoothly. Even Engels the bitter navigator deferred to her command as they plotted the course to Rabat. She hadn't yet fired the engines, however. They still hovered over the Brindisi harbor as most of the crew went to the mess, and Yasmeen asked the Vashons to bring Bigor up on deck.

Hands bound behind his back, his nose broken from Archimedes' fist, clothes askew, the marine no longer appeared buttoned up and straightened out, but still held his shoulders back, head high.

The Vashons pushed him to his knees near the cargo lift, and he kneeled, his expression flat—not resisting, not trying to escape, which made Archimedes wonder whether his sanity had broken or his pride was indestructible.

"Clear the decks, please," Yasmeen said.

The crew still on watch didn't hesitate. Archimedes wasn't crew—and he wouldn't leave her alone with the marine, anyway. He stood behind her, ready to back her up if needed.

When the last aviator had descended the ladder, she said, "Mr. Bigor. You understand that this has nothing to do with your following Captain Guillouet's orders today."

He gave a sharp nod.

"If you did *not* board *Lady Corsair* two months ago, slaughter my crew, and steal my gold, please say so now."

She wanted him to, Archimedes realized. Even though this meant she could avenge her crew, she didn't want it to be Bigor. Respect for him, perhaps—it was easy to respect such quiet strength.

"I did," he said.

If Yasmeen was disappointed, she didn't show it. Instead, she hardened. "Ordered by al-Amazigh?"

"Hired."

"Is that different than ordered?"

A nod. "Only my superiors give me orders. A man who simply possesses money is not my superior."

"And there's no loyalty to him, which is why you're telling me this now."

Another nod.

Yasmeen advanced on him, crouched a few feet away. "I'll trade you a story, Mr. Bigor. You tell me why al-Amazigh wants Hassan dead, and I'll write a letter to your wife and children that doesn't mention the slaughter of an entire ship, murders that *weren't* in service to your king."

"But they *were*, Captain Fox." The big marine stood.

Archimedes drew his gun. Yasmeen might not use hers as a warning, but by God, he would. "One step toward her and I pull the trigger."

The man didn't move, his eyes locked on Yasmeen's face. "They will receive a letter, Captain, but not from you. One that tells them how I was instrumental in assisting the French take their first step back into the Old World. That is an honor that needs no lie—and it is with that honor, I die."

Without warning, Bigor threw himself backward. *What the hell?* Archimedes rushed forward as the marine flipped over the rail. He didn't make a sound as he dropped into the harbor below. A splash swallowed him up.

Archimedes looked back in disbelief. Yasmeen hadn't moved, her face thoughtful as she looked out over the side of the ship. Her fingers reached for her sash—for her cigarillo case, he knew—and only when they encountered nothing did she shake her head, focus on him.

"It always seems a shame not to let a proud man go his own way," she said.

"You knew he'd do that?"

"I thought he might. And I am so tired of shooting people."

"Perhaps you should have." Archimedes looked over again. "You know what will happen now? He'll return when we least expect it and take his revenge."

She snorted. "That only happens in Archimedes Fox serials. His hands are tied."

"I returned from Venice," he said.

"So you did." Yasmeen pursed her lips, approached the side, and looked over. "If he bobs up again, feel free to fire. But don't wait too long for him to appear—you'll miss dinner."

Yasmeen would have been happy to miss the meal itself, but she'd always enjoyed sharing dinner with her passengers—and eating with Hassan and Archimedes for company was just as pleasurable. If she'd planned to stay on as *Ceres'* captain, she'd have eventually traded the stiff chairs for pillows around a low table, but this would do for the two or three weeks she intended to remain aboard.

The low thrum of the engines could be heard and felt from all the way aft, the conversation was entertaining, and for a short time, it was almost as if Yasmeen was exactly where she belonged again. In an odd way, Guillouet *had* put her back in her place.

But this lady wasn't hers, and so it wasn't quite where she belonged—and the only perfect thing was that Archimedes was sharing the table with her.

Tonight, they'd share the bed.

She could not stop imagining it. Not when he sat so close, so quick with a grin or a clever reply. Not when he swallowed his wine, and she couldn't take her eyes from the strong column of his throat, remembering how he smelled, how he tasted. The way he held his fork, the thickness of his hair, his rough jaw—every detail recalling what it was to touch him, to be touched, to be *loved*.

"You've grown quiet, Captain," Hassan said.

Lusting after my husband. Something that Yasmeen had never imagined herself doing, and yet she enjoyed every delicious second of it.

But of course she lied, and mentioned another matter that wouldn't have made for pleasant conversation during dinner but was acceptable over wine. "I am thinking of what Bigor said just before he jumped over. Did al-Amazigh have other French contacts aside from the *marsouins*?"

"Yes." Hassan sipped his—unpoisoned—tea. "For some time, he considered bringing in allies to help overthrow Temür, and to ease the transition from a Horde territory to an independent state. But I argued against it. I could too easily see that we might simply trade one occupying force for another, especially as the French had asked for portions of the city to be given over, so that their citizens could also settle here."

"One foot back in the Old World," Archimedes said. "After losing so much territory in the Liberé war, they've been feeling the pinch."

"Yes. Eventually, Kareem abandoned the idea, agreeing that the change needs to come from our own people."

"What of the two French officers I saw him with in Port Fallow?" Archimedes asked.

"We still must find friends in the New World," Hassan said. "To make certain that our trade routes are secure, that tariffs are reasonable, that our people will be able to travel without incident. We have met with a great number of men wearing many different uniforms."

"But al-Amazigh wanted to kill you," Yasmeen said. "Perhaps

he had returned to his original intention, and didn't want your opposition."

Hassan nodded thoughtfully. "Perhaps. But if he brings the French to Rabat's doorstep believing that it will accomplish anything, he has sorely underestimated Temür Agha."

"They could begin a siege, cut off trade to the city." If Yasmeen were to attack it, she would begin that way. Rabat was isolated; an ocean on one side, a desert and zombies on the other. They depended on goods brought in by the Horde and other sources. "They could try to starve Temür out—or wait until the starving people ousted him themselves."

"A siege with what? Sailing ships on the water, dreadnoughts in the air?" Hassan looked amused. "Wolfram did not destroy *all* of Temür's war machines. He has hidden them in the desert so they will not loom over the city, but they are accessed easily enough."

"Oh." She glanced at Archimedes—who was staring at her mouth. "I suppose Rabat has nothing to worry about, then. Right, Wolfram?"

It took him a moment. His gaze lifted from her lips to her eyes, then like a man dying of thirst, he threw back the rest of his wine.

"I suppose not," he said.

Guillouet had kept his papers in good order, so that her evening's entries into the records were not the chore she'd been expecting. On the opposite side of the desk, Archimedes was making his own records: a rudimentary map of Brindisi, an inventory of the items they'd gathered, the locations of the items they'd left behind. It had killed him to leave the clockwork man, she knew—but he'd agreed it was best not to bring something of that value aboard a ship with a new captain, on an expedition where mutiny had threatened and blood had been shed.

Even if they had been the ones to shed it.

"You are the perfect match for me," she said.

He stilled, then slowly lifted his head. His gaze caressed her face, emerald eyes dark and intense.

She leaned back in her chair. "But I think, for you, that is probably not enough."

"It is." His voice was rough.

"No. Not for Archimedes Fox, who throws himself into every danger, every excitement. 'A good match' would not be enough. It would be like drinking saltwater after wine. It is like lining up two people in bed like figures in a ledger. It adds up, but gold in hand is so much better."

He tossed down his pen. "What are you saying?"

"I'm wondering what you thought when I kissed you today. About to be killed by zombies, perhaps you thought it for pity—or to give you reason to hold on."

Wood shrieked as he came up out of his chair, braced his hands on the desk. His gaze bored into hers. "No."

"I could not blame you. Because what followed then? Crew and dinner and ledgers. Hardly the passionate responses of a woman who declared the softening of her heart with a kiss just that morning."

His jaw clenched. "Why are you saying this?"

"Because I am about to kiss you as I want to. As I would have, if zombies had not been at your back, and a new responsibility laid on mine the moment we stepped aboard." She rose slowly. Lifting her knee to the desk, she stalked him across its surface, put her lips almost to his. "Because I cannot believe I almost lost you today, because it still hurts, and I only have to close my eyes to see that door shattering again."

"Then don't close your eyes," he said softly.

"How can I not? Without that pain, how could I have ever known?" She breathed in his breath, loved the taste, the warmth, *him.* "So I tell you all of this because you are a man of deep emotion, Archimedes Fox, and I want you to know: *We are a perfect match.*"

For a long moment, his breath stilled. "So you are warning me."

Her lips curled. "Yes."

"And God help us both."

"There's no help for this," she said.

Rising up, she threaded her fingers through his hair. Silky and thick, unlike the rough scrape of his jaw beneath her lips. She tasted his skin, drank in his intoxicating scent, filled just by that, still empty and needing more.

And as her mouth opened over his, this was more than wanting, needing. It was *longing*, the slow, perfect pain of being so close but not yet having.

She had not had many things, had not wanted others, but here was both, having and wanting, built into a man who simply let her be who she was. Even Yasmeen had never allowed herself that, not completely. She'd never let herself be a woman who poured her heart into a kiss. She'd never let herself fall into the sensation of a man's mouth against hers, the stroke of his tongue, the tease of his lips, until she was hardly aware of anything else. She'd never let herself trust a man so much that when he lifted her with incredible ease, she did not even break from his kiss long enough to see where he was taking her.

Archimedes let her be, and she loved him for it—and she told him with her kiss.

He replied with his own need, his groans that said he loved her mouth on his jaw, her tongue tracing the straining tendons of his throat, the trail of openmouthed kisses down his chest. His stillness, his rigid abdomen betrayed his anticipation. Then his hands in her hair, his hoarse chanting of her name as his body shuddered beneath her tongue told her that she could do this forever, and never tire of his heady taste, his complete abandon to her mouth.

And he was magnificent as he rose over her, eyes so brilliantly green, his fingers strong, his body lean. Her thighs opened at a touch, her longing deep, having him, but not all of him yet, until he came into her slowly, so slowly. Her body arched as she fought to take him all, her nails digging into his shoulders, lips parting on a soundless scream.

His muscles bunched beneath her hands. He drove deep, and she'd never been this before, either, a woman crying out her lover's name, desperate to have him inside her again and again. She'd never brought his head down to hers, their kiss a frantic echo of each thrust, with everything wet—mouth and sweat and the slick push and pull.

She couldn't let him go. Her fingers and her body gripped him tight as she felt the end approach. Then she was gasping, shaking, trying to get away from each overwhelming thrust, opening wider to take more. He gave it, as hard as she wanted, needed, longed for.

Never this much before. Never this much.

She shattered beneath him, and he broke with her, shaking, shuddering. Through ragged breaths, she kissed him again, deep and slow, and let everything slip away.

No zombies. No airship. No treasure or ledgers.

But still her perfect match.

She'd warned him. Archimedes stared up at the ceiling, faintly visible in the predawn light through the porthole, and tried to think of anything, *anything*, that had been more exciting, more dangerous, more incredible than Yasmeen unleashing herself upon him. There was nothing. She'd probably ruined him for treasure hunts. Zombies wouldn't even raise his pulse. Hell, meeting Leonardo da Vinci in Heaven surrounded by nude singing virgins and endless hits of opium couldn't compare to the bliss of one kiss.

He was never going to leave the bed again.

Others on the airship had already left theirs. He heard the footsteps of the deck crew on watch above, the clatter of pots in the galley below. The engines rumbled, carrying him toward Rabat, the tower, and . . . nothing.

At his side, Yasmeen stirred. Eyes still heavy with sleep, her sleek body arched in a long stretch. Her knees cracked. She tensed, drew a sharp breath.

There. His reason to leave the bed. Archimedes could support her even when he felt almost nothing. He stroked his hand down her spine, smiled at her purr. She flipped her hair back, sat up, and stiffly straddled him, her knees popping again as they folded beneath her.

"Yasmeen—"

He broke off as she reached down, took his cock in a firm grip. Already roused by the morning and the memories of the night, he stiffened quickly against her stroking palm. She leaned over and kissed his lips, his jaw. Against his ear, she said, "I'm tired of pacing a cabin again and again. If you don't mind, I'd like to loosen my knees up another way."

Mind? He was already so hard he ached. "Use me," he said. "For as long as you like."

He felt her smile against his skin. "It takes me about half an hour."

Oh, God. His fingers gripped her thighs, and heaven surrounded him as she sank onto his shaft, softly biting her bottom lip, eyelids half closed as she worked herself down his length. He slipped his hand between her legs, thumb stroking through her dark curls.

"Oh." Her head fell back, the ends of her hair brushing his thighs. "By the lady . . . I can't even feel my knees anymore. Just . . . you."

And then she rocked, and before the half hour had passed, she'd ruined him for pacing a cabin again, too.

* * *

It was for the best that she'd drawn the line at the cabin door, but she still missed Archimedes' touch, his wicked replies, all the things that couldn't be said or done in front of a crew. At least she could read his smile and his eyes—and that morning, both were telling her that he was troubled.

He stood beside her on the quarterdeck, flying over the sparkling Mediterranean. A perfect sky lay before them, brilliantly blue, yet he looked inward, his eyes unfocused.

Perhaps he felt her gaze. He glanced at her, the corners of his lips tilting in the same smile that Yasmeen found herself giving when she met his gaze after a long time apart—not amusement, but simply the pleasure of seeing him, having his attention again.

"You looked very serious," she said.

His brows rose, and he nodded. "I suppose I am. I was attempting to judge our speed, and the distance to Rabat. We will arrive tomorrow, I think?"

Why guess when he could ask her? "Twelve hundred miles from Brindisi," she said. "A full forty hours, with this wind against us. We'll reach the city the morning after tomorrow."

"And how long until we are within range of the tower?"

Oh, lady. She had completely forgotten that he was susceptible to that signal. It was just . . . *impossible* to imagine him subdued in that way, with every strong emotion turned mild. Shallow happiness, shallow anger, no desire. She didn't know whether he could bed her, but he wouldn't *want* to bed her.

How could that ever be Archimedes?

"Rabat's tower has about a 250-mile radius," she said. "It will be late tomorrow night."

He nodded, watching the sky ahead. Terrified, yet not showing a bit of it. Such a man—and her line at the cabin door said nothing of hands. Silently, she laced her fingers through his, faced the oncoming wind. His throat worked.

"I will still love you," he said.

She squeezed his hand. "Yes. And it is only temporary. A few days, at most."

Not much time at all.

But the day felt as if it flew by, and though Yasmeen reminded herself that they would only be in Rabat a short time, she could hardly bear the thought of watching everything lively in him fading. Where was her heart of steel now? She skipped her recordkeeping and pulled him to the bed early, as if somehow she could sink deep inside him, put herself between his nanoagents and a radio signal. In the morning, she loosened up over him and then paced the day away on her quarterdeck, watching the height of the sun. When it began to slide west, she couldn't stay past the cabin line any longer.

With a clipped, "Mr. Vashon, the helm is yours," she asked Archimedes to accompany her to the cabin, and had barely closed the door when she was on him, tearing off his clothes, desperate to kiss him *enough* so that the next few days wouldn't matter, wouldn't hurt so much, wouldn't look so bleak. She leapt up around his waist, loved his hunger and ferocity as he pounded her back against the wall.

"Hard," she told him. "So hard we feel it until next week."

Pain, if nothing else. And that would have to be enough.

That would have to be enough.

Hassan appeared in a cheerful mood at dinner. Perhaps he enjoyed having his emotions castrated. Archimedes hated his own glower, his dim mood—but that would be cured soon, ha!

The older man's gaze rested on his face for a moment, then moved to Yasmeen's. She gingerly ate her beans one at a time, but she was moving everything gingerly. Archimedes hadn't been getting around so easily himself. He'd never have imagined it, but it was possible that they'd actually fucked *too* hard.

God, what a woman she was.

He glanced at the clock. A few more hours. They'd move into range just before midnight. Christ, he felt so maudlin, as if he were waiting to die. He should be sensible, instead.

"When the tower comes down," he said, "don't you worry that the people will have the same reaction they did in England?—the panic, the chaos?"

Hassan shook his head. "No, it is only the symbol."

"But when the signal suddenly stops, and they are flooded with emotion . . ." He trailed off as Hassan's brow furrowed. "What?"

"The signal is gone. It has been these past five years."

Next to him, Yasmeen dropped her fork. She put her elbows on the table, her face in her hands. Her shoulders shook.

Was this a joke? Archimedes stared at him. "Five years?"

"Yes. Temür reduced the signal gradually so that we wouldn't have the same panic. A period of several years at reduced strength, then gone altogether for the past five." Hassan gave him a strange look, as if suddenly wondering if he was talking to an idiot. Archimedes began to wonder, too. "Those towers are part of the reason the rebellion gathered such support. Why would Temür keep it on after he secured the governorship?"

"Why is the tower still *up*?"

"It is built on part of an old minaret, a site that many consider a tie to their past and the old religion—something from before the Horde. He did not want to antagonize the recent converts."

"But you will?"

"It needs to fall," Hassan said. "It is an old and valuable minaret, but Rabat would be stronger if we built something new in its place, together."

Not a joke, then. Yasmeen lifted her face from her hands, wiping her eyes. "Oh, damn. I can barely even *sit*," she cried, and then burst into laughter again, not bothering to quiet it, this time.

The older man's eyes were bright with laughter, darting from Yasmeen to Archimedes as if he was enjoying the hilarity without fully comprehending what had happened. Then his head tilted back, as if lifted by realization. "Ah, I see. He thought the tower would affect him."

Christ. "You talked of blowing it up, just like the Iron Duke had in England."

"And I see that you ran full bore with the assumptions you made from that, as per usual," Hassan said, and his laugh echoed in his air tank, reverberating through the cabin. "You fear more, you dare more—and now you love more. It will not be taken away from you in Rabat. Do you know, it was seeing what happened to you that prompted Temür to turn off the signal earlier than he intended?"

Yasmeen's brows rose. "Truly?"

"Yes. He'd always intended to power it down, but very gradually—over a generation, perhaps. We had heard of England and did not want a repeat of that. But when Wolfram was shot, when we saw the change in him after the infection . . ." He shook his head. "We have seen many who have lived beneath the tower, and then were released from it. The reaction of most warned us to go slowly. There was too much fear, too much wildness. But Wolfram was one of the first we knew who had been free, and then yoked by the tower. It was devastating. Even I felt the horror of it, and I was still under the tower's suppression. When Temür saw that bravery itself was squashed, he could not bear the thought that there was a city of brave souls, all squashed in the same manner."

"Temür Agha," Yasmeen repeated. "The same man who literally squashed a city of brave souls?"

Hassan frowned at her. "You break a man's neck with no regret before he carried out his intended rape, and yet you let the man who slaughtered your crew choose his own method of death. I love a man like a brother, yet I also know that the best thing for the city I love is to remove that man from power. We are none of us so easy to peg."

"I am," Archimedes said.

"You are the worst of us," Yasmeen said. "Everything you seek, every fear, every thrill, is something that is also gone like"—she lifted her fingers, *snap!snap!snap!*—"Done so quickly, and you run off to find the next. But you seek love, intend to run to heartbreak, and then you stick with love. You do not regret losing war machines that would lead to too many deaths, and then kill two marines following orders on their ship with barely a blink."

Mortally wounded, he flattened his hand over his chest. "I had to rescue my beautiful wife."

"So you did." She gave him a laughing look from beneath her lashes. "Perhaps next time I'll wait and let you break a neck."

He looked to Hassan. "Do you see? She makes offers like that. It would be impossible to fall out of love."

Chapter Fifteen

Two Horde outposts guarded each side of the mouth of the Mediterranean, overlooking the narrow entrance to the sea. Unlike a sailing ship, Yasmeen could detour around the outposts, taking a southern route directly over land to Rabat. A jewel of a city with a river running through its heart and nestled between the wall and the ocean, there was only one port that all airships and sailing vessels used—and it was under siege.

A fleet of French ships patrolled the waters, supported by two airships overhead. No airships were tethered at the port. They must have let all of the merchants leave, but no one through the blockade.

But unlike most of the airships, Yasmeen wasn't coming in from the west. She could approach the city from the eastern walled side before they could intercept her . . . though that offered its own dangers, and not only from the French fleet.

At the port, four of Temür's war machines stood at the edge of the sea, great hulking colossusi guarding the city. Two vaguely resembled elephants, with enormous bodies supported by sturdy legs, and at the front, a bank of long cannons that could be manip-

ulated, elongated to defend at a distance or contracted to fire a bar-
rage up close. The other two were equally bulky and enormous, like
an octopus brought out of the water—each tentacle working like a
giant grapnel, pulling down airships within range. All four machines
had firebomb launching stations, a battery of self-reloading cannons, rapid-fire guns that could be manned from inside or from one
of the stations connected by ladders and lifts surrounding the outside. Though at rest, with steam drifting lazily from the vents, they
would be ready to stoke at a moment's notice, pushing them into
lumbering mobility and engaging the electrical rail guns—and even
with boilers cold, could still use all of its weapons.

Manned by a crew of thirty men, protected by the thick steel
hide, a single one of the machines could devastate a city—or a fleet
of ships that came into range of its firebombs.

But Temür had not posted them only on the seaside. Two more
machines stood at the wall, overlooking the desert. Slightly shorter
than the machines at the port, but no less dangerous, they were
shaped almost like a Buddha sitting atop a giant mobile chamber
that rolled on plated tracks. A body squat and wide housed the bulk
of the weaponry, and it was so large that if it had hands instead of
two grapnel arms that could easily pull them down into the zombie-
infested desert, *Ceres* would have settled comfortably into its palm.

On the quarterdeck, Yasmeen lowered her spyglass and told the
aviator at the helm, "Take her in directly between those machines,
at the height of its shoulder. Follow the path of the river into the
city."

"Ma'am? Between the machines?"

"Yes."

Archimedes said, too softly for anyone to hear, "Are we out of
the tentacles' range?"

"No." She glanced at him. "No one has begun shooting yet.
They likely won't start for a sugar sloop."

"Even one with a Huguenot cross emblazoned on her balloon?"

A French symbol. That was unfortunate. "Do you think your luck is still holding up?"

"Well enough."

Hassan came onto the quarterdeck, peering across the city to the water in the distance. "So they have begun a siege."

"Yes."

He sighed. "Let me go to the bow so that they will see that I am aboard."

After sharing a glance with Yasmeen, Archimedes went with him. Yasmeen ordered the engines cut, and slowly, they sailed toward the city.

The great machines rose on each side. Though far enough away that Yasmeen couldn't have hit them with a thrown rock, their sheer size made it seem they passed at an arm's length.

And it was, she supposed. The machine's arm's length.

A shout rose from the starboard bow. And there she was. On a path from the city wall to the machine, zombies began to fall in the wake of a small figure robed in black. Moving with astonishing speed, Nasrin cleared the half mile between the wall and the machine's squat base in the space of ten breaths. Leaping up, she caught the edge of a ladder with gray fingers, flipped up onto the rolling tracks. She climbed to the torso, the shoulders, simply pushing with a foot, a hand, and launching herself higher with each push, so swiftly that she all but flew to the machine's shoulder.

The crew looked to Yasmeen, wild-eyed, as if waiting for her order. A few had started toward the gun stations.

"Attention!" she shouted. "A lady boards us. You will treat her as such. If you cannot stand as gentlemen, leave this deck."

Or die.

On the machine's shoulder, Nasrin flicked her wrist. Several of the men cried out as her hand detached and streaked toward them, trailing thin chains of mechanical flesh. Disembodied gray fingers gripped the gunwale. Nasrin leapt, the chain winding swiftly back into her arm. Within moments, the seam of her wrist sealed, and she climbed over the side of the ship with infinite grace. Her gaze touched Yasmeen, held for a long second, before moving to the men at the bow.

"Hassan, my friend," she said in Arabic, her voice like honey in spiced tea. "Have you been treated well? You appear sickly, as I have never seen you before."

Yasmeen curled her fingers to hide the trembling of her hands. The fate of this entire crew likely rested on his answers.

"Very well, Nasrin. The food and cold climes have not agreed with me."

"And are these friends?"

"Yes. Very good friends to me."

"And are you still friend to us?"

"Always. To Temür and to Rabat."

"I am pleased to hear that, Hassan." Her gaze moved to Archimedes. "Mr. Gunther-Baptiste. It is also good to see you in full, rather than peering at me through a peephole in a crate."

"You must forgive me," he said, grinning. "In the New World, men are taught that peepholes are the only proper way to catch a glimpse of a beautiful woman."

"Then you must have spent every moment aboard looking through a peephole." She looked to Yasmeen. "Is he yours, sister?"

"Every man aboard is, Lady Nasrin."

"Then I will call every man aboard a friend. You may enter our city without fear." On silent feet, she came up to the quarterdeck. "I will show you where to tether your ship. Will you tolerate the company of an old woman while we fly?"

Yasmeen would, gladly—but even if she wouldn't, it wasn't as if she had a choice.

* * *

Rabat was unlike any city she'd seen before. Though many things were the same—the smoke pouring from the factories along the walls and beside the sea, streets crowded with steam-powered vehicles and pedal-carts, people walking between them, it was also lusher than she expected, even with the presence of the river. As they flew over, there was hardly a building that did not have a garden on its flat roof. Goats and chickens were plentiful.

"If they plan to starve you out," Yasmeen said, "it will take awhile."

"Yes," Nasrin said. "Supplies from the east are not as plentiful, and Temür did not know if we could make friends with the west. So we prepared to have no friends at all. We have repurposed two of the salt factories into water factories to ease the burden on the river, and have spent years laying the pipes that bring fresh water to every part of the city."

"It is incredible."

"It has been much work, but well worth it."

But Nasrin did not smile in full, and her eyes softened as her gaze swept over the city—almost with longing, Yasmeen thought. A city that wasn't fully hers.

She pointed to a sandstone fortress near the sea. Tall walls surrounded a palace and the great tower, made of red stone and rising tall over the city, impossible to miss. One only had to glance that way, and their vision would be filled with that tower. It looked indestructible, immovable, imposing.

Perhaps Hassan was right. Perhaps such a thing would serve as a constant reminder . . . and even powered down, the fear that it might be turned back on.

"Come in over there," Nasrin said. "Near the *kasbah* wall, you may tether your ship."

Near a large section of the city under tents and stalls. "Is that a marketplace?" Yasmeen asked.

"Yes. But please understand—I know that some of the ports to the north are rough, Captain, especially as regards to the treatment of women. I see that there are no women on your crew, and so your men cannot have much practice with them. I ask that, unless necessary, they remain aboard the ship."

Yasmeen flushed. Because there were no women aboard, Nasrin thought that Yasmeen could not control her crew or depend on them to behave. But she had never been one to offer excuses. "Our supplies have spoiled along the way. If I may send my steward and one other man to restock them, it would be greatly appreciated. I will remind them to be gentlemen."

"That would be allowed. If they do not speak the language, I will be happy to send a guide to them, so that they might find everything more easily."

And keep an eye on them. Though Yasmeen bristled, in truth, she knew little of the crew's behavior at port except for what she'd seen in the Charging Bull.

To avoid any trouble at all, an escort might be a very fine idea. "Thank you, Lady Nasrin."

"Very good. Perhaps you would like to speak with your steward now, while I go and properly greet Hassan. As soon as you have tethered, perhaps you and Mr. Gunther-Baptiste would accompany me to the *kasbah*."

Such polite orders from a woman who had decided that Yasmeen was a complete barbarian. "We will."

The heat was welcome after so much cold. Though not sweltering, as he'd experienced it before in Rabat, warm enough to soak into skin and bones. He expected Yasmeen to lift her face to the sun after they came down the cargo lift and climbed up into the crawler's box, but the expression that he had seen aboard *Ceres* as she'd spoken to Nasrin—a tight combination of embarrassment, frustration—had given way to the cool amusement that tried to express everything was going her way.

On the padded seat bench behind Hassan and Nasrin, he gave her a searching glance. She met his eyes, gave a tiny shake of her head.

Well, they were not on her decks. He slid his hand into hers, offered the little support he could, and her amusement softened and warmed.

The crawler rumbled lightly and lifted its body from the ground on segmented legs. On its back, their small box of cushioned benches rose too, high enough that the steamcarts and wagons they passed would not belch into their faces. The rounded back allowed them to see over the driver, seated at the crawler's head, offering a perfect view of the green of the city, the blue of the sea— with the war machines and dreadnoughts the only marring.

Temür had rebuilt this into an amazing city. When last he'd been here, all had been yellow from the desert, a city baked and a people who simply lived and worked. But now, almost all of the buildings had been painted in whites and blues, and trees sheltered the streets from the sun. The people no longer looked so down-trodden. Several called up to Hassan with warmth. But on every face, there was still the wary glance, the tight pinch of a mouth— only the children playing seemed to lack it.

The gates in the *kasbah* walls were open, and Archimedes saw no guards. The enormous tower filled up the corner of the court-yard on Archimedes' right. A fountain spilled water on their left. Farther inside, only two guards stood at the palace entrance, and those not heavily armed—and not a single man wore the Horde's walking suit, that machine of steam and steel that could crush a body beneath its massive feet. A masjid had been built at the end of the courtyard, a simple dome and four minarets. He caught Yasmeen's eye. Her small nod said that she thought the same thing: Temür had been working very hard to bring the people to him. Judging by the small number who milled about, they hadn't been coming.

Nasrin turned in her seat. "I have forgotten to tell you, Mr. Gunther-Baptiste—I have greatly enjoyed your stories."

He was surprised. "You've read them?"

"Of course. We have many of the publications from the New World sent to us, and Temür and I have long followed the adventures of Archimedes Fox. We have missed a few chapters, however."

Yasmeen frowned. "You knew he was also Archimedes?"

"Yes. We were not certain at first, but in every story, a new brightly colored waistcoat for Mr. Fox was faithfully described as if dictated." Her laugh was delicate, the ringing of a silver bell. "We knew he could not be anyone else."

"I thought he didn't know," Archimedes said. "That the assassins only found me by luck—there were so few."

"Oh, no. Those are men who Temür deemed incompetent, but for one reason or another, it would have been . . . delicate, to dispose of them. So he sent them to find you, knowing they would not be returning."

Taken aback, Archimedes shook his head. "That's oddly flattering."

Yasmeen said, "So it wasn't regarding Archimedes' debt?"

Nasrin's brows lifted. "Archimedes? You use that name at all times now?"

"Yes," he confirmed.

Her gaze slipped to Yasmeen. "And you are Captain Fox. I thought you were untethered."

Untethered? After a second, Archimedes understood. Nasrin's

life was dependent upon Temür's continuing; she wondered if Yasmeen's life was tethered to his in the same way.

"She's not," he said, but Yasmeen added, "I might as well be," and he couldn't speak again immediately, so great was the emotion crushing his chest. She had not even said that she loved him yet, not in as many words. But now she declared, so very simply, that his death would be like her own.

It wouldn't be—and thank God for it, because that meant if he was ever killed, she would likely go on a tear of vengeance unlike the world had ever seen.

Nasrin's gaze held Yasmeen's. "Hassan has also been telling me of your journey, and how you came to captain the airship. I offer apologies for my insult."

"Thank you, Lady Nasrin, but there was no insult taken."

"You are very kind, and a liar."

"And you are fully altered."

The women smiled at each other for a long moment. Nasrin looked to Archimedes again, whose bemusement must have been clear. She said, "It is true. When you are fully altered, you have not much need to use lies as protection—though they are still useful when protecting others. Your name is a lie like that, I suppose, though you hardly needed protection from us."

"No?"

"Temür was angry after you destroyed the barge, it was true—but we also recognized that sending you out so quickly after you fell under the tower had been *our* mistake."

"He didn't care about the money?" Yasmeen said doubtfully.

"Of course that would have been of great use to us, but he did not *lose* money. He lost war machines—and as you must see, he already has more than most men could ever use. What are two or three more?"

Like Yasmeen's puddings. Like an extra five thousand livre. Archimedes couldn't ever recall falling into hysterical laughter, but he was afraid it might be coming. His brain felt as if it would soon explode. "So there was no debt?"

"Oh, there was a debt. But it was of obligation, an explanation." She gave him a disapproving glance. "You ought to have come to us. Every assassin we sent had the same message: come to us."

Now he did laugh, on a memory of slashing knives, quickly drawn guns. "I never let them get round to it. And I have spent ten years trying to find something of value enough to replace the money."

"If there was no debt, why did you steal the sketch?" Yasmeen asked. "It wasn't necessary."

"It was necessary to save his life," Nasrin countered. "One of those assassins would have eventually killed him. His luck cannot last forever . . . though I suppose with you at his side now, he does not need luck to protect him. And I knew that he would come for the sketch, so Temür and I let others know that we had it."

"Why didn't you just send him a letter, requesting him to come?"

Nasrin smiled faintly. "A request from Temür Agha is an order—and an obligation fulfilled under order is not one truly fulfilled. So my seeing him in Port Fallow was a happy accident, an opportunity opened to give him reason to come. I took it."

"Then you weren't there to kill him."

"Not at all." She looked to Hassan, and her smile was sharp. "I was only there to see why our friend Hassan was selling his jewelry."

That announcement killed any further conversation. Though Yasmeen could clearly read the resignation on the older man's face, there was not much to be done. Nasrin told them they would meet with Temür Agha after he'd spoken with Hassan and left for his audience with Temür. Yasmeen and Archimedes were escorted through the open, airy palace to a chamber that looked much like her cabin aboard *Lady Corsair*—though with many more pillows, a breeze that blew the silk curtains over the bed, and live birds singing in a small private garden.

"Are they going to kill us?" Archimedes wondered.

"I don't know," Yasmeen said. "It will all depend on Hassan, you realize."

"Yes."

"Do you think he was a true friend to Temür?"

"From everything I've witnessed between them, yes."

Yasmeen smiled faintly. "Then that might make Temür more lenient, or make the betrayal seem that much worse. It is impossible to know."

A serving girl bustled in, pulled a chain over a large marble tub. A clanking echoed through the floor, and a tile opened, spilling steaming water.

Yasmeen began unbuckling her jacket. "And it appears that if we are going to our executions, we are to be clean."

"Anything else would be rude. I hope we are also fed," he said and joined her.

Though she kissed him in the privacy of their bath, she dared not lose all awareness and make love. They were fed flaky pastries filled with beef and spices, a peppery stew over couscous, breads stuffed with honey and almonds. Yasmeen tasted each for poison, then for flavor, then his mouth after they drank the mint tea with rosewater.

She dared not do more, so she lay against him on the pillows, thinking of how she might possibly kill Temür if the man *did* intend to execute them. She would have to be quicker than Nasrin, to take the woman by surprise. After Temür was dead, she didn't know how quickly Nasrin would also fall. Hopefully it would be quick. Hopefully, if the woman had time to strike at all, she would only have time to strike at Yasmeen—and Archimedes would live.

"I ought not have come here with you," she told him.

He frowned. "What?"

She sat up. "We could have left Hassan somewhere safe. We didn't have to bring him back to the city. You know why we did: Kareem al-Amazigh might be here, and I need to kill him."

"I know," he said, and her chest squeezed almost to nothing.

Of course, he understood. Like her, he did not live in civilization, not truly. He did not live under the safety of rules and laws. No, the only rules and laws they lived by were their own.

But that also meant that when the seas ate up someone she loved, whether it was in lawless Port Fallow or the Ivory Market, whether it was aboard a ship on the ocean, that there was no one to seek justice. Murder was not illegal in a land without law, and so the only possible recourse for Yasmeen, the only loyalty she could show to her crew was to seek her own justice, to apply her own laws.

That didn't mean they had to be *his*.

"I could have come later," she said. "I didn't have to risk you. I should have been patient. I understand the *gan tsetseg* now, Archimedes. If the man I need to protect is hurt, a part of me will also die. I don't know if it is beautiful or barbaric, but I *know* it now."

"Yasmeen." Roughly, he took his face between her hands and kissed her—and kissed her again. "I will stand behind you. I will *always* stand behind you."

But he wouldn't, she knew. If anything ever threatened her, he would jump in front and take the first blow. Just as she would for him.

Hours passed. By the afternoon, they heard a growing commotion, of many voices shouting together. They had no view from their chamber, and so Yasmeen climbed quietly to the roof to look over, and saw the courtyard filled with men and women. Together, like this, the effects of the Horde occupation were still shouting as they did: almost every man and woman had been modified by the tools of the occupation. Legs had been altered into lifts or rollers, arms augmented with steel and iron or replaced altogether. But although they shouted, they did not seem angry. Determined, rather—and all of them seemed to be waiting, expectant.

Nasrin was waiting in their chambers when she climbed back down, her amusement plain. "We are sorry to have kept you here, but the talks were long, and the councilors have only just left."

The talks with the French? But Nasrin didn't say. She led them to a great columned hall that might have once held a throne, but now was only laid with a thick rug. Temür sat at the head, his legs folded beneath him. Hassan sat at his right side.

Temür gestured for them to sit on his left. Smaller than she'd always imagined, with shrewd eyes and iron gray hair gathered at the top of his head in a narrow tail, he was quiet, and still—much like Nasrin now, standing slightly behind him. He did not appear the clenched-teethed madman she had always pictured, ordering a city razed to the ground; nor did he appear the generous, impassioned man that had built another city up. He simply looked like a man, seated in front of a game of strategy—and she could not determine whether he was winning or losing.

"Our friend Hassan has told us of your journey, and all that you suspect of Kareem al-Amazigh."

Archimedes nodded, obviously relieved by the "our friend." "Yes."

"He is aboard one of the French ships laying siege to us now. They demand entry for their soldiers, and to allow al-Amazigh to destroy the tower."

He ought to have listened to Hassan, Yasmeen thought. Such an action might make him a hero, but he would lose the city to a foreign power.

Either way, he would not be a hero for long. Yasmeen pictured the line of ships. She would have to discover which he was on, and then fly *Ceres* close enough that she could infiltrate . . .

No. That wouldn't do, not unless she flew her alone. She could not risk the crew with this. She would not risk Archimedes—though she didn't know how she would stop him from risking himself.

"She is already determining how she will kill Kareem al-Amazigh," Nasrin said. "You had best talk more quickly, my love."

Yasmeen's eyes locked on the man's face. "You don't want me to?"

"An assassination aboard the French ships would be akin to shooting a first bullet. My war machines *will* destroy the fleet, but that would also destroy many of the trade agreements we have set in place with their allies in the New World. I do not wish to embroil my city in a war."

And a request from Temür Agha was an order. Yasmeen was not foolish enough to defy it. "And after he is not aboard the ship?"

The corners of his eyes lifted slightly. "Do as you like."

"How long will the siege last, do you think?"

"Not long. They will have no reason to stay, and their demands will shortly mean nothing. I am bringing down the tower tonight. Or rather—" He glanced to Hassan. "My friend will, after he steps into my place."

Shock silenced them both. Tears glistened in Hassan's eyes, sadness—the weight of responsibility.

He was a good man to bear it, Yasmeen thought.

Archimedes shook his head. "Truly?"

"Yes," Hassan said. "We are going out into the courtyard shortly, where we will make the announcement. I wanted to extend an invitation for you to see."

Yasmeen nodded, then glanced to Nasrin. "And you? What will you do afterward?"

"We will go somewhere. We have not decided yet."

"But for safety, and because it would not be expected, we would like to be aboard your ship," Temür said.

Yasmeen laughed. A rich, powerful man, planning to relocate using only *Ceres*? "She's a small ship. She can't carry much. She could probably not even fit your collection of robes."

"We will not take anything but what we wear."

"And perhaps we will read the wooden blocks in Goryeo," Nasrin said. "We will walk the flowered temples of Khmer, and bathe in the sacred river."

Yasmeen's throat tightened. Her eyes filled. She could not hear a word of Lady Khojen's tale without being overwhelmed—and it was more than a request. The iron in Temür's hair said that he would have more years, but they could not number many.

"All right." She nodded, then realized, "And your man is already putting the provisions aboard the ship. The one you sent as a guide for my steward."

"Yes. Your steward was very glad not to pay for anything."

So was Yasmeen. But that didn't mean she would take this job for free. "The price of passage—to wherever you like—will be Archimedes' sketch."

"Of course."

She glanced at him, saw his grin, and whispered, *"Fifty percent."*

"You will have it," he promised.

As the sun set, Yasmeen sat with Archimedes at her side, watching from the palace roof as the tower fell—not with an explosion, but pushed over by a squat war machine, under Hassan's first order.

Inside the courtyard, outside—the cheers rose over the rumble of the war machine and the crash of stone, just as Hassan had hoped. Then the people themselves rose up, sparked by the tower's fall—which Hassan had predicted, too.

But perhaps he hadn't anticipated the speed with which they would come for Temür Agha.

Yasmeen and Archimedes had cheered with the rest, but as the tenor of the cheers and the chants began to change, she rose uneasily to her feet. A crowd had started toward the palace, where the former governor stood at the entrance with Hassan's council.

She turned to Archimedes. "We need to get to *Ceres*. Quickly. Nasrin and Temür will have to catch up."

They returned to their chamber, where the sketch still lay in Archimedes' converted glider. He scooped it up and strapped it onto his back, and by the lady, Yasmeen was glad that he was a fast man, a strong man. He did not need to stop and rest as they raced through the palace. Behind them came shouts, the sound of stone shattering. They reached the palace wall, and he did not hesitate— not climbing the laurel tree as quickly as she, but just as sure-footed.

The gardens behind the palace were quiet. They were on the eastern side of the *kasbah*, and the mob at the west courtyard. Still, it would not be long before they would spill all through this area, searching for Temür.

A crash made her look around. The war machine loomed over the palace, giant arms swinging, breaking it open for looters. Also under Hassan's order? Probably not. But perhaps it would fulfill the same need as destroying Temür Agha. Cannons fired, crushing sandstone walls. People shouted over the rumbling, huffing machine. Steam spewed into the air as it squatted, lifted, and came down to crush the palace roof like a child stomping a grape.

"Good God," Archimedes breathed, looking back.

Yasmeen didn't dare look back again. *Ceres* hovered just outside the *kasbah*. Her eyes searched the dark for a gate, a tree, anything that would allow them over. The *kasbah* wall was too high, too smooth. Without a rope, Archimedes wouldn't make it to the top. Yasmeen wasn't certain *she* would make it.

"Can we signal them?" he asked.

She did not know with what. She and the crew of her lady had many signals, but she'd never established them with this crew.

"We might have to run through the crowd," she whispered. "We need to find robes."

Anything, anything to hide, anything to be safe—to make certain he made it to the airship.

"Find robes in there?" He looked to the palace again, eyes widening as the ground suddenly shook under an enormous impact. "Not in there. We'll knock someone out, take their clothes."

A dark figure in a robe swept past them, easily carrying a hooded man. "Come," Nasrin said. "We knew that they might storm the palace, but now they have taken over the war machine. So come quickly."

Hope lifted through Yasmeen again as they raced after her, until a shout from behind them gave away their presence. Nasrin reached the wall and leapt, flying halfway up. Her foot struck the smooth side and propelled her the remaining way to the top.

If anyone had doubts about who had been fleeing, they would not now.

"Nasrin!" Yasmeen shouted.

She turned, flicked her hand down to them. Yasmeen grasped the smooth mechanical flesh, held on to Archimedes. Nasrin wound them up with dizzying speed, and Yasmeen might have laughed if the mob were not closing in.

Atop they wall, they looked to *Ceres*. "She is too far away for me," Nasrin said.

People were in the streets below, but not rioting. Still cheering, many of them, others confused by the commotion inside the *kasbah*. She and Archimedes would be safe, for now, if they escaped here.

A rock whizzed past Yasmeen's head—thrown by a mechanical arm, altered and strengthened by the Horde.

Nasrin jumped from the wall, landed easily, then looked up at them.

"Jesus," Archimedes said. "I think she intends to catch—"

A rock slammed into the wall just below their feet, breaking apart in a shower of shards.

"You go first," he said.

Yasmeen laughed, turned to jump. The whizzing sound warned her, and she ducked. Pain shot through her brain, and everything went dark as she fell, instead.

"Yasmeen!"

Archimedes leapt for her, missed. Overbalanced, he toppled over, barely gripped the edge of the wall. He hung over the side, desperately watching as Nasrin caught her.

But, God—how badly had she been struck?

He flung himself away from the wall the moment Nasrin put her down. He crashed into her, and he felt her mechanical body warp beneath her robe, cushioning the impact. Still, it slammed the breath from him, and his chest was a molten hole as he scrambled for Yasmeen. Blood flowed heavily from her scalp, over her ear.

"She's alive," Nasrin said. "Pick her up. Let us go, go!"

He gathered her up, trying to let her breath and her heartbeat ease his fear. Behind them came shouts, the crash and huffing of the war machine. He ran, carrying his life, as he'd never run before.

They reached *Ceres*. Nasrin's hand shot upward, her arm

wrapped around his waist. They were carried up, onto the deck, where the crew waited, eyes wide as they looked over the *kasbah*. The war machine had begun rolling toward them.

The crew looked to Yasmeen, then to him. And holding her, *God please let her forgive him*, Archimedes took command of her ship.

Chapter Sixteen

When Yasmeen awoke, the morning sun was shining through the portholes. Bandages wrapped her head—so that was why it pounded so badly. She couldn't remember drinking *that* much.

Archimedes sat in a chair next to the bed, eyes closed, jaw rough, head in his hands. He looked exhausted.

"Idiot," she said. Her mouth felt parched, her tongue huge. She hadn't drunk too much; she *needed* a drink that much. "You should have slept."

He looked up. His eyes suddenly glistened—oh, beautiful man. She felt the smile curve her mouth, the one she could not help every time she saw him.

"Yasmeen," he said, and his voice was as rough as hers felt. He started for her, as if to pull her into his arms, before stopping himself. "How do you feel?"

She pushed up to sitting. Her knees cracked. She froze, then let the tension out on a sigh. "I feel like I need to loosen up—and I have to piss."

"Not at the same time, I hope." Gently, his arms slid under her.

"A whipping, I can take. But I am not quite adventurous enough for that."

She laughed, then had to stop at the ache in her head. He lifted her against him to carry her to the privy, but halted halfway across the cabin, suddenly shaking, holding her tight.

"I love you," he said. "Please remember that when I tell you—I have taken over your ship."

Yasmeen stared at him. Eyes bright, jaw tense, he appeared as if he were waiting for her machete at the back of his neck. "You ordered the crew to take her out of Rabat, I hope?"

"Yes."

"Which way have we gone?"

"North."

"Are we completely lost? Is the navigator dead?"

His tension began to ease. "No."

"All right, then. You have said you would back me up if needed, and you have done a perfectly fine job of it." She pointed to the privy. "Please."

He had her morning water heated when she was finished, the soap ready. And being injured was not so terrible at all when it was followed by Archimedes carefully washing her from head to toe, then drying her with slow strokes of a soft cloth.

Retrieving one of his shirts, he slipped it over her head, and put his arm about her waist so that they could begin to pace.

Outside the porthole lay a rolling plain covered in snow. They must have gone farther north than she'd realized. "How long has it been?" she wondered.

"Three days."

"And Rabat?"

"The mob stopped their looting after the palace. All is quiet again, and the French fleet is leaving."

She began to nod, then realized—"If you fled, how do you know this?"

"Ah, well. I ordered the ship south first, and then west, and then back north over the sea. And when we approached the French fleet . . ." He paused as Yasmeen choked. "We are obviously still alive."

Alive, and Archimedes would never be so stupid to approach them without a purpose. "Why did you do it?"

"We had a French academic aboard who had been part of a recent expedition that ended in Rabat, and he was seeking safe passage back to the islands. They recognized my name, of course—"

She snorted. "Of course."

"And when they saw the items we gathered in Brindisi, were happy to take them aboard—especially as Ollivier also knew the location of da Vinci's clockwork man."

Her breath left her. "You told him?"

"Well, yes. Because in a few days, he will be eager to meet another man he has heard is in their fleet, one who has possession of a da Vinci sketch . . . that Ollivier will recognize as a fake. And then that man is going to die a very natural-looking death. I made certain he knew that 'natural-looking' was most critical."

Al-Amazigh. Archimedes had arranged for Ollivier to kill the man who'd ordered the slaughter of her crew, yet do it in a way that wouldn't begin a war. And this man was hers?

Her eyes filled. "Thank you."

"I am sorry you couldn't do it yourself."

"It only matters that it is done." Finally done. It would not ease the pain of losing her crew, her lady, but the debt of their deaths had not gone unpaid. "And the French let you fly away?"

"I had a Vashon for a first mate, and this is an airship *very* loyal to their king. We even sport a Huguenot cross on our balloon."

That ugly, horrible thing. "And to think I said that Guillouet was treating her like a whore for it."

"She is definitely a lady," he said. "Are you sure you will not keep her?"

"She is not *my* lady."

"All right. We will buy another one." He stroked her back. "Temür Agha and Nasrin are waiting for you to awake before they go."

So soon? But it was probably for the best. "Then let us go see them off."

Ceres hovered over the edge of Paris, the sunlight glaring on her white balloon. A gorgeous day. The air above decks was crisp, zombies moaned below, and she had Archimedes by her side.

Temür Agha stood on the cargo lift, waiting for Nasrin. The *gan tsetseg* glanced at him before turning back to Yasmeen. "If the lady allows it, I will see you again, sister."

Perhaps. After learning that the Horde soldiers had been abandoning the outposts, Temür Agha had decided that, rather than wandering the empire on Lady Khojen's path, he would start at the outpost near Paris and begin gathering up rebels, slowly marching east. They would be in Europe for some time . . . and so, yes, it was possible that Yasmeen would meet them again.

"I look forward to it," she said.

Nasrin leaned forward, kissed her cheeks, then kissed Archimedes'. With a smile, she turned toward the cargo lift—but of course she did not go down that way. She leapt, and by the time the lift rattled its way to the ground and Temür stepped off, a mob of dead zombies littered the snow.

Yasmeen smiled, watching them begin their long walk before looking to Archimedes. "I would have chosen Lady Khojen's path."

"So would I. But for now, our path goes to Port Fallow." Archi-

medes took her hand. "Where does it go from there? I am an adventurer, you are a mercenary, but with the sketch, we will both have
money enough to do whatever we like. Will you still be with me?"

"Idiot. I just said, I'd have chosen Lady Khojen's path." She lifted
onto her toes, kissed him. Why not? This would not be her crew for
much longer. "That path is to go traveling the world with her man—
except I will not die at the hands of bandits. And I will still take
passengers, and make more money."

"I'll make it with you. And I will still throw myself into crypts
filled with zombies."

"Then I will throw myself with you," she said. "But first we
need a lady to throw ourselves from."

The Vashon shipyards seemed to be the perfect place to
find her. Three weeks after selling their sketch for five thousand
more than they'd anticipated, and four days after receiving a letter
from Ollivier confirming al-Amazigh's death, Yasmeen and Archimedes traveled to the New World to search for her new lady. They
took out a two-seater balloon, weaving around the airships tethered above Port-au-Prince's turquoise water.

"That would match my waistcoat," Archimedes said, pointing
to a bright orange balloon, then laughed when Yasmeen gave him
a look to kill. "You're right. The zombies would probably be leaping into the sky trying to catch us."

"And I would die of embarrassment before I ever stepped aboard."

He had never dreamed that choosing an airship would be like
taking his sister to buy a hat for her birthday. He only cared that
they had a cabin big enough for a small library and their bed made
of pillows, and that it wouldn't fall out of the sky on the first run.
"You have said that of most these ships."

"It is true of most." She pushed the steering lever and pedaled, circling around the orange envelope. A skyrunner appeared in front of them.

Archimedes had hope. "She looks like your lady."

"Too much," Yasmeen said, and her eyes softened as her gaze ran over its lines. "She is the same model, but I hate her for not being the same. And—*Oh*. There."

Had she ever looked at another person with such longing, Archimedes' heart would have broken. But he understood too well that the sleek airship was something else to her—a life with no walls. She felt the wind on her face; he ran from zombies. They could not choose what they loved, but he thanked God for his luck in finding a woman to share it.

They rode the two-seater to her decks, and he heard Yasmeen's sigh as her feet touched the boards. Her fingers trailed over the wooden rail as she walked along the side, and he saw the shaking of her hands as she stepped onto the quarterdeck and looked out over the bow.

A Vashon came up the rope ladder. Having seen several members of the family now, Archimedes wasn't convinced that Peter and Paul had been twins. They all looked alike: tall, dark, and trouble in their grins.

This one looked surprised, however. "This one, Captain Corsair? She is a sound ship, but she has been used before. You were supposed to be told of the markings on the tails that would indicate which ships were new."

"We were, and I don't care. Used only means that she has been tested—and she still flies, so she must have passed all her trials. How much?"

"Don't you want to see—"

"No. She'll need alterations. Rail cannons at bow and stern. More shelves installed in the captain's cabin. A different cargo lift, capable of raising . . ." She looked to Archimedes. "What is the biggest thing you have ever found, and wanted badly, but were not able to take with you?"

God, he loved her. "The bronze horses at the basilica in Venice."

Her brows rose. "Back to Venice?"

"Yes."

She turned to the Vashon. "Capable of raising four bronze horses, and to store them in her hold. You'll probably need to enlarge the exterior hold doors, as well."

"I would have to speak with the carpenters and recalculate the figures. The price will be—"

"Do it. I'll pay it."

"Yes, ma'am." He ran for the rope ladder.

Archimedes moved about the deck, looking down the hatchway, making his way to the quarterdeck, where Yasmeen stood with her eyes shining. Not tears now. Already feeling the wind.

"What shall you name her? She will be a lady, I think."

"Yes. Always a lady."

"Lady Luck? Lady Love?"

Her sneer was ruined by her laugh. "Those are horrible. You don't name your own adventures, do you?"

"No. Zenobia never allows me."

"I see why."

"She has named Lady Lynx's skyrunner *Steel Flower*."

Yasmeen smiled. "This one has the same feel about her: fierce, loyal. She will fly *so* well."

He grinned. "*Lady Caracal? Lady Tiger?*"

"Stop," she said, laughing. "Those are awful. Perhaps she will be *Lady Nergüi*—and she will be no one but my lady." She slid her hand through his. "You'll treat her well?"

His lady. "Always, my captain."

"Then we will see what adventures await us, Mr. Fox," she said, and met his lips for a kiss.